Loss of Innocence

SAMSARA-THE FIRST SEASON

Volume One - Book Four

JL Martin

Time Travellers Publishing House PTY LTD

ALSO by JL Martin

FICTION

SAMSARA- The First Season

That Fated Night- A Short Novella of Love and Loss

The Golden Glow

Unexpected Beginnings

Torn in Two

Loss of Innocence

Unconditional Love

Returning Home

Letting go

Soul Connections

Healing the Heart

Legacy and Love

Leo- Back to me!

Lilith- Utopia

SPAWNED OF SIN- Trilogy Series

Through Windows in the Sky I Fall

Tainted Blood, Poisoned Soul

The Ties That Bind Behind Me

Loss of Innocence

J. L. MARTIN

Published by Time Travellers Publishing House Pty Ltd 2021

The series is written in British English, as the Author is Australian and the books are based in Australia. My American friends will find U's where they have no right to be, Z replaced with S, and so many double L's you may feel like throwing the book against the wall. I apologise in advance, and hope one day we can all live in harmony...

National Library of Australia

Cataloging-in-Publication data

Martin, J L, 1971-.

Loss of Innocence

Samsara-The First Season

ISBN Print: 978-1-925852-28-8

ISBN Ebook: 978-1-925852-27-1

Cover design by Thea Atkinson

Editing and text design by Marianne Delaforce

Printed and bound in Australia by Ingram Sparks

A Note from the Author

IN READING THE SERIES 'Samsara-The First Season', I ask you to consider the era in which this work of fiction is set. In these more enlightened times, elements of this story may be considered homophobic, racist, and outright morally corrupt—along with being barbaric and downright ignorant. However; in 19th century Australia, they were not. Themes throughout the series are reflective of the times and are an accurate account of the attitude, bias and outright hate a large majority of society held towards the LGBTQI+ Community and our First Nations Peoples. In saying this, we no longer consider it appropriate for a fifteen-year-old girl to marry—forced or not—but 130 years ago, it was not uncommon.

The character of Leo is based on a real person. As outrageous, inappropriate and politically incorrect as he is—I love this soul. It is not my intention to stigmatise him or cause offence to anyone—only to remain authentic in my best effort to honour and immortalise a very dear man who left a significant imprint on my life—and who unfortunately was born without a filter and lacks all sensibilities; and can be very, very badly behaved.

Please be aware there are themes of violence, racism, and homophobia throughout this series; however, I have been mindful to write these scenes as sensitively as possible and with the utmost care.

I truly hope you enjoy 'Samsara-The First Season' just as much as I enjoyed writing it.

Dedication

To my sweet little Audrey.

May you carry in your heart the bond of family and know how much you are loved. You can be anything in life, but whatever path you choose to follow, go about it with kindness, discernment and joy, and know, I'm cheering you along and very proud of the lovely soul you are.

Chapter One

My eyes slowly fluttered open just as dawn broke, a smile touching my lips as I realised today was the anniversary of our arrival in Australia. We had been in Geelong for a year now and were looking forward to the celebration dinner, planned to take place this evening. I stretched my body like a cat, easing the tension in my back, then relaxed back into the soft, warm bed, listening to the resident kookaburra close by greeting the day. My body was returning to what it once was, and I found I could fit back into most of the clothes that I had worn before my pregnancy, causing Polly to threaten to skelp me as she was still struggling to lose the extra pounds she had gained while carrying Willie.

Thomas and Emmy had so far proven to be content weans, sleeping twelve-hours every single night since they were born, while allowing Mary to have a full night's rest and easing my guilt. She would bring them to us the moment they woke, and I would feed them while she stood over me to ensure I completed the task efficiently and to her very high standard. Once they had drunk their fill, we would play with them on our bed, the hours always passing far too quickly. Aaron would hold Thomas for a time, focussing all his attention on his son, then would swap with me and do the same for little Emmy. He was completely in love with his children and had modified his work hours to spend what he considered important time with them in the mornings, and occasionally the afternoons, if he could sneak away from Harry's watchful gaze.

Bessie now started at nine o'clock in the morning to give us time alone as a family. Once dressed, I would take the twins downstairs and place them in their perambulator near the hearth in the warm and bustling kitchen—taking them along with me as I went about my busy day. I would walk them to the village to see my friends, often staying to talk with the more experienced mothers to seek their advice, and to reassure myself I was doing everything correctly. Little Mary was a godsend, and what she didn't know about babies you could have written on a thimble. She loved and cared for the twins and would take them anytime during the day if I needed a rest or had something to do, and I appreciated her more than I could ever express.

Thomas and Emmy were two-weeks old, and I thought back to this time last year when I had arrived at the docks in Melbourne as a naïve girl, not knowing what awaited me—nor was I prepared for what I would find. I reflected on the previous twelve-months and how dramatically my life had changed in so many unexpected ways. As memories filtered through my mind, I smiled, realising in that very moment, my feet were on the right path all along—a road only I could travel, and all that was meant to be already was.

Hamish and I had returned to an easy friendship. He called on us as often as time would allow, visiting with the twins while we talked of family and the many mutual friends we shared, and almost always resulting in him forgetting the time and being late home. It was now comfortable between us. I could relax in his company once again and felt at ease when alone with him. I was relieved we had found peace and renewed our friendship.

I turned over and kissed Aaron's cheek. His eyes opened slowly, and he kissed me back, touching my ear with his fingers while playing with the diamond stud in my lobe. He caressed my back as I cuddled into him. I enjoyed the morning hours that we had alone together before the twins were brought in.

'What are ya plans for today, Abi?' He gently stroked my hair as I lay with my head on his chest.

'I'm taking Thomas and Emmy down to the village to see Amelia and Mathew, and then I will see where the day takes me. I was thinking of having a picnic down by the lake. Would you like to join me?'

'Yeah, of course. I've some work to finish off in the village, but it can wait. I'd prefer a leisurely lunch with you an' me nippers over that any day of the week, let me give ya the drum. I'll meet ya there at midday.' He closed his eyes, entwining his fingers in my hair.

'I'll be avoiding that bloody Mr Hinkle. That's one thing I know for certain,' I spat as his eyelashes fluttered open.

'What's the old bugger done now?' He chuckled to himself as I pulled away to meet his gaze, my cheeks warm.

'I was trying to be kind, and took some leftovers from the kitchen.' I stopped and put my hand up to silence him as he attempted to interrupt me. 'I know you've told me to stay away from the gatekeeper's cottage, but I was only taking a basket of food as a peace offering and to try, yet again, to introduce myself.' I lay my head back down on his chest.

'Oh, he knows who ya are.' He laughed loudly as I grimaced. 'What did he do to ya this time?'

'He saw me coming down the path beside the creek and shot at me.' I closed my eyes, my cheeks burning as his laughter subsided.

'He wouldn't have shot *at* ya. Only near ya, but I'll get Harry to go speak to him if he scared ya.' I raised my head, my eyes wide as I stared into his, twinkling with amusement.

'You need to stop defending that pig of a man or you will leave my bed now.' He threw back his head and laughed again, his arm around me tightening. 'I cannot believe how scared of the old bastard you are. Weak as a newborn wean, and as much backbone as a brown snake down in the scrub.'

'Oh, go easy, woman. Ya have to understand ya inherited the man from ya old aunt just like ya did this property. He won't have nothin' to do with me or me family since I married ya an' moved to the big house. It's no good me confrontin' him. Ya catch more flies with honey than vinegar, as me Ma says. He at least tolerates Harry, an' allows him to come as far as his front verandah if he needs a yarn.'

'I had no idea you and your family knew him. I barely see him, let alone interact with the cantankerous wee prick.' I relaxed against him, my anger dissipating a little as I tried to focus on my plans for the day and not allow old Mr Hinkle to ruin it before it even began.

'We know him as well as anyone in the district. Barely. By the time me parents emigrated to Australia, Willow Grove was not what it'd once been when ya aunt lived here, goin' by the gossip. It went quiet for over fifteen-years, an' the workers that remained kept to 'emselves.' He paused for a moment, a smile touching his lips. 'Dependin' which way the wind blew, there were times I'd hear what sounded like chisel on rock in the far distance, but me Da wouldn't allow any of us to step foot on the property to find out.' He laughed aloud, while I wondered how Mr Cavanaugh had prevented any of them sneaking off to explore Willow Grove given how wild they all were. 'We met old Hinkle in the early days when he'd come down to the boat a few times a week in his old jinker to buy fish to feed those left at the property. Going by the amount he bought, there were far more livin' here than we ever seen, but me father always said 'tis best to let sleepin' dogs lie. Old Hinkle never done any harm to anyone, an' 'tis best ya leave him alone. He's a hermit by choice, an' probably for good reason.'

'Never done harm? He bloody well shot at me!'

'But did ya die, Abigail? Are ya injured? He's tried to scare ya off before, an' he'll do it again if ya step foot near the gatehouse or his cottage. If he wanted to harm ya, he would have. He's a crack shot an' a bushy who can live off the land. Some say he used to hunt with the natives an' learned their ways, others say his mother was an Aboriginal woman an' his father an Englishman. There's even a few who believe he was transported over here as a convict when still a lad. For stealin'. You'll hear a hundred stories about the man goin' back decades, an' it's likely none are true.' He chuckled to himself while I pushed the thought of Mr Hinkle to the back of my mind.

'Are Patrick and Luke coming tonight?'

'Yeah. Ya couldn't keep Patrick away now he's openly courtin' Scarlett. He makes every excuse to come here, an' sometimes doesn't even have one. Ma says he never eats at home anymore, choosin' to come to the dinin' hall at every meal to wait for her to finish so they can spend all their free time together. He's livin' off our tucker an' doesn't even work here,' he replied with a grin.

He would tease Patrick relentlessly about being starry-eyed over a woman, much to everyone's amusement. I smiled across at him as I reached out and moved a lock of blonde hair that had fallen over his brow. I adored Aaron's brothers and found them all to be decent, honest men, just like him. Men who loved with their whole hearts and paid no mind to what anyone else thought, unless they loudly shared their unwanted opinion in earshot of the Cavanaugh boys—all skilled in the use of their fists and well known in the district for using them when words and a gentle approach failed.

'And your parents? I want to know how they like their new shop,' I enquired, feeling extremely happy for them.

Aaron and I had purchased a large commercial property on busy Malop Street in the heart of the business district in Geelong. Aaron's first priority had been to install cooling units to keep the produce fresh—a costly addition we discovered after they had been installed. The builders Aaron hired worked sixteen-hour-days for weeks remodelling the inside of the shop, then fitting it out with the best commercial equipment Aaron could source. It had only been finished last week and his parents were given the keys yesterday, leaving me excited and very eager to hear just what their reaction had been.

'They're the happiest I've ever seen 'em. Me father's over the moon about the shop an' the fishin' boat. He's already decided to put Patrick in charge of the new boat with Luke, an' is in the process of hirin' some local lads to work the other boats. I don't think I've ever seen me Da so pleased, or me Ma, for that matter, but for different reasons. Is she drivin' ya mad bein' here every day to see the twins?'

'No, not at all. I enjoy our afternoon teas and watching her spend time with her grandchildren. I never had people who loved me as much as Edith loves the twins. I don't ever want to stand in the way of that.'

'Abi, you're a beautiful soul to think that way. Most sheilas would despise their mother-in-law if she did what me Ma is doin'. The cheek of the woman pushin' herself on ya so often whether ya invite her or not.' He laughed and placed his large hand over mine as it rested on his chest, his strong heartbeat pounding against my palm, providing an overwhelming sense of comfort and warmth to my soul.

I smiled as Edith's face came to mind. I enjoyed my time with her each day, feeling as if I finally had my own mother coming to check up on me, always guiding and nurturing me, just as my sweet Sister Josephine had once done. It was such a joy to see her holding her grandchildren. I could feel the happiness and love vibrating from her body as she spoke softly to them while she held them in her arms. It seemed like they understood her and what was going on around them, staring wide-eyed at anything and everyone they came in contact with. Edith and I would talk throughout the afternoon, drinking coffee and eating sandwiches and cakes while she held her grandchildren—never once allowing anyone else to take them from her when she visited. She believed the sun rose only for those two children, and she was completely and utterly in love with them.

After the first week employed as their nanny, little Mary had come to me and advised she could not accept the higher wages we now paid her. She felt that she wasn't earning the extra money due to the twins remaining with me during the day and then sleeping through the night. I had responded immediately, advising her quite forcefully that she was worth every penny just by being available when I needed her, and that she was irreplaceable to me and must accept the wages without argument. She had been moved from the staff quarters into a guest room close to the nursery and was still acclimatising to the changes that had occurred swiftly and without warning. She slept in the nursery during the night, but told Leo she no longer recognised her life, likening it to a fairytale, only she was the princess with her own private bathroom. Dear Mary still marvelled at the large bathtub and modern commode only recently installed—still uncommon in these parts. It was almost unheard of for a person in service to have access to such luxury, and she appreciated it greatly.

'I've heard on the passionfruit vine there's gunna be a large turnout at the pub tonight,' Aaron remarked, jolting me from my thoughts. 'Seems there's a lot of blokes from surroundin' properties, an' even beyond the district, who intend on comin' here to celebrate with us. I gotta say I'm worried it'll turn into a shit show bein' the first time Dana's seen Hamish since Charlotte's death. They're both as bloody unpredictable as the other. I know she's improved, but I'm worried it's gunna set her back, ya know?' I had experienced similar thoughts for a few days now, but had not spoken them aloud. Aaron rolled me onto my back, then ran his hand lightly over my breasts, teasing me while sending tingles through my body. 'Let's worry about that later. We've some time before we hear that now familiar knock on our door.' He smiled before running his tongue along the inside of my top lip, then kissed me passionately again, and I let myself melt into him as all thoughts evaporated from my busy, busy mind.

Bessie stepped into the room and hurried to my side, taking Emmy from me. She kissed the top of her head as she cradled the wide-eyed girl in her arms, all the while murmuring sweetly to her as if they were the only ones in the room. Emmy grabbed her finger and held it tightly, making Bessie giggle in delight. She then did the same with Thomas as I smiled across at her. She appeared to find great joy in what was now her morning ritual, and she delighted in the twins every time she saw them. I had quickly become used to the fact the first ten-minutes of her working day was her special time with them without interruption or demands from anyone, including me. I now wisely chose to remain in bed until she was ready and indicated it was safe to approach her, preventing any further threats of harm directed at me when she was vexed.

Aaron played with the babies on the bed, once Bessie reluctantly relinquished them to their father. She busied herself in my dressing room, organising my clothes for the day. I kissed Thomas and Emmy, who seemed to be changing every day, almost by the hour. Thomas was gradually becoming more like his father, while Emmy was developing more radically into a small version of me.

When she first entered the world, the first thing I noticed was her green eyes, shaped just like mine. Although they were paler at birth, they were now like two shining emeralds. The rare hue she was fortunate to possess, a mix of green and blue with a touch of gold, mesmerised all who held her. They were exquisitely shaped, and quite large for a wean—with black eyelashes so thick and long, framing them perfectly. When you looked into her sweet little face and she gazed back at you, well, there was just no other love like it in the world. Thomas possessed the same eyes as his father, and they turned a brighter blue with each passing day.

Bessie placed my clothes on the end of the bed, before crossing the room to my dressing table. She silently pointed at the padded chair that sat before it, fixing me with a broad smile. I kissed my little family goodbye for the moment, then slipped on my dressing gown, crossing the room to sit down as ordered. She turned her full attention to me before attempting to tame my unruly hair. She brushed it thoughtfully as she gazed into the mirror, catching my eye, and then smiled again.

'They are the most beautiful children I have ever seen, Mistress, and oh so very well-behaved. I have never seen, or even heard of, weans who are so relaxed that they only sleep, eat and play. They are far less trouble than that childish Leo of yours. He's supposed to be an adult but behaves as if he is a two-year-old aristocrat demanding a golden spoon instead of the sterling silver one that sits in his big, fat, ungrateful mouth.' She frowned for a moment, obviously thinking of the trouble my favourite chef often caused her.

'They take after their father. He loves to sleep, eat and play, and he's relaxed all the time. Three out of three.' I erupted into loud giggles, and Aaron smiled at me from across the room, his eyes twinkling in amusement. The twins gripped his fingers and made sweet little noises while he held his face close to theirs, whispering softly to them and telling them his secrets. He was supposed to be at work now, but I didn't want to disturb his time with them by saying anything. He was so besotted with his children that it bordered on obsession, completely melting my heart to know just how loved our babies were.

Bessie finished my hair, piling it up on top of my head before pinning every curl into place securely, while leaving only a few small tendrils loose to frame my face. She helped me into one of my fashionable house dresses as Aaron watched appreciatively.

'I haven't seen ya in that one. It's an intense shade of orange, isn't it? It suits ya, though,' he called out as I crossed the room, winking mischievously at me. I picked up Thomas and cradled him in the crook of my arm as Aaron took Emmy and placed her upright against his chest, her face peeking out over the back of his shoulder. I beamed at her as I followed him out of the room, calling out our farewells to Bessie before making our way downstairs. We passed by the kitchen and moved towards the back door where I always kept the perambulator just outside under the verandah. Leo noticed us, and within moments we were swamped by the staff cooing over the weans and wanting to hold them, causing Aaron to be even later than he already was. We were finally able to excuse ourselves, much to my relief, and quickly placed the twins inside the perambulator before setting off toward the stables. Aaron proudly pushed the carriage as the twins lay side by side, touching each other's faces.

'I'm bein' a bludger, I know, shirkin' me work to come home all the time to see 'em, but they grow so fast, Abi. I don't wanna miss a moment.'

'You've already shown yourself to be a wonderful father, Aaron.' My leather shoes crunched on the gravel path as we wound our way through the garden, the autumn leaves carpeting the ground under the canopy of sprawling branches far above, some native while others had been planted by my aunt's own hands. I inhaled the crisp, cool air, the smell of eucalyptus heavy as I stopped beside a row of white roses—the petals already starting to curl and wither. Aaron stopped ahead of me and waited while I bent down and picked several sprigs of lavender, quickly placing them in my pocket before hurrying to his side. 'I am more than happy with how my life is turning out. When I arrived here a year ago, never in my wildest dreams would I have thought this was where I would be today. I truly believed I would be living in a small cottage with my friends, while allowing Hamish to court me—and eventually catch me in years to come. Then you came into my life out of nowhere and changed everything. All my plans were thrown out the window, and I took a whole new path that has made me happier than I ever thought I could be. You are my world, as are our children.'

He smiled as we came to the gravel track that separated the garden from the stables. He turned and took me in his arms, holding me tightly before kissing the top of my head.

'You're me world, too, an' always will be, as are these two precious little souls.' He stopped the perambulator in front of the large stable doors and bent down to lift them from the carriage, snuggling one in each arm. He stepped inside the warm building, the pleasant smell of fresh manure and hay filling my nose as I followed him to Goliath's stall—my heart beating faster as he stepped inside. I leaned on the railing that kept Goliath safely inside and watched him closely. I felt nervous allowing my babies around such a large and dominant stallion—one who did not possess the sweetest of natures as many a stable hand could attest.

He approached the horse slowly, whispering to him and ensuring he was calm before moving nearer. Goliath raised his head inquisitively at his master's voice, walked over, then sniffed my babies. I was terrified he would open his enormous mouth and take a bite out of one of them, but Aaron was careful not to startle him. He held the twins up to the enormous stallion, telling them of how they would ride their own horses one day and of all the adventures they would have once they could walk, which made me smile and brought tears to my eyes.

Aaron had decided to give Thomas and Emmy the twin foals born last year to the beautiful and placid Sugar Bell. After running a practised eye over them only last week, Aaron confidently told me that they were growing into a magnificent colt and filly and would be ready to ride in a year or two—leaving my stomach knotted up and my heart racing at the thought. Goliath pawed at the ground, startling me. I quickly entered the stall and took the twins from their father, who reluctantly handed them over after cursing under his breath, unaware that I heard every word. I did not want him to be delayed any further, or use us as his excuse yet again, as I was well aware Harry was far from impressed with his work ethic and had recently been overheard directing the blame at me. Aaron sighed before following me out to where their baby carriage waited, the early morning sunshine starting to cut through the heavy dew that had settled on the ground.

'What's wrong with you, misery guts?' He held open the cumbersome wooden door, allowing me to step outside before following me to the perambulator. He pried Emmy from my arms and held her to his chest, gently removing her bonnet before kissing the top of her head.

'I wish there were more hours in the day.' He placed her down on the soft, feathered mattress Margaret had made for them before kissing Thomas. 'I hate bein' away from you an' the nippers. I never thought I would say it, but I wish I was their Ma an' got to stay home, an' ya were the Da who had to go out an' work.' I giggled at the scandal such an arrangement would cause as Harry opened the door and brought Goliath out. He had kindly saddled him, aware just how behind Aaron already was and would continue to be if I didn't leave and stop distracting him.

'It's only a couple of hours until we see you at the lake, so cheer up, my darling.' I gently touched his cheek and smiled as Harry returned to the stable and slammed the door behind him. Aaron smiled back, then bent down and kissed me goodbye before kissing the twins once again. He expertly mounted his horse, and I waved to him cheerily as he reluctantly kicked him forward and rode away.

Both babies looked around wide-eyed as I set off toward the village, pushing the heavy perambulator with both hands and a great deal of effort. I stopped at the top of the hill and loosened their blankets so they could kick freely, finding I had over-wrapped them now the autumn sun had started to gather its strength. The perambulator Aaron had purchased was the best he could find. Imported from England and identical to the one Queen Victoria had used for her children half a century ago—and now used for her grandchildren. The wheels were large and the carriage well made, making it only slightly easier to push over the thick grass and undulating paddocks. The body of the carriage had high sides, and there was a shade cover at the top that could be pulled down to stop the sun from shining on their vulnerable skin. The summer sun in Australia was fierce and like nothing I had ever experienced. It would burn a white man's skin in a very short time, leaving it bright red and blistered, even if only exposed for an hour or two. I made sure its harsh rays never directly touched the twins, whatever the season, their skin, unfortunately like mine and not their father's, who turned golden brown almost immediately.

I turned the perambulator towards Amelia's shop, whistling to myself as we passed the terraces while cheerfully greeting the residents who were out in their front gardens—delaying me more than half-an-hour. Most were friendly and loved to have a natter, making it difficult to get away without being rude, especially when you had somewhere you needed to be.

I saw Amelia engaged in conversation with Polly through the window as I approached. She had kindly offered to help her a few days a week as the store had become so busy, Amelia struggled at times to run it on her own. Working at the general store suited Polly as it gave her something to do, provided some extra pocket money, and she could take William with her. They both greeted me warmly as I pushed the carriage through the front door. They fussed over the twins before we sat at the table behind the counter to have tea. I held William to my bosom, who stared back at me with his big, brown eyes and his father's smile.

'Are you and Angus coming tonight?' I asked Polly, who held Emmy on her lap. She stared down at her, gently touching her cheek before kissing her on the forehead.

'Yes, of course. We are taking Willy up to the main house to stay with little Mary and the twins. This will be the first time Angus and I have been alone since he was born, and I'm so excited. Can you believe we've been here a year?' She shook her head in disbelief, tickling Emmy's tummy with a finger. Amelia came back with our tea and joined us. She picked up Thomas, who had been frantically kicking his legs in the air, and settled him in her arms.

'I suspect that Jenny Pickering is pregnant,' Amelia interjected, her voice low as I helped myself to a scone spread with jam and thick, sweet cream, then started to eat.

'What makes you think that?' I asked, forgetting I had food in my mouth. She leaned in towards us to avoid being overheard, despite there being no one else in sight.

'Lately, I've noticed that when she's serving food, she looks positively green, and on more than one occasion, I've witnessed her drop everything and run out the back door to the privy with no warning,' she replied smugly. If true, I believed that starting a family together would be wonderful for her and Harry—especially Harry—who had been alone for a long time. I couldn't help but notice my stomach clenched at the thought of him having a child with another woman, leaving me feeling ridiculous and highly embarrassed.

We chatted about our children while Amelia got up to attend to the shop throughout our morning tea, always returning to the conversation when she was finished and her customers had departed feeling satisfied with the service and their purchase. It was soon time for me to meet Aaron for lunch, and I quickly rose to my feet. We prepared to part ways, hugging each other goodbye on the front verandah.

As I neared the lake, I noticed the twins frantically sucking their fists and realised they were hungry—again. My breasts felt heavy and full and were becoming uncomfortable. I still wore the dresses Catherine had made me when I was carrying, finding them the most comfortable of all the dresses in my extensive wardrobe. Due to the stretch of the material, they had shrunk back to fit my shape, and although a little loose around the stomach they allowed me to expose my breasts and feed them without having to undress. I refused to resume wearing corsets, much to Bessie's chagrin, and wore nothing but my shift and petticoats under my dress now. It was a battle that was ongoing between Bessie and me, and I was winning so far, but the war was not over yet, and I knew it.

Aaron had a blanket laid out at the lake and the basket he had collected from Leo beside him. He stood as I approached and came to take the babies from me.

'Stop. Wait. I have to feed them first. I'm sorry, but if you want to start eating, go ahead.' I stopped the carriage and picked up both babies before sitting down on the blanket. They still didn't cry, even when hungry, and I again wondered if something was wrong with them.

I pulled open the top of my dress, exposing both breasts as Aaron sat down beside me and touched the babies, gently stroking their heads while murmuring sweet words only for their ears. I organised myself to feed them as quickly as I could, then reached over to pick Thomas up. I attached him to my breast and grimaced for a moment as he sucked hungrily, then reached out for Emmy, who immediately did the same. It still hurt for the first few minutes when they would suckle, having made my nipples so sensitive and sore, but even if given the choice, I wouldn't have changed a thing because they were both growing and were healthy in every way. I relaxed as I felt my milk start to flow out of me and slow relief as the tightness in my breasts began to subside. Aaron watched me intently, then reached over and gently touched my face.

'Is it wrong to watch ya doin' the most beautiful thing in the world, an' find it seductive?'

'Aaron, the things you find aesthetic do not surprise me anymore,' I teased, rolling my eyes. The sounds of the native birds above filled the silence around us while the clear water lapped gently at the sandy banks of the lake. Harry had told me in passing only last week that an underground spring-fed into it, and the water held minerals that were good for the body inside and out. I had tried it the last time I was here and spat it out immediately, finding it tasted like metal.

'Why? Do ya think the things I find erotic strange?' He attempted to feign horror but did not quite achieve it as he broke into a wide grin. 'Just remember, I find *you* to be beguilin'. That'd make you strange.' He chuckled to himself, glancing down at our babies to ensure they were drinking their fill.

'I stand by it, Aaron. Who in the world finds toes stimulating?'

'Toes in general don't rouse me appetite all that much, but I do find *your* toes stimulatin'. There's a difference.' He smiled, taking off my shoes and wiggling my toes with his fingers. Thomas and Emmy had both gone slack in my arms, their eyes firmly closed, and suckled only occasionally, now their bellies were nearly full and sleep beckoned. Aaron took Emmy and rubbed her back until she burped loudly, then placed her in the carriage, already sound asleep. I held Thomas on my lap; however, he had no interest in burping or doing anything other than sleeping like his sister. Aaron took him from me and tucked him up next to Emmy, kissing them both on their cheeks before sitting down beside me and making himself comfortable. He kissed me for a long time before pulling away and gazing into my eyes. 'Hello, Abi,' he whispered, and I leaned in and kissed him back.

'Hello, my handsome man. I miss you too, you know, when you're away from us and working.' I reached up and placed my hand on his cheek, running my finger along his jaw. I began to unpack the food and dish it onto the cast-iron plates Leo had packed, feeling ravenous. We ate our lunch companionably, looking out over the water to the island. I could see why Aaron had told me it would be an ideal place to lay our old bones, as it was lovely and peaceful there. The gumtrees that dotted the island appeared to be hundreds of years old, and I had recently spotted a group of koalas up high eating their leaves. The strange little island was filled with native shrubs and trees, which I found beautiful.

Several months ago, Aaron had rowed me over the day the boat had been delivered, and we had walked around most of the small, man-made island, taking our time to explore the thick brush and native flora and fauna. The surrounding lake was of a decent size. I wondered how many men it had taken to dig it when the property was being quarried for the basalt rock—or bluestone, as most referred to it—over twenty-years before. I wasn't certain how deep it was as I hadn't swum there, but Aaron had told me it came up no higher than his shoulder.. He didn't believe it was suitable to swim in compared to the rivers and billabongs running through the property filled with fresh water and was highly concerned the minerals could cause harm, not only externally—believing it would weaken our bodies and cause disease if ingested.

He had refused to take me to Devil's Point to show me where Leroy was buried, avoiding that side of the island entirely. In fact, Aaron had earmarked the island for a cemetery well before we thought we would ever have to use it, and now it had become one, only nobody but us knew about the hidden grave. We had found an old, weathered headstone, the name unreadable, however, were able to decipher what appeared to be a short poem inscribed that had faded and would soon be gone if left to the weather. The grave was now shrouded in mystery over who, in fact, it belonged to, and how the poor soul came to be buried on the island, then seemingly forgotten by all who once knew him.

The short pier usually had our row boat tied to it, but it was conspicuously missing today, bringing my thoughts back to that awful night. To my knowledge, no one had been here looking for Leroy, and I doubted anyone would. He was on his own in England, and the only people he may have known there were other criminals. I doubted they would be bothered to follow him halfway around the world. They didn't seem the kind to go out of their way for anyone unless it benefited them.

I still believed what Aaron had done was right, but I knew that it haunted him. He would sometimes wake during the night in a cold sweat and have trouble getting back to sleep; however, he would never speak to me of his dreams.

While I packed up the leftovers and put everything back in the basket, Aaron leaned over his offspring, sleeping in their pram. I saw a slow smile spread across his face as he gently stroked their heads before going to Goliath and attaching the picnic basket behind his saddle. That done, he took me in his arms, completely encompassing my body, and looked down adoringly into my eyes.

'You have a lovely day, whatever ya end up doin'.' He adjusted the leather hat atop his head, the brim wide to protect his face from the sun, before slipping on his woollen coat, his long pants held up by thin leather braces, his light brown linen shirt hiding the two layers of long underwear beneath. 'Thoughts of you are always close, even when we're apart for a short time. Ya look even more beautiful today than ya did in that orange dress the day I met ya, Abi. Motherhood suits ya. It's what ya were born to do. Me Ma told me she's so proud of ya for not hirin' ten nannies to look after her grandchildren. She was worried we wouldn't provide 'em with a normal life 'cause of the money we have. She was anxious it'd go to our heads, especially mine, after we married. Ma thought we might start socialising in the same circles as ya wealthy friends, an' that we'd always be away from home all the time, allowin' strangers to raise our nippers.' I shook my head and rolled my eyes.

'Surely your mother doesn't believe I would leave my children or raise them like that?' I was astonished she would even consider such an idea.

'Of course not. Ya know what she's like when it comes to her grandchildren. She has a vivid imagination that runs wild sometimes—somethin' me' father reminds us of whenever she's scatty.' He chuckled and continued to hold me close against his broad chest. Reluctantly, I pulled away, not wanting to be the reason he was constantly late for work. He kissed me on the forehead before bending down and kissing his babies.

He mounted Goliath and smiled at me before turning the stallion's head and kicking him into a gallop. He waved over his shoulder, and I waved back. I checked on the children, placed my hands on the handle of the perambulator, and headed for the village, feeling full and very grateful for my lot in life.

I knocked on Maisie's front door and stepped back to wait, unsure if she was at home. I could hear someone hurrying up the hallway to the door before a beaming Maisie swung it open, not surprised at all to see me. She welcomed me in, and after I had managed to get the bulky carriage with its sleeping beauties inside the entrance, we embraced warmly. Within days of their birth, I realised that everything took twice as long once you had children. We became fast friends after she gave birth to Henry. Since I'd had the twins, we had become even closer.

'How are you, Mistress? Thomas and Emmy have grown so much already. They change every time I see them. I feel like they're my own niece and nephew.' She admired them both before going to the kitchen and placing the kettle on the stovetop to boil. Henry was sleeping in his crib as I entered the front room and sat on the lounge. The place was cosy and clean, and again I thought how easily I could live in one of these terraces with Aaron and the babies.

'How is Mr Masters enjoying his new role as a father?' I asked while she prepared refreshments for us.

'Oh, he's wonderful. He comes home after being on his feet all day, and the first thing he does is pick Henry up and take him to his chair to read while holding him close. It brings a tear to me eye to see it.' I couldn't imagine it despite the look of utter adoration on her face whenever she spoke of her husband, but I would take her at her word despite never witnessing Mr Masters behave any other way than stiff and formal.

I heard my babies stirring and made my way to their side, taking them from the carriage before placing them on the comfortable settee. They lay quietly on their backs and gazed up at the ceiling, their feet kicking in the air, their arms intertwined as they made soft little noises, as if they were talking to each other. Maisie and I sipped our tea, talking about motherhood and what it was like for her to stay at home after working so hard for so many years.

'I love being with Henry, but I find I need something to do during the day and to mix with other people. I have spoken to Margaret, who has agreed to take care of Henry for a small fee so I can return to my position, if that's suitable to you and Aaron?' She offered me a slice of cinnamon cake as I nodded thoughtfully. Despite having eaten my fill at lunch, I couldn't refuse, as that would be rude. And I could always make room for cake.

'Of course. You can start back when you're ready.' I bit into the moist, buttery cake she had only baked this morning and closed my eyes in bliss. I chewed slowly, savouring every crumb. We talked about the orphanage where I had been volunteering and how I decided to stop, as I didn't want to spend time away from the twins.

A week after they were born, Mother Hannah had been to visit, and we had sat in the garden while she cradled them in her arms, saying a special blessing over them. I explained to her how I felt, and she had smiled and said how much they had appreciated my help and company, but it was now time to care for my own. I promised to continue helping financially and that I would keep in contact, and Mother Hannah had given me her blessing, gently touched my cheek, and advised she would pray for my family daily before kissing me goodbye.

'I'm a bit worried about Jenny. She's been feeling so unwell of late, and she won't see a doctor.' Maisie appeared concerned about her neighbour and close friend.

'I'm sure if it gets worse, she will. She's a grown woman, Maisie, and Harry won't let her get too sick before he calls for Dr Richards. There's nothing to worry about,' I reassured her, not wanting to gossip. I organised myself to go, informing her that our friends would start to arrive soon and I wanted to be there to greet them.

I waved to Maisie as I walked up the street, pushing the pram, my babies still wide awake, and wondered if Catherine had returned to the house by now. She had left early this morning to ride the property with Colin, and I had gotten the feeling they planned to make a long day of it. I stopped at the end of the cobblestone street to gather my strength, gazing up at the top of the undulating hill before taking a deep breath, my hands holding tight to the carriage as I bent forward and pushed, smiling down at my babies as they closed their eyes, ready for their bed.

Chapter Two

When I arrived home, I found Catherine—exhausted but clearly happy—reclining on the oversized couch in the sitting room. I placed the twins on a lounge, sidled up close to her, then pounced, pinning her down with my body.

'So, tell me every single detail and do not leave anything out, or I will lick your face,' I threatened, sticking my tongue out only inches from her nose, making her squeal and giggle.

'Get off me, you big oaf. I will tell you everything. You are like a child sometimes, Abigail. That Leo is such a bad influence on you,' she squealed, pushing me away while still laughing. I moved away, flopping down heavily a few feet away from her in the lounge. She sat up, a dreamy look on her face as she reached across and held my hand. 'He kissed me today for the very first time, and it was so romantic,' she whispered, closing her eyes for a moment as if savouring the kiss all over again. 'We were down by the beach eating lunch, and he just leaned over and did it. It was lucky I had just swallowed my food.' She laughed at his timing, and I smiled. Her face was shining as she described what a gentleman he was. 'We are taking it slow because I don't want to relocate to Geelong until the end of the year. We will see what happens then when I am out from under my parents' control.' I was glad she was choosing her own path and didn't care what anyone thought, but worried for her if this budding romance did go farther and how her parents would react. I already knew

William's feelings on the matter, as he had made his opinion quite clear from the beginning.

I picked up the babies, then lay back on the lounge, placing them on my breasts to feed. When they had drunk their fill, they both fell asleep. I left them on my chest with a blanket tucked over them. I silently listened to Catherine as she told me her hopes and dreams. A little later, Aaron stuck his head through the door.

'There ya are. I've been lookin' for ya everywhere. Mary wants to take the twins once they've been fed so ya can have a kip then get ready for tonight.' He stepped inside and crossed the room in several strides before stopping next to the lounge and picking them up, holding them in the crook of each arm. I followed him to the nursery, finding little Mary folding clean clouts, the room immaculately clean and organised without a thing out of place.

'I was wonderin' where you were. Have they been good?' she enquired as we placed the twins in their cribs so I could change them again before they fell asleep. I told her of our adventures today, and she seemed pleased. 'Plenty of fresh air is the tonic for a growin' wean,' she advised knowledgeably, then waved us off the moment I had finished and the twins were sound asleep in their beds.

'I've got somethin' to tell ya,' Aaron remarked quietly, his face grave as we left the nursery. I must have shown alarm as he smiled, placing his hand on my arm to stop me. 'Settle down. It's nothin' bad. I found a dingo today all alone out by the river. I looked around the scrub to find its mother, but couldn't see hide nor hair of her, so brought him home. I'm gunna call him Dingo,' he said proudly. I stared up at him as we stood beside a timber sideboard in the wide hallway that held several of my great aunt's treasures, my eyes sparkling in amusement.

'That's *so* original, Aaron. Where is he now?'

'Down in the kitchen gettin' all the staffs' attention an' being fed beef an' beer pies.'

Aaron took my hand and led me down the grand staircase and to the kitchen to show me. In a basket was a tiny yellow pup that was so thin I could count his ribs that protruded under his short coat. They had placed a bowl of warm milk in with him, which he had lapped up within moments and licked the bowl clean. He didn't look more than a week old and was so small and fragile. If Aaron hadn't found him, I was sure he would have died. Someone had cut up a warm beef pie into tiny pieces and placed the bowl next to him. He ate it as if he had never seen food before and wouldn't again. I didn't want to pick him up in case I hurt him, so stroked him gently. He was a sweet little thing. I had never been this close to a dingo, having only seen them around the property at a distance.

They were native to Australia and lived in the outback, usually in the north, and were rare in Victoria. I was uncertain if Aaron planned to release him when he was older and more robust, as dingoes were generally not kept as pets. We left him with his warm beef pie and returned upstairs.

'Ya need to rest for a bit. It's gunna be a late night,' Aaron remarked, pulling me down on the bed with him. For someone who had been nagging me to sleep, he kept me awake for much longer than I expected. Afterwards, I cuddled into him, drifting off into a land full of giants, seashells, and snakes—the Southern Cross high above them.

I heard Bessie come scurrying into the room and slowly opened my eyes.

'Time to get up, Mistress,' she called out cheerfully, then swiftly flung open my heavy drapes, flooding the room with light. Aaron, who could sleep through a hurricane, was still snoring softly beside me as I slipped out of bed and put on my dressing gown.

'Now, I don't want to wear anything fancy tonight, Bessie. Maybe one of the new dresses that Catherine brought down for me that I haven't seen yet?'

She nodded and headed for the dressing room. Based on my old measurements, Catherine had made me some dresses in the new cloth she had managed to purchase from London. She promised me they would be as comfortable as the dresses I wore while carrying my babies.

Bessie returned with a plain dress in emerald green, her favourite colour. She helped me into it, and I was pleased as I studied my reflection in the full length looking glass. As Catherine had promised, it was extremely comfortable but looked fashionable. I sat at my dressing table for Bessie to do my hair. I rarely wore hats unless I was leaving the property as no man or woman went out publicly without covering their head, no matter what their social standing. Bessie bluntly refused to let me wear my hair down if I planned to step foot off the soil of Willow Grove, but did compromise by allowing me to be free at home. She enthusiastically took a hairbrush to it as she told me of recent gossip, leaving my hair in shiny waves that hung around my waist. I noticed that Aaron had awakened, and I turned to find him staring across at me with an odd look in his eyes.

'Ya look beautiful in that dress with ya hair like that.' He wiggled his eyebrows wickedly as I laughed aloud.

'Thank you. It's one of the new ones that Catherine made for me, which reminds me, I must still pay her for them. Don't let me forget,' I said, watching him closely as he got up to get dressed. He nodded before disappearing into his dressing room, leaving me ready and waiting on him for the first time since we had married.

We found Polly and Angus, along with William and Catherine, in the sitting room—Leo only having joined them a few minutes before. They lounged around comfortably as they gossiped. Well, Leo gossiped and they sat silently, their eyes wide. They all listened in fascination, wondering if some of his rumours could even be possible, let alone true. We sat down next to Catherine to wait for the others to arrive, the mood in the room jovial as they bantered and teased each other.

The Cavanaugh family were the next to arrive, bringing Victoria, and there was lots of kissing and back thumping while they greeted each other. They all found a seat and quietened down. They were rowdy when they were together—so loud, in fact, you could often hear them coming from a mile away.

'How's it feel to be a Da, old mate? You've aged twenty-years already,' Aiden said as Victoria sat down next to him, smiling up at him adoringly.

'Maybe ya should try it. Ya might like havin' someone else to think about other than yaself all the time, ya selfish dickhead,' Aaron retorted, causing Victoria to blush bright red. They were very much in love, with Aiden being the only man she had ever allowed to court her. She had been pursued by several very eligible men but rebuffed all who displayed any romantic interest. I knew she would marry Aiden as soon as he asked her, but, unlike his brother, he was a slow mover.

Martin and Dana arrived. She had started to regain the weight she had lost after Charlotte's death, and even though she was nowhere near back to her usual self, she was certainly doing much better than before.

Soon Tamara and Brian joined us. They had made the trip from Melbourne and were staying the night, as were Elizabeth and Eric, who hadn't come downstairs yet. We chatted while we waited for Amelia and Tommy, who came rushing into the room shortly after, apologising for their tardiness. They had left little Mathew with Margaret from across the road, and he wouldn't settle, causing their delay. Amelia embraced everyone present, many of whom she had not seen since staying with us when George had beaten her, and they were all genuinely pleased to see her again and find her well.

Mr Masters entered the room and informed us that dinner was served, causing everyone to stand at once to join him in the dining room. Once we were all seated and ready to begin, Hamish rushed through the door.

'I'm sorry I'm late,' he apologised, crossing the room to sit next to Angus. I saw Dana freeze when she heard his voice and her body tense. She sat motionless, looking away as he made himself comfortable and joined in the conversation. She refused to look at him and kept her head down, focusing on her plate. I noticed Martin place his hand on hers in support, and she looked up at him and smiled weakly.

'So, what do you think of your new shop?' Martin asked Mr Cavanaugh, whose eyes lit up with excitement.

'We've never seen anythin' so modern. I think we'll make a good trade there,' Gavin Cavanaugh replied before they descended into deep discussions regarding business that went above my head.

Tamara sat opposite me, her face glowing. She had recently found out that she was with child, thanks to the week when Brian had made love to her—now many months ago—and was over the moon. I was happy for her. It was something she had wanted so desperately in the hope a child would improve her marriage. She had somehow managed to get her own way again despite her husband not wanting to have an intimate relationship with her. Elizabeth and Eric had just returned from their honeymoon and only had eyes for each other. He sat with his arm protectively around her as we waited for dinner to be served.

Mr Masters supervised the footmen, who began carrying serving bowls around the table, stopping beside each guest to offer them the first course. I noticed Dana's hand trembling when she served herself some roasted asparagus with salmon smoked by my own father-in-law; however, she soon regained her composure and started to eat, but only once her plate held the appropriate amount of food deemed acceptable for a lady to eat in public. She quietly chatted with Polly and even managed to smile a few times at Leo, who was acting like an idjit, as usual. Aaron smiled at me and winked. He had been watching Dana, too, and had been nervous about how she would react tonight.

Halfway through dinner, Polly stood up and tapped her crystal glass with a spoon, demanding we stop talking and pay attention to her. This was unplanned and surprising—she didn't like to speak in front of groups. Even the footmen stopped while our guests sat back in their chairs expectantly, the room silent. It took her several moments to calm her nerves before she began.

'It was one year ago today that Abigail, Bessie, Mary, Leo, and I arrived here on these shores with an unknown future, along with some of you sitting here with us tonight. You are all dear to us. Well, not so much Leonardo. Only his absence would make this night truly perfect.' I heard someone snigger and looked across suspiciously at my brothers-in-law. 'Anyway, one thing we did know for certain was whatever the circumstances, we would be all right because we had each other. Today, we still have each other, except the bond we share has only become stronger.' Leo narrowed his gaze, then stuck his middle finger up at her. She decided to go on, ignoring him. 'Since being here, we have made friends who have become like family. Abi has turned a large, empty, stark mansion into a home. Not just for us, but for the people who work here, too.' She smiled at me before continuing. 'This house may be fancy, but because of you, Abi, it's filled with love and happiness. It isn't like most grand estates. You have turned it into something unique and special, whether people agree or are comfortable with it or not. I love how we live, and I can't imagine being this happy anywhere else, or being surrounded by better people. I would like everyone to raise their glass in a toast to us, and the many happy years we will all spend together here at Willow Grove.'

They cheered, then drank deeply, many charging their glasses more than once and clapping for Polly, her cheeks flushed while tears glimmered in her eyes, while many around the table had tears in their own. When she sat down, Angus slipped his large arm around her proudly. We continued our repast, with everyone laughing and talking, until the delicate glasses of crème brûlée arrived. After we had finished our coffee, we retreated to the sitting room.

Mr Masters stood at the liquor cabinet in the corner of the room preparing drinks and serving them on a sideboard, ensuring that no glass was left empty for more than a few moments. I loved being with everyone. There was so much to talk about, and all present seemed to be enjoying themselves, even if they did imbibe to excess at times.

After some time, Mr and Mrs Cavanaugh excused themselves for the night, saying they were too old to be out this late. We laughed at them but let them go. They were only in their early forties, which did seem old to me; however, Aaron had explained they were young in comparison to some of his mates' parents.

We led them up to the nursery so they could see the twins, and when Aaron could finally pry them away, we stood in the driveway and waved their carriage off as they headed toward home. Aaron stopped me from going inside, gently grabbing my upper arm as I went to step through the grand entrance.

'Stay with me for just one-minute, Abi.' He pulled me into his arms as I reached up and brushed the hair from his eyes. 'I need some time alone with ya. It's tense in there with Dana an' Hamish, an' I'm just waitin' for 'em to start bluein' in front of everyone,' he said, breathing in the scent from my hair.

'I know. I feel the same way. She seems to be calm enough, but that could change in a split second. He will only have to say one word wrong and she will jump across the table and kill him with a butter knife,' I replied, hoping that tonight no blood was shed. He kissed me for a long time before letting me go.

'I don't wanna think about what could happen. I'm lookin' forward to spendin' the evenin' with ya an' enjoyin' the company of our friends.' I nodded, swallowing hard as he ushered me back inside and into the sitting room to join the others.

I excused myself, raising my voice to be heard over the excited banter. It was time to give the twins their last feed for the night. Aaron rose to his feet and followed me up to the nursery, walking side by side while speaking quietly about Dana. Thomas and Emmy were wide awake when we picked them up and carried them to our room. I lay back on the pillows and offered them my breasts, both latching on immediately and sucking frantically before slowing their pace. I had found this was their usual habit now; however, it still caused me a great deal of discomfort.

'They're such good little nippers. Is it usual for 'em to be this quiet? I see the new mothers in the village, an' they haven't slept for days. I hear babies screamin' an' squalkin' all the time down there, but not these two. Do ya think they're all right?' Aaron asked, appearing worried.

'Dr Richards says they are perfectly healthy. They are just content and like to sleep,' I replied, feeling slightly concerned myself. I stroked their bodies while they drank their fill. Once they stopped suckling and their tiny bodies had gone limp, Aaron lifted Thomas up while I fixed my dress. We carried them back to the nursery and kissed them goodnight before tucking them into their cradles. Willy was sound asleep in a crib in the corner while little Mary sat on the bed, knitting a thick scarf for the approaching winter. She smiled and bid us goodnight as we waved, the kerosene lamp beside her casting a romantic light across the room before we closed the door behind us.

Dana was by my side as I strolled along the well-worn path beside the stables and over the hill towards the village pub.

'How are you feeling? Tell me the honest truth.'

'I'm much improved, Abigail. I am up every morning and running my house and back in touch with my friends and acquaintances. I am attending my first social function next week,' she replied, reaching out and taking my hand in hers. She wore no jewellery anymore and still dressed in black; however, she wore no veil anymore, and the colour had returned to her face.

'How are you coping with seeing Hamish for the first time?' She stopped at the top of the hill, allowing others to pass us before turning and looking me straight in the eye.

'I will be honest with you, Abigail. Out of respect for you, I'm trying to keep my temper and not harm him. I know that you are still friends, and I would never put you in a position where you had to choose between us, but I *hate* him. I will never forgive him for using my Charlotte, then discarding her and their unborn child like they were shit on his shoe.' Her voice faltered as tears welled in her eyes. I squeezed her hand as we navigated our way down the hill, the charming village lit up brightly tonight.

'Has anyone told you that Hamish was planning to do the right thing and marry Charlotte? He just needed a little more time.'

'No, I have not heard that before, but it makes no difference. He took too long to decide, didn't he? Fatally too long. He did not at any point give Charlotte a shred of hope that he was even considering marrying her. I am sorry, but I blame him completely, and I always will.' I squeezed her hand again as we passed the terraces, tears trickling down her face.

Aaron came up behind me and cheekily squeezed my backside before putting his arm around my waist and chuckling. I knew he was looking forward to seeing everyone, having a drink with friends, and listening to music.

When we arrived at the pub, Angus and Hamish pushed as many tables together as possible, allowing everyone to sit down. Bessie and Danny joined us, and she sat down heavily in a chair next to me, her eyes bright and her face beaming with joy.

'Just think, Mistress, this time last year, we were all unmarried and had nowhere to live and look at us all now.' Aaron placed two bottles of whisky on the table and several jugs of beer. It looked like it was going to be one of those nights, I thought with a smile, as they began filling the empty glasses.

The music began, and Aaron led me to the dance floor where other couples were dancing slowly, their bodies so close you couldn't see a sliver of light between them. He pulled me against him, and as he wrapped his arms around me.

'I desire ya so much, it's driving me mad,' he whispered, kissing my face while we danced. I felt the same way, but Dr Richards had been very strict about us not resuming sexual relations for at least six-weeks. I felt fine and was sure I would be all right, but Aaron had taken the doctor's warning very seriously.

'It's only a month, and it's not as though we aren't doing other things so stop complaining.'

'The next four-weeks are gunna take forever,' he griped. I said nothing more, resting my cheek against his chest while we danced through several slow songs.

The mood in the pub was festive, with workers from other farms arriving to celebrate with us. Aaron and I returned to the table just as the music changed and the rhythm quickened. Half the room got up to dance, except for Martin and Dana, leaving only us on the table to keep them company.

'Look at him up there dancing with that *girl*,' Dana snapped bitterly, nodding toward Hamish and Ruby, who appeared to be having a great deal of fun. She glared across at him hatefully; however, he hadn't noticed her even looking at him. 'As far as I'm concerned, he might as well have killed Charlotte with his own two hands. That's how responsible he is for her death,' she spat, taking a long sip of whisky. I placed my hand on hers and gently said her name, making her look up at me, her eyebrows arched inquiringly.

'Hate is like drinking poison and expecting the other person to die. It only affects you. I hope in time it will lessen for you, Dana, but tonight I'm proud of you. You are controlling yourself well.'

Thinking it might ease her pain, I suggested she pay a visit to the medium in Melbourne she had mentioned long ago and ask her to try contacting Charlotte in the hereafter. While I didn't fully believe such things were possible, my own experiences with clairvoyance and the golden glow convinced me that we were much more complicated and mysterious than we thought.

'I will consider consulting with her again one day,' Dana replied, 'but it's too soon for me to travel that far. Besides, what if I find out she was sent to the depths of hell for killing herself? I couldn't stand knowing she was suffering more than she did in this life.'

'Dana, I do not believe Charlotte is in hell. She had too many good qualities to end up there because of a tragic mistake. All I know is that when I have a chance, I'm going to pay Madame Zvezda a visit myself. I have some serious questions that need answers, and maybe she can provide them.' Dana nodded miserably before returning her attention to the glass in her hand.

Many had returned to the table, hot and thirsty and ready to celebrate some more. Colin had joined us, and he and Catherine were absorbed in conversation with William. Harry and Jenny sat down with us, and Aaron poured them a drink. Since he had become involved with Jenny, Harry was the happiest I had seen him, and she seemed just as besotted with him, despite the age difference.

'I wanna thank you for allowin' Jenny to move in with me,' I overheard him say quietly to Aaron. Jenny excitedly talked to me about how she had decorated their home, and how lovely everything was now that it had a woman's touch. Harry appeared embarrassed, his handsome cheeks slightly flushed. 'I don't know what it is, but I have a morbid fear of marriage,' he continued. 'Although I wanna marry Jenny, and I love her more than anythin', I can't bring myself to do it.'

'All I can say, mate, is once ya do get up the nerve to go through with it, it'll be the best thing ya ever did,' Aaron replied, smiling and thumping him on the back.

I was standing at the bar when I saw Patty frown as she rushed around trying to get everything done at once all alone.

'What's wrong? Can I help?' I asked before making my way behind the bar. I was only drinking lightly tonight in case the babies needed me when I got home. She looked at me gratefully.

'Thank you, Mistress, it's just that it's so busy in here tonight. I've never seen so many people, and I can't leave the bar unattended. There's a box in the second storeroom in the back with some glasses in it, and I'm running short. Would you mind getting them for me, please?' she asked, almost apologetically.

'Of course not. I'll get them now, but only if you stop calling me Mistress,' I replied with a smile.

'Okay, then, Abigail, but only because I'm desperate for the extra glasses.' She giggled to herself as I walked through the pub, greeting people I was starting to get to know well, then opened the door leading to the storerooms.

Once closed, I made my way down the narrow hallway to the second storeroom and opened the door. I gasped loudly and immediately froze, unable to move a muscle. Only a few feet away from me stood Samuel and Brian engaged in a sexual act. They heard me gasp again; however, I was still unable to move or look away. I had never seen men have sex before. Although it shocked me, it also fascinated me, and I wondered if it felt the same as it did between men and women. Brian looked up at me in horror, quickly pulling up his trousers, while Samuel did the same. A lamp burned on a table, illuminating the room far too brightly for my liking. Samuel couldn't look at me. He stood stone still, his face the colour of beetroot, staring at the ground. Realising what this meant, I knew I must leave before anger got the best of me. I turned and ran back up the hallway, slamming the door behind me as I stepped back into the pub.

I returned to the table, sat back down next to Dana, and picked up a glass of straight whisky, downing it in several swallows. Now I understood why Brian was so cold to Tamara. It wasn't because he had another woman; it was because he was a homosexual. I saw Samuel slip out the door and walk to the bar, where he casually talked with some friends from a neighbouring property. Brian returned to the table not long after and sat with the other men as though nothing had happened.

Now that it was safe, I cautiously went to retrieve the glasses for Patty, making sure I knocked on every door I went through. Poor Leo. He thought he had found the love of his life in Samuel and had no clue he was being betrayed. I was so angry with both men. I felt like sacking Samuel on the spot and announcing what I had just discovered to the entire pub. But I knew I couldn't humiliate Tamara or Leo like that and would have to think carefully about what I would do with the information.

I returned to the bar with a box of glasses for Patty, who thanked me profusely and handed me a glass of lemonade with raspberry syrup that she kept hidden in a cupboard just for me. I returned to the table and sat on Aaron's lap, putting my arms around his neck and squeezing him tightly. He would know what to do when I talked to him about it later, but for now, I felt it would cause them too much pain if I told Leo and Tamara. On the other hand, what were the consequences for them both living with liars who were blatantly betraying them while appearing ignorant of their true natures? I felt awful for Tamara. She was expecting their first child this year and hoped it would bring her closer to her husband, who showed no interest in her and never would. I was confused and still in shock that they would do this to the people who loved them.

'Are ya all right, Abi? Ya body's all tensed up,' Aaron asked, massaging my neck.

'Yes, I'm fine. I will talk to you about it later if you're not too drunk.'

'I don't plan to be too pissed to play later,' he whispered in my ear, sending shivers up my spine. I kissed him with the promise of what was to come, a slow smile spreading across his handsome face when I pulled away.

Hamish was sitting at the table drinking whisky and talking animatedly with Ruby when Liza approached and threw her beer all over him. It happened so quickly that no one had time to react, including him.

'That's what you get, Hamish Makenzie, breakin' a girl's heart like that. You promised me a future and led me on, only to throw me over for other women. You step out with them for a short time, using all of us, then move on to the next. Watch out, Ruby. He'll do the same to you as he has done to me and so many others. Do you really think a lowly kitchen maid would be welcome at the great Makenzie table? He's just using you until he finds a bride with the right breeding who his parents will approve of. You have no heart, Hamish, and you have a black soul. I hope you rot in hell!' she screamed, then turned on her heel and fled the room.

Hamish wiped the beer from his hair and face with Ruby's help, appearing calm but perplexed. He shook his head in disbelief that Liza would act in such a manner in public.

He really didn't have a clue when it came to women and the trail of hurt he was leaving behind—or maybe he just didn't care. I silently wished he would find his women away from here and resolved to tell him so. Now I would have to deal with two warring maids and, inevitably, two broken hearts. Whenever I looked at Hamish, I still saw all the good and lovely qualities I knew he had—qualities he would never show to others. I loved him, but I wasn't in love with him anymore, and I prayed he would find happiness somewhere that would allow him to act like the person I knew he was. Hopefully at a neighbouring property rather than here at Willow Grove given the trouble it caused.

Fortunately, Dana and Martin hadn't witnessed Hamish's latest faux pas. They had left hours ago because, after a few drinks, Dana began feeling tempted to jump across the table and strangle Hamish. Martin thought it best to leave before any public outbursts or murders occurred in front of a room full of witnesses.

We gathered outside the pub and said our goodbyes. Most were tipsy, some more than others. A few staggered up the street toward home, drunkenly singing an Irish song they seemed to have learnt tonight.

As Aaron and I walked together hand in hand, Hamish came up alongside us. Aaron shook his head and placed a hand on his shoulder.

'Hamish, what're ya doin', mate? Two of our maids?' he asked incredulously. Hamish looked down at the ground, unable to hold my gaze.

'Aye, I know, an' I'm sorry fer it. It just happened that way, an' now I've made another mess fer meself. Ye'd think I'd have learnt me lesson.' I nodded slightly in silent agreement. Aaron slapped him on the back, and Hamish walked on ahead of us to catch up with Angus.

'Did ya have a good night, Abi?' Aaron asked. He kept his arm around my waist while we slowly trudged up the hill.

'Yes, I did, and it made me realise how much my life has changed in a single year. I'm a wife and a mother now. I didn't plan on doing that for years, but it has all turned out better than I ever would have expected.'

Colin and Catherine walked behind us hand in hand, much to William's disgust, but he tried to ignore them and continued talking to Polly about her next trip to Melbourne. We passed the stables, and I let out a deep sigh. It had been a long night, and I was feeling tired now. As we arrived at the house, Aaron and I went inside with the others, while Catherine and Colin stayed in the garden.

We headed to the warm kitchen to eat leftovers, which turned into a feast as Leo continued to bring food to the table, heating the savoury dishes in the hot oven. I took plates out to Colin and Catherine while the others sat around the large table eating as if they hadn't seen food in a month. After I had finished three desserts, I was so full I sat back on my chair, barely able to move.

'You realise in most grand houses like this, Abigail, if the master is hungry, the servants get up to serve a hot meal no matter what time of night it is?' William remarked haughtily. I rolled my eyes at him before raising my glass of lemonade in a toast.

'But isn't this more fun?' I replied, smiling as the room filled with laughter, and William raised his own glass in good cheer, smiling back at me.

Aaron and I crept into the nursery to kiss the twins before we retired for the night. They were sleeping peacefully next to each other; however, Aaron could not restrain himself from picking up Emmy, his head bent as he caressed her sleeping face. I slowly bent down and gently kissed Thomas, then Emmy, when Aaron placed her back in the cradle. They were so sweet and were becoming little miniatures of Aaron and myself. Emmy's hair was exactly like mine and had grown significantly since she was born.

We sneaked out of the room, leaving little Mary softly snoring, and made our way down the hallway to our room. This was our sanctuary, the place where we came when we wanted to be alone together, and now the place where we came together as a family. Aaron helped me undress.

'Let me choose ya nightgown,' he said, heading off to the dressing room. He came back with a black negligee that was more see-through lace than silk. I slipped it over my head, still feeling as if I were naked, then climbed up into bed. 'Dana held it together tonight.' He appeared surprised as he stripped off his shirt and trousers, letting them fall into a heap at his feet in the middle of the room before sliding into bed beside me.

'Yes, I was very proud of her, knowing how much she hates Hamish,' I replied, yawning widely. He pulled up the heavy quilt, covering us both before making himself comfortable.

'Surely, she's gunna realise Hamish intended to do the right thing an' forgive him, won't she?' He did not really know Dana that well, and it would be improper if he did. Men and women were not able to be close friends with another's husband or wife. They were expected to be polite and correct towards one another, but to form a close friendship would cause a scandal.

'Dana will never forgive Hamish for as long as she lives. We spoke of him tonight, and she made herself very clear Charlotte would still be with us if she hadn't had the ill fortune of meeting him on the ship.' My only concern was that hate would eat away at her until there was nothing left, and I would lose my friend forever.

'Talkin' about it is as useful as a third armpit. I don't wanna dream of the dead.' He gathered me in his arms, whispering wicked things in my ear. He pulled me up on top of him, instinctively making me move against him as I settled myself comfortably on his thighs. He looked up at me and raised an eyebrow. 'No, Abi. We're not doin' that. I just wanna look at ya.' He touched the lace against my skin, rubbing it gently between his large fingers, his eyes glinting in the dim room, the hearth providing the only light in the room as the fire burned warmly. 'How many nippers do ya want now ya have two at once to care for?'

'Twelve,' I replied immediately. Ever since I could remember, I had always wanted a dozen bairns at my feet, all raised in a happy home, and all mine.

'Lucky for you then ya not a sea hag an' I don't mind helpin' ya achieve that goal in the future,' he said, pulling me down and kissing my lips for the longest time. Later, as I lay naked in his arms, I dreamed of a powdered wig, a police officer, and a giant tiger snake.

Chapter Three

I WOKE UP EXCITED for the first time in my life. I hated Christmas at the orphanage, watching the village children in their new clothing, flaunting their sweets and playing with their new toys, while we trudged through the streets to attend mass and thank the Lord for providing the little we had. Tomorrow would be the twins' first Christmas, and being nine-months-old, they were starting to notice what was going on around them. Aaron and I had bought them toys from a shop in Geelong, and I couldn't wait to lay them out tonight and fill their stockings.

Our loved ones planned to enjoy Christmas lunch here with us. We had bought presents for all our friends and family, placing them under our enormous Christmas tree, which we had decorated with the sometimes help, sometimes hindrance, of Emmy and Thomas. Aaron had cut down a Geebung tree, deciding to follow the tradition of his parents, who had used the native plant due to its pine-tree-like leaves and its yellow flowers that bloomed around Christmas time. Given they could grow to around twelve feet tall, I understood its attraction. Aaron's memory of their first Christmas in Australia was of his father proudly dragging a Geebung through the front door and advising them the round, fleshy fruit was ripe to eat once they turned a deep purple in winter—deciding then and there to plant a number of them along the boundary of their property to attract a variety of mammals and birds throughout the year.

Catherine had been here all week. She was over the moon as I had surprised her and purchased a substantial building in the centre of Geelong town, a difficult task given she needed room to set up her sewing machines and work areas behind the large shop front. It was a magnificent building encompassing sweeping views over Corio bay, along with an entire floor above that she decided would be converted into an apartment she would use as her primary residence. When I had first taken her there to show her, she had burst into tears and embraced me tightly.

With her parents' blessing, Catherine had decided to call the business Montague's, continuing her father's legacy and honouring the gift he had so obviously passed down to his daughter. She planned to live with us until the building works were finished in the next few months. She was still seeing Colin and came to stay often. They were getting along famously, and their romance was progressing slowly, just as Catherine wanted it to, while Colin had been a perfect gentleman.

We were having a baby boom on the farm. Amelia and Tommy had just welcomed a little girl, while Harry and Jenny were blessed with a son several months ago—and three of the farmworkers' wives had recently fallen. Tamara had delivered a girl and was overjoyed she was pregnant again. She had somehow managed to manipulate Brian into performing his husbandly duties once more. I never did tell her and Leo what I had seen that night in the storeroom. After consulting with Aaron, he had wisely advised me that Samuel and Brian would trip themselves up and get caught by themselves without my interference and was worried I would be blamed for the repercussions if I said anything. Daylight began to break, and I could hear the kookaburra nearby start his morning song.

'G'mornin', beautiful,' Aaron murmured, slowly opening his eyes as I gazed back at him sleepily.

'Good morning, my love,' I replied, kissing his lips. I ran my hand down his chest and over his belly, then realised he was definitely wide awake. 'Really? Is there ever a time of day that you don't want it?'

'Nah, never. Only 'cause there's somethin' real special about ya. Must be ya incredible femininity an' lust for life. An' ya slow kisses an' curvaceous arse are a factor. When ya next to me, I can't help but want ya.' A slow smile spread across his face before he closed his eyes again, sighing contentedly. For a former fisherman, Aaron possessed a great deal of poetic talent.

'Well, we might have to do something about that,' I replied before slipping my arms around him and kissing him firmly on the mouth.

He stroked my bare back, relaxing my entire body as I thought about the twins. He had been so excited the day I handed them up to him on his horse and he took them for their first ride. They had enjoyed every moment, giggling as their father held them tight and they bounced along. He was a natural-born father, and he couldn't wait for them to walk so he could do more with them. He would come home several times throughout the day to see them and play with them before heading back to work.

They adored him as much as he did them and were so affectionate towards us. They loved little Mary, too, and I was more content now to leave them with her at times during the day if I needed to, as I saw how much she cared for them. They were primarily happy babies. They still slept through the night, even though their personalities were starting to emerge more and more each day as they became quite demonstrative.

I felt I had a perfect life, but there was something deep inside me waiting for it to go wrong. Waiting for something terrible to happen. I pushed it to the back of my mind, as I usually did when I didn't want to think about something, and tried to focus on happier thoughts. I was confident it was only my deep-seated fear that no life could remain as perfect as mine. I felt I didn't deserve what I had been given, nor the right to experience such pure happiness, as deep down, I was still the orphan nobody wanted.

We had recently held the twins' christening, and Hamish and Catherine were now Thomas and Emmy's godparents. They had looked beautiful in the handmade lace gowns with matching bonnets that Catherine had sewn for them.

I couldn't keep Hamish away from the twins; he would drop in every day to play with them and give them a treat. He was proving to be an admirable godfather and uncle, and a close friend to Aaron. It was evident to everyone that Angus and Hamish were now Aaron's best mates. They saw each other every day and did everything together. When it came to me, Aaron and Hamish had been able to put everything in the past, even though Aaron would tell me that Hamish still loved me deeply and would never stop.

This would always make me feel sad, and terribly, terribly guilty. There had been times where I noticed Hamish looking at me like he used to. When I would catch him, he would quickly look away and regain his composure, acting normally around me again. He was still stepping out with numerous women—he had told me himself—no one special, but sometimes quite a few of them at once.

There had been an economic bust in Victoria, with people losing money on stocks. Lots of businesses closed, putting thousands out of work, and many banks shut down.

A depression ensued, with so many having no work or a place to live. Some of the wealthy I had met lost everything, returning to their families in England, shattered and with their lives in ruins. We had taken on as many workers as we possibly could, but we still had a steady flow of people knocking on our door asking for work each week who we were forced to turn away.

Mr McPhee had advised me that I had been fortunate due to how my trust fund was managed, giving himself credit where I felt none was due. I had not lost as much as others, he had proudly informed me, clearly taking all the credit. We still had the money under the house to fall back on, and the way it was looking down there, we could live comfortably for years without touching another penny in the bank.

We had decided to give the staff and workers a ten-pound Christmas bonus this year and hoped it would be a pleasant surprise, along with the individual presents we had bought each of them. I felt overwhelmed with excitement about the holiday, as I got to share it with my babies. I vowed they would always look forward to and enjoy every aspect of their lives and the special days of the year that we would celebrate with them. I wanted them to have everything I had missed out on when I was growing up, and was doing everything in my power since the day I laid eyes on them to ensure they did.

They were such beautiful children. Thomas looked exactly like his father, even inheriting similar personality traits. He was calm and sweet and didn't have a temper. Emmy, however, was like me; she would become fiery if she didn't get what she wanted. Her hair was auburn like mine and grew like weeds, with it now curling down below her shoulders. Her eyes were like sparkling green emeralds, framed with beautiful, long eyelashes.

Just as I was thinking of them, there was a knock on the door, and little Mary stepped inside, the two freshly changed babies held against her chest before she hurried to the bed and placed them in our arms. She set a bottle for each on the nightstand. They squealed in delight at seeing us, and we kissed and hugged them. They were crawling now, and there was no stopping them. We had to make sure the doors were closed to any room they were in, or they would climb the stairs if we didn't watch them. They had started to pull themselves up on the lounges, on which they would stand and wobble before falling on their bottoms. Emmy was a lot smaller than Thomas and fine-boned, while Thomas was tall and solid for his age and had his father's bright, blue eyes.

After we lay them both on the bed, Aaron began tickling them, and they giggled in delight. Both were saying Dada and Mamma now, which melted my heart when I heard it. Soon Aaron pulled them onto his lap, and they relaxed into him, knowing with certainty what was to come next.

Every morning Aaron would carry out this ritual, as he had done since the day they were born. He would place them on his chest with his arms wrapped around them and tell them stories of the wild ocean and the creatures that lived there—stories of the stars and far-off lands we had never visited. They would sit still and listen quietly as if they understood. I believed they really just loved the sound of his voice. I knew I did as I lay back and listened to today's story about an octopus with six legs instead of eight and the quest to find his lost legs deep on the ocean floor. I giggled along with the twins when Aaron would make his voice squeaky, then deepen it, making sounds like a monster or a growling dog. I cuddled into his side and placed my arm over the three of them as he went on, kissing my forehead before I lay my head on his shoulder and closed my eyes.

Bessie came rushing into the room and kissed the twins before organising my clothing for the day. I called out that I wanted something festive, and she emerged from my dressing room with a bright, green dress with small, red berries printed on it, which I thought perfect. Aaron smiled as he fed the twins their bottles while Bessie helped me ready and styled my hair.

'Having the little ones now will make it a merry Christmas indeed. For all of us,' she said, her eyes shining as I watched her in my mirror. 'It's so lovely the twins are aware of their surroundings. They love everything that sparkles, exactly like their mother.' I laughed aloud, watching closely as she applied a hairpin with natural diamonds to the top of my head that was highly sentimental to me. Dana had given it to me as a present to celebrate being in Australia for a year.

I was looking forward to seeing Dana tomorrow. She had nearly returned to herself, although she was probably the best she would ever be. I believed most would inevitably lose something of themselves when someone they loved was ripped away so suddenly and without explanation. She was not civil to Hamish in any way, but she was no longer antagonistic towards him, either, choosing to ignore his presence whenever they were in the same room.

Bessie patted the back of my head, indicating I was ready and went about straightening the room and sorting through my clothes while I went back to Aaron and the twins. He and I had been eating our breakfast in bed at seven o'clock every morning for the last few weeks, but I was feeling hungry already, and it was only just after nine o'clock. We would often stop in the kitchen for a second breakfast before he went to work if we weren't too late getting down there.

We carried the twins downstairs to the kitchen, where the staff whisked them away to entertain them in their perambulator while waiting for me. Aaron kissed me goodbye and reluctantly went off to work. I sat at the table, looking around for any leftover food.

'I'm hungry, Leo. What can I eat?' I asked, feeling my stomach rumble. He sat down beside me and looked at me in mock despair.

'Don't you ever stop, butterball? If I ate like you, I would end up with an arse like the back of an elephant. My bum wouldn't fit through that door, and yours won't for much longer either if you keep this up, Roly-Poly. Now, what do you want, something savoury or sweet?' he asked, sighing deeply as I smiled fondly at him. I settled on buttermilk pancakes with butter and maple syrup. He made a stack of them in case anyone else was hungry. He set the plate down in front of me and took a plate for himself. We started to eat our pancakes, drowned in maple syrup when he began to look serious.

'I thought Polly-Wolly was a song? Not used as a slur against the more rotund.'

'It is. Polly Wolly Doodle to be more accurate.' He lowered his voice and leaned closer. 'It's a Yanky children's song. I only know of it because an old friend of mine was in New York when Dan Emmett and his Virginia Minstrels performed this annoyingly repetitive ditty at the Bowery Amphitheater sometime back in '43. He was old when I met him and is likely resting six feet under in a London graveyard now, but he told me it's often credited to a man named Emmett.' He sat back up and smiled across at Erin, who did not look impressed having to run around cleaning up his mess.

'Am I even meant to care? No doubt whatever it's about, you will turn it into something offensive.'

'No doubt. But back to me. As unbelievable as this sounds, I feel like Samuel is losing interest in me.' I was not surprised in the slightest but bit my tongue.

'What makes you think that?' I asked, sounding sympathetic while seething inside about Samuel's infidelity.

'He doesn't want to do romantic things with me anymore and turns his back on me in bed,' he replied, shoving another forkful of pancake into his mouth.

'Isn't that a good thing?' I teased, and he smiled weakly.

'Abigail, in normal circumstances, yes, it would be a good thing, an open invitation, really, but in this case, no. The shop is closed,' he told me adamantly. I was tempted to tell him the truth about Samuel and Brian, but I couldn't bear the pain it would cause him. I ate my second plate of fluffy pancakes drowned in syrup as we talked about what he would do.

'You do know you are always welcome to move back into the house? He can rack right off back to the staff quarters if it's not working and you're unhappy,' I offered, hoping he would accept. He nodded his head and said he would think about it, then kissed me goodbye to go on with his work in the kitchen. The staff brought the weans back in their carriage, stopping it beside me while I finished my coffee then stood to leave, bidding all farewell before stepping out the back door and into the bright summer sunshine.

I huffed and puffed, pushing the perambulator over the hill and down to the village to see Amelia while the twins sat up, looking around curiously as we went. She was at home while Polly ran the shop today and opened the door with daughter Maddison in her arms. Mathew was toddling around playing with his toys, and I couldn't believe that soon he would turn two. Maddie favoured her father, just as her older brother did, her blonde hair almost white, while possessing lovely cornflower blue eyes. She was only a month old and was already smiling. I thought she was beautiful and held her while Amelia made the tea.

I had managed to predict the gender of every wean that had been born at Willow Grove since we moved here. I would place my hands on the mother's stomach, and my palms would go warm and start to tingle. I would then see a male or female child in my mind before I took my hands away. What had intrigued me most of all was the pictures I saw of each child in my mind were precisely how each child looked when born. It hadn't worked on me, even though I tried almost every day. I didn't even know I was carrying twins, let alone a boy and a girl. I could not understand why I had this gift or why people around me had golden, grey, or black auras, but I was determined to make sense of it even if I was forced to speak to someone who had some knowledge of the supernatural. Although, the only spiritual advisers I knew of were members of the church and

I was concerned they would form the opinion I was possessed by a dark force and have me sent to the asylum in Ararat.

Emmy and Thomas sat up in their carriage, giggling as they ran their hands over the other's face then pulling away and screaming *Boo*. As long as it kept them occupied, who was I to interfere? I smiled to myself as I watched them play together, feeling such deep love it physically hurt my heart. I had placed two stuffed toy cats we had bought snugly beside them so they could touch the pure sheepskin from which they were made.

Amelia brought our tea, making herself comfortable at the table beside me as she spoke of the money she was earning now—a generous sum that allowed her to hire Polly full time—and granted her the privilege to remain at home with the children for as long as she liked. She confided in me that she could even afford a nanny again if she so wished, but did not want to appear snobbish to the other mothers, so chose to stay home for the moment as much as possible now Maddie was here. I listened to all the latest gossip directly from some of those who kept the Willow Grove's passionfruit vine alive after a number of friends called in to join us for tea, before politely excusing myself and bidding them farewell, making my way to the shop next door.

There were no customers inside when I stepped through the door, calling out hello to Polly, who had recently found out she was pregnant again. So far, she was not sick like she had been with William, for which we were all grateful. We had recently talked of how much she hoped this child would be a girl, and that she did not gain as much weight as last time. She smiled down at me from the verandah where she reclined on a well-crafted wicker chair recently purchased for a farmhand who showed talent in the art of making furniture—her arm outstretched and rocking Willy back and forth while he slept in his perambulator. She had the same model as I did. When Aaron purchased ours, he had also ordered one for her. They were the best infant carriages on the market he had told us proudly at the time, although I found them heavy and cumbersome to push.

'Tell me, sister. Are you excited about Willy's first Christmas?' I asked, feeling more enthusiastic as the day drew closer.

'Of course, but I'm not like you, Abi. You act like Saint Nick is coming down the chimney for real and bringing presents for the first time in your life. We all know how much you love presents. I've never seen so many decorations in my life. Every room in your house looks like Christmas has exploded in it. The tree is enormous, and there must be hundreds of presents underneath. Did you wrap them all yourself or get help?' she asked, her mouth twitching in amusement.

'I chose every one of them and wrapped them all myself, thank you very much, Pollyanna. I am not that lazy to make the staff do my personal chores. I even love that part about Christmas. The secret is to start buying everyone's presents throughout the year. By November, you have everything done.'

She rolled her eyes at me then grunted. Polly was not the most organised person when it came to preparing ahead and left nearly everything to the last minute.

'Stop trying to turn me into you. One Christmas freak is enough around here.' She rose to her feet and shook her head at me. 'I have to go inside while Willy's sleeping now while no one's here so I can finish doing my own Christmas shopping and wrapping,' she said, making me laugh aloud. She narrowed her gaze before descending wide wooden steps to kiss the twins goodbye. I hugged her before turning and heading for home.

Aaron's family had been incredible since the twins were born. Of course, they were that way when I first met them, but they had been especially so since Emmy and Thomas arrived. Aaron's brothers would visit several times a week to play with them and catch up with Aaron. Gavin would hold them every Sunday during our family lunches and would not hand them over to anyone, much to the twins' delight, who adored their grandfather beyond measure. Edith still visited most days to spend time with me and her grandchildren, who were the light of her life.

The elder Cavanaugh's new business was booming. He found that despite running two boats, he was selling out every day, complaining that even octopus was gone by lunchtime—a delicacy most were unaccustomed to. He would explain to his customers how to cook the produce they bought, and after they tried it, they would come back to him for more advice and something different. His shop was known throughout the district as the place to buy fresh seafood, and word of his recipes soon spread.

As a surprise, Aaron had ordered another two fishing boats for him. The boats, to be captained by Aiden and Luke, would be delivered in three-months. Many of the young men in the district wanted to work for them, as they were known to pay decent wages and treat the men well. Finding able-bodied crew members to work the boats had not been an issue like they thought it would be when initially considering expanding the family business.

Aaron was becoming more comfortable spending money, while I was still careful. I was more than happy to spend it on others; however, I found there was very little I needed when it came to myself. Aaron wasn't wasteful, but he would buy things of quality and was generous with his family and our friends. We both felt that we had been blessed with so much that it would be shameful to sit back and watch our friends and family struggle financially while our money built up in the bank. We agreed there was more there than we could ever spend on ourselves in our lifetime and wanted to ensure those around us were just as comfortable.

I continued to support the orphanage in Newtown and visited as often as I could, always taking a cake to Sister Mary Teresa and meeting with Mother Hannah to see what financial aid I could provide that month. I would receive letters regularly that had been written every second day from Sister Josephine, who held onto the hope I would travel back to England sometime soon to visit her.

We were so busy here on the property, we had no plans to go back until my thirtieth birthday to settle my financial affairs with Mr Malcolm. If we were to be away for an extended period, we would be forced to hire a manager to replace Aaron—something he was reluctant to do in the near future.

Our horses were highly sought after. So popular, in fact, that we could not keep up with the demand. Aaron was hoping that he could expand the operation in the next few years enough to ensure he could fill the orders of all who sought to buy from us.

We decided that to celebrate my thirtieth birthday, we would take ship with the children to France, London, and New York, staying at The Delmont in each city for several weeks. Aaron promised me by then, our Martarino stud would be where he wanted it to be, and he would have quadrupled our stock while reducing the other beasts we ran on the property. Only then would he agree to take the six-months off that it would take to travel there and back. I was content to stay home with my little family, surrounded by friends, and not sailing around the globe like we could afford to do at the drop of a hat.

I found the kitchen staff extremely busy when I arrived back at the house. One of them took the twins while I sat down to a cup of Leo's freshly brewed coffee.

'Are you excited about Christmas?' His body tensed immediately as he straightened up, then placed his hands on his hips while glaring at me from across the room.

'Fair suck of the sausage, Abigail! I suspect you've gone madder than you already are? Do you have any idea in that butter-head of yours the amount of time, effort and love I must give to put a feast on the table for twenty by lunchtime?' he asked, clearly exasperated. 'You seem to think you're the queen of Willow Grove, but really, I am the only royal worth mentioning within cooee of the place. Without me, you wouldn't be able to hold the fabulous parties and dinners that you throw, so start to appreciate me. If I stopped, this whole house would stop, and it would be chaos—chaos, I'm telling you. You're rude, obnoxious and self-centred and I will have more to say on the matter when I'm not so busy.'

I knew I shouldn't have asked such a simple, seemingly harmless question when he was so anxious. I smiled at him, though, as I knew he was always like this when he had to cook something special for a crowd.

'I'm sure the dinner will be the best ever. This feels like the first real Christmas I've ever had because of Thomas and Emmy,' I said and saw him soften a little. We resumed drinking our coffee companionably, and I reached across the table and took his hand in mine.

'I've thought a little about what we talked about this morning, and I think I'm going to do it,' he said, quickly glancing around to ensure no one overheard. I stared back at him, feeling confused as I raised my eyebrows. We had spoken for a long time, and there were many things he had told me he might do—one being to smother Samuel in his sleep and another to slice off Samuel's equipment with a blunt razor blade. I was of the opinion the sooner they were separated, the better, at least for Samuel's sake. 'I'm jack of him and plan to move back into the house, and damn that scungy boozer to hell.' He abruptly stood, snapping his fingers and waving his hand around my face, making me giggle. 'He'll be as cross as a frog in a sock, but I'm telling him tonight. We will be out of the terrace by tomorrow.'

'Are you feeling all right about this, Leo? You're not sad?' I was concerned he may be trying to mask deeper, more painful emotions and was only pretending to be his usual, cheeky self.

'Not bloody likely. He's treated me like shit for far too long, and it's time I take back my fabulous life.' He appeared happy enough as he sat back down beside me. I nodded, believing it best to change the subject and distract him from his own thoughts.

'Aaron, the twins and I will eat lunch here in the kitchen if it's okay with you?'

'No worries. I love having my babies here. And my Goliath of a man. He's one of the few I can gaze upon while thinking indecent thoughts with no repercussions, as he thinks I'm only being polite. It's quite a delightful place to be when you eat in the kitchen. It makes it so much easier for everyone when you're in here with Goliath. And *my* servants adore every part of it.'

He laughed, and I couldn't help but join in.

Mary met me in the bustling kitchen. I strode across the room and opened another window that looked out onto the kitchen garden where Leo grew the herbs he needed at hand. I found it far too hot in here once the weather warmed, and the large ovens that burned from dawn till dusk didn't help. I continued walking around the large room, opening several more until I could feel the warm breeze touch my skin. Mary smiled at me, shaking her head in amusement as she placed the babies in their feeding chairs while I hurried back across the room, dodging and weaving in between the busy kitchen staff. I pulled out a chair, scraping it on the floor and causing several people to glance over disapprovingly. I sat down and patiently waited for Aaron, placing my chin in my hand as I watched the twins interacting with anyone who would pay them mind. Leo had prepared a large bowl of mash with so many kinds of vegetables, I lost count when he told me. He ensured the children ate a wide variety of vegetables at least twice a day with finely chopped meat, along with a fruit plate in the morning and one in the afternoon. They had such large appetites and ate everything we offered them five times a day—on top of two bottles of milk and four to six bottles of water or juice—all of which made them little eating, peeing, and shitting machines.

I couldn't stand the thought of them being in wet clouts and changed them often, leaving the staff with a mountain of dirty clouts to launder each day. I felt terrible about foisting such a distasteful job on to others; however, Aaron was firm in his belief I wasn't to do anything other than care for our children. He often pointed out we had a dedicated laundry house a hundred feet from our backdoor the size of an average cottage that housed a family, and only had to remind me once that the five maids who staffed the bluestone building would no longer have a job here if I took to doing our washing, a situation I certainly didn't want. It always annoyed me that those who held strong opinions on certain matters often didn't have to carry out the tasks involved, leaving me feeling extremely sorry for my maids.

Aaron stood in the doorway, his tanned skin glowing golden as he removed his hat and hung it on a hook beside the back door before stepping into the kitchen. He crossed the room, whistling to himself before stopping beside the twins. He bent down to kiss them as they giggled in delight before strolling over to the table and seating himself beside me.

'I've missed ya, *mo anamchara*. Any chance after lunch we can have some time alone?'

'Of course. I'll leave Thomas and Emmy with little Mary for a while,' I replied, my voice low as he grinned at me, the blonde stubble on his face glinting as the sun streamed through the windows.

Leo had announced he was in charge of feeding the twins today, kindly encouraging little Mary to take a break. She hurried away and disappeared into the staff quarters while she had the chance to take lunch with her friends. Leo was overly protective of the twins. He didn't like even Mary looking after them, complaining that the standard of care we were providing was not up to his expectations.

I left him as he prepared to feed them and turned my attention to Aaron, who placed his hand on my thigh under the table. We enjoyed the mouth-watering ribs, the meat falling from the bones, and mashed potatoes. For dessert, he proudly served us apple and rhubarb crumble with thick, clotted cream, finding it didn't impede our lively conversation about the running of Willow Grove.

After a time, I glanced over at Thomas and Emmy sitting quietly in their high chairs. Their mouths were open as they gazed up at Leo, who stood in front of them staring back down while eating from their bowl. My eyes widened as he fed himself the entire lot without giving either of them even one spoonful. Aaron followed my gaze and immediately saw what was occurring right in front of us before turning back to me, his eyes twinkling in amusement.

'That gives new meanin' to the old sayin *easy as stealin' from a baby*,' he snickered, then collapsed into loud laughter, his head bent as he put his hands over his face.

Unlike him, I was *not* amused. If I hadn't caught the greedy shite, I wouldn't have known they hadn't eaten as neither made a sound or complained. They looked over at us, silently questioning what we would do about their food being stolen from their mouths. I watched Leo take the bowl to the sink before taking a loaf of freshly baked bread and slowly cutting two slices.

'What are you doing, Leonardo?' I called out, my anger increasing as I looked at my sweet, starving children.

'Oh, I'm just cutting the twins a piece of bread. They still look hungry,' he called back, buttering the second slice indifferently. I felt fury rise in me. He expected my children to eat bread and butter for lunch like povs', and something snapped. Polly and I had used the term since as far back as I could remember—referring to anyone living in poverty—and that was how we viewed ourselves throughout our time at the orphanage.

'You selfish idjit. I swear, I'm going to fix you for this,' I roared as Aaron's grip on my thigh tightened. The twins stared across at me, their eyes wide, while Emmy raised her hand and pointed at Aaron. They had never heard me raise my voice before. I always tried to keep calm when Leo frustrated me, having to summon my strength and practice self control so often each and every day I lost count.

'Mama?' Thomas called, narrowing his gaze at his father, who continued to laugh.

Leo glanced across and saw the look in my eye and promptly ran out the back door, with me close behind. I could hear Aaron's uproarious laughter behind me as I chased him toward the stables. He let out a piercing scream as I got closer, while I shouted all the obscenities I could think of as I tried to grab his arm and pull him back so I could strangle the little shite. Before I could grasp him, he jumped up onto the stable door and clambered up onto the roof. He gasped, trying to breathe as he pulled himself unsteadily to his feet, his boots planted firmly on the ceramic tiles. He gazed down at me, terror in his eyes as he clutched his throat, panting loudly. I remained with my feet planted firmly on the ground, my hands on my hips as I glared up at him. The sun was high in the sky, its strong rays touching my face while several cockatoos flew down to sit on the large chimney to watch. I raised my hand to my eyes so I could see him.

'Come down now, you evil, wicked dunny rat. How dare you take the food from my babies' mouths? I don't know where your brain is sometimes,' I roared as the birds spread their white wings and flew up into the snow gum that sheltered the stables, their loud squawks piercing my ears.

'Abigail, stop being so dramatic,' he called down, a smug smile spreading across his face. My hands turned to fists at my sides. 'I was going to fill their stomachs. What does it matter if they are full of vegetables or bread? They don't know the difference at their age. Let's face it. They're greedy little beasts, just like their big, fat arsed, wombat headed parents, who will eat anything. I am confident if I served them shit on toast, they would gobble it down.'

I went white with rage, my hands trembling. 'You funt! How dare you say that? If I could get my hands on you now, you would be the one eating shit until you choked to death on it.' I bent down and picked up a large piece of broken bluestone that lined the garden near the entrance to the stable—I assumed, discarded during the construction of the mansion. I aimed at his head, threw it as hard as I could, and hit him on the leg. He let out a piercing scream and fell back onto the roof on his backside.

'You are a vicious, malevolent woman,' he shouted back. 'I don't know how Goliath can stand you. With his face and arse, he could have any woman in the world, yet he chose a bad-tempered, fat-arsed, mean-spirited, foul-mouthed shrew like you, who could not behave like a lady even if her life depended on it.'

'Oh, just you wait. I'm going to shave your eyebrow off the moment you fall asleep. I will be watching you,' I growled as he flinched. He raised his hand to his dark hair and nervously smoothed it back into the leather binding at the nape of his neck.

He struggled back up to his feet, his hands haughtily placed on his hips as he gazed down his long nose at me. He knew I couldn't climb up there after him, and he was safe. For the moment.

The stable door opened slowly, and Angus and Harry stepped outside to see what the commotion was. They were soon doubled over, both laughing loudly before moving off to the side to watch. I was so infuriated I picked up another rock and aimed it at Leo's knee. I threw it as hard as I could, striking him in the shoulder, and he let out a loud shriek. I turned to see Aaron casually walking towards me, a broad grin on his face, giving Leo the opportunity he had been waiting for as he caught sight of him.

'Goliath, come get your mad wife away from me and drop her off at the Ararat asylum, please. It is far enough away to keep us all safe, yet close enough for you to visit her four times a year with your new wife.' I grunted, stamping my foot in frustration before bending over to pick up another rock. Leo ignored me, focussing all his attention on my amused husband. 'You cannot do anything wrong around her children, or she acts like an insane washer woman. I couldn't help tasting my vegetables, and they were so good I ate them all. I was hungry, too. Do any of you ever think of that? What about me? I have to eat occasionally. It's always about Abigail and keeping her quiet by giving her everything she wants without question. She eats a hundred times a day and then chastises me for eating a bowl of vegetables. She behaves like she is the master and I am her slave. I'm sure she would whip me with the cat-o'-nine-tails if she had the chance and thought she could get away with it. I am just a poor, abused servant who is denied the most basic of rights. A simple bowl of vegetables. She is the most selfish woman I have ever met.'

I picked up a second rock and raised my right arm, aiming for his head again. I planned to throw the second missile seconds after the first, only this time I was aiming for his bollocks. I felt Aaron's hand on mine, swiftly knocking the rock from me. Jerking away, I shrugged him off.

'Harry, can you please get me the ladder? I'm going up there to kill him right now where he stands.'

Leo looked down at me fearfully as Harry and Angus continued to laugh. Angus held his stomach and stared up at the spectacle on the roof with tears running down his face.

'If I were you, Leo, I would make myself scarce for a few days and go and camp by the billabong until the fiery wee wench has calmed down,' Angus called up warningly. 'I don't know what you did, but if it had anything to do with her children, there will be hell to pay. You know she goes berserk and behaves like a lioness protecting her cubs. When will you learn?'

I continued shouting threats as Aaron came up behind me, picked me up by the waist, and carried me toward the house.

'Ya don't need to be fightin' me. I didn't eat their tucker,' he chuckled as I struggled against him to no effect. He carried me up to the house and through the back door then stood me on my feet in the middle of the kitchen, knowing I would have to appear calm in front of the twins. Mary was feeding them from a large bowl filled with mashed vegetables and shredded chicken. They were like little sparrows as she spooned it into their mouths, eating hungrily and clearly happy again that all was right in their world. Aaron sat down and pulled me onto his lap. 'Now, ya know ya can't go killin' him,' he warned me thoughtfully. 'I don't wanna be visitin' ya in gaol, an' I don't wanna go hungry, either. Ya know what he's like. He would've had that first taste to test that it wasn't too hot an' found he enjoyed it. Then he got distracted an' wouldn't have given the twins a second thought till he finished the bowl. You've punished him enough, so calm yourself down an' concentrate on the nippers. They're content now, an' no damage was done—except for where ya struck Leo. I know ya both well enough now to know you'll be best friends again within the hour.'

He chuckled and kissed my temple. We watched our babies eat every last bite of their lunch, then little Mary fetched a crystal bowl filled with creamy egg custard.

'I will fix him, don't you worry about that,' I vowed as he laughed out loud.

'Righty-o, me hot-headed little sweetheart.' He rose to his feet, stopping to bend down to kiss the top of my head before straightening his trousers and tucking his shirt back in, adjusting his braces over his broad shoulders. 'I gotta get back to the stables to see what's become of Leonardo. Please don't make me come home to bloodshed of any type—yours, his or any of the innocent bystanders forced to endure ya bullshit. Stay right away from him if he crosses ya path. Dr Richards is gettin' tired of me callin' him here to the house when ya have accidentally hurt each other, or harmed the other on purpose. I'm sick of tryin' to explain the idiotic things ya both get up to. I need to speak to ya, so I'll meet ya in our bedchamber in fifteen-minutes.'

I hugged him tightly, feeling much calmer, before pinching his backside as he strode towards the children. He kissed Thomas and Emmy goodbye, causing several of the kitchen staff to smile to themselves. They both gave him a toothless grin, their mouths filled with custard, causing him to chuckle before he rubbed them gently on the head then called out his goodbyes, stepping out the door and heading back to the stables to keep Leo out of my way.

I left the twins with Mary, who had nearly finished feeding them. They behaved like hungry baby chicks, their mouths wide open and heads turning from side to side following the spoon, continuing to eat until the bowl was empty. They had a healthy appetite like their parents, causing me to grimace as I kissed them goodbye.

As I sat at my dressing table waiting for Aaron to arrive, I gazed around our room. I adored the various shades of purple throughout, complementing the solid, wooden furniture, and remembered the décor was chosen by my late great-aunt Isabelle. The more I thought about her, the more I realised what a remarkable woman she must have been. After nearly two-years, I had completely settled into the mansion, feeling I now truly had a home. Not only that, I had a family—people who cared what happened to me and needed me as much as I needed them. Never in a million years had I ever dreamed things could turn out to be so wonderful. I had somehow found what I considered a perfect life, and it wasn't just because of the money. It was nice having it, though, as it took all the worry away that most had to deal with on a daily basis.

It was the people in my life who made it perfect. I could have lived in a two-room humpy as long as I had them by my side. I heard the door open and looked up to see my beautiful husband had arrived. He sat on the bed, and I quickly joined him.

'Hello, my love. You were longer than you thought you would be.' He narrowed his gaze, his handsome brow furrowed.

'Well, I would've been here sooner if I didn't have to climb a ladder an' carry ya best friend down from the roof of the stable slung over me shoulder, shriekin' like a feral banshee, too.' He sighed deeply, shifting uncomfortably on the bed before stretching his arms out wide, grunting to himself. 'I go back out there to find him cryin' like a lass on the stable roof, wailin' how he is terrified of heights an' can't get down. Harry put the ladder up, but he refused to move unless I went up an' helped him.' He shook his head before narrowing his gaze at me. 'I get up there, an' he throws himself into me arms an' clings to me, an' won't bloody let go, the wanker. It was less hassle, in the end, to carry him down. Why do I always end up bein' the one who has to come along behind youse an' clean up ya mess?' I slipped my arms around him and gave him an apologetic kiss.

'I am sorry. He just makes me so mad. I always think that nothing he does will surprise me anymore, yet it always does.'

'Ya gotta admit, Abi, it was funny. The blokes are still laughin' at how volatile ya are an' the foul mouth ya have on ya for a woman—a lady, no less,' he chuckled, pretending to bow to me.

'What did you need to talk to me about? You looked so serious before,' I asked, ignoring his teasing as we made ourselves comfortable on the bed.

'I heard somethin' on that passionfruit vine of Leo's. I dunno if it's fair dinkum or not, but if people are talkin' about it, it may get back to those involved,' he said, appearing concerned as he swallowed hard. 'I heard that Adelaide is sneakin' next door to see John on the nights that Patty is workin' at the pub, an' they're having an affair.' I sat bolt upright as the shock hit me in the chest, leaving me unable to breathe.

'Where does Neville think Adelaide goes on the nights she isn't working at the pub?' I asked, hoping it was just a rumour. On a property as big as this with as many people as we had working and living here, gossip was unavoidable. I found that some had a seed of truth, whereas others were completely inaccurate.

'From what I was told, she tells him she's needed at the pub, an' 'cause he has the nipper to look after, he's stuck at home an' can't check on her—an' why would he feel the need to? He suspects nothin'. Neither does Patty.' I knew Aaron held strong views on marriage and fidelity and would be furious if I ever spent time alone with another man unless it was Leo.

'If this gets out, and only if it is true, by the way, there could be two marriage breakdowns,' I said, and he nodded disapprovingly.

'Enough about other people's marriages. How about ours? I think it's time ya did some unspeakable things to me.' He pulled me close to him, his face only inches from mine. 'I don't care if I'm late back to work,' he added, undoing my dress and removing his clothes.

'I don't care if you are, either,' I replied with a giggle and helped him take off his pants.

I found Aaron's mother in the sitting room with the twins, patiently waiting for me. She had been told I was busy and would be down shortly. She would be horrified if she knew what I had really been doing up in my bedchamber with her favourite son. She beamed at me as I went to her side and kissed her cheek.

'Why don't we take the children into the garden, under the shade of that big gum tree?' she suggested as she held them on her knee. They cuddled into her, gently touching her face. It was quite warm outside, with Australian summers being brutal, but today was milder in the shade, so I agreed. I never left my children in the direct sun with their ivory skin, as I was scared of them burning or becoming dehydrated. I grabbed a large blanket as she gathered up the twins, and we headed outside. The twins didn't stay on the blanket long, crawling off to explore the manicured gardens and play with Dingo, who was very gentle with them.

'How are things going between you and Aaron, now that the babies are here?' Edith asked, her cheeks slightly flushed.

'Good. Great, in fact. Ah, what exactly do you mean?' I asked, confused by her expression. She smiled shyly.

'Well, sometimes after you have had a wean, it takes a while to get, you know, that side of things back on track.' She stared out over the garden, the bees weaving in and out of the plants and flowers, settling on the lavender at the foot of the rose bushes before returning to their native hive nearby.

'Oh, that side of things. I can tell you we are fine. In fact, steaming down the railroad track at full speed ahead when it comes to that, so you don't need to worry,' I replied, gently squeezing her hand in reassurance.

'My son does look happy. He can't keep his hands off you whenever you are together, but I thought I should ask you, not having your own mother and all,' she said kindly, and I felt a tug at my heart.

'Thank you. I really do love and appreciate you. I enjoy our time together so much when you visit. You have made me feel like I have my own mother, which I will always be grateful for. I always want you to feel you can come here anytime for as long as you like. I enjoy your company and want you around the twins.'

'You're such a sweet and lovely girl.' She turned to me, her eyes filled with tears. 'I have listened to my friends' talk of their daughters-in-law, and all I hear about is hurt feelings and the resulting misery. Fights and arguments, turning son against mother. You know how it goes, Abigail. I am so relieved it isn't like that between us. I know you love my son and look after him and the children extremely well. I am so proud of the woman you have turned out to be. When Aaron came home that first day after meeting you, he told me then he would marry you. I was doubtful that a marriage between him and such a young girl would work, but I have never seen two people so happy. Thank you for allowing me to be the grandmother I want to be to Thomas and Emmy.' She leaned forward and kissed me on the cheek.

She was such a thoughtful woman, and, despite intimate subjects never being spoken of so openly, I felt touched that she would raise the matter with me given how uncomfortable it obviously made her feel. When she talked to me, it was always from the heart and would bring tears to my eyes, stirring emotions deep inside me. I hugged her appreciatively and went to collect the twins from the garden, catching them just as they tried to eat the lavender. She looked at me thoughtfully as I sat back down on the blanket with both babies cuddled against me. Dingo had no interest in playing with me, so he wandered off, looking for his master.

'It looks like you might lose one of your kitchen maids soon. I think Patrick is going to propose to Scarlett,' she said, her face breaking into a lovely smile, her teeth straight and white. Edith couldn't wait until all her children were married off to nice girls. She wasn't judgmental and didn't care what any of their backgrounds were, only that they loved her sons and treated them well while raising a loving family like they themselves had experienced. The only prerequisite to marrying into the Cavanaugh family was that you always put family first and were caring and considerate towards one another.

'That would be exciting.' We could always replace a kitchen maid, but to gain a sister-in-law would be wonderful. I had always liked Scarlett and found her outgoing and friendly, with a wicked sense of humour.

Edith stood to leave, carrying the twins in each arm as we made the short walk to the stables. When Harry brought out her horse, she handed Thomas and Emmy over to me, and I placed one child on each hip. They babbled to their grandmother as she kissed their little faces, then embraced me. I kissed her goodbye before she mounted the big, black Martarino mare we had given her for her birthday and waved as she cantered down the driveway toward home.

Chapter Four

'HARRY HAS THE CARRIAGE ready and waiting. Let's go and see how much they've done,' I announced, surprising Catherine. Her face lit up as I led her from the kitchen towards the front entrance, hurrying down the wide hallways until we arrived at the door, both out of breath and filled with excitement. The builders had already begun to transform the large shop in Geelong into what she envisioned her new business would look like. She had spent many hours with them, designing the shop and the work area out in the back. The apartment upstairs was large, with many grand rooms, and I had estimated it was three times the size of an average house in town.

We climbed up into the carriage with Harry's assistance, helping each other with our long and cumbersome skirts once inside. We chatted animatedly the entire time about how wonderful it was that she would soon be a permanent resident of Geelong. She had neither asked for nor expected me to buy the building for her or pay for the renovations, but I knew she was deeply grateful; and slightly embarrassed.

'This has changed my life, Abigail. I no longer have the threat of a landlord increasing my rent year after year until I can no longer afford to run my business, and the money I make will be mine. I do not know how I can ever repay you for your kindness. I wish you would agree to let me pay back the money you have spent,' she said, and I squeezed her hand.

'No. We have already talked about this, and it is a gift to help you start your life exactly the way you told me you wanted to the day we met on the train. Seeing how happy you are is thanks enough.' We embraced before the conversation turned to men and romance, the two not necessarily going hand in hand, much to our amusement.

The carriage stopped abruptly outside the shop in Malop Street, Geelong. Catherine had talked incessantly about the business and how fortunate she was to be the proud owner of such a prestigious building, given she had only just turned eighteen. She believed with her heart and soul that her business would become just as prominent as her father's in the coming years. I felt pure happiness for her because I knew she could do anything she set her mind to, and I was beyond proud.

We stepped down from the carriage, nodding our heads politely at the well-dressed passers-by who greeted us, some familiar to me. Catherine continued to chatter unremittingly while I looked across at the shop, an imposing double-fronted, two-story stone building painted white with intricate lead light panes above the large windows, admiring just how much it suited the business she was opening. The area downstairs alone was big enough to accommodate two businesses. We had again utilised Eric's construction company, thrilled with his work on our own property, which greatly pleased Elizabeth. She adored her husband and was incredibly proud of how talented he was and that his buildings' were already renowned in Melbourne.

We stepped inside to find several carpenters busy erecting walls and building large dressing rooms, along with refurbishing a small factory area that would be used to store cloth and produce the garments out of sight of the glamourous shop. She took my hand excitedly and led me up the stairs. They had already erected frames for walls where all the rooms were going to be. Catherine had ensured that her bedchamber and washroom were spacious with an enormous walk-in wardrobe and dressing room, along with several guest rooms and a possible nursery in the future. As we walked from room to room, I could see the apartment was going to be colossal. She wanted it modern, and that was what Eric and his men had delivered, including a small staff quarters with rooms off the kitchen for her seamstresses if they decided to live in, and a housekeeper, if she chose to have one later on.

She still could not believe that Aaron and I had purchased the building in her name, but we had explained again for the fiftieth time that we only wanted to ensure she did not have to worry and could concentrate on doing what she loved without being a slave to the bank. It eased my mind that all she had to focus on was the business side of things and could follow the dream she had held onto since she could first remember, which was more than enough thanks for us. Her face glowed as she gazed around at all the progress being made.

'This is bigger than my father's shop. I have room for ten seamstresses if and when I need them,' she gushed.

I knew what she did was arduous work at times, but I also knew she was remarkable and ahead of her time. I was confident she would have this shop up and running in no time, with racks full of designer dresses and many employees under her supervision. I had no doubt in my mind she would be successful in her own right, out from under her father's shadow, and she would become legendary in her field across Australia, possibly even beyond.

It was late afternoon by the time we returned home and I arrived to collect the twins, interrupting them as they played with little Mary in the nursery. I brought them down to the sitting room to meet Catherine just as Leo came in with a beverage he called eggnog. He stopped at the door and eyed me suspiciously.

'Now, I'm not coming any closer until I know you will behave yourself, Abigail,' he warned me, remaining where he was. 'If you dare hurt me again, I will slap you so hard it will make your butter-head rattle. I'm not like the other men in your life, you know? I *will* hit you and not feel a drop of guilt.' Catherine's giggles filled my ears as I narrowed my gaze at him. He placed his hand on his hip before continuing, refusing to venture further than the door. 'I will scratch your eyes out if you try to cause me an injury like you did with those rocks. My beautiful skin will be black and bruised for weeks because of your uncontrollable violence. I wish I was an African man. Then you wouldn't notice all the scars and injuries you've caused. I adore dark complexions, and I can only imagine how beautiful I would be if I had been born there. Now, I'm being serious, Abigail. Back to me! If you move a muscle when I come near you, I won't be serving you this delicious beverage that I learnt to make one Christmas in Paree.' Catherine laughed louder, clutching her stomach, while my mouth twitched in amusement.

'It's all right, Leo. You're safe. There were enough vegetables left for Mary to feed them lunch, although I still think you're a greedy pig. I promise I won't hurt you.'

He entered cautiously, placed two large glasses on the table, and then poured eggnog into each, not once taking his eyes from me. He left the jug, went over to the twins, and kissed them.

'Now, I have apologised to Thomas and Emmy and explained I was hungry, so they have now forgiven me. You now must do the same, as I am your best friend. You seem to keep forgetting that, which is something you should keep in mind, Catherine.' He waved to the twins before hurrying back to the kitchen without another word, leaving us smirking at each other. After nearly two-years of friendship, Catherine had become used to Leo and his ways, finding it all quite entertaining.

I picked up my glass and took a sip. It was delicious, and I drank the mild-looking liquid down quickly, enjoying every mouthful. Catherine did the same, and we repeated the process several times before lying down on our lounges, sipping more rounds poured from the second jug Leo had brought in. We chatted as the twins kept themselves occupied on the floor with their toys and each other, sometimes stopping to kiss, leaving saliva on each other's face. I loved that they were so affectionate and hoped they would remain close as they grew up.

Soon, I felt warm and heavy all over, and Catherine and I started giggling about the silly things we were saying. Leo brought in another jug, and we continued drinking. I enjoyed the creamy, sweet taste and the bite of the nutmeg as it travelled up my throat and to my nostrils.

'Leo, this is our new Christmas tradition on Christmas Eve. I don't know where it started or who invented this magical drink, but it has to be served every year,' I slurred at him, and he giggled.

'They're potent, aren't they? I made these full of brandy to get you drunk on purpose, to prove you are both not ladies. Real ladies wouldn't be caught dead drinking hard liquor like you two do, and in the afternoon as well. Shame on both of you. I don't know what to do with you, Abigail, as you certainly wouldn't have made it as a nun, and you still show no signs of becoming a lady at all.'

'Hey, you're the one who makes things for me and doesn't say what's in them until I've finished. I didn't even know there was brandy in this, and neither did Catherine, so you can take that back. Catherine is definitely a lady, and I don't give a fat rat's arse if I am or not,' I articulated slowly as he pranced out of the room, appearing pleased with himself. Catherine lay on her couch giggling for no reason, which started me off, causing the twins to look over at us curiously. Shortly after, Aaron came in, sat down on the lounge, then kissed me. I struggled to sit up beside him.

'You're maggotted—the both of ya. You should see yourselves. An' with the nippers here an' all.' He threw back his head and chuckled loudly before picking up the twins and kissing them. He placed them back on the floor to play, then returned to my side and gazed across thoughtfully at Catherine, who was snoring softly, then back at me. I grinned up at him. 'What've ya been doin'? Drinkin' a bottle of brandy straight? I could smell it as soon as I walked in.'

'No, it's something called eggnog, and it's delicious. I think it smells like Christmas,' I mumbled. As the room was spinning, I shut my eyes and lay back on the lounge for a quick minute, which turned into an hour.

I woke alone and still drunk. I assumed Catherine had retired to her room for the night just as Aaron walked in. He came to my side and looked down at me with a grin.

'I gave the twins to Mary an' just put Catherine to bed an' was comin' to get ya.' He lifted me up and carried me to our bedchamber. He was so solid and comforting when he held me close to his hard body, and I let myself melt into him as he climbed the stairs. He lay me on the bed fully dressed, climbed in onto his side, and gathered me into his arms. 'Come here, woman, an' kiss me. I love ya kisses when you're drunk, not that I don't like 'em when ya sober, but they're especially sweet when you're drunk.' He chuckled before kissing me on the mouth, exploring every part of it gently with his tongue. 'Ya taste nice. I'll have to get Leo to make me some eggnog. Go to sleep now before everyone gets here for dinner.'

He cuddled into me, and I felt myself drift off in his arms, dreaming of a barrel, a boat, and a gavel.

'Time to get up, Abigail. Aaron is already downstairs with your guests,' Bessie called out as she vigorously shook my shoulder. I still felt slightly tipsy but not sick, for which I was grateful. I groaned before dragging myself out of bed and slowly crossing the room to sit at my dressing table. Bessie quickly fixed my hair and straightened my dress, and I was ready to go. I made my way to the sitting room, finding no one there, and moved on to the dining room.

I stepped inside to find Amelia and Tommy, Polly and Angus, along with Leo, Catherine, Hamish and Aaron looking straight at me from their chairs around the table. Thomas and Emmy, who were sitting in special walnut highchairs made especially for them by Luther Fiske, a talented stable hand, stared at me in silence.

He had carved the arms and back following the exact style of our dining-room chairs. I had cried when he presented them to me as a gift when the twins were four-months old. I had only spoken to him on a few occasions, and we weren't well-acquainted. It showed me how many truly beautiful people there were in the world, and especially here, living among us at Willow Grove.

Each chair had a large, wooden tray in front, keeping the twins restrained while allowing them to feed themselves and interact with others at the table beside them. The exquisite chairs had been built to fit under the table, seating the babies far higher than the dining chairs, while the tray sat just over the top, preventing them from leaving a mess on the fancy tablecloth. I never wanted my children to have memories of eating separately from their parents, like so many of our friends, and made sure they had at least one parent with them at every meal. I was so pleased with the high chairs, I paid Luther to make two more for the kitchen so we didn't have to move them around each day.

Mr Masters and the footmen served dinner while everyone talked and caught up on each other's day. Leo had prepared veal in a creamy sauce that melted in the mouth accompanied by roasted vegetables. It was so delicious I could not resist serving myself a second helping, well aware this would not encroach on my appetite for dessert. I eyed the large meringue topped with whipped cream and an array of berries with a sweet sauce sitting on the sideboard waiting to be served. Eating this food was certainly making me feel better after drinking all that eggnog. I turned towards the door to see Leo carrying two jugs of the potent stuff on a tray as he carefully made his way to the table.

Aaron smiled when he saw me watching everyone fill their glasses. I thought it wouldn't hurt to have another one. Just one, given they tasted so good. I helped myself to another and took a measured sip. It made me feel even better than the food. Hamish sat down beside me while everyone else relaxed around the table and talked.

'How are ye, Abigail?'

'In the best of health, Hamish, and you?'

'The usual. Same shite, different day. Me father gripes about me helpin' over here every day when I should be workin' his property. He's a black hearted mongrel, an' I prefer the company at Willow Grove.' He looked over at Thomas and Emmy and smiled fondly. 'The twins are really growin'. I hope ye dinnae mind, but I went tae see them in the nursery before dinner an' was shocked tae see they're almost able tae walk,' he remarked, clearly surprised. They both were eating independently with silver spoons; however, more was ending up on their trays than in their mouths. They eventually gave up and started eating with their hands, one copying the other, and he grinned broadly at them.

'I know,' I laughed, 'imagine those two running around. I will never keep up with them,' I remarked as he nodded thoughtfully. 'So, are you seeing anyone special?' I added, looking at him intently. He seemed happy enough and was as kind and caring towards me as a friend could be.

'Naw one special, but there are two o' them right now I cannae decide between. There will never be anyone truly extraordinary again fer me. Me heart will only ever belong tae one person, an' I can naw help it. Try as I might, I cannae change that,' he blurted, then looked embarrassed. I shifted uncomfortably in my chair. He had never said anything inappropriate to me since I had married Aaron, and I didn't know what to say to him. He looked at me apologetically. 'I'm sorry, Abigail. I never should've said that. I dinnae even know how I let that happen. Please forget it fer the sake o' our friendship.'

'It's already forgotten, Hamish,' I replied, smiling at him. He looked deep into my eyes for a moment, and I saw his pain. He stood quickly and returned to his seat. It would create enormous trouble for him if he didn't let go of me. All I wished for him was a happy life, with a wife and children like he had always wanted.

We retreated to the sitting room, where they sprawled on the lounges and chatted amiably. Aaron carried Thomas and Emmy in on his hips, then handed them around to their aunties and uncles, who lavished attention on them. When he sat down with me, we watched Emmy giggle as Angus threw her up in the air, then expertly caught and tickled her while Hamish played with Thomas.

We admired the Christmas tree we had chosen to put up near the hearth, while going against tradition and proper etiquette, we were harshly reminded by Mr Masters. The sitting room was the most frequently used in the house as we had made it the most comfortable, with big, heavy lounges facing each other and space for a large group to socialise. There was nothing in here the twins could hurt themselves on, except possibly the fireplace, and the ambience was perfect.

The space under the tree was filled with presents I had lovingly and carefully wrapped myself, and their bows and ribbons twinkled in the light. I could feel the holiday excitement welling up in me again. I had experienced my first Australian Christmas last year, but I had been pregnant then. This year felt different. I had my own family, with children whose happiness I was responsible for. It was as if I, too, was a child experiencing their first real Christmas, taking in all the cheery decorations and joyful atmosphere.

It was time to put the twins to bed, so Aaron and I bid our friends' goodnight before making our way up the staircase. He held Emmy while Thomas clung to me as we chatted quietly between ourselves, winding our way through the hallways and towards the children's wing of the mansion. In the nursery, we changed their clouts and waited for little Mary to bring their bottles. She arrived shortly after, and Aaron fed Thomas while I sat with Emmy on my lap, feeding her.

After Emmy drained her bottle, her eyes started to close. She would open them wide, fighting sleep, but she finally succumbed. I cuddled her on my shoulder, letting her burp softly before putting her down in her crib, her limbs heavy. Thomas was asleep in his father's arms with a bit left in his bottle that Aaron was still trying to get him to drink. I took the bottle from Aaron, smiling, and he placed Thomas in his own crib next to Emmy's before we kissed them both goodnight.

They were getting too big to sleep in the same crib, although they wanted to, and would cry for each other when they woke up alone. We were trying to get them used to sleeping by themselves; however, we would give in and put them in together if they wouldn't settle. Now, though, they were both sound asleep and didn't have a clue, which made me smile. I kissed them both goodnight again, and Aaron took my hand as we made our way to our bedchamber, where I asked him to undo my buttons so I could undress.

'I saw Hamish talkin' to ya at dinner. For a split second there, it looked like he wanted to kiss ya,' Aaron observed, eyeing me intently. I walked naked to my dressing room, thinking a hundred things at once, before returning with a long nightgown on and climbing into bed. I told him what Hamish had said to me while he kicked off his shoes. 'He's not lyin',' he remarked, stripping off his clothes. 'I see it all the time in the way he treats women. That's why ya don't see him courtin' upper-class sheilas like his mother is always tryin' to force him to do. That's too much hard work, especially when he just has to walk into a pub an' have all the girls flockin' to him like starvin' galahs. After you, he doesn't want commitment. He wants easy.' Slipping into bed next to me, he kicked off the heavy quilt and pulled the linen sheet up over us. 'How about ya go an' put on one of those racy negligees that Catherine makes for ya instead of that old thing that me granny would wear?' He smirked, trying to pull it off me.

'That old thing, as you say, is comfortable,' I replied as he tried to convince me of the merits of changing for him. I couldn't see the point in wasting my time putting one on, but I did anyway, trudging back into my dressing room and changing into a short purple nightgown that clung to the shape of my body. The lace was so soft and comfortable that I knew I could sleep in this. If he would let me.

'Stop,' he said before I could climb up on the bed. 'Let me look. This one's a ripper. God bless Catherine.' He laughed, then pulled back the sheet for me to climb in.

'So, it doesn't upset you. About Hamish, I mean?' I cuddled into his shoulder as he let out a deep sigh.

'Out of everyone in this world, I'm probably the only other bloke who understands what it feels like to love ya so deeply,' he murmured, a tinge of sadness in his voice. 'Nah, I can't blame Hamish for somethin' he can't control. I know he'd never touch ya or do anythin' wrong by me, so there's nothin' to be upset about. If anythin', I wish I could help him, or he would meet someone he could fall in love with. It's six of one, half a dozen the other, but I don't think that's gunna happen either.'

I nodded silently before he kissed me, gathering me in his arms. I closed my eyes and drifted off to sleep, dreaming of a large brass key, a platypus, and a golden harmonica.

Before I even opened my eyes, I felt overwhelming excitement bubbling up inside me. It wasn't even daybreak yet as I turned and kissed Aaron full on the mouth despite him being deeply asleep.

'Merry Christmas,' I whispered, putting my arms around him.

'Merry Christmas, *mo anamchara*,' he mumbled, kissing me back before sleepily opening his eyes then running his hand gently down my back. 'I wanna give ya your Christmas presents from me this mornin' while we're alone.' He pulled me in close and smirked as he slipped my purple negligee off over my head, and I grinned right back at him. Later, as I lay naked in his arms, I remembered my gift and quickly sat up. I reached over to my bedside table and pulled out a wrapped, flat box.

'Happy Christmas, my love,' I said, passing it to him. He sat up, unwrapped it, and pulled out a thick, gold chain. I held it up and pointed, bringing it closer so he could see. 'Look here on the bottom. I had Mr Dawson intertwine three solid-gold hearts into the links representing me, Thomas, and Emmy. The fourth heart, made of white gold, represents you, my darling.' I showed him each one in turn as he nodded. His face lit up in delight, and he gently touched the links in the burnished chain. 'That way, you always have our hearts next to yours.' I smiled and placed it around his neck, securing the gold clasp. He kissed me on the lips and stroked my cheek.

'Thank you, Abi. I love it. I'll never take it off,' he promised, reverently running his fingers over the links now around his neck. 'Now, it's your turn.' He grinned and handed me a small box. He loved giving presents as much as I did. We always gave each other gifts for anniversaries, birthdays, and special celebrations during the year; however, we would often surprise each other with gifts for no reason at all. We had appointed Colin Dawson our unofficial jeweller. He was so good at what he did, we refused to go to anyone else. I opened the box and pulled back the tissue paper. There lay a solid gold, filigree watch. The exquisite piece had diamonds scattered throughout the solid band, with twelve of them on the face. I gasped when I saw it.

'It's beautiful. Where did you find something so exquisite?'

'I asked Mr Dawson to make it, of course. He remembered ya ring well. In fact, he still had the sketch so he designed ya timepiece to match the look of ya weddin' bands,' he said proudly and helped me take it out of the box. When I snapped the band closed, it fit my wrist perfectly, the diamonds glittering in the dim morning light. It was faultless, and I kissed him in thanks. He lay back, his hand resting near his neck, lost in thought as he rolled the thick, square chain between his fingers while I fidgeted with my new watch.

We had laid out the twins presents from Santa in the sitting room during the night. I couldn't help but compare their childhood to my own and how different their experiences already were. Too excited to wait any longer, I rose and slipped on my silk dressing gown.

'Abi, the sparrow hasn't farted yet. The nippers aren't even awake,' he teased, his eyes sparkling in amusement. Seeing my determination, he sighed and struggled to sit up before yawning widely.

'I know, but it's Christmas morning, Aaron. It only happens once a year, and I don't want them to miss a single minute of it.' He grimaced before throwing back the quilt and rising to his feet, groaning loudly. He put on his robe before following me to the nursery.

The twins were still sound asleep. I bent down and kissed their faces until they sleepily opened their eyes and smiled up at us. When we took them downstairs to the sitting room and showed them their presents, they were more interested in ripping off the wrapping than what was inside. Aaron and I laughed at them as they scrunched up the paper and threw it around the room while we played with their toys.

After a time, we took them up to bed with us. I lay down next to Aaron, who snuggled Emmy and Thomas against his chest for a Christmas story that featured emus and kangaroos, platypuses and crocodiles, and a big gum tree decorated in tinsel far off in the outback of Australia.

We met Catherine and Leo downstairs for breakfast. Leo had been true to his word and packed his possessions then moved them to the house early this morning, leaving Samuel screaming abuse at him because he would be forced to return to the staff quarters. Catherine had invited Colin to Christmas lunch, and she seemed to be full of anticipation.

'Have ya settled back in, Leo?' Aaron asked as we all started to eat the feast he had so thoughtfully laid out before us. Leo had prepared everything himself, from bacon and eggs to fried tomatoes and mushrooms. He had cooked pork sausages made with his own hand, which were Aaron's favourite, and had even made sweet, creamy porridge for us to start with. I drank my freshly squeezed orange juice before tucking into my food with deliberate concentration.

'I have settled back like I never left. I don't belong in a workers terrace. If anyone deserves to live in a mansion, it is I, being the blue-blooded man I am. At least I know how to act like a lady,' he told us, his perfectly shaped eyebrows arched, and I wondered if he even knew what he was talking about sometimes. I heard Aaron snort in amusement. Little Mary took the empty bowl of porridge away from the twins, and I filled two plates with warm breakfast food and placed it in front of them to eat with their fingers.

They enjoyed food as much as their parents did and would happily sit up in their special highchairs if it meant they would fill their bellies, which pleased me greatly because the chairs kept them from wandering off halfway through a meal. Not that either ever tried to escape when there was food to be eaten. I was impressed how they would eat anything offered to them, even black pudding, which I despised.

We chatted while we ate, being mindful that our friends and family would be arriving soon. Once finished, Aaron and I picked up Thomas and Emmy and went with Catherine to the sitting room. It really felt like Christmas now as I sat with the twins on my lap, looking up at the tree. They climbed down and crawled over to their new toys, which they hadn't played with yet, having been so fascinated with the paper that they were wrapped in. I went and sat on the floor, and they climbed onto my lap, holding some of their toys.

The Cavanaughs' arrived first, with Aaron's parents immediately focussing on the twins, taking them from me and kissing them all over, much to their squeals of delight. It wasn't long before they were passed around by their uncles, who played rough and tumble with them on the floor, making them laugh loudly, which thrilled me. They were already enjoying Christmas and, even as young as they were, I could see they both knew there was something different about today.

Tamara arrived shortly afterwards with Brian, who wouldn't look me in the eye, and their adorable daughter, Madeline. Tamara was in the early stages of her second pregnancy and was glowing. She embraced me.

'Thank you so much for inviting us. I need to speak with you privately when you have time.' I smiled at her and nodded discreetly. Elizabeth and Eric followed them, looking more in love than the last time I saw them. They always seemed so comfortable together, appearing relaxed and happy. Eric squeezed her hand as they sat together on the lounge.

Hamish bounded in with an armload of presents and placed them under the tree, then greeted everyone. Amelia and Tommy arrived with Mathew and Maddie in tow, moving around the room to kiss everyone hello. When Martin, Dana, and Victoria entered the room, Dana greeted everyone but Hamish, who tried to stay out of her way and not antagonise her.

We passed out our gifts and sat around chatting as we opened them. Hamish loved the new saddle we had bought him, and Dana, her diamond bracelet. While I adored the opal earrings I received from Catherine. Polly and Angus joined us with Willy, setting him down on the floor to play with his cousins. Leo brought in hors d'oeuvres and drinks for everyone, and we relaxed on the lounges together to talk and enjoy Christmas morning. Time passed quickly, and Mr Masters entered the room to announce lunch was being served.

The dining room was decorated beautifully with flowers, candles burning on every surface, and the table laden with an enormous amount of food. There were roasted meats of every kind, including pork, beef, and lamb. Leo had gone to even more trouble and prepared what he called *white meat*—an enormous roasted turkey along with half a dozen chickens and a range of seafood, along with vegetables picked from our own garden and cooked in various ways. The potatoes were roasted, and there was a tray of finely sliced potatoes and pumpkin, baked in a thick sauce of cream and cheese until it was soft and golden on top. Condiments were plenty, the apple sauce made from fruit picked from our very own orchard, and rich gravies, along with the mint sauce, made straight from our garden to go on the dark golden roasted meat that was so tender it fell off the bone.

We bowed our heads and said a prayer before the room erupted in rowdy conversations. We cheerfully helped ourselves to the food laid out in the middle of the table, just as I had asked. This was how we preferred our Sunday lunches and celebrations of any kind—the food dished up on large silver platters from which we could serve ourselves. It came close, but it wasn't quite the same as I remembered the Malcolms' family lunches. The food served here was far more decadent because of Leo and his expensive tastes, not to mention the fact we employed numerous staff to help prepare such a huge feast.

The Malcolms only had Mrs Shank to cook a wonderful repast all by herself; however, despite the larger scale, I wanted to recreate the same feeling of my first-ever family Sunday lunch with them. I knew I had succeeded when guests commented how much they enjoyed helping themselves to a second or even third serving without the household staff hovering around. The table held bottles of wine, whisky, and beer, along with ginger ale and fruit juice, the footmen replacing the empty bottles as swiftly as the guests drank them.

Mr Masters was not as happy about it as we were, but he tolerated what he referred to as my countrified eccentricities. The mood in the room was jovial during our meal. By my second helping, I was full, while my dining companions had also started to push away their plates. The leftovers were promptly removed, and a gargantuan plum pudding was brought in, flaming in brandy and carried by a proud Mr Masters, followed by the footmen with trays holding large bowls of custard and cream to serve. Samuel gave Leo a withering look as he set the four bowls of thick cream on the table, spacing them out before abruptly leaving the room. I could see there would be some tense moments in the house now that things had turned sour between them. I had given the staff the day off after lunch to enjoy their own Christmas dinner in the dining hall tonight and spend the day with their friends and families.

'Leo, the tucker was top notch. I haven't eaten this much in as long as I can remember,' Aaron told him appreciatively. Leo smiled at him.

'Well, if it wasn't for you saving me from your bush pig of a wife yesterday, then no one would be sitting here eating.' His eyes went wide as he pointed his finger at me, raising his voice shrilly. 'She tried to kill me for the fiftieth time and nearly succeeded.' He went on to inform everyone present of his version of what had occurred yesterday.

I felt my face flame up like the pudding in front of us as they all started to laugh and tease me good-naturedly. I hated the fact that I was hot-headed, although I tried as hard as I could to control it, feeling embarrassed when I did lose my temper. When it came to my children's welfare, though, I couldn't help it. If anyone did anything I thought could harm them, it unleashed something frightening in me. As Polly would say, I would lose my mind and go berserk, directing my angst at Leo most of the time, as he was by far the principal offender who did stupid things around them. I knew he loved them; however, sometimes, they were more mature than he was.

'Crikey, Abigail. I'll have to remember that when the twins come an' stay with Ma an' Pa,' Patrick said, chuckling to himself. Aaron's parents smiled at each other, then down at Thomas and Emmy, who sat on their laps eating from their grandparents' plates with their hands. I couldn't believe how much they had eaten, demanding Mrs Cavanaugh refill her and her husband's plates with their favourite things several times.

'Yeah, nah. I don't want ya comin' after me like that when ya lose ya marbles again,' Luke said with a wink and a smirk. I felt myself blushing deeper. Aaron laughed along with the others. He found his brothers' teasing the funniest thing he had heard in weeks as they continued to talk about me like I wasn't there.

'Well, you should all know by now how protective Abi is of the twins. It's only an imbecile like Leonardo who never learns his lesson,' Polly said in my defence, and I smiled weakly at her in thanks.

'Where's yer daughter, Tamara? Is she unwell?' Hamish asked, appearing concerned, even as he ate his plum pudding with relish. Tamara stared across at him for a moment, confusion crossing her face.

'She is with her Nanny, where all children should be at that age. She is being fed in the kitchen now. Surely you would know that Hamish, being brought up the same way as I? I love Abigail and Aaron, and they can raise their children as they see fit; however, I will bring mine up in the way I believe they should be reared,' she replied matter-of-fact. I noticed several members of the Cavanaugh clan glanced at her in pity, but they remained silent.

'I think I've changed me views about that since Thomas an' Emmy were born,' Hamish replied, spooning a large piece of pudding into his mouth before chewing thoughtfully. 'I'd hate tae think at mealtimes when we're all sittin' together an' enjoyin' ourselves that they'd be isolated with Mary in the kitchen. I know we've been brought up the supposed correct way, Tamara, but the older I get, the more I wonder if it was the right way.' I smiled over gratefully, adding custard and cream to my bowl before taking a bite of the sweet, sticky pudding I adored so much. It was lovely to see such a change in him since he first arrived in Australia. He hadn't been exposed to people other than his own class and had very set views on how things should be done. He was far more relaxed now, joining us for breakfast on occasion before they started work. He could also be found a few times a week eating dinner with us, also in the kitchen, unless we had guests who were uncomfortable eating anywhere else but in the dining room.

'Tell me, when you finally marry and have a family, are you going to allow them to eat in the kitchen with the servants and treat them as equals?' Tamara asked, clearly shocked.

'Aye. Now I think about it, I would. I see how content an' loved the twins are, an' witness daily how this house is filled with happiness an' laughter, even from the servants. That's rare, Tamara, as ye well know. I've never heard o' anyone workin' here bein' dissatisfied. The workers at Willow Grove know there's a hundred people tae fill their boots if they dinnae work hard, an' the simple fact is they like Aaron an' Abigail. They respect them an' appreciate the way they're treated an' looked after here. 'Tis known throughout the district what wonderful employers they are. There's a constant stream o' people seekin' work here, an' they've employed so many with families tae support,' he told her thoughtfully before continuing. 'There's naw other property I know o' set up like this that provides conditions like the servants have here. The fact they dinnae pay tae live in brand new houses an' all their food is supplied is well above any standard I know fer any labourers or servants alike. The quality of the meals in the dinin' hall is as good as the meal we've eaten today. The amount o' money put back in tae Willow Grove tae keep the standard o' livin' high is enormous, an' I believe that is why they have the most loyal an' hardworkin' servants in the district. I'd seek work here meself if I was o' that class.' Tamara stopped eating and placed her spoon down as she stared back at him in disbelief, as did Brian.

'Hamish, how dare you say my food is of the same standard as Jenny's? I am a world-renowned chef, and she is a simple cook,' Leo complained loudly, causing me to spit my food across the table as I giggled.

Tamara dropped the subject and returned to her food, realising they were never going to agree. I continued eating my pudding despite having eaten my fill simply because it tasted so good. When I was finished, I sat back in my chair, feeling like I could sneak off for a nap. I closed my eyes and listened to my loved one's talk, laugh, and tease each other and wondered if I could be any happier than I was right at this moment.

We met our staff in the back garden to present them with their Christmas gifts and bonuses—a surprise they were unaware they would receive today after a long year of hard work for each one of them. We had provided refreshments of beer, wine, and fruit juice, and they all stood or sat in groups with their friends and ate afternoon tea from the trays on the table. They seemed to be having a good day so far, appearing relaxed and happy. They had their Christmas dinner to look forward to tonight, and then free drinks at the pub paid for by Aaron from the farm account. We had experienced enormous profits from the sales of the Martarinos recently, all due to their hard work.

In the middle of the festivities, Aaron stood and shouted to get their attention. They settled down and listened quietly as he wished everyone a Merry Christmas and thanked them for their hard work all year, with many of them clapping and cheering. They all got along with Aaron exceptionally well. As I had requested, they had brought their families with them. I had purchased gifts for every child who lived here, and was bursting with excitement to see their faces when they opened them. The fourteen terraces were occupied now, all with families, and the village was now filled to capacity. Additionally, we housed the unmarried workers in the sleeping quarters above the dining hall, in the rooms above the stables.

We were employing far more than we needed due to so many being out of work due to the depression in Victoria. When they came to the house asking for work, I listened to all their stories. We made sure to hire as many men supporting young families as possible, given many other employers preferred to hire single men so they didn't have to worry about the cost of accommodating families. There had been several single men I had felt great sympathy for and decided I wanted to hire based on their personal circumstances and not just their working ability. Aaron said I was too soft-hearted; however, he always gave a job to someone if I really dug my heels in. I was more than aware we couldn't employ everyone, but I also knew how many terraces we had available at the time and was confident Aaron would find something for them to do around the property to earn their keep and wages.

Aaron asked them to come up one by one, calling to them by name, then handed them and their wives and children wrapped presents, their names on small squares of cardboard I had so painstakingly cut out with my new scissors. It had taken me months to organise all the presents, with so many trips into Geelong and shopping at Amelia's store to ensure I purchased the perfect gift for each person.

Once they had their presents, Aaron then handed an envelope to the man or woman who worked for us. The joyful looks on their faces when they opened them was all the thanks I needed. I saw what a difference it made to them all. The extra money would buy them something nice they would typically be unable to afford.

I knew Jenny and her kitchen maids had been working nonstop since yesterday to prepare a magnificent meal for tonight for every man, woman, and child who lived here. It made me feel good to know they were getting the same luxuries we were on such a special day. I decided that I officially loved Christmas and wished we celebrated every month, despite it being such hard work. I moved around the garden, mingling with the workers and their families before they slowly began to head back to the village, ensuring I wished each and every one of them a merry Christmas.

Once they had gone and the house staff had joined them in the village, my family and friends relaxed in the garden on large sun lounges that fit two or three people sitting side by side or one person reclining. I loved the lounges, the cushions so large and soft I would occasionally fall asleep on one when relaxing in the shade on a warm day. Remembering Tamara had wanted to talk, I went and sat next to her, far enough away from the others to not be overheard.

'How are you, lovely lady?' I asked, kissing her on the cheek. She gazed at me reticently and lowered her voice, looking around to make sure no one could hear us. I pulled my bare feet up under my skirt and made myself comfortable.

'Well, I have not been good, and that is what I wanted to speak to you about. It is all so humiliating, Abigail, but I cannot talk to my friends in Melbourne as they would gossip and cause a scandal. You are my only friend who doesn't mix in those circles, and I know I can trust you. All right, I'll start,' she said nervously and took a deep breath. 'Several months ago, days after I gave birth to Maddie, I finally found out why Brian doesn't like to touch me or make love to me. You were right. It was not my fault. When I walked in on him unexpectedly at work, I found him... Oh, I cannot even speak the words.' She stopped for a moment, trying to regain her composure. 'I found him doing perverse and immoral acts with his valet in his office.' I shifted uncomfortably in my seat, avoiding her gaze.

'What will you do?' I reached over and took her hand in mine, feeling terribly guilty. I gazed up at the trees, several cockatoos squawking above and causing me to flinch.

'Don't fret. I have already done it. I remembered what Dana told us on the boat about her first husband, so I did the same. Only I didn't steal all his money. I am making him give me what I always wanted. I demanded he provide me with four children, all close together in age, and the freedom to do as I wish. He can go off and carry out his unnatural and despicable acts with other men as long as my good name and reputation are protected. The only thing that concerns me is that my children and I are kept in the lifestyle we are accustomed to, which I have ensured we will be. In exchange for that, I will keep his filthy secret and not destroy the disgusting little faggot.' I did not like how she referred to homosexuals at all; however, I did understand her outrage, given what she had gone through.

When I had met her, she had certain expectations of marriage, one of which was that her husband would adore and worship her. Sadly, it hadn't turned out that way, and she was now in a situation from which she couldn't escape. I was impressed by her strength and determination and knew divorce was never an option for her. She had been forced to take control of her own life, and I was proud of her bravery.

'Once I've finished having my children, I am going to take a lover, as you suggested.' She smiled wickedly, making me giggle. 'I'm going to find someone who has a body like your Aaron. Then watch out.'

Catherine and Colin had decided to take a ride around the property, and Elizabeth and Eric joined them, as did Aiden and Victoria. Everyone I had ever met who had ridden a Martarino horse fell in love with them instantly and never again felt the same riding another breed.

Patrick had left to attend the village to spend the rest of the day with Scarlett, as he was utterly besotted with her. Aaron's parents were preoccupied with the twins, so Aaron took the opportunity to lead me away from the garden.

'What's wrong, Aaron?' He took me in his arms and kissed me passionately.

'Too long without this,' he said, holding me close. My head rested on his broad chest as he held me so tight I thought he would never let me go.

That evening, after we filled our stomachs again with leftovers until we felt we would burst, our guests began to depart. The Cavanaughs' bid us farewell after tucking their grandchildren into bed for the night, and Martin and Dana prepared to leave.

'Thank you so much for having us, my darling friend,' Dana said and embraced me. I could feel she had regained the weight she had so dramatically lost as I hugged her tight. 'Don't forget the luncheon I have planned for us at my home next week,' she reminded me as they climbed up into their carriage. I nodded and waved them off.

As the night wore on, people began to retire. Elizabeth and Eric had gone to bed early, exhausted from riding all afternoon, while Polly and Angus returned to their cottage along with Hamish, who planned to stay overnight with them.

We said goodnight, left everyone else in the sitting room and slowly made our way up to our bedchamber, hand in hand. Aaron and I both let out a deep sigh before I went to my dressing table and started to brush my hair, then plaited it into one long rope that curled at the bottom.

Aaron came up behind me, kissed the back of my neck, and undid the back of my dress. I dragged myself to my dressing room and slipped on a negligee I knew he liked. As I crawled into bed, I watched him as he took off his clothes and placed them neatly over the back of the chair. He was magnificent naked, making me wish he could walk around like that all day.

'Peace at last,' he said, climbing into bed beside me. 'I feel like I've hardly seen or spoken to ya today. You've been runnin' around like a blue arsed fly. Ya needn't have bothered puttin' on that slip of a nightgown as I'm only gunna take it off.' I placed my arm across his chest, and he ran his hand gently down my spine until it stopped on my bum, where he left it. 'Did you have a good Christmas, me darlin'?' he asked, kissing the top of my head.

'Yes, Aaron. It was exactly what I used to read about in books.' I let my body relax into the thick, feathered mattress. 'I never imagined I would ever experience such a lovely two days as we have. Christmas Eve is just as important to me, as we have already started our own little traditions with the twins and our family and friends. My favourite new Christmas tradition is drinking eggnog. I don't know how to describe how I feel because it goes further than happiness. It's like I finally belong somewhere. Willow Grove has become much more than a house to me. I'm a part of something bigger than me, and I have a purpose. I'm a wife and a mother first, but I have all these new people who have come into my life in so many ways. I always thought I would end up alone and childless, and I'm so grateful that my worries and fears never seem to come true.'

Much later, as he held my naked body close to his and the full moon shone through our windows, filling the bedchamber with a soft glow, I drifted off to sleep, dreaming of colourful paper, an orphanage in Scotland, and a giant bull ant intent on eating me.

Chapter Five

I WOKE TO FEEL a warm northerly breeze blustering through our open windows, blowing the sheer curtains straight out while causing them to billow and swirl. I quietly got out of bed and closed each window, pulling the thick drapes closed to keep out the sun. It had only gone daybreak, and I could already feel the heat in the warm air that filled our room.

It was the first week of April 1893 and still stinking hot compared to Scotland. I didn't think I would ever get used to Australian summers despite it now being autumn and still far too warm for me. I climbed back into bed, slipped under the sheet, and lay quietly listening to Aaron snore softly beside me.

The twins had turned two last week and were running around everywhere, even going to work with Aaron sometimes when I could part with them for that long. They would sit up proudly in front of him on the saddle and giggle when he rode fast. They really were the most adorable creatures I had ever seen, even though I was somewhat biassed. Aaron was the most loving and protective father a child could want, and the three of them adored each other. The twins were talking now, putting rudimentary sentences together, which delighted us because now we could understand their wants and needs. They were both consistently using their own small chamber pots. I was so relieved they were out of clouts. Now, there was no need for the maids to carry out the distasteful job of laundering them, and I could stop feeling guilty for not doing more.

I glanced over at Aaron's face. He seemed so peaceful and looked so handsome that I couldn't stop myself from kissing his sculpted lips. He slowly opened his eyes and gave me the sweetest smile, and I couldn't stop myself from kissing him again.

'G'mornin', *mo anamchara.*' He yawned before gathering me in his arms and pulling me close.

'Good morning. You looked like you slept well,' I said, stroking his face.

'An' you didn't? Ya must have been awake to have been watchin' me,' he replied, yawning again before rubbing the sleep from his eyes.

'I slept all right. I just kept waking up at times throughout the night.'

'Ya should have woken me up, *mo anamchara*. I know a few ways to help ya get back to sleep.' A slow grin spread across his face before he pinched my nipple without warning. I reached over and squeezed him back in retaliation. He rolled his eyes in mock ecstasy. 'C'arn, Abi, do it again.' He laughed out loud, and I smacked him playfully. He settled back, turning his head to stare into my eyes. 'I saw Aiden yesterday down the back paddock. He an' Vicki are stoked their house is done after all the kerfuffle, an' now all they have left to do is wait for the nipper to come,' he remarked as I cuddled into his chest. They had married over a year ago, and as a wedding present, we had sectioned off two acres next door to Aaron's parents' property and built them the home they had both dreamed of. They had lived with Aaron's parents during construction and moved in two-weeks ago, just in time to settle down and await the arrival of their first child, who was due any day now.

Dana was overjoyed at becoming a grandmother for the first time and was staying with them until the birth. Knowing how Aaron's mother was towards her grandchildren and knowing Dana's personality just as intimately, I could see there would be some real battles of will coming up in the near future.

Patrick and Scarlett had married a few months ago and were also living with Aaron's parents, forcing us to employ a new kitchen maid, Nellie, who was now working in the village with Jenny. I loved having sisters-in-law, and I saw them often, becoming close to them both. Victoria and I had already established a solid friendship since meeting on the ship, and Scarlett was so outgoing and easy to get along with we had become firm friends very quickly. They treated me like a sister, and I loved them the same way, always enjoying the time we spent together during the week, whether it be a short visit to enjoy a cup of tea and scones, or a night out at the pub with our husbands.

We had offered the same to Patrick and Scarlett, and they had accepted after some deliberation, although their house was only in the initial stages and the foundation had only been laid last week. Aaron felt by building the houses next to his parents' home, it made it easier for them to combine work and family responsibilities. Everyone was pleased with the arrangements, none more so than the family-oriented Edith Cavanaugh, who wanted all her children and grandchildren close by. To Aaron's parents, their family was everything. It came before anything else in the world. I loved that about them and finally felt like I, too, was a part of a family.

'The nipper's filly and' colt are growin' into the pride of the stable, Harry tells me,' Aaron remarked proudly before gently covering my face in kisses. The day his children were riding alongside him would be one of the happiest of his life. The horses had inherited the sweet nature of Sugarbell, their mother, and their sire's magnificent muscular build and stamina. Personally, I was terrified of my babies being on such massive horses and would have preferred if he had started them out on ponies, but Aaron was adamant.

Because of their placid natures and despite their size, he assured me that Martarinos were the only horses he would trust with his precious children. He told me of many incidents of nasty horses he had encountered during his life, eventually convincing me to allow the twins to ride them. They had begun their riding lessons a few months ago, led around on Sugarbell together by their proud father, much to their delight. I would go down to the stable yard and watch, terrified that they would fall from such a great height, but it hadn't happened. They both seemed to have great balance and knew how to stay upright without any help now. Aaron had already ordered the children's saddles, wanting them as soon as possible and couldn't wait to pick them up from the saddler in Geelong. I was less enthused about the whole situation, but kept a smile on my face and tried not to show it.

'Hey, Ab's,' Aaron said, running his hand down my body and raising his eyebrows wickedly. 'Do ya wanna play?'

We ate our breakfast in the kitchen, with the twins sitting at the table eating their porridge. Aaron looked at them lovingly while he ate, reaching across and helping them at times.

'So, Leo, what's new?' I asked, biting into a piece of hot toast spread with honey from our own hives. He stood at the kitchen bench, ordering everyone around as Sally brought him a sizeable ceramic jug from the icebox.

'Oh, I feel like I'm part of Gilbert and Sullivan's *Yeomen of the Guard*. It was one of the first dramatic productions I ever saw in London at the Savoy Theatre in '89. It's no different living here, always some shemozzle going on somewhere on the property, which I must admit is very much how I like it,' he confessed with a bright smile. 'I am playing a bit of a cat-and-mouse game with one of the farmhands.' I giggled as he raised an eyebrow in amusement, knowing full well who the mouse really was. Leo kissed the twins, placed two cups of milk on the table for them, and then joined us. 'I don't know how Neville is coping with the children after Adelaide's death. I feel so sorry for him,' Leo remarked, and I nodded my head, remaining silent.

Adelaide had recently died in childbirth, leaving Neville to care for their two-year-old son, Ian, and their newborn, Molly. It had been a horrendous time, with me calling Dr Richards to attend her after she had been in labour for nearly a full day. I sat with her throughout the time and tried to help her. Dr Richards had manually turned the unborn child, causing her enormous pain. As the labour went on, Adelaide became weaker and, with no warning, suddenly took her last breath and died. Dr Richards immediately performed a caesarean section and delivered their baby, who was healthy and large—too large, Dr Richards told me later, for Adelaide to have given birth naturally.

Neville was devastated. He was left struggling to care for two children on his own—and struggle he did—particularly with the wean. Aaron had given him time off from work while still paying him his wages. Adelaide's death had sent shock-waves through Willow Grove and surrounding areas and had sent Neville and John from next door, with whom she had been having a torrid affair, spiralling into grief. I was off to see Neville this morning as I had come up with an idea that I wished to discuss.

'Hey, Leo, can I ask a favour, mate? Would ya mind makin' up some of Abi's favourite foods an' packin' 'em in a basket for me to collect before lunch?' Aaron asked before glancing sidelong at me. Leo turned to him, raising his hand to stop him from saying another word.

'Is it a special occasion? Why am I the last to know everything around here? You know I like to be the first to hear the gossip, Aaron. I know it's not time for cupcake day, as we had that two-weeks ago,' he teased, causing Aaron to chuckle as he chewed his toast.

Without fail, Aaron still brought me my anniversary cupcake each month, after spending time in the kitchen eating most of them. The kitchen staff had come to enjoy his early morning visits—most stopping to laugh with him as he sat drinking coffee and eating whatever came out of the oven, before quietly returning to our bed at daybreak to spend a few hours with me.

'I want ya to meet me at the lake today without the nippers.' I agreed, questioning if everything was all right, to which he nodded. We were spending all our time with the twins, and it was rare that he wanted to meet me alone without them during the day.

'What's your favourite food today, Abigail?' Leo asked, his eyes sparkling in amusement.

'I will leave it with you, Leo. I trust your judgement.'

'Well, you make that easy when everything you eat becomes your favourite. You would eat shit on toast and enjoy it if served at this table as a delicacy, or sprinkled in sugar.' He laughed to himself before placing a pot of freshly brewed coffee down on the table for us to share.

I pushed the perambulator along the street towards Neville's house. Thomas and Emmy loved sitting up in the bulky, heavy pram that took all my energy to push, especially now that they were getting bigger. They would sit there for hours if I let them as they loved being driven around the property in such comfort and luxury. They were walking proficiently now, and I felt the time was nearing to retire their carriage and give me back my freedom.

When I knocked on Neville's door, he opened it within moments, holding Ian on one hip and little Molly in the crook of his arm. I took Ian from him and entered the house. Once he was seated, I handed Ian back before I went to get the twins. The house was a mess, no longer the spotless home that had been lovingly kept with pride. There were unwashed clouts in the kitchen, giving the place a pungent smell. I went to the sink, opened the window, and put water on to boil for tea.

'How are you coping, Neville?' I asked, placing the dirty clouts in a bucket. I filled a large pot and put it on the stove to boil to at least soak the clouts in laundry soap.

'I'm about to throw it in, Mistress.' His eyes filled with tears, and I noticed his hand tremble as he gently touched Molly's cheek. 'When one stops cryin', the other starts, an' I'm gettin' no sleep. Some of the wives in the village have been good to us an' made me burden a little lighter; bless 'em. They visit durin' the day an' try to help in whatever way they can, but they've families of their own. Margaret's been wonderful. She's such a carin' woman an' has a natural way with the bairns. She only has to pick mine up, an' they stop fussin' immediately. She's been very generous an' kind, as has her husband, Sean, in allowin' her to spend so much time helpin' me. I feel like such a burden, Mistress, as I can't expect 'em to drop their own lives to raise me children an' tidy me house.'

I placed the twins on the floor to play with Ian while I changed Molly and prepared a bottle for her. When I returned with the tea and the bottle full of warm goat milk, I sat down with Molly in my arms and started to feed her. She was so sweet, and my heart went out to both children, who would never know what a lovely person their mother was.

Adelaide and I had become friends and confidants over the years. She had confessed her affair to me, telling me she loved both men and couldn't choose. I had kept quiet on the subject and not broken her confidence. I knew there had been rumours, but these stopped when Aaron confronted the gossips' and ordered them to stop or they risked losing their job. It had all gone quiet after that, and the affair had continued with neither of their partners finding out.

John was grieving just as profoundly as Neville. Of course, he was unable to show it or those around him would have become suspicious. He had spoken to me of his love for Adelaide only because she had told him I knew of their affair but would not betray them. Even though I disagreed with what they had done, I understood how it happened and had sympathy for all concerned.

John and Adelaide had become friendly while living next door to each other, so when the women started running the pub, Adelaide would go and help him on the nights his wife, Patty, was working. It inevitably turned to love as they became close, and they started sleeping together. John believed Molly was his child; however, he couldn't tell anyone. She had bright red hair, as did he, and he was so sure of it that it was breaking his heart.

'That's why I've come to see you, Neville. I hired a Nanny who will also act as a housekeeper for you. She's arriving today. We need you back at work, and we are willing to employ her to care for the children and the house. Her name is Trixie Moffat. She has come from a grand house in Melbourne and is said to be wonderful with children.' I was firm in my manner, knowing what his response would be. Like most of the men I had met in Australia, he was a proud man and extremely stubborn. He looked surprised at first, his face softening as he stared at me intently.

'Thank you, Mistress, but I can't accept such an offer. It'd mean you're payin' two wages to support us when you don't have to. Maybe it's easier for everybody if I move on from here an' the memories of me poor, darlin' Adelaide.'

He started to cry and placed his head in his hands, his shoulders trembling as he tried to pull himself together. I sat Molly up on my lap and burped her as she sleepily looked around to see where the noise was coming from. My two chattered nonstop with Ian, with me only understanding half of what they were saying. Ian was looking at them both wide-eyed as he held a small wooden boat in his hand.

'Neville,' I said gently, giving Molly the other half of her bottle. 'Maybe it would be a good idea if you moved into one of the other vacant terraces and start afresh, given that Adelaide died here and all the memories you have of her in this house.'

Although the terraces were all spoken for, some families had recently moved on, so I would be able to move his family into another one and have this one cleaned up for the new occupants who would arrive in the next week. He stopped crying, wiping his face with the back of his hand before turning to stare out the window at the neighbourhood children playing on the cobblestone road. Minutes passed before he turned back to me and smiled weakly.

'You dunno how much I appreciate what you an' Mr Aaron have done to help me. I'll be eternally indebted to you for your kind actions. Yeah, I'll move into another terrace, return to work, an' try to raise me children as best I can. Thank you, Mistress.'

I nodded silently as I placed Molly down to sleep in her cradle, put the dirty clout in the bucket of hot water with laundry soap I had brought with me, and returned to drink the rest of my tea. We spoke quietly about the children, and I suggested he return to work next week once he had rested. I waved goodbye as I pushed the twins back up the street toward home.

'I lub my mama,' Thomas said to Emmy, and she nodded with enthusiasm, then smiled sweetly at me as I huffed and puffed and shoved the bloody heavy baby carriage up the hill.

I found Hamish waiting for me in the kitchen, talking to Leo, and, although they were polite to each other, I could see they would never be friends.

'There's me big laddie an' me bonny princess,' Hamish called out. The twins ran into his arms, squealing as he lifted them both up, placing one on each thigh.

Hamish had been courting a society woman for several months now—a Miss Angelique Promenade, in fact, and seemed happier in himself than he had since arriving in Australia. I had met her briefly years ago at Elizabeth's wedding, and Hamish had recently brought her to the house. She was from a wealthy family and was extremely beautiful, and I was pleased to see him doing better. His parents were thrilled that he was finally courting a woman of substance and quality. It helped she was from a prominent family that would assist the Makenzies' in their climb up the social ladder. Predictably, they approved of their wayward son's choice in this possible future bride, and had welcomed him back into the fold. Hamish looked across at me and smiled.

'How are ye, Abigail?' He bounced the twins on his knees, who giggled hysterically, making me laugh. I told him how we had just come from Neville's, and the offer we had made to help him return to work so he could support his children. We could have just let him stay home and paid him to care for his own children, providing free accommodation and food, however, we were well aware that would rob him of any pride or self-worth he had left. 'That's good o' ye an' Aaron tae do that fer the poor man. If it was one o' me father's workers, he would've moved 'em on by now. Naw that he employs anyone with bairns unless they reside off the property. Business is business, as he says.'

I had become increasingly affectionate after marrying Aaron, always hugging my friends or holding their hands to comfort them when things went wrong. Many times over the years, when Hamish and I would sit talking about his problems, I had wanted to pat his hand in comfort. I always held back, frightened of the reaction my body would have if we touched.

'How are things with Angelique?' I asked, and he gave me an odd look.

'All right, I suppose. O' course, me parents are happy I'm no longer seein' women o' low breedin', as they put it.'

'Are you happy, Hamish?' I asked intrusively.

'Aye, I'm the happiest I've been in a long time, but naw the happiest I've ever been, an' there's a big difference.' He gazed deep into my eyes for a moment, giving nothing away before he focussed his attention back on the twins. 'She's hard work, Abigail. Always complainin' about somethin', even when there's nought tae complain about. She'd never sit here in yer kitchen with servants around her, treatin' 'em as equals. She'd be mortified. In fact, I doubt she's ever seen the inside o' a kitchen or knows where hers is.' He smirked, and I laughed at the thought of Angelique sitting here with us. I couldn't imagine it, either.

I would call her proper, and that was a kindness, and although I had found her agreeable, I could see she looked down her nose at the way we lived and how we treated our staff. It wasn't too many years ago that Hamish behaved and thought the same way. She found my children disdainful, and I would watch her cringe when they approached her, although she hid it well from Hamish, who was too enraptured with Thomas and Emmy to notice her reaction to them. Aaron did not like her at all, finding her uppity and rude. He felt she was a suitable match for Hamish, though, as he needed to improve himself and be a better man—a gentleman even—as there would be consequences between the families if he treated her poorly.

'I've come tae help Aaron with a job, so I must go an' find him. He'll be waitin' fer me.' He kissed the twins goodbye then placed them down on the stone floor. They ran to Leo, who went to his secret jar that was no secret from my children, handing them both a toffee to suck on. He lifted them up onto the bench so they could watch him cook. He would let them stir the mixtures and lick the spoons from the desserts, and they loved helping him. They would sit there for hours if I let them. I said goodbye to Hamish as he called out his goodbyes before stepping out of the room and through the back door, leaving me thinking about his current situation while I finished my coffee. I sighed deeply as I took my empty cup to the sink then made my way over to the bench in the centre of the room, bending down to kiss my overexcited babies.

'Why are you over here?' Leo asked. 'Don't think you're taking my children in the middle of a cooking demonstration. Oh, they love it, Abigail. Look at them watching so quietly, but see how they concentrate only on what my hands are doing?. I'm starting to think they actually might have a brain in their little heads. As you know, I don't like the screaming monsters at all; however, these two are different. Quite fabulous, really. They're nothing like the unfortunate-looking children who live in the village. These two take after me in looks and are perfect examples of what true physical beauty is. All the other children do is scream and complain, throwing tantrums in the street.' He stirred his pot faster as his emotions intensified. 'I can't stand children at all and often wonder why you breeders have so many of them,' he went on. 'They drain you in every way possible, and take all your time, energy, and money while they are young; then, after everything you have given up for them, they don't make you the centre of their universe. They do not show you any attention or love once they have sucked you dry and you are old and need them, which really is the only purpose of having the horrors when you think about it. They just wait for you to shrivel up and die so they can inherit all your worldly goods, which they never worked for, mind you, and basically tell you to stick it up your clacker, and not in a good way.' I scoffed at his diatribe.

'You do so love children, although I must admit you aren't very good with them,' I said, dipping my finger in the bowl to taste his concoction. 'The children in the village don't like you at all. They've told me you tease them when you walk by. I really hope that isn't true, Leo. You can't go around calling a five-year-old an unfortunate looking grommet.'

'Oh, give it away, Abigail.' He smirked wickedly before turning his head to look down at me, his hand moving at great speed as he whisked the ingredients. 'You obviously saw that child for yourself since he lagged on me. Would you say there was anything remotely beautiful about him? His face is like an emu's bum. Anyway, you shouldn't be paying attention to anything I do in the village in my spare time. If I want to go and have some fun and the little wombat turds get in my way, then, of course, I'm going to tell them what I think. They really need to know at a young age that they're a disappointment to everyone around them, including their parents, so they can get used to it. Then no one will be disillusioned when they turn into adults with no prospects. You should be grateful that I actually like the fruit of your loins . Not in the literal sense, either, you dirty-minded little moll.' I laughed hysterically, and the twins joined me, although they didn't understand what Leo had said.

'Can you please just stop talking? You are so offensive to everyone, no matter how old. Talk about something else other than unfortunate-looking children,' I told him through my giggles.

'All right, then. I see you and Adonis are still getting along. You haven't had an argument with that man since you married Goliath. I want the gossip. Do you think he is serious about that Angelique? I have only met her a few times, but she is totally up herself and looks down her nose at everyone, including me. I mean, how the duck dare she? I wonder if she does have webbed feet? Just a thought.' He paused for a moment to yawn. 'Back to me, Abigail; your mind is wandering. I would love to twist her nipples off, but I doubt she would take that in good fun. I haven't really decided yet whether I like her or not, as some who've been hit with the ugly stick—you, as an example—are quite fun to be around.' He whacked his spoon on the edge of the pot for emphasis. 'If I could have one wish to turn an abnormal person normal, I would choose Hamish. He is just as delicious to look at as Aaron; however, he would have to romance me, as I still haven't forgiven him for betraying you. He is acting so sweet and lovely to you, yet he won't whisper anything romantic in my ear. I will wait and hope that he realises he is normal before he hitches his wagon to that Angelique. Let me know the next time you see her if we are going to like her or not.'

I rolled my eyes, picked up the twins from the bench, who yelled, 'Goodbye, Uncle Leo,' in unison, and hurried out of the kitchen and down the hallway before climbing the stairs to the nursery to find little Mary.

A few minutes later, I learnt Trixie Moffat was waiting for me in the parlour and made my way through the enormous hallway until I came to the door.

'I am sorry you were asked to wait in here. I had to put my children down for their nap,' I apologised after stepping inside. She stood and curtsied to me politely before I invited her to sit back down. I crossed the elegant room that we rarely used and took a seat opposite her. She was a pretty girl, no more than twenty; however, she had hard eyes. Everything else about her seemed lovely, and I dismissed what I had seen, kicking myself for being so judgmental. I explained what had happened to Adelaide and the situation that Neville now found himself in.

'Oh, my goodness, that *is* heartbreaking. I hope I'm able to ease their pain in some way and take the burden from him, the poor man,' she said, appearing quite emotional. We discussed her duties, then I asked Mr Masters to take her to meet Neville's little family and settle her into the new terrace that they were moving to later today. As I watched her depart, I hoped she would be a good thing for Neville and his children, and the healing would begin for all of them.

I ambled across the property towards the lake, enjoying the green paddocks and animals as I passed. I watched eight kangaroos grazing in the distance, who all raised their heads when they heard me, but made no move to bound away. We had so many native animals at Willow Grove that still fascinated me. I had never seen wildlife like that before. Some were very odd-looking specimens, like the emu. You couldn't get too close to them. Being wild, they could really harm you if they attacked with their strong legs and large claws. Kangaroos also could hurt you if they decided to kick. They would lean back on their long muscular tails and kick out hard with their feet. I still loved all of them but wisely kept my distance.

As I drew closer to the lake, Dingo came running up to me for a pat. Aaron had nursed him back to health and would take him everywhere, carrying him in the front of his shirt when he was young, then on the front of his saddle as he grew. Now he was Aaron's constant companion and had the loveliest nature for a wild dog. He was fantastic with humans; however, not so great with other dogs. He would fight with the farmhands' dogs, with them coming off second best most of the time. He slept on a mat at the back door, waiting for Aaron in the morning, and then curled up there when their day was through. Aaron would give him a big meal and pat him goodnight before leaving him to guard the door.

Aaron was by the pier waiting for me and already had the basket and blankets in the rowboat. His face lit up when he saw me.

'Ya looked like a gypsy princess comin' through the paddock in that dress, an' with ya hair all loose. I'll bet ya have no shoes on,' he said, slipping his arm around my waist as he bent down to kiss me. I giggled and lifted my leg so he could see my foot. 'See, I knew it. I know ya better than ya know yourself.' He kissed me again, this time firmly on the mouth. He helped me into the boat as Dingo stood on the pier, whining. 'No, Dingo, you're stayin' here, mate. I want time alone from everyone, includin' you.' He grinned as he rowed us toward the island, leaving Dingo barking loudly on the pier, seemingly contemplating whether to jump into the water to follow or stay dry. Aaron tied the boat up at the dock on the island and helped me up, collecting all the things he had brought with him. We walked to the big gum tree that stood tall near the edge of the water—a place we always gravitated to when visiting here. He spread the blanket out on the ground under its shade and motioned me to sit and make myself comfortable.

'Now, what's this about?' I asked suspiciously, leaning back and looking out over the water. He placed everything he was carrying down by my feet. 'You never miss a chance to see the twins, then suddenly today it's all a mystery, and you want to see me alone.'

He grinned at me again, sat down, gathered me in his arms, and kissed me for a long time, taking my breath away.

'I just wanted to spend some time alone with ya today. We're always so busy with Thomas an' Emmy. I only wanted to be with you,' he said, kissing me again.

'You are so romantic to me still, even after a couple of years of marital imprisonment. I was worried you would be sick of me by now and wished you hadn't been stuck with a nagging wife,' I teased. He chuckled, raising his hand to move a strand of hair from my face.

'Ya might be a pain in me arse when you an' Leo get up to mischief, but you're far from bein' a nag. I've seen naggin' wives, an' I hear about them all the time from the blokes here. No, me precious girl. A nagger you ain't.'

I giggled. I didn't have to nag him because there was nothing to nag him about. He looked after the children and me like we were the most precious things on earth, and I had no reason to be unhappy with him. We had our fair share of disagreements, especially when Leo got me in trouble or tried to kill me, but other than that, we agreed on most things.

We ate our delicious lunch and lay back on the blanket listening to the birds while he made love to me under our tree. We then wandered over to the other side of the small island, hand in hand, to pay our respects to Adelaide. Neville had wanted her buried at Willow Grove, and we thought the island would be the perfect place, as it was beautiful and serene. Few people knew it was already a cemetery with the mysterious grave and Leroy; however, we made sure she was buried on this side of the island, not far from the pier, so it was easy for Neville and the children to visit her gravesite.

I picked some wildflowers and placed them on her grave, silently telling her that her family would be all right now and there was nothing to worry about. Aaron and I walked back to our tree in silence, both lost in our own thoughts. She had only been twenty-years old when she died so tragically. Far too many women died in childbirth, I was coming to realise now, and was glad I didn't have this information before giving birth to the twins. Aaron leaned his back against the trunk of the enormous gum tree, and I sat between his outstretched legs so he could massage the knots out of my shoulders.

'I love ya more now than the day I married ya, if that's possible,' he whispered.

'I love you completely.' I turned and kissed him on the cheek, a flock of seagulls squawking above before they excitedly flapped their wings and flew away, back towards the ocean at the end of the property in search of food, finding no leftovers here.

I wondered how the new buildings were progressing, and had decided to go and see for myself. We had recently come to the conclusion we needed a school as there were so many children living at Willow Grove now. The labourers were in the process of constructing a small house for the teacher, a schoolroom, and a school hall with a playground outside for the children. I had found a teacher who was reputed to be the best in Victoria, having taught at several prestigious private schools in Melbourne through a friend of mine, Janet Russell. We had met at Dana's wedding and became firm friends, corresponding through letters every few weeks. I had even taken the thirty-mile journey to Shelford with the twins to visit for the day. She was knowledgeable when it came to the education system, and had a number of contacts in the area due to her benevolent work with charitable organisations—all while running her property, Golf Hill, single-handedly. She had advised me of a friend of hers, a Miss McGinty, whom she had known since she was a girl herself. After contacting her with an offer of employment and outlining the living accommodations and benefits, I had received a letter back a month later advising she was agreeable to the employment terms offered and would commence work when the school was complete.

I was happy that Emmy and Thomas would be educated here among the children they would grow up alongside and would have the best education we were able to provide. We could have sent them to several prominent private schools in Geelong, and there were some decent public schools in the district, but we had agreed it was better for them to be educated at Willow Grove.

The buildings had progressed reasonably fast and were nearing completion, with the framing of the house already up and the school hall completed. I walked over to where several men were building a playground. One of our workers, a young man named William Hargrave, had agreed to design and build equipment for the children to play on. He had shown me some of his sketches that he liked to do at night when in his quarters—one he referred to as a box kite—telling me proudly this invention of his would help him fly. Despite me thinking him quite mad, I was impressed and asked him where he had seen items like these, as I certainly never had. He blushed and told me shyly that he had just set his mind to thinking about what he would like to play with if he were young again, and suddenly he was creating things that had never existed before. Aaron had agreed to pay for all the materials required and allow him to work full time on the project, assigning three farmhands to help him. I waved to them all as I watched them work, and they happily waved back.

'I wish I were a child again so I could play on all these wonderful things,' I called out, and they laughed.

'You're still small enough to fit on them, except for your long legs,' Mr Hargrave called back. His workers suddenly stopped what they were doing and looked at him in shock. You didn't speak like that to a woman about any part of her body, especially not your boss' wife. William's face turned a deep shade of red, and he appeared quite horrified.

'Yes, I know. They should have been a foot shorter,' I called back, dismissing the sin he had just committed. I smiled at them all and waved goodbye, and they waved back, appearing relieved.

On my way home, I decided to visit Polly. She had given birth to a little girl they had named Isabelle Abigail—calling her Bella—who was about to turn one. The twins loved playing with Willy and Bella while Polly and I gossiped and spent time together. Her relationship with Jemima had deteriorated even further in recent times, finding her cold with the children and a troublemaker, always trying to come between her and Mrs Makenzie. Harriet would visit Polly and Angus up to five times a week, and since our friendship had remained strong through all the trouble and strife, I would stop in to take tea with her as often as I could.

I found Polly sitting at the table on her back verandah. It was her favourite place, and I always knew where she would be if she wasn't in the house.. When she saw me, she smiled brightly and stood to embrace me.

'It's so good to see you, Abi. It's terribly busy here now with all these workers and their families. You seem to spend your days running around after them and fixing their problems.' She frowned before sitting back down and inviting me to join her.

'Well, who else is there to do it?' I made myself comfortable in the seat next to her, noticing a beautiful white lace doily she had been working on. 'Aaron is far too busy to waste his time on squabbles between housewives in the village and making sure all their medical needs are attended to. They don't seem to realise that we pay Dr Richards to visit and care for all at Willow Grove, but they somehow think they will be left with an exorbitant bill, even though I have reassured them a hundred times that will not happen. They still refuse to call for a doctor until a person is really sick—or dead.' Polly gave a nod of understanding.

'You have to remember the people who work here are like us, Abi. If our lives had gone a different way and we were working for some powerful, aristocratic family who promised us more than we expected or asked for, we wouldn't trust them either. We were brought up to believe the rich are callous, cold and selfish; for the most part, that has been confirmed by many people we have met over the years. They will start to believe as soon as you have paid for him consistently for a while longer. Don't even worry about it. It will sink into their heads that there are no strings attached and they don't need to be suspicious. It just takes time.'

I knew she was right. I would be apprehensive, too, if I were being offered extra benefits, wondering what motive was behind it.

'How are you, my dear sister? You seem quite upset,' I said, noticing she looked a little tired. She then explained that Jemima had told Harriet that she had been moaning that her mother-in-law had been visiting far too often. Of course, it was untrue, but Mrs Makenzie had taken great offence until Polly went to her and told her it was a lie.

'But who is she going to believe, her own flesh and blood or me?' She appeared troubled as she poured me a mango juice from a large jug on the table.

'Jemima is a spiteful girl, so do not put up with her bullshit.' I screwed up my nose in disdain, remembering my wedding day and the unexpected, threat-filled visit I had received from her.

Little Mary arrived and immediately took the twins inside and placed them on the floor with Willy and Bella, leaving Polly and me to chat. I was sure Mary followed me around on my daily rounds. She would often appear without warning and be where I was without reason, before quietly taking over the care of the children if I wasn't looking. Last week, I took tea with Amelia at the shop when little Mary came walking in and took them from me, disappearing back to the main house without a word. She behaved as if I were stealing my own bairns away from her. We laughed at the children playing together on the floor when Angus came rushing in, his usually tanned face drained of all colour.

'Abigail. You're needed up at the house. Aaron's had an accident, and the quack is on his way,' he said, breathing heavily. I immediately rose to my feet, and Polly grabbed my hand.

'Abi, leave the children here, and I'll have Mary bring them to the house when they're ready for their dinner.' I nodded as she urged me to leave, shooing me away with some urgency.

My heart was in my throat as I ran as fast as I could to the house, gasping for breath. I stepped through the back door and ran into the kitchen where I found Leo boiling an enormous pot of water.

'He's in your bedchamber with Hamish,' he said calmly as I hurried past him. I took the stairs two at a time, running as fast as my shoes would allow until I arrived at our door. I pushed it wide to find him stretched out on our bed, his face white, his lips tinged blue. I rushed to his side and threw my arms around him.

'What happened?' Hamish lowered himself into a chair near the fireplace as I stroked Aaron's forehead.

'We were down in the south paddock fellin' trees when one came down the wrong way an' pinned Aaron by the leg. I managed tae get it off him, but I tell ye, he roared with the pain. I finally got him up on Goliath an' rode back here slowly 'cause every step was painin' him. I've called fer Dr Richards.'

Hamish was just as dishevelled and filthy as my husband, his face streaked in dirt and sweat. Aaron's left leg showed no signs of any deep wounds, only superficial cuts and abrasions; however, he was in pain, so I assumed his leg was damaged in some way. I removed his boot while he groaned in agony. His foot was swollen, as was his lower leg, so I attempted to make him as comfortable as possible while waiting for the doctor to arrive. I elevated his leg on a pillow as he tried not to cry out, then went and lay next to him, stroking his face and talking to him.

Hamish seemed uncomfortable, and I immediately thought back to the last time he had been in here alone with me, feeling self-conscious. I hurried across the room and stepped into the washroom, rummaging around in frustration until I picked up the small bottle of laudanum, returning to his side to administer a spoonful to ease the pain. Within fifteen-minutes, he was sound asleep. Hamish gazed across at me intently as I sat on the bed next to my unconscious husband.

'Ye dinnae have tae be nervous around me, Abigail. I'm naw goin' tae touch ye or leap on ye when yer naw lookin',' Hamish teased quietly as Aaron snored softly beside me. I arched my eyebrow inquiringly but said nothing. 'Ye get a certain look on yer face sometimes when yer alone with me, like yer either ready tae run away or defend yerself from me unwanted advances.' He seemed amused, while I could feel myself blushing.

'I don't mean to, and I certainly do not intend for you to see it,' I replied, my face becoming warm. 'It's only that sometimes you look at me in a certain way, or you say something that brings back a memory.'

'Ye do that tae me constantly, Abigail, but I'll be honest with ye. If you were married tae anyone but Aaron, I'd still pursue ye until ye let me catch ye. Unfortunately fer me, I've too much respect fer the man tae betray him. Ye dinnae need tae worry that I'll ever do anythin' tae ye. Naw while yer with Aaron, an' happily, I see. It gives me peace that yer loved an' content,' he said with a grin. I smiled back.

Dr Richards arrived and placed his bag beside the bed, then started to examine Aaron's leg, waking him up. He was groggy and disoriented as he stared up at the doctor, who slowly ran his hand down his leg, stopping several times. Aaron cried out when he placed pressure on his leg below the knee, so he stopped and felt around a little slower. He mumbled to himself before straightening up and glancing sympathetically at me then focussing his attention on Aaron.

'I'm sorry to tell you this, Aaron, but you have fractured your bone in several places. I will have to set it, but it means you will have to stay in bed for several weeks until it's healed,' Dr Richards said to a drowsy

Aaron. I was relieved that he hadn't been seriously hurt or killed and kissed him on the cheek. The doctor made his way to the washroom, his large leather bag in his hand.

'Oh, me beautiful, Abi. I love ya so. Ya have nothin' to fear when I'm beside ya, 'cause I'd fight to the death to keep ya safe. Isn't she lovely, Hamish?' He stopped for a moment, his eyes closed as the awkward silence hovered above. 'Oh, of course, ya know she is. I'm sorry, mate. I feel strange with that stuff Abi gave me. I've never had it before,' he slurred. Hamish and I exchanged smiles as Aaron opened his eyes for only a moment then closed them again and muttered softly to himself.

There was a knock on the door, and I turned to find Bessie, who had come to help.

'How is he?' she asked, hurrying to my side. I told her what the doctor had said. 'Hmm, these boys think they're invincible. Then something like this happens, and you realise it could have been very bad. Very bad indeed,' she said disapprovingly. I agreed with her wholeheartedly.

Hamish asked where the twins were, and when I told him, he excused himself to go visit with Angus, Polly, and the children. I thanked him for what he had done for Aaron, and he nodded and quietly left. Aaron had dozed off again. Bessie and I undressed him, which was a feat in itself, and leaned him back on the pillows so the doctor could treat his leg. Bessie then hurried off to get tea for the doctor and Aaron while I lay beside him, holding his hand.

'I'm sorry, Abi. I do love ya, ya know?' he said, sounding as if he were dreaming and in another world. I put my head on his chest, and he stroked my face until Dr Richards returned and went about his work.

Aaron was going to hate being in bed. I knew he would demand crutches before the week was out—while not putting it past him for a moment to hobble down the stairs to the kitchen, then go about his day within the confines of the house, while possibly falling and injuring himself further. He bit down on his lip during the bone-setting, his groans so loud Dr Richards administered a hefty dose of heroin, a derivative of opium, into his bare backside with a glass syringe. When it was all over, I felt his body relax back into the bed. We put his leg up on pillows and tucked him in. I walked Dr Richards out and thanked him.

'He is fortunate, you know? If that tree had fallen anywhere on his upper body, he would be dead. You could be a widow right now as we speak,' he said matter-of-fact, making me instantly feel like I had been punched in the stomach. If I had lost him, I wouldn't have known what to do. I said goodbye to this strange, blunt doctor and returned to the bedchamber.

'Are you in pain?' I asked Aaron before gently kissing his face.

'Nah, I'm feelin' pretty good after that injection. Whatever it was, it's fabulous, as Leo would say.' I smothered a smile and kissed him again before he slowly sank into a deep, painless sleep.

Chapter Six

I MADE MY WAY downstairs to see if Richard Malcolm had returned from his office in Geelong. He had arrived from England with his wife and son to stay with us not long after completing his law degree a year ago at Oxford. When I finally saw him disembark from the ship with his family, I was so overwhelmed with joy I felt my heart would burst. He was still as handsome as ever, but he had a confidence that he lacked when we had last seen each other. He had turned into a man. We had embraced for the longest time, tears spilling down my face, I was just so pleased to see him.

He had shaken Aaron's hand and introduced us to his wife, Jasmin, and Daniel, their son. With hair the colour of wheat, she was truly beautiful, possessing bright, blue eyes that gazed adoringly at her husband and son, who favoured his father in every way. They had meant to stay with us for two-months before returning to England, but they liked Geelong so much that two-months turned into four, then six, which pleased me greatly.

Aaron and I eventually sat down with Richard and asked him to open a law practice to manage my trust fund and business interests. I didn't get along with Mr McPhee, nor did I trust him—a feeling that proved to be well-founded. Richard, I trusted entirely in every respect. Richard and Jasmin soon decided that Australia was where they wanted to raise their children, and that this opportunity was too good to pass up, soon accepting our offer. As he had no money behind him, we purchased a building in Ryrie Street, Geelong, and furnished it so he could open his practice.

Mr McPhee had not been happy when Richard met with him to advise he was now acting as my lawyer and required all documents relating to me to be handed over by the end of that day. Mr McPhee had refused and ordered him from the office, adamant he would remain the legal guardian of my trust fund until I attained the age of thirty. Richard had calmly advised that if he did not quietly accept the new arrangement and do as asked, he would be exposed for stealing thousands of pounds from my trust fund. Aaron had been the one to discover the theft and immediately spoke to Richard, who looked over the records and confirmed his suspicions. He had agreed to confront Mr McPhee in my absence while making it clear that charges would be filed if he refused to cooperate. After some thought, Mr McPhee quietly bowed out of my life forever, much to my relief.

Richard would not accept the offer of money as a gift to build a house for his family; however, he did agree to an interest-free loan that he intended to pay off as it suited him. He and Jasmin were building a grand house not far from ours where they had purchased twenty hectares, as neither wanted anything as big as Willow Grove to manage. Until it was finished, they were staying with us, much to my delight.

I got along famously with Jasmin, who suited Richard perfectly. He would have kissed the ground she walked on while Jasmin adored him just as much as he did her. Daniel favoured his father in looks and personality, being a sweet, placid boy. I found Richard in the sitting room with Jasmin, who I affectionately called Jas, talking and playing with Daniel.

'We heard Aaron had an accident. Is he going to be all right?' Richard asked, coming to sit on the opposite lounge to where I had made myself comfortable.

'Yes. He is away with the fairies thanks to the injection Dr Richard's administered, but he is going to go mad and drive everyone else insane given the fact he is to stay in bed for four-weeks to allow the bone to heal. Even I am not looking forward to that,' I said, and they laughed, knowing what he was like if left idle. 'How is your practice going, Richard?' I asked by way of changing the subject.

'Slowly, but I'm getting there.' He brushed the dark hair from his handsome face and smiled, his straight, white teeth almost blinding me. 'We would be stuck if you hadn't given me your trust to manage and business to oversee. I am starting to secure new clients every week. Although much of it is mind numbing, like drawing up wills and contracts, I am starting to get some criminal cases.' Jas looked at him proudly, placing her hand on top of his.

'How was your day, Jas? I didn't see you all day.' I was surprised as we always saw each other daily while the children played together and during mealtimes in the kitchen; however, they had missed breakfast, and I hadn't been here for lunch.

'Yes, I left early and went to the village to help Amelia in the store. Now she's pregnant with her third, she is just so tired. She's so busy that she plans to hire a local lass from one of the farms to assist her. She's not feeling well either with this pregnancy,' she said with sympathy, and I nodded. I told them that I would not be down for dinner but would eat with Aaron and the children in our room.

'Then I will go and let the staff know we'll eat in the kitchen tonight. Saves all that dining-room fuss,' Richard said. 'And I'll let Leo know you want your dinner sent up.'

I nodded appreciatively, and he and his family left, leaving me wondering just how much of a pain in the backside Aaron would be now he was incapacitated.

I went to the nursery to see the twins, who were freshly bathed and in their nightgowns, playing with their toys. I scooped them up in my arms, their loud giggling and squealing filling the room before I lay down on the bed with them to play. Soon after, little Mary helped me carry them to our bedchamber, placing Thomas on her hip while I took Emmy. Aaron was still sleeping but woke as soon as he heard his children excitedly calling out for him. He sat up sleepily as I placed them on the bed, where they quickly went to him and started jumping on his chest.

'No jumping on daddy. Daddy has a sore leg. Thomas, lie down next to daddy, there's a good lad. No more jumping, Emmy,' I said, grabbing her mid-air and placing her next to her father. They cuddled into Aaron while he told them a story about something called 'the dreamtime' as I lay beside them and listened.

There was a knock on the door just as he finished his story, passed on to him from a native friend when he was very young. Leo came prancing into our room carrying Aaron's dinner, followed by our two footmen, Jonathon and Samuel, both carrying trays. They placed mine and Aaron's trays on our laps. Samuel handed another tray to little Mary before quickly departing, while Jonathon followed after wishing Aaron well. Leo pulled a chair up next to Aaron's side of the bed and looked down at him, his eyes sparkling in amusement.

'So, Goliath. You *are* just a mere mortal like us all. And here I was, believing you to be a God of some sort. You do have the backside of a Goddess,' he remarked, slapping his hands down on his knees before bursting into hysterical laughter. Little Mary came to my side and took the twins, sitting them at the table and placing their dinner in front of them.

They refused to let anyone feed them anymore and were still learning how to use a knife and fork without much success, often becoming frustrated that they couldn't get enough food in their mouths, before reverting back to using their fingers. Today was one of those times. I watched them gleefully pick up the food with their bare hands and place it hungrily in their mouths, making me smile across at them. If we had eaten that way at the orphanage, even at their age, we would have been reprimanded severely.

'Unfortunately, Leonardo, I'm not invincible like ya seem to believe. Can't say I'm enjoyin' it much, though. I do enjoy when ya cook this Mediterranean tucker for tea, though. Thanks, mate.' He enthusiastically began to eat his Moussaka and Greek salad, although he appeared drowsy, his actions and reactions slow. I enjoyed it, too, being one of my favourite dishes, especially when it was warm outside. I loved the salad. The cucumbers, tomatoes, onions, and lettuce were picked this morning from our garden. Leo transformed them with strong feta cheese he bought from a local farmer and pickled black olives that he processed himself from our olive trees.

'Are you in a lot of pain, Goliath?' Leo asked sympathetically, patting him on the shoulder.

'Yeah, nah. The injections the quack is givin' me help a lot, an' that laudanum stuff Abi keeps fillin' me full of. I feel like I'm pissed an' can't sober up.' he said, and Leo giggled.

'Give me some, Abigail, just for fun,' he demanded. Aaron chuckled as he finished his meal, then went on to his dessert of chocolate peppermint cheesecake. The twins had finished their dinner and ran to me. I put my arms around them and helped them up onto the bed.

'Now, you have to be careful of daddy's leg. Emmy, don't try to jump on him,' I said and grabbed her just before she threw herself at Aaron.

'I want Dadda,' she told me firmly, her arms stretched out to him. Aaron passed his tray to Leo and opened his arms out for her.

'Come to me, sweetheart. It's all right, Abi, I'll take her.' He lifted her onto his lap, where she cuddled into his chest and placed her little arms around him tightly. He lay back on his pillows as he stroked her long, wavy hair. Thomas came and joined her, also snuggling into his father's lap. Aaron placed his arms around them and closed his eyes briefly as he again started to tell them a story, much to their delight. They stayed silent and unmoving as they listened to the tale of men walking on the moon. Emmy fell asleep listening to her father's voice while Thomas was wide awake, staring at his father in awe before his eyelids began to droop, and he, too, nodded off. I was disappointed not to hear the end of the story and learn how the men got back from the moon. Little Mary and I carried the sleeping children to their cots and covered them in their soft, warm blankets, kissing them both goodnight.

Aaron was awake when I returned to the room. 'Are you sure you want me to sleep in here? I might knock your leg or hurt you accidentally,' I said with a frown.

'The day I don't want ya to sleep with me is the day I die.' He smirked to himself as he closed his eyes again. 'Now get in here. I'm bored.' I felt this was not the last time I would hear these words in the next few weeks. I went to my dressing room and picked up a nightgown, crossing back to the bed before asking him to unbutton my dress. He groaned at me as I fixed him with a stare.

'It's your leg that's broken, not your bloody arms.' I smiled at him, and he chuckled. Once changed, I got into bed carefully, trying not to move his leg, and made myself comfortable. He kissed me then pushed my hand down under the quilts, guiding my hand down past his stomach.

'Surely not,' I said to him, my eyes wide.

'Why not?' he asked, widening his own eyes and protesting his innocence.

'Because the movement will throw your leg around and undo all the good work the doctor did setting it.'

'Not if you're the one doin' the movin'.' Later, as I snuggled into his arms, I dreamed of a kookaburra with babies in a golden nest, a crystal chandelier, and a boat.

I woke to hear Aaron complain, 'I'm starvin',' and abruptly turned to glare at him, shaking my head in disbelief. Over the next few weeks, I could see he would be an immense pain in my arse. I knew he would be missing his early morning visits to the kitchen where he usually had his first breakfast, and I did feel a pang of sympathy for him; however, only slight.

'Do you want me to go and get you something?' I asked, yawning and stretching my body under the warm covers, not wanting to get up. It wasn't even daylight yet, and I pondered over what had possessed me to marry an eating machine for the hundredth time.

'Would ya? I'll love ya forever,' he chirped and lay back on his pillows, wide awake.

'You'd better.' I dragged myself out of bed and pulled on my dressing gown while muttering to myself. I made my way through the dimly lit house then stepped into the brightly lit kitchen, the warm room bustling with staff going about their duties. The kitchen was frenetic as usual, while Leo stood at the central bench preparing a cake batter. He saw me and started to giggle.

'I assume you are down here because Goliath can't be, and he's hungry. Am I right, or am I right, or am I right?' he called out with a smirk.

'Surprisingly enough, you're right.' I laughed and kissed him good morning. I sat down to a hot cup of coffee while I waited for Leo to cook something for the Whining Laird of Willow Grove and smothered a smile. By the time I had finished my drink, he had a tray of hot food and cold apple juice ready for me to take up to the bedchamber.

'Tell him we miss him parading his god-like body in front of us all, especially that backside.' Leo sighed as he gazed out of the window into the blackness.

'I'll be sure to do that,' I replied as several maids giggled. Leo moved towards me and placed his hand on my shoulder.

'You know what? If you like, I will take his tray up to him and comfort the poor boy while you stay down here and out of my way.'

'Leo, he told you the other day to stop flirting with him. If I send you up there when he is lying helpless in bed and unable to defend himself from your advances, he will divorce me.' His face fell in disappointment, sending several more maids into a hysterical giggling fit.

'Abigail, you are so selfish trying to keep him all to yourself. You don't know how to share,' he yelled after me as I picked up the tray and made my way out of the warm room, the kitchen staff calling out their good wishes as I left.

I found Aaron waiting impatiently as I stepped back into the room. I placed the tray on his lap and put the juice and coffee on his bedside table. He was wide awake and ready to eat.

'Thank you, *mo anamchara*. I could eat the crotch out of a low flyin' duck,' he said, starting on his omelette and bacon with tomatoes and mushrooms. 'How are they all down in the kitchen?' he asked wistfully, and I knew he missed his morning routine.

'They said to tell you they miss you already and to get well quickly,' I replied, smothering a smile at the thought of Leo as I climbed back into bed carefully so as not to hurt his leg. He sat back against his pillows, appearing pleased. I knew he wouldn't look so happy if I repeated the actual conversation in the kitchen when he wasn't around. When he had finished, I removed the tray while he drank his coffee and got back under the covers.

'Are you in much pain?' I asked, studying his face intently.

'Nah, but I think the medicine ya give me is keepin' the pain at bay,' he said, relaxing back into bed and patting his full, muscular stomach. I turned to try to go back to sleep: however, he wouldn't allow it, tickling me, talking, and generally annoying me until he got my attention.

'Aaron, what do you want?' I asked crossly after this had gone on for more than half-an-hour.

'You,' he replied, pulling me towards him.

'All right, but then you have to let me sleep,' I said firmly as he smirked and kissed me.

When I exited my carriage outside Montague's in Malop Street, Geelong, I stood for a moment admiring the window display of fashionable ballroom and wedding gowns. Catherine was becoming known for her bridal wear and was getting a steady stream of orders from across Australia. Women would send their measurements and a description or a picture from a magazine of their dream dress, and Catherine would design them, then pass them to her seamstresses to sew.

Colin had left us to train under Catherine to become a tailor. They were secretly living together, with her family believing him to be an employee when they visited—all except William, who had kept her secret so far. Her grand apartment above the shop had turned out better than expected, and her parents were impressed that she was living in such luxury so soon into her career. She employed several seamstresses and Colin as her apprentice tailor, two shop assistants, and a housekeeper who cooked all her meals and looked after her.

As I pushed the door open and stepped inside the shop, a bell tinkled above my head. The shop assistant went out the back to tell Catherine I had arrived, and soon after, she came bounding out to greet me. She led me upstairs where her housekeeper, Mrs Mary Swan, had morning tea waiting for us. I greeted her warmly before we withdrew into the drawing-room to enjoy it. I adored Catherine's apartment. It was so warmly decorated, with the most exquisite furniture throughout. I had offered to pay for the decorating and furnishings, which she hadn't wanted to accept; however, I had insisted. I made sure she chose precisely what she wanted, despite the cost. I had told her if she was so determined to pay me back, she could be my private dressmaker and supply my clothes for free, to which she readily agreed, promising to make me the finest-dressed woman in Australia.

I sat on the oversized couch next to her, kicking my shoes off as I tucked my feet up under me and looked at her intently.

'So, how is everything going, Catherine? Have you settled in all right?' Her face shone with happiness, and she looked beautiful, with her blue eyes shining and her long, blonde hair falling loose around her face.

'Things couldn't be better, Abigail. The business is thriving, and I'm making a fortune in my own right, but it's more the fact that so many women want to wear my creations that thrills me,' she said, her porcelain complexion flushed with excitement. 'Colin is wonderful. He shows a talent for fashion and is thoroughly enjoying every minute of it. I must say, I enjoy having him around, too.'

I smiled. She was completely in love with him, as he was with her. The fact he was living with her secretly as husband and wife, without the legal paperwork, would infuriate her family should they ever find out. To them, Catherine was their eighteen-year-old virgin daughter who one day would marry an affluent man—hopefully, one with a title and impeccable family connections.

They had great expectations that she had no intention of living up to when they weren't around. As she didn't see them often, it had been easy to hide her living arrangements. William had changed his views towards Colin, having fallen in love with a working-class woman himself. He loved Catherine and would never betray her, knowing his parents' reaction if he did. When she gave me a strange look and started to blush, I wondered what was wrong with her.

'Those things you told me to do in bed when he first started sleeping here are really working. Now I understand why Aaron can't keep his hands off you.' She giggled self consciously, and I smirked at her wickedly.

'Well, you need to thank Dana for that. If it wasn't for her, Aaron and I probably wouldn't have a sex life, given neither of us knew what we were doing at the start.' We both collapsed into loud laughter. Once I managed to compose myself, I told her what had happened to Aaron and how he was already restless, and she nodded sympathetically.

We discussed how our Sunday family lunches were growing by the minute, with friends marrying and having children, and the fact that Richard and Jas were living with us had only added to the increase. Hamish brought Angelique with him now, who I still hadn't made my mind up about. Catherine was disappointed to not see the twins with me, but when I explained I had left them at home to entertain their father, she laughed, knowing what Aaron was like.

'From now on, I am making my sample dresses in your size.' Catherine nodded to herself as if the arrangement was now set in stone. 'I always make up the design of a dress first to see how it looks and to keep it in my collection. I have a copy of every dress I have ever made. When the ladies come to me for their one-off dresses, what they don't realise is I have already made the exact dress to keep here. I will let you choose what you like from the samples, then modify them a bit to make them uniquely yours. That way, you will have the fanciest wardrobe in the world. I will continue to make your house dresses; however, you will have so many magnificent gowns to wear to events, you will never have to think about your wardrobe again.' I looked at her in disbelief.

'You can't be doing that,' I gasped. 'Those dresses are worth a fortune and take so long to make. I couldn't accept. When I agreed to you making my dresses for free, I meant only my house dresses as they are plain and don't take so much cloth or time.'

She shook her head in defiance. 'You will agree, or I will hand this shop back to you,' she threatened. 'It is the only way I can show you how much I love and appreciate you for everything you have done. Without you, I would still live in Melbourne with my parents and under my father's thumb. I would never have been able to have anything like this without you, Abigail, or a chance to make a name for myself. Colin wouldn't have had the opportunity to train as a tailor, as he never thought he would ever have the chance to better himself. He always hated hard labouring work but had no other options available to him until now,' she told me, tears welling in her eyes. 'What you have done for me has changed so many lives. I have five seamstresses, two who solely work for Colin, and I'm able to afford to employ as many workers as I need. I have taken a leaf out of your book, and I pay them above what they would get anywhere else and make sure they are provided with enough breaks. They seem to love working here, and I find that they are very loyal and hardworking, not wanting to lose their jobs because of how I treat them. Making the sample dresses for you is the only way I can even try to repay you, so you have no choice but to accept.' I looked at the stubborn set of her face and grudgingly gave in. She was the loveliest person I knew and such a good friend to me. I could feel the excitement already bubbling up inside me at having Montague dresses fill my wardrobe. 'How are Richard and Jas? Is their house nearly finished?' she asked, abruptly changing the subject. She also got along exceptionally well with them and now counted them both among her close friends.

'They are well. I love them staying with us and hope it takes forever to finish their home. Unfortunately, it won't be long now.' I frowned as she laughed.

'You would have all of us living with you if you could, Abigail. Not that your house wouldn't fit everyone in it comfortably.' She laughed aloud as Mrs Swan carried a tray into the room and set it down in front of us, smiling sweetly as she poured out tea and offered me a slice of sponge cake with passionfruit icing. 'It's wonderful that Richard is establishing himself here as a lawyer. I have asked him to act for me in any legal matters I might have, and he has happily agreed. He told me I can come to him with anything to do with my business, and he will assist me. He is one of the nicest people I have ever met, and so is Jasmin. You are fortunate to have him looking after your business and money, as there is no one better you could trust after what that wicked Mr McPhee did to you.'

'Yes,' I said, nodding thoughtfully, 'he told me the other day he's already had to employ two junior solicitors to keep up with the work he's getting. I can see he will do well here. As for my money, now I don't even have to think about it, as I trust him completely. Aaron meets with him weekly to discuss our finances. Sometimes I stay and listen; however, I find it too overwhelming, so I just leave it to them.'

'You're hopeless.' Catherine grinned widely, shaking her head in mock disgust. 'I make sure I oversee every part of my business, down to the last penny.'

I smiled proudly at her. Unlike me, she was a businesswoman and had the intellect for it, whereas it was something I preferred not to think or worry about.

After spending several hours gossiping, Catherine walked me out to my carriage, and we embraced warmly.

'We will see you Sunday. Give Aaron our love. I hope he is not too much of a pain for you.' She was still giggling to herself as my carriage pulled away, waving until she lost sight of us before returning to her shop.

I arrived home just before lunch, wondering what devastation awaited me in my bedchamber, while knowing full well the twins would be running loose in there. I was relieved to see Bessie sitting at the table watching them play on the floor with some toys while Aaron lay back against the pillows. He appeared melancholy as I made my way across the room.

'What's wrong with you, sunshine?' I asked as his face lit up at the sight of me.

'I've been waitin' for ya. I'm bored. It's like watchin' paint dry layin' here,' he moaned. I rolled my eyes. He was seriously getting on my nerves already, and if he continued like this, I would break his other leg before the week was up. I picked up the twins and kissed them, then sat on the bed next to Aaron. Thomas put his arms around my neck and kissed me back.

'I love you, Mama,' he said sweetly. Emmy crawled off my lap and over to Aaron while I kept my arms around Thomas.

'I love you, too, my darling little man. You are the sunshine in my day and mean everything to me.' He smiled up at me while Aaron looked over at us lovingly.

'Me sit on you, Dada,' Emmy demanded. He lifted her up and placed her on his lap. She cuddled into him while looking across at me and giving me the sweetest smile.

I had just turned eighteen, and I had never thought for a moment I would be a mother and wife at this age. The three of them meant more to me than anything in the world, and I adored them with every part of my being. I didn't know what I had done to deserve my own perfect family, but whatever it was made me incredibly grateful.

Aaron and I played with the twins while Bessie looked on affectionately, sometimes laughing at what she would hear them say. Soon they wanted to get off the bed, and I helped them down so they could resume playing with their toys.

'Stay with me for a while, Abi? Little Mary will look after the nippers, an' it's their lunchtime now anyway,' he pleaded quietly.

'All right. But just for a little while as I want to go and eat lunch with them. They never eat without one of us being there,' I reminded him, and he nodded.

'Bessie, do ya mind takin' 'em to the nursery for half-hour an' let Mary know Abi will be down to eat lunch with 'em?' Aaron asked. 'They aren't starvin' 'cause they both ate as much as I did for mornin' tea so the delay won't hurt 'em.'

She nodded and picked them up, placing one on each hip as she walked out the door, kicking it closed behind her. I walked around the room, putting things back in their proper places since the twins had decided to redecorate. He watched me as I went about tidying the room, which looked like a hurricane had struck.

'Ya look beautiful in that dress. I admire how Catherine makes clothes to fit snug to ya body while showin' off ya assets. By assets, I mean ya tits an' ya arse.' I ignored him; however, I spoke of Catherine's offer to make my gowns, and he lay back against his pillows, appearing impressed. Once I was finished and the room was clean and tidy once again, I sat down on the chair beside the bed and narrowed my gaze at him.

'What do you want me to do for you, Aaron? I can't think of anything more that would help?' I tucked my legs up under me and grimaced. It had only been a day since the accident, and he was already starting to drive me mad.

'Ya could take off ya dress an' come an' get in beside me.' A cheeky grin spread across his face as he patted my side of the enormous bed.

'Aaron, I'm not going to have sex with you every time I come in here just because you're bored.'

'That's not the reason, Abi. I need to have ya close to me. I miss talkin' to ya,' he complained. 'I've more time now to spend with ya, not by choice, I must admit, but I don't wanna waste it.' I felt myself softening towards him as I looked at his beautiful face, his blue eyes pleading with me.

'Oh, all right, but only till lunch. We agreed the twins wouldn't be left for others to look after all the time, especially at mealtimes,' I reminded him again, and he nodded.

'I promise I won't keep ya any longer than half-hour.' He smirked as I climbed up onto the bed, then patiently undid my dress. Soon after, I was naked beside him, and he pulled me over onto him and kissed me passionately. 'Just remember, you're havin' sex with me 'cause ya enjoy it an' can't keep ya hands off me, not 'cause I'm bored.'

I found Richard sitting at the table in the kitchen, the twins beside him secured in their high chairs. He stood when I entered the room, greeting me with a kiss on the cheek. I took a seat next to him as Leo brought our lunch of something he called spaghetti bolognese to the table and sat down to join us.

'Where's Jas?' I enquired, serving his meal before the twins.

'She's up in our bedchamber with Daniel. He isn't feeling well, so we've sent for the doctor. I doubt it's serious. Jas is keeping him upstairs so Thomas and Emmy aren't exposed to whatever it is. Just a chill, I think, but he's running a fever, so I didn't think it would hurt to have him examined.' I nodded, setting a cup of barley water on each highchair.

We had been fortunate with the twins so far. They were blessed with the same strong constitution as their father, who rarely took ill. There had only been one incident when they were teething where they both became unwell with fever and were up crying through the night. They stared at me expectantly as I served out two bowls of bolognese and cut the pasta up into tiny straws. When I placed the food in front of them, they eagerly picked up their spoons and started to eat.

I would have to clean them up after such a messy lunch but smiled at them adoringly when I saw how much they were enjoying it. I served Leo then myself, and we began to eat. Leo poured two glasses of guava juice for the twins that he had only pressed this morning, which they both immediately chose over the water, finishing so quickly he poured them another.

'So, how is my Goliath?' Leo asked. 'I feel so sorry for him lying up there all by himself with you swanning around down here, not giving him a second thought, you cold cockatoo. If you like, I can go and keep him company after lunch while you go about your business around the property like you are the queen of the castle.' Richard burst out laughing while I continued eating until he regained his composure.

'Leonardo, do you ever think before you speak?' Richard asked. 'I hope you don't talk like this in front of strangers as you would be arrested and placed in gaol on suspicion of being a homosexual. Of course, everyone here knows and loves you how you are, but please be careful. I can't warn you enough of how violent and harsh the treatment for men like yourself outside the protective bubble of Willow Grove.'

'Oh, I know, Richard. I'm not ignorant. How do you think I've lasted this long? I've travelled the world and haven't been beaten or thrown in gaol yet because I'm careful. You all see me here, but when I go out in public, I act like a strong, fearsome man no one would dare cross.'

He chuckled at the image, and I could see Richard doubted Leo's contention.. I, however, had observed Leo in public on many occasions when we visited Geelong together and, although he came across as effeminate, he did make an effort to tone down his behaviour and ensured he blended in with the other men by how he dressed. We didn't mind how flamboyant he was with his wardrobe here at home, with Catherine making clothes for him in bright colours and ostentatious styles. However, when he left the house, he wore plain shirts and trousers with an understated jacket.

'Well, Goliath is bored,' I said, 'but he told me to warn you to stay away unless I'm in the room to protect him from you.'

By the time I had finished eating, the twins had eaten a second helping and were both staring at me again. Emmy gave me the sweetest smile.

'Crème brûlée,' she said as clear as day, and Leo choked on his food. Richard thumped him on the back and handed him a glass of water. It took him some time until he could speak again.

'I cannot believe what I just heard. Like mother, like daughter, right, my little Miss Em?' he said and stroked her hair. He went to the icebox and returned with a tray of individual bowls filled with crème brûlée that he always kept on hand for me. He placed two crystal bowls down in front of Emmy and Thomas, who giggled, picked up their spoons, and quickly started to eat. They had never been given a whole serving of their own before, with them being fed from my or Aaron's dessert dish. I laughed as I watched them swallow spoonful after spoonful, not stopping until they had finished every last morsel. Richard looked at me, clearly impressed.

'I can see your children take after you, Abigail. I seem to recall crème brûlée being your favourite when you first tasted it in London all those years ago,' he said, his eyes twinkling.

'Have you had your eyes closed for the entire time you have been living here, Richard?' Leo asked impatiently. 'Oh, my goodness gracious me with a tiddlywink on the top! Have you not seen their father eat? It takes all my time to keep this mob fed, including the twins, who eat as much as me.' Richard chuckled, then turned to me, his face becoming serious.

'I need to have a chat with you in private now that Aaron is out of action. I don't want to disturb him, especially when he is being given medication for his pain. I don't imagine he can think clearly right now. I went to see him yesterday after it happened, and he was extremely groggy, so, unfortunately, you are stuck having to talk business with me.'

'I will ask Mary to stay with the twins,' I said, and he nodded. 'It's fine to talk business with me as long as you remember to tell Aaron everything you tell me after he improves, as I might forget. If I'm not interested in something, I find my brain instantly shuts down.'

'I promise it won't be that bad.' He smiled reassuringly as Leo snorted.

'Not that bad? Have you not realised Abigail and business do not get along at all? They actually despise each other,' Leo said smugly, and I quickly twisted his ear, making him shriek.

'Stop talking like I'm deaf and dumb. Of course, I understand. I just choose to have nothing to do with it,' I told him crossly as he held his ear in pain and glared at me.

'Just for that, I'm going up to get into bed with Goliath and give him the sympathy he deserves for being married to such a moll.' He abruptly stood, leaned across the table, and yanked my hair as hard as he could before running out of the room.

Richard sat back in his chair, laughing so hard he had to hold his stomach, while the twins giggled at me. They were used to seeing ear twisting and hair pulling and found it amusing. Usually, I would be in hot pursuit of him, trying to pay him back. Today, I was too full of food to run and knew it could wait. I was finding the longer I took to seek my revenge, the more effective it was as he would let his guard down a few hours from now, thinking I'd forgotten. There were times when he could be a little shit and drive me insane, while other times he was loving and kind—always such a dedicated and faithful friend when he wasn't misbehaving. I sighed deeply and rubbed my scalp where he had nearly pulled my hair out by the roots.

'I see you have the five-year-old brother you always wanted.' Richard teased, and I smiled weakly at him.

'You're not wrong about him acting like a child. Sometimes when he speaks, he makes so much sense and is intelligent and sensitive, while he's such a ratbag at other times, I could kill him with my bare hands. I suppose I'm fortunate to have you to represent me if I ever murder the little shite.'

'Oh, well, Abigail. As you say, you can't choose who you love.' He chuckled to himself before embracing me tightly.

I let Richard sit in my oversized leather chair behind my ornate desk in the grand office I rarely used. I preferred the more comfortable chair opposite him. He wanted to get the official business out of the way and immediately adopted his professional courtroom demeanour.

'All your businesses have turned a profit, Abigail, although the Melbourne Delmont only just due to the economic bust here in Victoria, but we do believe it will bounce back in the near future once this blows over,' he said matter-of-fact. 'Your trust fund here in Australia is growing rapidly, and I wonder if you are getting enough of the interest paid to you each month because I can increase it. I only release thirty percent of that profit to you each year. There would be no objection from me should you request a higher percentage to be paid to you annually. It only means your trust fund will take longer to grow, and you will have less money at your disposal when you attain the age of thirty.' He shuffled the pile of papers in front of him before looking up at me inquiringly. I tucked my feet up under me and smiled at him fondly.

'No, Richard. We are more than satisfied and live well enough, as you know.' I thought of the money under the house that we were still using to pay our staff, along with other bits and pieces. We also had the farm account that Aaron managed, which held a substantial amount of money in it from which we could draw, along with my bank account that was growing at an alarming rate. 'So, are you excited about your new house?' I settled back to talk about anything else but money. He became Richard the friend again, smiling at me warmly.

'You have no idea how happy we are.' He leaned back in his chair and relaxed. 'It's now nearing completion, and I still can't believe we could ever own a house as grand as this. My parents will be stunned when they visit and finally see it. They will be so proud of me, Abigail, which they haven't been to this point, as you well know. The house is nearly as big as yours, and I never dreamed I could own such a place. We have loved every minute of being here and staying in your beautiful home, and we don't really want to leave. That's why we purchased the land just down the road from Willow Grove. We want to remain close to you and your family.' He reached over the desk and took my hand 'Without you, Abigail, we'd still be back in London, and I would no doubt be slaving away on menial tasks and trying to earn a living as a junior solicitor. Instead, we're here living like we're wealthy in our own right. I can never repay in money how generous you have been to set us up like you have and help me establish my law practice. I can only be eternally grateful. But I will repay you every penny you have spent on the land, the house, and its furnishings.'

'When does all the furniture get delivered? I know the inside is nearly finished,' I asked, still trying to get away from the subject of money.

'In the next few weeks, I've been recently advised. I really wanted to tell you, I know I have made the right choice to stay here. You and Polly are my younger sisters, and although we became close in London, since I have been here, I feel like a protective older brother. I never had sisters, as you know, but for the first time in my life, I really feel like I do.'

It was clear his words came from his heart, especially when he walked around the desk and embraced me for the longest time.

'Well, I feel the same way.' I pulled away slightly to look up into his eyes. 'I never had real siblings, but I always considered Polly to be my sister, something I have never questioned and just accepted. When I met you, I knew we would be friends; however, ever since you've been here, I do feel like I have an older brother looking after me. My life has changed so dramatically in the last three-years, and I really do have a family now. Some don't have the same blood as me, but it makes no difference. You are my brother and always will be.' He gently kissed my cheek before letting me go and returning to his chair.

We sipped some brandy, and the time flew by as we talked of how our lives had turned out so differently from what we expected when we first met. I swallowed the last of my brandy before looking at my watch, reminding us both of our present-day responsibilities. We said our goodbyes before parting abruptly, Richard hurrying off to find Jas and see how Daniel was faring while I went to find my babies.

After Aaron finished telling them their bedtime story, I put Thomas and Emmy down to sleep in the little wooden beds Aaron had asked Luther Fiske, the farmhand who had made their highchairs, to build for them. The beds were low off the floor so the children could easily get in and out by themselves. I had ensured they had the best mattresses with small quilts and covers to keep them warm. They were in the same bedchamber, just off the nursery, as they didn't want to sleep apart. It was hard enough to get them to stay in their own beds, and I often found one of them had slipped into bed with the other during the night. I sighed deeply and kissed each one goodnight as they finally closed their eyes, then waited for them to fall asleep. They were both breathing regularly within moments, and I quietly left the room, stopping to talk to little Mary as I passed through the nursery.

'Mary, if you want to go downstairs to the staff lounge and spend time with your friends, it's okay. Thomas and Emmy come straight to our room now when they wake, so you need to go and have some fun.'

'Are you certain, Mistress?' She placed her knitting on her lap, appearing to hesitate for a moment. 'I would hate for anything to happen if they woke up, and I wasn't here.'

'Honestly, they'll be fine. I will check on them, but they're already in a deep sleep. From now on, after they have been bathed, I want you to have the rest of the night off until you're ready to come back up and find your own bed. They're always with Aaron and me until bedtime anyway, so there's really no need for you to wait around in the nursery when you could be downstairs with the others who've finished for the day. You have many friends here, and they would love for you to be with them at night in their lounge. Anyway, it's not a suggestion, Mary, it's an order.' I tried to smother a smile. If I didn't stand my ground with her and give her an official direction, she wouldn't do it if it meant leaving the twins. She stood up and formally addressed me.

'All right, Mistress. As you wish. May I please have permission to come and check on them throughout the time I'm downstairs, though? I promise I will only pop my head in, then return to my friends.' I nodded my assent, and she smiled. If it gave her peace of mind, then so be it.

'We are agreed, then. Off you go.'

I giggled softly to myself as she hurried away, her footsteps echoing down the long hallway. I left the doors open in case one of the children should wake and make their way to our bedchamber. They had the freedom to come and go rather than being locked in a cot with bars—reminding me very much of the cellar in *that* tavern at the docks so long ago. They rarely woke during the night; however, we had experienced the odd occasion when we heard little taps on our door in the middle of the night. I would go and open it to find two sleepy little angels who wanted a cuddle. If one woke, the other would, too, and walked hand in hand to our room. I secretly loved when they found their way to our bed and slept with us and, although Aaron would complain I was spoiling them, I knew he loved it, too.

I made my way to our room and found Aaron still awake but groggy. He gave me a wide grin just as Bessie hurried in to help me change for bed.

'I feel like you've kept me waitin' here all day for ya,' he complained.

'Aaron, my darling but oh-such-a-pain-in-the-arse husband,' I called out from my dressing table, where Bessie brushed and plaited my hair. 'I have spent every minute of my spare time today in here with you, not to mention what you keep asking me to do. I would hate to embarrass Bessie, but I feel I have done my duty.' He chuckled, and Bessie touched the back of my head to indicate she was finished. I stood up to see her glaring across the room at Aaron, her brow furrowed.

'I know very well what you would have been getting her to do, boyo. Just because you must stay in bed doesn't mean Abigail is your sex slave. I'm telling you now to cut it out. You're a demanding little shite, and I will foot you up the backside if you don't stop,' she told him firmly as she helped me out of my dress and into my nightgown.

Aaron appeared drunk as he lay across the bed, chuckling to himself. Bessie bid us goodnight and shook her head at Aaron before wishing me luck with such an imbecile of a husband, leaving me giggling as I closed the door behind her. Aaron stared at me as I climbed up onto the bed as carefully as possible, trying not to knock against his leg. I pulled the covers up and cuddled into his side, placing my hand on his bare chest.

'How's your pain now?' He had been waiting for the doctor to come when I put the twins to bed. He smiled at me dreamily, his eyes glazed.

'What pain? The quack was just here an' gave me another one of those injections so I'll sleep. It's all good,' he said, his words slightly slurred. Good for me, too, as that meant I might get an uninterrupted night's sleep. He kissed me deeply, taking my hand from his chest and sliding it down his taut stomach.

'Aaron, not again? You are meant to be resting, and you're out of your mind on those injections. You're not meant to move your leg.' He shook his head then kissed me deeply again.

'I know somethin' ya can do where me leg won't move at all.' He slowly pushed my head down gently towards his belly as I rolled my eyes in disbelief.

Later, as I lay contentedly in his arms, I fell asleep and dreamed of a stolen horse, the side of a cliff, and strawberries.

Chapter Seven

I WOKE TO THE sounds of crashing waves and it took me a moment to remember where I was. Aaron had brought me here to the honeymoon cottage yesterday afternoon as a surprise for our fifth wedding anniversary.

It was the first week of August 1895, and we were experiencing a bitterly cold and wet winter. When we arrived, the storm broke within minutes of Goliath being unsaddled and let loose in the paddock. We had gone inside to find the fires burning warmly and our dinner waiting for us in the oven. We had sat in bed watching the storm pass and reminisced about the past five-years we had spent together.

Aaron had given me a book as part of my anniversary gift, *While the Billy Boils* by Henry Lawson, and it was full of engaging short stories I had only just begun reading. I had looked through page by page when he had presented it to me, knowing how much I appreciated and loved books. I didn't want to just skim through it, wanting the experience to last as I read each page as slowly as I possibly could, cherishing every word. This had only just been published, a special first edition that I would keep with my collection. I treasured my books, caring for them as though each was priceless. I had them all lining the walls of my library, where I would spend my quiet time reading the new books I had ordered. Books were the one thing I spent money on, just for myself, as they brought me so much joy. I still had many shelves to fill, although I knew that I would run out of room one day at the rate I was going.

Thomas and Emmy were with Aaron's parents for the weekend, which they often were—Mrs Cavanaugh ensuring she collected them on a Friday afternoon for their two-night stay. They would then bring them home when they came for Sunday lunch. Thomas and Emmy were four now and loved going to the Cavanaughs' as they got to play with not only their doting grandparents and aunties and uncles, but their younger cousins, too.

Aaron had surprised me as we were waving his parents and the children off in their brand new carriage, drawn by two of our horses, and had taken me to the stables where he had Goliath saddled and waiting impatiently. I had asked him where we were going, and he wouldn't tell me, only lifting me onto the horse and swinging himself up behind me.

When we arrived at the honeymoon cottage, our clothes were already there and our dinner was warming in the oven. We sat outside drinking champagne until we were drunk, then went to bed and made love. He had given me my book wrapped in beautiful paper with a love letter enclosed, melting my heart.

He then presented me with an enormous crystal that had been carved into a Martarino horse. I was overwhelmed with the gift and would treasure it my whole life. I had never seen anything so beautiful, the way it caught the light and glimmered, casting brilliant shards of colour onto the walls as the light reflected from and through it. I placed it on my bedside table, reaching out often and gently running my fingers over it. It had been carved to look like my Delly, which delighted me.

I had given Aaron a new saddle, handmade from the finest leather, and a solid gold pocket watch. He was thrilled and teased me that I was trying to turn him into a gentleman, something I knew to be impossible, leaving me in fits of laughter.

It had just gone daybreak, and I could hear someone rattling around in the kitchen. As Aaron was still sleeping soundly next to me, I knew it wasn't him. I carefully slipped out of bed and put on my dressing gown then crept out of the room, gently closing the door behind me. I found Leo in the kitchen putting our meals out for the day and a box of cakes and creamy tarts along with lemonade and beer.

'The sparrow hasn't even farted yet. What are you doing? Aaron told me not to disturb you both, so don't tell him I woke you.' He giggled as he smacked me on the bum then picked me up off my feet in a hug. He went and sat at the table, indicating for me to join him. 'So, did you and Goliath root like root-rats last night?'

'Oh, stop being rude. It sounds even worse when you use that Australian slang, so enough now. I'm not allowed to tell you anymore, anyway. You blabbed to Aaron about me bragging about our sex life, and he has now banned me from talking about it. He thinks you do dirty things to yourself while thinking about him because I've described his naked body to you.' I narrowed my gaze as he pushed his chair away from the small table. He was such a big mouth at times. He always seemed to be getting me in trouble with Aaron and Bessie. It was never my fault, despite Aaron always blaming me. Leo started to giggle, and I smiled even though I didn't want to.

'Well, he's not wrong.' He leaned back further in his chair, still laughing. 'My nights are split between Goliath and Adonis, depending on which one looked the most attractive on the day. You know, most of the young women in the district despise you for marrying Aaron? I heard on the passionfruit vine that so many wanted him to court them, and some even threw themselves at him, legs wide open and everything, but he declined each of the filthy scrubbers. I have no idea what he saw in you, but he was besotted from the first day I met him. It has to be those bewitching eyes that are the colour of real emeralds. I've seen people in my lifetime with green eyes, but they're a very pale green—nothing like yours. I wish I'd been born with lavender eyes. I think that would be the most beautiful colour on me, especially if I was black. I know you will tell me I'm perfect as I am, but I know that already; thank you very much. It would be nice to add to perfection.' He looked smug as he rose to his feet and crossed the large room to the stove to pour our coffee.

'So, what about you? I know you don't always sleep alone,' I told him just as smugly when he returned with our cups and added some cream.

'Oh, I get my bit. Nowhere near the quality that you get to shag ten times a day, but enough for me.' He made himself comfortable again in the chair opposite then grinned at me. 'You'd be surprised just how many so-called heterosexual farmhands are not that at all. They come to me because I'm my authentic self here, so everyone knows my true inclination. Some hate me for it, while others secretly feel they are no longer alone. It's not just about the sex, and I'm being serious here, Abigail. I'm fair dinkum this time. Just listen, or I'll smack your face if you don't keep your attention on me.'

'I *was* listening, but because I glanced toward the window for a moment, you assume I'm not. I can do several things at once, unlike someone else I know.' I shook my head then fixed my gaze on him.

'As I was saying,' he went on, sniffing daintily as I picked up my cup and inhaled, 'it's nice to know you're not alone, especially when there's so much hatred directed at anyone who is different. Look at you. You haven't conformed to the pressure you're constantly under to attend these high-society events just because you're a wealthy woman. You're bright enough to know they don't like you much, anyway. I admire that in you, and I love it about myself, but not everyone's like us. I've met several men who've worked here for years and kept their secret hidden, having no one they could trust or talk to. Now they have, as we are getting to know each other in secret, and friendships are being formed. We don't go around having sex with everyone in our group. Some of us have met others we like and have taken things farther, while many are just friends. You think all homosexual men are like me because you're still such an innocent. You can't always tell just by how people look or act, Abigail.' I nodded, impressed by his clarity and sincerity.

He had always been wonderful to me, explaining homosexuality from his perspective, as all I had ever been taught was to hate it like so many others. I had never hated him and only ever loved him from the moment we met, but he was right that I was innocent in the ways of the world, unlike him. He had taught me so much over the years, and I had formed my own opinion on the matter.

'I'm happy for you, and for them. It's like you're finally finding your tribe.' He seemed relieved that I understood what he was trying to say and relaxed back in his chair, appearing thoughtful.

'It would be wonderful to be part of a tribe of natives. The Aboriginal men fascinate me, although I do find the way they're treated beyond appalling.' I nodded sadly, knowing full well they were treated worse than the beasts in the fields and valued far less. Some of the stories I had heard around the traps over the last few years of massacres, rapes, beatings and slavery of their people sickened me. 'They have such beautiful, dark skin and the loveliest eyes. The groups that wander through Willow Grove or work here are so gentle and shy, aren't they?' he asked, and I nodded.

'Yes, they are beautiful people. They know they're welcome to camp here anytime, and they won't be hunted down and killed if they take a beast from our paddocks. I do find it horrible that their land was taken just because they don't use it the same way as white men, and now their food sources are diminished by farming, and they're punished if they steal a sheep from an area where there was once native meat and what they call 'bush tucker' in abundance. I find it all very unfair but feel helpless to speak up as everyone around me thinks this is acceptable.' He nodded again, tears stinging my eyes as he reached across and patted my hand. 'I do love to ride out and sit around the fire with them and talk. They tell the most interesting stories of Australia and the land. I had no idea there were hundreds of tribes, all distinct and unique. From the little I do know, we are living on Wathaurung land, but the tribe who seems to roam through here the most lately is the Yaawangi, who originate from the You Yang Hills area. Did you know they have this belief that when they die they go to some place or another in the afterlife where they're turned into white men, and they then return to this world again for another existence? They think all white men previous to their death belonged to their own tribes and then returned to life with different coloured skin.'

'Reincarnation? Sounds like they have a few kangaroos loose in the top paddock, if you know what I mean?' He grinned as he pointed his finger towards his temple and moved it in a circular fashion while pulling a face that would have him committed to the Ararat insane asylum immediately.

'It's interesting, Leo. In cases where they've killed whites, it's generally been because they imagined them to have been enemies in their past life, or because they belonged to tribes they warred with.' He stared unblinking at me, nodding on occasion and encouraging me to go on. 'It's one interpretation of what they call the eternal dreamtime, and from what I know, it can vary widely.' It was rare we could speak so bluntly given so many around us had no compassion for the first people of this country we now considered our home—a country Leo and I felt had been stolen from them. 'Aaron has started to take a couple of sheep carcasses from the hanging shed for them to cook when he knows they're here, and they always, without fail, invite us to stay and eat with them. I even tried a witchetty grub a few weeks ago,' I told him proudly, and he giggled.

'I can't say I'll put them on the menu, but what did it taste like?'

'I don't know. It was slimy and had a nutty flavour. I would eat it again because they told me it was full of goodness,' I replied, and we both giggled. I drank my creamy, sweet coffee as he looked across at me mischievously then put his hand to the side of his mouth so no one could hear him, despite there being no one else in the room.

'I have come up with a trick we can play on Mr Masters.' I smirked but shook my head, not willing to be drawn into his shenanigans again.

'What this time? He got really cross when we hid his spectacles. He couldn't do his paperwork for a whole day, not to mention I got the entire blame yet again.' I leaned back in my chair and sipped my coffee, remembering how bad I felt for weeks afterwards that we had been so cruel.

Aaron had suspected it was us and eventually pinned me down on the bed until I admitted to it. He had then marched me downstairs with the glasses, forcing me to hand them back with a sincere apology. I had been mortified. Leo had been the one who stole his eyeglasses, and I was only holding them for him. It was yet another prime example of him getting me into trouble, and now everyone believed it was solely my idea to steal them. I had noticed the household staff glancing at me sideways and thinking I was a common criminal—a thief just like Aaron had called me.

'We won't get caught this time, I promise. The next time you meet with him, bring me along and tell him you're divorcing Aaron to marry me. When he realises I would be his boss and he would be answerable to me, the look on his face would be priceless. I have no doubt he'll fall off his chair. Please do it, Abigail, just for me. You know how I like to see him flustered.'

'No. Absolutely not. I would look like an idiot, and Aaron will find out we've been playing games with people again. Nothing you say can convince me this time. You're always getting me in the shit, claiming every time we won't get caught, but we always do. I won't do it.' I finished my coffee and took our cups to the sink.

'Oh, you'll change your mind when I come up with something else that we can't be connected to. You're such a wet blanket and are no fun anymore. I've no doubt if I murdered someone, you wouldn't help me hide the body, which makes you a terrible friend.'

'I have never understood that metaphor or how it seems to be the standard scenario in which to judge a true friendship. I mean, if you were in trouble, I *would* lie to the police, help you hide evidence, whatever you need, but asking me to dig a hole just sounds like too much hard work.' He threw his head back and laughed loudly.

'We're two peas in a pod, you and I. You should have married me when you had the chance, so we wouldn't have people always looking over our shoulders, Aaron in particular. We could have been the boss of everyone, with no one allowed to tell us off or we could sack them on the spot. It'd be my dream come true. Now that I've thought about it, I really think you should consider divorcing Goliath. You and I would be the perfect match.'

I snorted with laughter. 'How is it going back at the house, you twit?' I strode back across the cosy kitchen to his side and ran my fingers through his hair, tidying it up after his ride to the cottage.

'All my servants are delighted at having half a weekend off,' he said, standing up and organising himself to leave. He kissed me goodbye, and I walked him out to the front of the cottage, where Delly was waiting. He was the only other person I would let ride her, as he was gentle and kind to her. I went and stroked her neck while he mounted her, then waved back at me as he trotted away.

I returned to the kitchen, grabbed a sweet pastry that was still warm, biting into it as I slowly made my way to the bedchamber before quietly slipping back into bed. Aaron turned over on his side, facing me.

'How's Leo?' he asked sleepily, trying to wake himself up.

'Good, I think.' I bit into the delicious pastry that was filled with sweet apricots, finding it far more interesting now the aroma of cinnamon and sweet fruit filled my nose. 'He didn't stay that long, so we only talked for a short time.'

'You're such a lady. I hardly understood a word of that.' He chuckled, leaning over and kissing the crumbs from my mouth. 'Mmm, ya taste like apricots,' he said, kissing me again and running his tongue across my lips. I slipped my arms around his neck, still holding my pastry, and kissed him back.

'So, what do you have planned for today after such an incredibly romantic night?' I asked as he smiled sweetly at me, grabbed my pastry, and swallowed it in one bite.

'We've a full day an' night of no interruptions, an' we can make as much noise as we like. What could be better than that?' He smirked wickedly, and I smiled back. He turned and lay on his back, pulling me to his side and playing with my hair. 'Five-years ago today, I was at me parents' house gettin' ready to meet ya at the church,' he said quietly. 'I was the most excited I'd ever been in me life, but also the most terrified—terrified ya wouldn't love me as much as I loved you, an' worried sick I would fail ya as a husband. I thought I knew everythin' there was to know back then, but now I know I really knew nothin' at all. I didn't know what true, deep, passionate love was, or what it is to create a tiny human bein' an' have ‘em love ya like no other.' He gazed at me adoringly as I caressed his cheek with my fingers. 'You've made me life beautiful beyond belief. You're lovelier than the day I met ya, an' me happiness grows day by day, if that's even possible. I love ya, Abi.' He kissed me again and handed me a small box. 'Remember, though,' he added, 'the tenderness we feel can't be packaged up into a small box.'

Ah, his poems and poetry, often kept hidden, would emerge at times like this when we were alone, and I appreciated that side of him. I opened the box, tears threatening to spill over, to find a small diamond bracelet. It was dainty and flawless, and I couldn't believe he had saved a present to give me on the actual day of our anniversary. We had swapped gifts last night only because I was too excited to wait.

He helped me put it on my right wrist, which I then held up in front of us to admire.

'Aaron, it's beautiful. I can see you bought it from Mr Dawson.'

'Only the best for you, precious girl, an' he's the best. He now imports the most brilliant diamonds an' priceless stones that he can find. He knows how much jewellery we buy from him each year, includin' for Emmy, an' gifts we give to family an' friends. He told me that in the five-years we've been his customers, his wealth has increased a hundred times. I'm happy for him. He was such a small jeweller when we first went there an' got him to make our weddin' bands. That's the reason I'm loyal to him 'cause he stayed up all night doin' nothin' else but creatin' our beautiful weddin' rings so we had 'em by the next mornin'. Of course, the other reason is he's the best jeweller I've ever seen, creatin' masterpieces' every single time. A kinder man than Colin Dawson I haven't met an' doubt I will. He's as honest as the day is long.' I couldn't have agreed more.

'I wouldn't know the difference between diamonds and cut glass, so I just have to trust him, which I do.' I smiled to myself as I ran my fingers over the delicate chain with dainty diamonds scattered along its length. Because of Aaron, I was covered in diamonds, which I rarely took off. I had forced Polly to pierce my ears again so I could wear my diamond studs in the second holes and, in the first piercing, vary the beautiful earrings Aaron had given me over the years. 'I love you, my darling husband.' I held him close to me for a moment. 'Thank you for giving me the family I always wanted. These five-years have been the happiest of my life. All because of you. Looking back, I was just a child when we married and were blessed with the twins, but I wouldn't change a minute of our lives together. You are my love, my heart, and my joy, Aaron, and always will be.' I lay comfortably in his arms as he gazed into my eyes.

'Me precious Abi. I knew nothin' then, either, but we've grown together. If I knew then what I know now, I would've made ya agree to marry me the first day I met ya. There's no way I could've waited the two-months we did. I would've made love to ya within the week.'

'Well, I would have taken you to my bed the first night and not wasted any time.' I laughed along with him before he leaned forward and kissed me again, slipping off my negligee in one graceful movement.

We stayed in bed all day and into the late afternoon, only getting up to bring food and drink from the kitchen back to the bedchamber. We lay in our deep, warm bath while Aaron massaged my feet and played with my toes. I didn't know how he had managed to have such a large bathtub built, and I felt sorry for the household staff who were expected to come down here once a day to heat the water over the fire and on the stove to fill it. He hadn't set up the same system installed in the main house to all the washrooms where water was now warmed over a fire and piped through a tap to fill our basins and baths at will, a complex system I still didn't quite understand.

I felt terribly guilty that they were forced to carry heavy buckets just so I could luxuriate like a queen with my husband, the warm water filled with bath liquid that smelled of sandalwood, but obviously not guilty enough to refrain from bathing. I relaxed my head back on the edge of the tub, my hair piled on top of my head as I had only washed it yesterday.

'I love Thomas and Emmy, but it has been blissful here without them,' I said dreamily, stroking his strong legs that were on each side of mine. The water came up to my neck as I lay back but only lapped around his chest.

'It's not over yet, an' there's no chance of 'em turnin' up,' he said, pulling me up onto his lap and kissing me. Much later, when the water started to cool, we both got out, and he wrapped me in a large, fluffy towel before drying himself off.

I went to get a nightgown out of the small bag that Aaron had packed for me. I wasn't surprised to find that the only nightwear in there was an assortment of the risqué negligees that Catherine had made for me, and nothing else at all. And there really was nothing. He hadn't even packed me a change of clothes to wear if I wanted to dress. Given it was the middle of winter, I felt I could have benefited from one of my thicker nightgowns, but Aaron was not always practical when it came to things like that. I grunted to myself as I slipped on my nightwear and hurried back to him.

He was silent as he leaned down at the fireplace in our room, putting as much wood as he could fit onto the fire. I stood watching his naked body gleaming in the firelight, his well-formed muscles rippling under his skin as he moved. I knew I was a fortunate woman to still lust after him as much as I did and have him show the same desire and raw passion for me.

I thought of Tamara and how, after having her four children, one after another, she had taken a lover. She was currently having passionate sex with her driver, which amused me no end. I had never seen her so happy and content with her life and herself. She basically ignored Brian's existence, although when she did speak to him for the children's sake she was always very polite and proper in her dealings with him. It seemed the marriage suited him as well. To the world, he was a respectable married man with children, and people were unlikely to suspect his true inclinations. I liked Brian and found him to be a nice, quiet man without a mean bone in his body. We weren't close, as that would have been improper and would have shamed Tamara; however, we did get along well when we were all together as a group, which was often.

Aaron came over and ran his hands down my body, feeling the silkiness of my negligee.

'I like this one. Have I ever asked the Lord to bless Catherine?' He gazed down at me, his eyes twinkling as he grinned.

'Every single time I put on any of these thingamajigs.' I laughed and placed my hands on his face and allowed myself to melt into him.

Aaron was reluctant to leave, dragging me to bed one last time before we departed. Finally, we mounted Goliath and headed for home. Our family and friends would be arriving soon for our Sunday lunch, a day I looked forward to all week.

We rode up to the house to find the entire Cavanaugh clan in the back garden with the children playing on the lawn. We dismounted, and Aaron left Goliath with Harry before we went to greet his family. Harry still had that lovely, golden glow surrounding him and, although I liked him very much and was drawn to him, I wouldn't say I loved him in the same way I did my friends. It was a different connection I had with him that still completely confused me.

I walked hand in hand into the garden with Aaron, and I kissed and hugged everyone hello. Aiden and Victoria had a bonny lad named Robert, two and a half, and a little girl, Charlotte, who had just turned one. I loved being an aunty to Willy and Bella and the Cavanaugh children. They all seemed drawn to me, too, and loved my cuddles with them. Both sets of grandparents doted on the children. Dana often visited, coming to stay for days at a time, during which I would get to see a lot of her.

Patrick and Scarlett had moved into their home and were the proud parents of a daughter who had just turned one, named in honour of Scarlett's best friend, and our maid, Ruby. Scarlett was now six-months along with their second child. Both of Aaron's brothers appeared to be in happy marriages, and I loved spending time together with them as a family. They had embraced and treated me as one of their own since the very first day we met.

Soon Catherine and Colin arrived. They were still living together without her family's knowledge, and Colin was now a full-fledged tailor in charge of designing and fitting all the men's clothing. He was working alongside Catherine, not below her, which I thought would only result in a stronger relationship. He was also earning more money than he ever imagined he could and was becoming wealthy in his own right. Catherine was famous for her designs and was always busy, but she loved it so much she didn't mind the hard work and long hours she was required to sacrifice. And she loved Colin. He treated her like she was something precious while constantly looking after her. They were happy together, even without marriage.

Hamish arrived with Angelique, who was dressed as if attending a grand gala event. Hamish went straight to the children, grabbing Thomas and Emmy in his arms and rolling around on the grass with them as the other children joined in, jumping on his back while she looked on disdainfully. They had been courting for years, but there were no signs of marriage in the near future.

We had been expecting an engagement announcement that hadn't come for the past twelve-months now, and I wondered how much longer she would wait. I was surprised his parents had not forced him to wed her by now. I knew Aaron was right. I needed to keep my opinion of her to myself, but there were so many times I wanted to pull Hamish aside and tell him he was making the biggest mistake of his life.

William had graduated from Melbourne University and was a junior solicitor working at a Melbourne law firm, limiting his visits to an occasional weekend. He wasn't able to be with us today. Beatrice was fifteen and still wouldn't speak. She was cared for full time by Nanny in Melbourne. Her parents rarely stayed at the residence, and when they were present, they had little time or affection for her.

Richard and Jas came walking into the garden carrying their children, Daniel and little Jenny. They had moved into their large home nearby in Grovedale, and his practice was going very well. They had a houseful of staff and farmworkers to run their enormous home and small farm, leaving Jas a lady of leisure and giving Richard all the time he needed to focus on his practice. Their living situation had impressed his parents and brothers, with Richard sending photographs of the mansion and his growing family and receiving letters from each of them, congratulating them on their good fortune.

Aaron had purchased photography equipment that only he and Leo knew how to use for this reason alone. We had so many friends and workers who had left family behind they were likely to never see again in this lifetime. Because these new cameras were so expensive and unavailable to most, Aaron and Leo were more than happy to take photographs of our friends, workers, and their children, and record special moments to send back to family across the ocean.

Leo had sent a photograph to his family of me standing by his side with my arms around him, telling them I was his wife. I had often wondered what the reaction had been the day they received it. To my knowledge, they hadn't written back, wounding Leo deeply.

Richard was earning himself a reputation as a fine lawyer, and he was starting to get more criminal cases that he so desperately wanted. He was happy and settled in his life, he had told me recently. He treated me as his younger sister, as he did with Polly, and was always there for me when I needed to talk about anything. He was indeed my brother, and I loved him.

Amelia and Tommy arrived with Mathew and Maddie and sat down to talk with everyone while all the children ran around the garden squealing. They were chasing Hamish, who would then turn around and pretend to be a monster, scattering them in all directions as they screamed and ran away. We were only waiting now on Martin and Dana, who were always the last to arrive. Aaron strolled over and sat down behind me.

'I wish we were back at the cottage. There are too many people here,' he whispered, and I laughed.

'Well, most of them are related to you, so stop your whining.' I grabbed his face in my hands and kissed him.

Mr Masters marched out to the garden to announce lunch was ready, just as Martin and Dana walked around the side of the house. They greeted everyone warmly, except for Hamish and Angelique. Dana went to pick up her grandchildren, Robert and Charlotte, and we walked in together, carrying all the children to the dining room. Once seated, with the children settled in their own chairs or on their parents' laps, Mr Masters and the footmen placed the last of the enormous trays of meats and steaming vegetables on the table.

We began to serve ourselves and pass the trays around to each other, laughing as we helped the person next to us serve their food before doing the same in return. I noticed Angelique didn't look happy and refused to take any tray handed to her, waiting instead for Hamish to serve her, which he did. She stared across at me, a judgmental glint in her eye.

'In all the grand houses I have been privileged to attend, you never serve yourself,' she said loudly. 'Do you not realise that is what your servants are here to do? I have been a guest at some of the grandest mansions in Victoria, including Werribee Park, and there really is nothing grander than being hosted by the Chirnside family. You must understand, the children of these dynasties are rarely seen in the main house during the day, and *never* eat in the dining room when guests are present. Don't any of you have nannies or governesses like those you so obviously aspire to be like? It's quite odd and far removed from normal?'

An awkward silence hung over the room, while Hamish was stone still, his face blank. Angus straightened up in his chair, his broad shoulders tense, a dangerous glint in his eye.

'I would say to you, Angelique, an' as politely as I can, this *is* normal.' He raised his large hand and swept it around the room while not breaking her stare. 'What is *not* normal is to leave the bairns in the sole care of nannies to be raised not ever knowin' their parents' love. Ignorant, arrogant people like you who think that's the right way to raise the next generation should be hangin' their heads in shame. You'd be the first to complain when you're old an' they're runnin' the country an' inflictin' their own punishment on you without compassion.'

He tousled Willy's hair as he sat by his side, heartily enjoying his food. Thomas and Emmy were seated next to him, and I saw the confused look that passed between them.

'How dare you speak to me that way, Angus Makenzie! I am going to be your sister-in-law in the very near future. Apologise to me now or Hamish and I are leaving,' she spat, turning slightly towards Hamish, silently demanding he defend her. However, he looked away, remaining silent. It was obvious to all present just how embarrassed he was. I knew he would never go against his brother over a woman, especially if he agreed with his opinion.

'No,' Angus roared. 'You need to apologise to every single person you've offended here at this table. You're a rude an' unfeelin' woman, an' as cunnin' as a dunny rat.'

Polly quickly covered her mouth with her hand, unable to hide the smirk spreading across her face. She couldn't stand Angelique and didn't get along with her at all. Angelique's pretty face, her skin usually like porcelain, had turned the colour of beetroot, and she appeared ready to explode just like 'the bags of mystery' Leo liked to cook.

'I only commented as I have formed the opinion that not one soul here knows the correct etiquette or proper manner in which to behave when you are the owner of a grand home like Willow Grove. You have servants in every corner waiting to do your bidding, yet you live like you are staying at the local boarding house in Geelong,' she remarked haughtily, her back straight as an arrow while she glared down her nose at Angus.

'I've heard just about enough,' Aaron interrupted. 'If ya think Willow Grove is such a slum an' we live so poorly, why do ya even bother to come here?' His demeanour was calm and amenable, although his hands had curled into fists planted firmly on the table each side of his now forgotten plate laden with food. 'Ya don't like the nippers, an' ya certainly don't like Hamish havin' any mates. You're jealous of Abi an' how she looks, how she acts, an' the generous nature God gave her, makin' everyone love her. You're so green with envy, ya put her down at every opportunity. You're invited here into our home an' treated like family when all the while all ya do is try to tear down everythin' she says or does. You're an unfortunate sheila with an unfortunate character, an' I apologise to everyone here for ya bein' as rude as ya are, an' the fact I've allowed it.'

All the blood had drained from her face, her cough the only sound in the room as she choked on her own saliva. I watched in fascination at the extremes of colour in her cheeks in such a short time, the shade deepening moment to moment. She glared at Aaron hatefully, unable to speak as she continued to cough into her lace handkerchief. She took a small sip of water before turning her attention back to my husband, her perfect nose wrinkled in disdain.

'How *dare* you speak to me that way as a guest in this house! Why would I be jealous of your wife? Everyone in the district may say she is exquisite and a rare beauty, but I have seen nothing special in her, and I have looked. Do you really think I'm jealous that she's still in love with Hamish? Her obsession does not concern me. He didn't want her before and cast her aside for another without a second thought, and he doesn't want her now, I assure you. Especially now she has two brats tied to her hip and has that many men chasing her like she's a bitch in heat. You need to keep your eyes open, Aaron. She has a number of close, male friends, as she calls them. She's even friends with the servants, male and female. I've seen her down at the stables talking with your foreman as though they are intimately acquainted. You don't have to be well-bred to know how inappropriately your wife behaves.' I watched Aaron slowly put down his glass and push himself away from the table. I reached out and placed my hand on his thigh to prevent him from standing, his anger palpable. Hamish appeared beyond furious and slammed his fist down on the table, breaking the silence while startling everyone and making Bella cry.

'Enough! Ye've said too much, an' ye need tae leave,' he roared at Angelique, who jumped in fright, appearing stunned.

'But Hamish, I didn't mean....' she trailed off.

'What ye said is untrue an' offensive. I've known this side tae ye since we met; however, until now, I've chosen tae overlook the vindictive, malicious, an' plain nasty side tae yer character, which I can naw longer do. Come with me, an' I'll put ye in the carriage fer home.' She glared at him, confusion crossing her face for a moment.

'What? You're not going to escort me back to my parents? What kind of gentleman are you, Hamish Makenzie?' she spat, her eyes wide as he rose to his feet and took her firmly by the arm.

'I'm sorry fer it, Angelique, but ye dinnae deserve a gentleman.' He led her out of the room, the silence louder than thunder.

We had finished our lunch by the time Hamish returned, his face relaxed and his manner now calm. Although we had finished eating long ago, we remained where we were and continued chatting while he ate.

'My dear, Dana. When are you coming to stay with Victoria and Aiden again?' I smiled across at her as she held little Charlotte on her lap.

'I plan to visit later in the week for a few days, so we will all catch up, Abigail. We adore it when you bring the twins over to play with their cousins and, of course, to gossip with you,' she said, then leaned over to whisper in my ear. 'So, it's been five-years now. How's it all going in the bedchamber? Is it still as passionate as it first was?' I looked up at her and smirked, then cupped my hand around her ear and leaned closer.

'More so,' I whispered back. 'He is wonderful in every way. It's like we were meant to be together. He is a part of me now, and I am part of him. The things he does to me sends chills through me just thinking about it.' Her face lit up as she winked at me.

'I'm happy for you, Abigail, and my Victoria as well. You are both leading beautiful lives in honour of my Charlotte, who didn't get the chance to leave a lifetime of memories beyond childhood. I hope that if she were still with us, she would have found happiness just as you both have.' She kissed little Charlotte on the head before quickly wiping her eyes with her handkerchief. I squeezed her hand, and she squeezed back.

We lounged around the garden for the rest of the afternoon, with some choosing to ride the magnificent Martarinos to explore the property, while others decided to sit in the sun to talk and play with the children. We were lucky today that the weather was fine. The sky was clear, and the winter sun shone down on us, leaving me feeling blissfully happy and deeply content as I lay back and relaxed. Aaron was in deep conversation with his father before leaving the twins with his parents and sitting with me.

'Do we really have to go to the openin' night for the new theatre this week, Abi? There's goin' to be so many uppity people there, an' I have so much to do here,' he griped for the fiftieth time. According to instructions in great-aunt Isabelle's Will, we had built The Cosmopolitan Theatre on the corner of Flinders and Russell street in Melbourne. It was finally finished after years of planning and construction, and the grand opening was this coming Saturday night. Aaron didn't want to go, and had been trying to get out of it with every excuse he could think of ever since he found out about it. I personally wouldn't have built it, given the hard financial times Victoria was still going through, but Richard had explained what the Will stipulated and that it must move forward.

Richard had done a magnificent job of managing all aspects of the building and the decorating of the theatre. He had taken us there last week, and I was beyond impressed, having never seen anything so luxurious and fancy in my life. The building was enormous and spanned some five stories, including the rooftop, with elaborate exterior work, and the foyer alone was something to behold. Elegant velvet lounges lined the room, with chandeliers hanging throughout that radiated a soft, warm glow. I was mesmerised and looking forward to opening night to see my first show on the grand stage.

Upstairs, there was a large area where refreshments could be purchased. Off that were numerous balconies, each of which could hold eight people in comfort. Each booth was lined with heavy velvet drapes to close them off from the room behind, so patrons could watch the show in privacy and comfort.

Downstairs, the seating sloped up from the ground floor higher and higher until the last row ended two floors up. The theatre consisted of four generous levels; however, because of the space required for seating and the height of the lavishly decorated ceiling, it only had two distinct levels inside.

'Aaron, anything short of death and you're going. Colin has already made your new suit, and I have a new evening gown from Catherine, and you're obligated to go, whether you like it or not. We financed this thing, and it would look bad if I attended opening night alone.' I leaned over and kissed him as he shook his head in disbelief and muttered to himself.

Little Mary appeared from nowhere to take the children in for their baths before dinner, or tea as the Australian's called it, before going home with the Cavanaughs'. Everyone was staying, all except Gavin and Edith, who were taking all their grandchildren with them so their parents could have a night out at the pub. Little Mary had kindly offered to care for Polly and Angus' children, and they had accepted so they could come along with us.

We went to the pub nearly every Sunday night to enjoy the music. All our friends and family were here, and no one ever wanted to go home after lunch, except Aaron's parents. They occasionally joined us at the pub, although several times Aaron's father had to be carried home, which had irked Edith no end.

Aaron and I excused ourselves, promising to meet them in the kitchen at seven o'clock to eat leftovers before leaving. We had given the house staff the night off, something they were becoming accustomed to and had started to look forward to.

We walked Aaron's parents out to their carriage, chatting jovially all the way. Aaron held our nephew and niece, while I led Thomas and Emmy by the hand.

'Mummy, I love going to stay at Grandpa and Grandma's house. They give us treats like you do,' Emmy told me happily as we walked across the paved driveway.

'Well, I know they love it when you come and stay with them, even though Mummy and Daddy will miss you,' I replied, smiling down at her. Aaron walked beside me, an amused glint in his eye.

'Oh, Mummy, there's no need to miss us. We're only down by the back paddock. You can come and stay with us if you like,' she offered thoughtfully.

'Ya Ma won't miss ya for long, Emmy, I can promise ya that. Mark me words, me little princess. I'll be carryin' her home on me back tonight. You'll take after ya daddy an' never get so drunk that ya can't walk,' Aaron told her, chuckling loudly as I smacked him on the arm.

'Why does Mummy get drunk, Daddy? You drink the same yucky stuff and don't act like you belong in the asylum?' Thomas asked, and I felt myself starting to flush.

'Ah, the problem is ya Ma is what's called a two-pot screamer, Thomas. While I can have two nips an' be perfectly fine, she has the same amount an' her legs don't work, while her mouth works only too well,' he explained to our small son, who smiled up at him.

'Does that mean Mummy is a dirty little alcoholic like Uncle Leo says?' Aaron threw back his head and laughed aloud.

'Now, I've told ya both ya not to listen to ya uncle's stories about ya Ma 'cause a lot of 'em aren't ridgy-didge.' I was overwhelmed with the need to smack Leo when I next saw him. In his soft parts. Hard. We arrived at the carriage and kissed everyone goodbye before picking up the twins and hugging them. 'I want ya both to be good for ya grandparents—no talkin' back or bein' disobedient. We love ya, but we love when ya go on ya little seaside holidays, too.' He kissed them goodbye, and they giggled at him.

The poor things had only come home today, and already we were shipping them back to their grandparents so we could go out and get drunk. I was starting to doubt how responsible Aaron and I really were to be in charge of these precious little angels.

We stood together, Aaron's arm around my waist, and waved them off. Mr Cavanaugh raised the long reins and smacked the horses into motion, the carriage moving forward abruptly as the children hung out the windows, calling out and waving back at us.

'Another night of peace, which I wasn't expectin'. Tomorrow mornin' we can stay in bed till we wanna go down for breakfast, an' I'll have ya all to meself.' He guided me up the stairs to the grand front entrance that we rarely used unless we had guests. Soon after, we arrived at the bottom of the grand staircase where he roughly picked me up and slung me over his shoulder before making his way to our bedchamber.

'What are you doing, you duffer?'

'Just gettin' in some practice before tonight. You're so little. I just wanna hold ya all the time. Ya weigh practically nothin' so I like to throw ya around like Dingo does with the soft toys ya gave him?' he explained, causing me to burst into a fit of giggles.

'Dingo does more than that to those poor toys, especially the large teddy bear that he is having a love affair with. If it were a real female, it would have had five litters of teddy dingoes by now.' He chuckled loudly as he shut the door behind us with his foot and continued to hold me in mid-air against his body as he crossed our bedchamber.

'I love Sundays, but it's hectic, hey?' He appeared relieved as he set me down on my feet and kissed my forehead.

'Yes, but I wouldn't miss them. Sunday has always been my favourite day since I arrived here. I love how we spend the day together with everyone, then go to the pub to dance. It's an enjoyable day for me.' I moved over to the bed and lay down to wait for Bessie, who had agreed to help me ready for our night out. Aaron sat me up and undid my dress.

'We've plenty of time before Bessie gets here. Now, I'll be Dingo, an' you'll be that teddy bear over there.' He smiled sweetly, which melted my heart and made me smile, and always made me agreeable to anything he would suggest.

Chapter Eight

I WOKE UP TO the sound of Bessie charging through the door. Aaron snored softly beside me, sleeping so deeply a herd of brumbies stampeding through our bedchamber wouldn't have woken him. She narrowed her gaze when she saw we were in bed yet again.

'Time to get up, you two. Sleeping through the day, I don't know. Anyone would think you're Lord and Lady Muck,' she called out, smiling to herself as she went to choose a dress for me. Aaron laughed softly at her.

'She's such a submissive little servant. I'm shocked ya chose a ladies maid who's so obedient, Abi,' he remarked loudly as he opened his eyes.

'Oh, and you can be quiet, thank you very much,' she called back, her voice muffled from inside my wardrobe 'I'm a ladies' maid, being exactly what it says. I'm not here to clean up after your sorry backside, or look at your bare arse, boyo. I've told you a hundred times to keep yourself covered. I'm not paid enough to have to look at your hairy bum, but you don't care. You just get up naked, proud as can be, flashing your sausage and eggs at me, which I don't appreciate. It's bad enough I have to look at them at home without putting up with it at work. And while I'm on the subject, you can stop farting in front of me and corrupting my innocent Abigail to do the same. She's meant to be behaving like a well-bred lady, and you have her farting like a drunk at the local tavern. Stop it now, Aaron, and I mean it.'

I laughed so loudly my stomach hurt while he stared across at her, his blue eyes sparkling in amusement.

'So, ya don't fart, Bessie? Before ya say anythin', I'll know if you're lyin' to me,' he warned her. She started to blush, and I laughed harder. I had loved Bessie from the start and still did, but her reactions often would send me off into peals of laughter. She wasn't just my maid; she was my friend and always would be.

'It is no business of yours what goes in or out of me, laddy. You are such a crude little shite, I should wallop you across the ears.' She hurried to my side, and I quickly stood and slipped my dressing gown on before crossing the room to my dressing table so she could attend to my hair.

'Bessie, please leave it down tonight,' Aaron pleaded. 'We're only goin' to the pub, an' no one there cares. I love how Abi looks with it swingin' around her waist.'

She glared at him, but he gave her such a charming grin that she relented, placing two tiny plaits in my hair and tying them at the back. She looked across at him as he got out of bed naked and stretched in front of her. She promptly raised her arm and threw the hairbrush across the room, striking him on the bum and leaving a red imprint on his backside.

'Ow. What was that for? I didn't show ya me front out o' respect, an' ya go abusin' me, Bessie. Come on, now. We're friends, aren't we? I sometimes don't know how me mate Danny puts up with such a hard woman.'

He strode across to his dressing room and pulled his pants on before coming back out shirtless, rubbing his backside.

'If you're not careful, I'll be giving your wife here some lessons on toughening up with you,' Bessie threatened, her brow creased. 'She lets you get away with murder, with you treating her like a sex slave, too. You should be ashamed of yourself, Aaron. I will tell your mother.' He laughed as she finished my hair and touched the back of my head, indicating I was ready to dress. 'Are you happy now that she's going around like an eight-year-old with her hair flying all around her?'

'Yes, thank you, Bessie. It's lovely,' he replied, giving her a quick hug before she could get away or slap him.

After we had eaten leftovers in the kitchen, we headed for the pub. I could hear the music in the distance from the hill as we all strolled towards the twinkling lights cast from the numerous lanterns. The village was cheerful, with lamps burning brightly in the windows of the terraces and the dining hall as people were still eating dinner. Aaron talked to Angus about the week ahead while I walked side by side with Hamish.

'Are you all right after what happened today?' I asked, still feeling perturbed.

'Tae tell ye the truth, I feel embarrassed about what Angelique said in front o' everyone. Especially tae ye, given how tolerant, patient, an' kind every soul here has been towards her. She's an ungrateful bitch with an evil tongue. As fer finishin' with her, aye, I'm perfectly fine with it. Thank ye fer bein' concerned about me an' askin'. Me parents will be furious, as will hers, an' it'll create some problems fer a time, but like everythin', it'll eventually go away. I dinnae love her, ye know?' I stared back at him in disbelief. He had been courting her for a number of years now, and had seemed happy enough to me.

'Why did you stay so long with her, then?' I glanced sidelong at him to find he appeared genuinely sad.

'It was more fer me parent's sake. They were happy with her an' expect grandchildren from me, so I come tae the decision she would do. They're friends with her parents, an' her father is a very powerful man. I knew I'd never be happy an' thought someone should be, so I went along with it. Tae be honest, I feel relieved it's all over now. She had more qualities that I dinnae like, than the few I did.'

I wanted to reach out and put my hand on his shoulder in comfort, but I couldn't bring myself to do it. I loved him as a friend, and he would always have a place in my heart; however, I wasn't in love with him anymore—at least that's what I tried to make myself believe every time I was with him. I couldn't understand how he could still tug at my heartstrings when I was so deeply in love with Aaron. But I felt relieved that he wasn't going to spend his life with a cold, and often cruel woman who would have mistreated him.

We walked the rest of the way to the pub in silence. I followed the others inside to find people already dancing—the room filled with laughter and music—while Patty served large groups of men at the bar single-handedly. Angus ordered drinks for everyone while Aaron took my hand and led me to the dance floor where we joined in, laughing and dancing to the fast-paced Irish music. After some time, we returned to the others, thirsty and ready to relax. Hamish stood at the bar while a number of our household staff swooned around him, and I assumed he had already told someone he was unattached again. I sat on Aaron's lap next to Dana and Martin, finishing my glass of beer in one go to quench my thirst.

'Slow down, or I'll be carryin' ya home an' you'll shame ya children. It'll be a repeat of that tomato juice incident.' Aaron grinned while I grimaced. He never would let me forget that.

'How is everything with you and Martin?' I asked Dana.

'He's like a comfortable couch that you just don't want to get out of,' she replied, smiling at me, 'and he makes me cry out in bed like no other.' She smirked as I giggled.

Trixie, who had arrived here as the Nanny for Neville's two children after their mother died, was now his wife. They smiled as they came to sit with us. I drank another beer while I chatted with Trixie about the children, and Neville spoke with Aaron. I was finding that I had a real thirst for beer tonight and was drinking them like water.

I went to get another and sat with Catherine and Colin, who were happily chatting away like they had known each other their whole lives. I thought what a wonderful couple they were and how she had helped him start a new vocation and better himself. He had loved her unconditionally from the beginning. It was such a shame the Montagues' held such a negative attitude towards people of other classes and their strong opinions regarding who should marry and what was right and proper. Catherine didn't adhere to any of that, doing things her own way while trying to respect her parents by sparing their feelings. Nothing they would say could change her mind, though, and it would only cause a rift that might never heal if she didn't play her cards right.

Colin rose to his feet and approached the bar to order more beer for the table. I was already quite drunk, and I could feel Aaron watching me. I poked my tongue out at him then sipped my next beer, pretending to slow down. He shook his head and smiled at me, probably thinking he *would* have to carry me home.

Sally danced nearby with Jonathon, her new husband. She had started as a scullery maid the day after we arrived in Geelong and had moved up the ranks to assistant cook under Leo's supervision. She now was responsible for all the basic food preparation and was in charge of the kitchen maids and the organisation of the kitchen itself. Since Jenny Pickering was entirely responsible for the dining hall where she was head cook with many hardworking kitchen maids to assist her, it had taken the burden from Leo. An enormous number of house staff and farm workers ate there three times a day, with the dining hall holding the title of the busiest kitchen at Willow Grove.

I made sure I sat down with Jenny weekly to ensure she was happy and had enough workers to cope with the demand. She had requested two more kitchen maids, to which I had agreed, allowing her to conduct the job interviews and select her own staff. She had her own menu and made sure she catered to everyone. I had never had a complaint about her as a person or regarding her cooking. She was the loveliest person I knew, and we had become close friends.

The workers and staff raved about how well she fed them. She used only the best ingredients, which we supplied in ample amounts. The storage room beside the kitchen was stocked full of dry goods, including flour, sugar, rice, wheat, and legumes, among the other staples she requested. We supplied her every day with fresh meat from our own property, along with eggs and all the vegetables and fruits she required. I enjoyed eating her food. Although it was just as good as Leo's, it was different, which I loved.

It also meant that Leo could have more time off. Although we tried to eat at the dining hall at least twice a week, he was still responsible for all our other meals, including weekends, where we often held large dinner parties. He had been training Sally well, and it was getting to a point where I couldn't pick who had cooked what. I was proud of Sally. She was my age and had been fifteen when she started here and had worked her way up through sheer hard work to become second in command of the kitchen, all within five-years.

Jonathon was still happy in his job as a footman, although since moving to the village with Sally, he had to walk to work in the dark to get there on time. I watched them dancing slowly just as they did on their wedding night, held here at the pub. Following that celebration, Aaron and I had sauntered home at daybreak after too much wine and dancing. It had been a happy night for everyone, including us.

It felt like we were a family here at Willow Grove now, where everyone looked out for each other. If someone got sick, the other wives would look after the children and take their meals to them until they were back on their feet. Margaret had been minding the working mothers' children for years and earned herself a good reputation and income. She lovingly looked after them like they were her own, and the children were thriving.

Aaron led me to the dance floor and took me in his arms. 'You're pissed as a parrot,' he remarked. 'I don't dare bring' ya up here for a fast dance. You're likely to fall down on ya arse without me holdin' ya up.' He chuckled, and I smiled sweetly at him. He loved when I got really drunk, often teasing me that I became overly affectionate and said things I wouldn't usually say. He stared down at me intently as we danced. 'Ya know, I can see in ya big, green eyes how much ya love me. It could be the beer, but I think I see it,' he whispered in my ear.

After several slow dances, we sat back down, and I drank a few more beers while talking with Luke, who was the only single brother left. After hours had passed, Aaron suggested it was time we find our beds.

I agreed but first went up to the bar, my head spinning and my memory starting to fade. I was there for a time before someone helped me back to the table and sat me down next to my sisters-in-law. Victoria and Scarlett laughed at me as I tried to tell them something important, but my words wouldn't come out straight. Aaron grabbed my hand, stood me up as best he could, then walked me outside with his arm around my waist.

'I'm all right to walk,' I slurred, staggering when he let me go. I heard him chuckle as I tried to stand up straight, holding onto the wall of the pub for support while everything spun around me. I felt like my body was numb, and I couldn't feel my nose when I touched it.

'Here, jump on me back.' Aaron leaned down in front of me, waiting for me to respond. I couldn't jump anywhere in the state I was in, although I tried and missed, with Aaron quickly grabbing me by the shoulders to ensure I stayed upright. He bent down again in front of me with his back towards me. I flopped forward onto him, and he placed his hands under my legs as I wrapped them around him, my arms around his chest. I rested my face against the side of his neck as he strolled down the cobblestone street toward the hill, the others all walking and chatting around us. 'Are ya feelin' crook yet?' he asked, sounding amused.

'No. Pleasantly and happily drunk. Do you know, Aaron, you are the best husband anyone could ever wish for? I don't know that my life could go on without you in my world, and the way you adore your children melts my heart.' I sighed, nestling my face deeper into his neck. He slipped his hands under my backside and squeezed.

'Thank you, Miss. Abigail. I think your blood's worth bottlin', too,' he replied as Hamish drew up beside us.

'She's goin' tae be sick tomorrow,' he warned Aaron, a broad grin spreading across his handsome face.

'Yeah, I know. I'll try to get some water into her before she sleeps. How ya goin', mate? I'm sorry about Angelique, but I won't piss in ya pocket an' tell ya it's rainin'. I think it's for the best. She would've only brought ya misery an' strife. Maybe the old Hamish would've been fine with nannies raisin' the nippers an' havin' staff all over the house, but as ya are now, ya would hate it an' come to despise her. Ya not the snob I first met five-years ago, cobber. You've changed more than anyone I know. You'd never been in a kitchen before ya came here, an' look at ya now. I have to put up with ya ugly mug most days at breakfast. Ya spend more time workin' at Willow Grove than ya do at ya own property. Isn't ya old man gettin' annoyed with ya?'

'He naw gives two shits, the old bastard,' Hamish murmured, almost to himself. 'He's never there, so 'tis naw like he wants tae work the property together with me. I've given up tryin' tae make suggestions tae him, so now I do things the way I want since he's naw interested. The bludger shuts me down every time. He has a new mistress an' hasn't been home fer weeks. He has his foreman runnin' the show, an' more workers than he needs, makin' me redundant. I'd rather be here with ye blokes an' helpin' out where I can. At least ye have a vision fer this place, unlike that cranky auld cockhead.'

'I'm gunna have to start payin' ya for the hours ya work, but we'll sort it out tomorrow, hey?' I listened as Hamish refused his offer while Aaron insisted, and it continued to go back and forth between them the whole way up the hill. Hamish finally agreed he would discuss it tomorrow, said his goodbyes and dropped back to walk with Angus and Polly.

'How ya feelin', precious girl?' he asked, shifting me higher on his back and taking a firmer grip on my backside to hold me up.

'I'm feeling happy and fine. You have no idea of the unspeakable things that I'm going to do to you tonight. They will have to be seen to be believed,' I slurred, and I heard him laughing at me somewhere in the distance. I watched the moon while he spoke to Richard, who had also consumed too much of something. Richard teased him loudly about the theatre opening, which he, too, was obligated to attend, while I giggled to myself.

In the kitchen, everyone helped themselves to what remained of the leftovers as Aaron called out our goodnights and continued on to the hallway. I waved far too late, unable to yell out or speak coherently as he carried me up the stairs to the bedchamber, where he undressed me and put me straight to bed. He went to get a jug of water with raspberry syrup and a glass, then placed them on my bedside table before taking off his clothes and climbing into bed beside me.

'Now, about those obscene things you were yapping about,' he whispered.

Later, as I lay encased warmly in his arms, the room spinning, I could hear Aaron murmuring to me. I fell into a deep sleep, dreaming of a flock of sheep, a barrel of beer, and an incredibly intricate snowflake.

I woke slowly, sensing someone staring at me. 'What?' I opened one eye to test my reaction to the light. It was overcast outside, and a strong, cold wind was blowing. Aaron lay on his side next to me, appearing highly amused, while I lay unmoving on my back, feeling unwell.

'Nothin'. I was just waitin' for ya to wake up to see if I'm still the best husband in the world. By the way, ya wicked woman, those obscene things were highly obscene. Just in case ya don't remember,' he teased. I smacked him on the arm. Hard.

'I remember everything, thank you very much, even how grateful you were by the end of it, so shut that hole in your face,' I replied softly, my head pounding in time with my heart, and he laughed.

I jumped as little Mary noisily ushered in the twins, all ready for school. Their grandmother had brought them home early this morning so they wouldn't miss their schooling, which they both loved. They sat on Aaron's knee while he told them a story. Bessie came hurrying into the room with a fresh jug of lemonade and raspberry syrup.

'I hear you were acting like no lady last night, having to be carried home drunk like the tarts in the taverns.' Emmy and Thomas stared up at her wide-eyed while I choked on my own saliva. 'Surely, Mistress, you know you should be setting an example to the workers you employ. Imagine if all the wives went and got as rotten as you did at the pub. And in public, mind you. I will never be able to send you to a high-society event without worrying myself sick you won't behave yourself. You're lucky that people don't carry picture cameras to record your shameful shenanigans.'

'One day they will, Bessie,' Aaron interrupted helpfully. 'With progress, the cameras will become smaller an' more affordable like everythin' does in time. I imagine in a hundred years from now, every house will have its own camera.'

She scoffed at him. 'You and your silly ideas and stories about men walking on the moon and being able to fly in the sky from one country to another in bird-like machines. I don't know where you get your imagination from, Aaron, but it does keep these two entertained.'

I sat up on the side of the bed and poured myself some juice. I only had vague memories of last night, and there were large chunks of time I couldn't recall at all no matter how hard I tried. I remembered some things, like arriving home and going to bed, but the rest was confusing and my memory fragmented. I finished the glass and drank another before standing and carefully walking to my dressing table and sitting down.

Bessie came up behind me and started working on my hair, glancing at me disapprovingly in the mirror and muttering crossly under her breath. I remained silent, not wanting to be chastised again. Once she had finished my hair, she helped me into a house dress before storming out of the room and slamming the door behind her. I sat back down on the side of the bed, my head pounding while my thoughts were fuzzy.

'I think you're in for a bit of strife.' Aaron threw back his head and laughed before focussing his attention back on the twins and finishing their morning story then kissing the tops of their heads. When he rose to dress for the day, I hugged my babies and kissed them all over, making them squeal as I held them down on the bed.

'Mummy, your eyes aren't shining at me like they always do,' Thomas remarked, gently touching my face and running his fingers along the tops of my eyelids.

'That's only 'cause Mummy's eyes were sparklin' a bit too much last night with all the dancin' an' drinkin' she did,' Aaron interjected, throwing himself down heavily next to us and placing his hand on my face.

'Mummy, can you please ask Uncle Leo to stop making us sit on the lounge to watch him sing and dance?' Emmy asked. 'Thomas and I are sick of his terrible voice and the awful jumping up and down. He has the worst voice in the whole wide world but makes us pretend he is the best performer that ever lived, and we have to clap and cheer each time he finishes a song, or he won't let us go and play and threatens not to cook for us ever again.'

I erupted in uncontrolled giggles, unable to stop myself as I stared down at her serious face, clearly not amused by any of it.

'When did he do this?' I asked as they both stared up at me, unblinking and unable to see the funny side at all.

'Every time you and Daddy are eating in the kitchen, he tries to steal us away into the drawing-room so that no one can stop him from hurting our eyes and ears,' Thomas complained, making Aaron laugh so hard he had tears running down his face.

Leo thought he was the most gifted singer who had ever drawn breath; however, he was very wrong. He also believed he was a natural dancer who should be performing at The Cosmopolitan Theatre on opening night. I found it hard to believe he really was unaware of how bad he truly was. Now he was torturing the twins, who didn't appear happy to be used as his test audience.

Thomas and Emmy were both articulate children and quite advanced for their age. Aaron believed it was because we had talked to them constantly since they were born. They used words that were well above where their vocabulary should be; however, I also believed it was because they were always around people and loved to talk just like their father.

Aaron helped them both off the bed, lifted me to my feet, then guided us down to the kitchen, talking and laughing as the twins told us about their overnight stay with Aaron's parents. We hardly ever ate breakfast in the dining room anymore unless we had guests. Even then, some of our friends liked to eat in the kitchen, too.

Leo greeted us as we sat down and kissed the twins on the head. Within minutes he had served us a hot breakfast and special pancakes for the twins with chocolate in them.

'Thank you, Uncle Leo. I love your special pancakes. This makes having to listen to you sing a bit more bearable.' Emmy smiled sweetly at him as he leaned forward and took her face in his hands. She looked so cute with her hair up in pigtails.

'Well, I love you, my little princess. Unfortunately, you look like your mother. You would have had a much better chance in life had you favoured your father. Oh, well, at least your brother will be handsome. I'm sure he will always look after you as his spinster sister with a hundred cats.' He kissed her forehead while she continued to stare up at him, her face blank.

'Don't say things like that to her, Leo,' Aaron said, pushing him away. 'Emmy is beautiful, an' I have no doubt I'll be fightin' off the boys from Willow Grove an' the surroundin' district by the time she's fifteen. Em is exactly like her mother, who, despite what ya think, is the most beautiful woman I've ever seen, an' every bloke I know agrees with me. You're an imbecile openin' that mouth of yours without engagin' ya brain. Just stay quiet for the rest of the time the twins are here.'

Emmy smiled up adoringly at her daddy. Thomas hadn't been listening, too engrossed with his pancakes, just like his father. I wasn't much better, eating hungrily as a silenced Leo put more pancakes on the table. Once they had finished and drunk all their milk, we walked them out the back door, but not until they had received many hugs and well wishes from the kitchen staff, who loved seeing them every morning.

Aaron and I watched Thomas stop, pick up a stick, then throw it, while Emmy picked flowers as we strolled over the hill and down toward the village. The school was beyond the pub, dining hall, and shop. It was far enough away that the children had wide-open space, but close enough to the village that they could eat lunch in the dining hall each day. Richard and Jas' children attended school here, as did the many village children and some from neighbouring properties. On my friend Janet Russell's recommendation, I had hired Mrs McGinty as the headmistress and found her to be outstanding. She was in her early fifties and, although she was firm with the children, she was not cruel. I had watched the children blossom under her teaching. When we arrived at the school building, Thomas and Emmy went running to their friends, then remembered to come back and kiss us goodbye before they went in for the day.

Aaron would always be here at the end of the school day to accompany them, even though they could walk home by themselves. They were both riding their twin horses, Rainbow and Majestic, by themselves now, pleasing their father no end when we rode together as a family.

'They grow so quickly, don't they?' Aaron remarked as we walked back to the village hand in hand. 'I feel like it was only yesterday we were countin' down the days till they were born, an' look at 'em now. They're like little adults. They don't need us as much, an' they argue back a lot now, have ya noticed?'

'Yes, very much so. Emmy refused to wear a pair of shoes I had picked out for her the other day, and nothing would convince her. I even tried chasing her around the room and putting them on her by force, but I couldn't catch her.' I smiled at the memory as he chuckled to himself.

'Stubborn like her mother. She even stamps her foot the same way ya do when ya get upset, an' she points that little chin out at me in exactly the same way.' He reached over and pinched my cheek teasingly, stopping in the town square to kiss me. I enjoyed their emerging personalities—Thomas being so much like his father already, while Emmy was sweet as sugar but strong-willed when she didn't get her way. When we arrived at the stables, I sighed, put my arms around his neck, and hugged him tightly.

'Well, I'd best leave you to get to your work.'

'All right, *mo anamchara*. I'll see ya for certain at lunch. If you're not in the kitchen, I'll be comin' to look for ya.' He smirked and kissed me goodbye before I floated off towards the house.

I stopped in at the cottage to see what Polly was doing and inquire if she felt like company. I found her in the sitting room playing with Bella, who was still too young for school, unlike William, whose father walked him there every day. She smiled up at me as I greeted her.

'How do you feel this morning, Abi, especially after all that beer you drank last night?' She laughed aloud as I sat down beside her.

'Better than I thought I would, actually,' I replied, cuddling into Bella once she had settled herself on my lap.

'You were so funny. The way you climbed onto the bar and did that Irish jig that we were taught on the ship. Well, I thought I would wet my pants. Aaron came and got you off because we were all scared you would fall down and break your neck, even though we were laughing.' She continued to giggle as my eyes went wide and I stared across at her in horror.

'I did not,' I insisted, although some vague memory of standing above the crowd did come to mind for a moment.

'Ask anyone. Didn't Aaron tell you?' She slapped her knee as she continued to laugh.

'No, he forgot to mention it,' I replied darkly, trying to think of what I could do to pay him back for not telling me about my outrageous behaviour. 'Did I do anything else?' My voice faltered slightly as I leaned back against the large lounge, trying to collect my thoughts.

'Other than telling everyone how much you love them and how sweet you are on Aaron, no, you didn't embarrass yourself further. As long as you had a good time, and you seemed to, that's all that matters.' She smiled at me, noticed the look on my face, and quickly changed the subject. 'How about Angelique's form yesterday? I'm so glad Hamish has finally seen the light and thrown her over. She is horrible, hates my children, and looks down on where we live. I've never liked her, but I put up with her for Hamish's sake as it was keeping him on the straight and narrow. Can you imagine if they had married? I would have had Angelique and Jemima as sisters-in-law. I can't imagine anything worse. I would sooner walk naked down the main street of Geelong than have to bear that.' She pulled a face before we fell about laughing, while poor Bella looked up at us, appearing confused.

After talking for a time, I excused myself as Tamara was arriving with her children to stay for a few days. I kissed Polly and Bella, then hurried back to the house. Finding she hadn't arrived yet, I went to the warm kitchen to see what Leo was cooking. He always prepared snacks throughout the day, from little pastries and cakes to savouries. Today he had made what he called curry puffs, and I bit into the flaky pastry and tasted mince meat and vegetables in a sweet curry sauce.

When he had first started cooking for us, I asked him how he had acquired his recipes. He told me he had worked with chefs and cooks from around the world and made sure to record how to prepare the foods from their homelands—dishes that no one in England had ever heard of.

'How are you feeling today, Abigail? Are you up to doing a jig on the breakfast table?' He laughed, and I tried to swat him on the side of his head, but he ducked out of my reach.

'All right, Leo. I've heard all about it from Polly.' I rolled my eyes, arriving at his side where I picked up a small chunk of cheese and popped it into my mouth.

'But what you don't understand is how funny you are when you're drunk. You say and do the silliest things, and I've decided that you need to drink like that every day. I'm in love with the boozer Abigail.'

'I thought you loved the sober me, too,' I complained, trying to look hurt. He squeezed my shoulder affectionately then followed me to the table where he sat down next to me while I bit into a cheese pastry.

'Not since I've discovered the wicked and wild woman who can't handle the grog. We could have so much more fun if we got drunk like that together every day. Imagine what we would get up to because we wouldn't care about getting caught by Goliath and his constant reprimands. Boring. You could have chosen a less intimidating husband, you know? If it's not him watching us, it's that bloody Bessie.'

'What about bloody Bessie, you cheeky, wee shite?' I heard Bessie say as she stepped into the kitchen. Leo cringed, and I smirked at him.

'I said, 'Bloody Mary', you earwigger. You know? The drink that Abigail likes to get blind on in the mid-afternoon.' She narrowed her gaze at the back of his head; however, he didn't turn to face her. She rolled her eyes at him, then addressed me.

'Mistress, I only wanted to let you know that Maisie has opened a wing of the house for your friend Tamara and her children. It's the north wing.' I nodded and thanked her. It was amazing how Maisie and her maids whipped through the house so quickly and thoroughly. Bessie strode up behind Leo and smacked him hard across the back of the head without warning before turning on her heel and silently walking out. I had heard her speak of wanting to hit him in the past; however, she had never actually carried out her threat. His mouth hung open, his eyes wide as he rubbed the back of his head.

'See what I mean? We can't even talk privately without getting into trouble from your hatchet maid or angry husband. Aaron threatened to ban me from you when he heard us talking about taking the stable cat up to the loft and dropping it to see if it's true that cats always land on their feet.' I glared at him, my eyes widening in horror.

'That was you talking about doing that. I never said a word, other than you could hurt it, and Harry would be upset, as he loves that cat. How dare you get me into trouble again? I didn't even know Aaron thought I was part of your evil plan against cats. I told you that you can't go around experimenting on live animals or people and that you would have to find another way to prove your theories.' His face fell in disappointment as I rose to my feet. 'I'm going out to spend some time in the garden and pick white roses. I will leave you to prepare lunch, as I know I'm holding you up.' I kissed him goodbye, and he went back to work, still rubbing the back of his head. I took my basket and a knife to cut the stems and walked out the back door, breathing in the pure country air as I stepped outside.

I met Tamara and her four children at the front of the house—Madeleine, Charles, Frederick, and Edward—all born one after the other. Tamara did not travel lightly. She had brought each of her children's nannies and a ladies' maid with her. Usually, I would get my housemaids to look after any guests, but Tamara liked to do it her own way, in her own style. I showed her to a guest wing that held six rooms for the children and their nannies, as far away from Tamara's room as possible just as she had requested. I asked Bessie to show her ladies' maid to the staff quarters, to which she obliged. Soon after, Tamara and I retired to the sitting room and made ourselves comfortable.

'Thank you so much for having us, Abigail. I just had to get away from that pathetic excuse of a man. I find the faggot so repulsive, I can't bear to look at him. He just carries on with life, pretending to everyone that we're happily married. He goes about his business in Melbourne no differently than any respectable married man, but he's far from it, and the people that surround him don't have a clue he's a raging sodomite. I must admit he is a good father, and I give credit where credit is due, but he is shit in every other way.' She appeared disgusted as she described Brian, and I wondered how she acted when they were together.

It was nearing lunchtime, and I sent a prayer to Sister's God for Mr Masters to hurry up and knock on the door to announce it was ready, just so I didn't have to listen to her horrible words any longer. Before Tamara's arrival, I had warned the staff that everything had to be done correctly during her stay, much to Mr Masters' delight, including taking every meal in the dining room with all the pomp and ceremony that went with it. I had explained to them formality was required by all given that was what made Tamara comfortable and was all she knew, and they understood from what I could tell.

Soon after, Mr Masters did knock on the door as expected, and we followed him to the dining room. I had barely sat down when Aaron rushed in, kissed me, greeted Tamara, and quickly seated himself opposite me. He appeared to be in a hurry today, and I wondered why but remained silent, concerned whatever was going on would not be for Tamara's ears. Leo wandered in, as did Angus and Polly, and lunch was promptly served. I noticed Angus rushing through his meal but said nothing, preferring to engage in frivolous conversation with my friend, until Hamish joined us halfway through lunch and took Tamara's attention, while Leo, Aaron and Angus hurried back to work, leaving me alone like a shag on a rock.

Hamish and Tamara decided to go for a ride around the property after lunch, and I waved them off to the sound of their laughter. I decided to visit Amelia in the village before picking up the twins from school. I found her at home as she had recently employed a young girl from a neighbouring property who was working in the shop today. We embraced before sitting down together at her kitchen table. We chatted about family for a while, then she prepared afternoon tea.

'I have that French shampoo and scalp conditioner for you. I ordered an entire box of the stuff so you won't run out anytime soon,' she remarked casually as she placed the teacups and scones on the table before turning to go and retrieve the teapot.

'Thank you, Amelia. I will have to come back tomorrow to pay you for it.' I picked up a scone and nibbled on it, watching her pour the tea before sitting down opposite me.

'Just take what you want, then pay me the next time you visit. Don't go making a special trip. I trust you. Besides, you can't escape. I know where you live.'

We chatted about the shop, and how well it was going. She talked of financial security and how she now had enough money in the bank to buy a house if she ever needed to—not that she intended to move from the village. The terraces were full now, and I knew from Leo's passionfruit vine that our workers were content and happy living there, most telling us they felt they had everything they needed at their fingertips. I could easily have lived in one of the terraces with Aaron and the twins and knew I would love to be part of their community. Even though I was friendly to everyone, not all the wives wanted to be friends with me, some feeling I was above their station and shouldn't be mixing with them. It hurt my feelings; however, I had pushed it to the back of my mind as I usually did when I didn't want to think about something.

Amelia and I strolled to the school together to collect our children. I saw Aaron waiting at the gate and felt myself light up at the sight of him. Amelia and I parted ways when she went to speak to some of the other mothers, and I joined Aaron.

'What was wrong with you at lunch? You were in such a hurry.' I stood on my toes as he bent down to kiss me and placed a hand on my waist.

'One of the blokes nailed his finger to a post. He's not the brightest button in the box. We pulled it out, but he kept faintin' every time he looked at it. We were in a hurry to get back an' make sure he hadn't fainted to death,' he said with a wry smile. I burst into a fit of giggles. I could just imagine how supportive they would have been. They were likely to have fallen down laughing at the poor boy, especially Angus.

The children came running from the schoolhouse to the gate, where we embraced them before turning to start the journey home.

'Daddy, I learnt arithmetic today,' Emmy said proudly as Aaron smiled down at her.

'Did ya now? That seems a little advanced for ya first year of school. Ya must have a brilliant mind. You'll be able to go to university an' never have to have a husband.' He tousled her hair teasingly as she narrowed her gaze at him, frowning slightly.

'I don't want a husband, Daddy. I want a wife like you have Mummy.' Aaron glanced across at me, appearing startled, and I shrugged my shoulders.

'Girls can't marry girls, Emmy. Ya can only marry a man when your daddy says it's all right.' She stopped walking then placed her hands on her hips. I halted abruptly beside Aaron and turned to look at her.

'I just told you I don't want a husband. Are your ears painted on?' I cringed as she repeated word-for-word something I would occasionally say to them when they wouldn't listen to me.

'No, Emmeline, me ears are real—an' I do hear everythin' ya say. I'm not happy with how you're talkin' to me, though. Ya can stop stampin' ya foot right now an' stop stickin' ya chin out at me. God, you're the spit of ya mother. It's fine that ya don't want a husband, but ya can't marry a girl an' that's the end of it.' I smiled at her as she stomped away towards the village, then took his hand in mine reassuringly.

We stopped in at the general store, and she soon forgot how cross she had been with her daddy when he let them choose some sweets to eat on our walk home. They unwrapped a raspberry drop each and placed it in their mouths, then ran along ahead of us while we chatted about our day.

'Are ya drinkin' beer again tonight?' he asked nonchalantly as we walked hand in hand up the hill toward the stables.

'No,' I snapped defensively.

'Damn.' He feigned disappointment, which made me laugh despite myself.

Aaron took the twins up to the nursery to little Mary so they could play with Tamara's children before dinner. Hamish and Tamara had returned from their ride, and soon after Tamara joined me in the garden, her face flushed. She sat down next to me, positively glowing.

'Oh, Abigail, there is something I have to tell you.' She raised her hand to her throat as she tried to catch her breath. I smiled at her encouragingly, then took a sip of my cranberry juice. 'I enjoyed a wonderful ride around your property. It really is magnificent.' She stared across at the swimming pool we rarely used, several rainbow trout breaking through the surface in their search for food. Aaron had decided to breed them on a small scale and now provided our kitchens with his favourite freshwater fish. 'Hamish decided to rest the horses under a tree after we had been riding for several hours. Suddenly, he is kissing me, and then he's on top of me. With that chiselled body and a face carved by the angels themselves. Well, I couldn't help myself.' She stopped for a moment and quickly looked around to ensure we were alone, her face flushed pink. 'I let him do it to me. It wasn't that good, though. He tends to look after his own needs as a priority, but I enjoyed his company. Do you think I should keep him as a lover when I come down here to keep me occupied?'

The last thing I wanted to hear or visualise was Hamish and Tamara fornicating. She was my friend, and so was he, but I had nearly married him. A small part of me would always feel a slight pang of jealousy when I would see or hear about him with another woman—ridiculous even to me given how happy I was with Aaron. Some things in life didn't make sense to me at all.

'I don't think I should be the one giving you advice on Hamish.' Confusion crossed her face for a moment.

'Why not? You are one of his closest friends. Would he try to destroy my marriage or force me to leave my husband?' I sighed. She was obviously taking no notice of me, her eyes sparkling while her thoughts vague.

'You would have to talk to Hamish about that. I don't know what he thinks anymore.' Ever since we broke up, Hamish had been unpredictable, and although it was rare for him to be alone, I had never known him to step out with a married woman before. I was unsure how he would behave towards Tamara or if he would use her, then reject her as he had done to sweet Charlotte.

It would probably suit them both, with him not wanting to have a serious relationship and Tamara only wanting an affair. I hoped he treated her better than he had most of the women I had seen him with. He had taken up with several of our maids; however, he'd also had affairs with many women he had met at the pubs around Geelong, always leaving broken hearts and tears behind him. Aaron joined us, sitting down behind me and putting his arms around my waist.

'I invited Hamish to stay for dinner, an' he's decided to stay the night if that's all right with you.' I rolled my eyes, feeling like an accomplice to a crime, and I again hoped that Hamish wouldn't hurt Tamara. Despite her bravado about taking lovers, was still very innocent and inexperienced in bed. Hamish was charming and had a way of drawing women in—just as he had with her, from what I could see.

'He knows where the guest rooms are. He can stay in whichever one he likes,' I replied just as he stepped out the back door and made his way over to us.

'Why are all the bairns bein' fed separately in the kitchen tonight instead o' with us?' Hamish asked, appearing confused.

'Because that's what nannies are for,' Tamara replied, smiling up at him.

Polly, Angus, and Leo joined us in the dining room for dinner, and despite having already eaten, Emmy and Thomas were there, too, waiting patiently for dessert. Leo had taken extravagance to a new level when preparing his menu for Tamara, with her praising his talents over every course and asking him to work for them as her personal chef. She attempted to sway him by offering to pay him twice what he was earning here with us.

'Even if you paid me triple, Tamara, I couldn't leave Willow Grove. This is my home, and everyone here is my family,' Leo explained, causing me to reach over and squeeze his hand. 'Plus, Abigail wouldn't know what to do without me. Her children would be unfed, her house wouldn't run as smoothly as it does, she would be starving and complaining, driving Goliath mad. I couldn't do that to him. He has to put up with enough, especially having a wife who brazenly displays herself by dancing on top of a tavern bar. I need to stay here for Goliath as he relies on my support, often consulting with me over his wife's behaviour. He couldn't cope without me here as, in actual fact, I am more of a wife to him than Abigail. I raise his children, making sure they're fed and healthy, and I have his food on the table five times a day. I would go and make his bed for him, if you know what I mean, but he won't let me. Goliath likes to play hard to get.'

Tamara stared at him blankly, and I heard Hamish snort in amusement. Aaron stared at Leo for a time before sighing deeply.

'Listen, ya little... ya lucky me nippers are here. I'll respond to this later, but one thing I'll say is I've never consulted ya over me wife's behaviour. The only reason I go to ya is when you've got up to mischief with her, an' I've hunted ya down to give ya a tongue lashin' for your part in it.' Leo rolled his eyes dreamily, then turned to gaze down the long table.

'I would love a tongue lashing from you, Goliath.' Emmy and Thomas looked across at their father inquisitively, Emmy raising her hand to speak as Aaron shook his head and hushed her.

'Stop,' I snapped, glaring down the table at him, my cheeks hot. 'You are always complaining I don't know how to behave in public. Look at you. You're being awful—bloody stop talking! You have made everyone uncomfortable, and now my children are confused and will ask me what all this meant. Thanks, Leo. Now I have to tell them, as I won't lie to them. Don't even answer me. I don't want to hear your voice.'

Tamara smiled across at me gratefully, as did Aaron. Everyone resumed their banter while continuing to eat. Tamara gazed dreamily at Hamish, who ignored her completely, while Angus studied them both, a puzzled look on his face, and clearly wondering what was going on. The fun begins, I thought darkly to myself.

Thomas and Emmy sat next to Aaron and were now talking quietly between themselves. I respected Tamara's choices in how she parented her children, but I had very different ideas about raising mine.

Several people had recently commented on my unlikely friendship with Tamara, given she wasn't an easy person to get along with. I loved her and had never had an argument with her, always seeing the real Tamara deep within, and found she was a sweet and lovely person. Others seemed to find it difficult to look beyond her arrogance, whereas I accepted that it was all she knew so far. She had told me herself she had never met anyone who raised their children without nannies constantly caring for them, leaving me deeply sad for her.

'Oh, well, Leo,' Tamara called out cheerfully. 'I admire your loyalty to Abigail and Aaron, if that was what you meant? I do find it hard to follow along with what you say sometimes. I hope that one day I find a chef as talented as you, who *will* agree to come and work for me.'

'I have tae ask, Tamara,' Hamish interrupted. 'Why dinnae ye allow yer children tae dine with us when they're at Willow Grove? I understand ye want tae keep everythin' proper when yer in Melbourne an' entertainin' yer friends, but bein' here should be a holiday fer them. They've freedom they dinnae have at home an' so many things tae do. I can take them out on the horses, if ye like?' She stared across at him, her manner cold, her tone icy.

'It looks to me, Hamish, that you yourself have spent far too much time at Willow Grove on holidays and have forgotten your breeding,' she remarked, her tone clipped and proper as always. 'You only have to listen to that Scottish brogue you've let yourself fall back into. When we met, you spoke like a perfect English gentleman.' She paused, wrinkling her nose in disdain. 'You and I were raised correctly, just how my children will be raised, and I'm sure when your time comes to be a father, you will do the same. It is the only way if you want them to turn into adults who will make a good match with a good family, not like the local larrikins who don't know how to behave in public.' He frowned. I could see he didn't want to argue with her given she was a guest in our home, so he wisely dropped the subject and finished his coffee.

After dessert, little Mary collected the children, and we all retreated to the sitting room, where we spent an hour talking and drinking wine. I started to yawn by my third glass, causing Aaron to stand up and gently pull me to my feet. I embraced Polly and Tamara goodnight, then said goodnight to the boys, kissing Leo on the cheek, before Aaron led me up to our bedchamber.

It felt so good to stretch out naked in bed under the heavy covers. Tamara seemed to have settled in since her arrival this morning, enabling me to relax. I was always anxious when trying to ensure our home met her high standards.

It was so cold outside, we had lit fires in all the rooms that were being used. Aaron threw some kindling and logs onto the smouldering embers, then turned and ran to the bed, shivering while complaining loudly.

'Come here an' warm me up.' He grabbed me roughly then pulled me on top of him.

'No, let me go. You're freezing.' I tried to get away to no avail as he held me against his cold body.

'I know somethin' that'll warm ya up quickly,' he suggested, and I smirked at him. Later, as I lay in the warm room wrapped in his arms, I dreamed of a large gum tree, an army, and a bottle of silky shampoo.

Chapter Nine

'COME HERE, *MO ANAMCHARA*. You're havin' a nightmare. It's all right, I'm here. I've got ya,' Aaron murmured sleepily, putting his arms around me. I didn't know what I'd dreamed, but I'd awakened in a cold sweat. I must have been whimpering loudly to wake Aaron, who was a deep sleeper. It left me with a feeling of dread in the pit of my stomach, and I didn't know why. I lay there quietly to allow Aaron to go back to sleep, but after some time, he turned to me. 'You're not sleepin'. What's wrong, *mo anamchara*?' He rested his head on his hand while he stared intently at me.

'I don't know. Nothing. I just have a bad feeling.' I was unable to articulate my emotions, and I didn't want to. He looked at me sympathetically.

'It's only a dream. Here, lay ya head on me chest.' I nodded, moving closer, my cheek against his heart before he placed his hand on my head and stroked my hair.

I lay unmoving, hoping to drift off while considering rising from our bed at this godforsaken hour to write to Sister Josephine. I still wrote to her every second day and received the same back every month when the postie would deliver a bundle of letters all at once. It was February 1897, and she had recently sent me a handmade card for my twenty-second birthday with roses from their garden pressed into the paper. She had included a scarf with all the colours of the rainbow she had knitted herself. I was excited to wear it, but since we were in the middle of summer, I had months to wait. I looked out through the pane glass window at the full moon shining in, casting a romantic glow across the room. I had left the large windows open so the cool night breeze could flow through the room. I breathed deeply, the air filled with lavender and roses wafting in from the garden below.

'*Mo anamchara,* if you're not gunna sleep, come here.' I lifted my head from his chest and moved up the bed to kiss him—the letter to Sister Josephine left unwritten and now forgotten.

Thomas and Emmy sat on a bench in the kitchen watching Leo cook their eggs, while Aaron and I sat at the kitchen table, talking and drinking coffee. They joined us when Leo served their breakfast and gave them a glass of milk each, then kissed them both on the head. They were six-years-old now and thought they were so grown up. I heard the back door open, and Willy and Bella hurried in, kissed Aaron, me, and Leo, then sat down for breakfast. The four of them walked to school by themselves every morning, having decided they were too old to have their parents accompany them anymore.

It had really affected Aaron, leaving him feeling rejected. He enjoyed walking them to and from school each day, but they were determined. The first day, Aaron followed along behind them, embarrassing them when they caught sight of him in the village while they were with their friends. They complained to me, so I made Aaron promise in front of them that he wouldn't do it again. To my knowledge he hadn't—or he was just being more discreet.

They went every Friday after school to stay with Aaron's parents until Sunday lunch. Either their grandfather or an uncle would ride over to collect them, and they would ride Rainbow and Majestic back to be with their aunts and uncles and cousins. Luke had married Adele, a local girl, over a year ago, and they had just moved into their own house next to his brothers' homes.

The fishing business was booming, initiating a discussion between Aaron and his father regarding a processing plant. They had spent many a night over the last three-months talking of building the factory and how many jobs it would provide the locals, while securing great wealth for the family for generations.

Leo placed our breakfasts in front of us, making sure Willy and Bella were eating and drinking their milk.

'Aunty Abigail, can you please make sure Uncle Aaron stops following us to school?' Willy enquired, his hand going up into the air to get everyone's attention. 'We saw him yesterday followin' along behind us, thinkin' we didn't know or see the fatty. He's too big to miss.' I was about to answer when Angus crossed the room then settled his large frame next to his children.

'What are ye complainin' about now, Willy?' He smiled down at his curly black-haired son as Leo went and organised breakfast for him.

'Just Uncle Aaron, Dad,' he said, and Angus nodded knowingly.

'Aye. Your Uncle Aaron. Is he still followin' you to school then?' The four children all nodded, appearing quite annoyed. I looked across at Aaron, who was suddenly preoccupied with his food.

'Yes, he is, and he won't stop, Mummy,' Emmy complained as she ate her eggs. 'Yesterday we saw him in Bessie's backyard watching us walk up the hill. He is *so* embarrassing. You have to do something about him before our friends tease us to death.'

I couldn't help but giggle at the thought of Aaron hiding in Bessie's backyard as he would have a clear view of their entire route home. Aaron continued to eat in silence while Angus laughed so hard, tears ran down his handsome face.

'I think Daddy needs to be sent to Coventry, Mummy. It's the only thing that'll stop him. Our friends are laughin' at us, for Christ's sake,' a frustrated Thomas yelled, making Leo gasp.

'Thomas, don't let me ever hear you curse like that again.' He raised his hand to his throat while waving his finger in Thomas' face. 'Oh, heaven help us and praise be. I hope you haven't inherited your mother's foul mouth, young man. Having been sent to Coventry myself, I don't think you are being very fair to Goliath here. Coventry is the worst place to be banished to—a dark place that torments your soul.'

I laughed aloud, unable to contain myself any longer. Sending someone to Coventry was a term we used when a person would do something seriously upsetting. We would send them to Coventry by ignoring their presence until they were able to do right, and apologise for the wrong they had done. To date, Leo had been the only one who holidayed regularly at Coventry, much to his disgust. He hated being ignored, and when he was, especially by everyone at the same time, he would throw tantrums and shriek at us until he got sick of the sound of his own voice and stormed away. Angus smirked at Aaron, then focused his attention on the children.

'Well, I may have a solution to your problem without you havin' to send your father, and uncle, to Coventry.' They stared up at him in silence, Willy nodding on occasion while encouraging him to continue. 'I'll come here every day for breakfast and keep him here while you walk to school. That'll give you plenty of time, Bella, so stop your fashin'. When you finish school, I'll keep him busy at the stables until I know you're all safely home. I'd hate to see a mate of mine sent to Coventry.' They all nodded, seemingly satisfied, then quickly finished their breakfasts.

'I think you lot better get out of here and go to school,' Leo ordered, handing them all a wrapped toffee. They kissed us goodbye then ran out the kitchen door, their excited voices filling the room long after they departed. Angus, still chuckling, also said goodbye then made his way to the stables. Aaron went to stand up.

'Where do you think you're going?'

'I just have something to do.' I saw the guilt in his eyes as I reached over and took his hand in mine, pulling him back towards the table.

'Didn't you hear anything that was just said? Stay here with me and have another cup of coffee until you have to go to work. The children will be fine.' I smiled, and he reluctantly sat back down.

'I wasn't gunna follow 'em. I was only gunna watch 'em walk over the hill.' I patted his hand and nodded while smothering a smile. Leo, his back to us as he stood at the sink, giggled to himself just as Mr Masters appeared in the kitchen doorway.

'Martin has arrived to visit with you, Mistress. He says his business is of an urgent nature. He refused to let me show him to the parlour and has chosen to wait at the front entrance.' He grimaced, just as he did every single time he was forced to announce our friends and family by their first names. Before he could escort me to the front door, Martin burst into the kitchen; sweat pouring from every part of him as he stopped in front of me and tried to catch his breath. Mr Masters, who found this most uncivilised, promptly turned on his heel and left. Martin collapsed in the chair next to me, his face pale.

'What's happened? Is everything all right?' I enquired, my heart in my throat. He shook his head, placed it in his hands, and began to cry. I felt fear rise in me and I started to shake, even as I tried to push it back down.

'The coppers came to our house this morning and arrested Dana and took her away,' he said through his sobs, his voice like gravel. I turned my head sharply to stare at Aaron, who had also gone a lighter shade of pale, before I turned back to Martin.

'What was she arrested for?' My hands continued to tremble, my heart pounding so hard I thought it would explode.

'Bigamy,' he replied softly, then hung his head and cried some more.

Aaron arranged for Harry to ready the carriage, and we hurriedly made the journey to Geelong to meet with Richard. We knew he would be able to find out what was happening to Dana and, given that Martin wanted to retain him to represent her, it was the only place we could think to go. Poor Martin was in a terrible state. He didn't know where she was or if she had been harmed when taken into custody, and was clearly distressed.

We arrived at Richard's Ryrie Street offices and rushed inside. He heard us in the waiting room and came out of his office, appearing perturbed.

'Something's happened. It's written all over your face.' He smiled sympathetically before guiding us into his office and inviting us to sit down. Martin explained as much as he knew, and I told Richard what Dana had revealed to me on the ship about her relationship with her English husband. Richard listened silently, waiting for us to finish. 'It's likely she will go before the Court of Petty Sessions at the Geelong Courthouse any time after ten o'clock this morning. We had better hurry over there so I can see her before she goes before the police magistrate,' Richard said calmly, grabbing his leather bag before rising to his feet and stepping out from behind his desk.

When we arrived at the courthouse, Richard confidently strode over to the front counter and spoke to a neatly dressed officer, who then escorted him to the holding cell to interview Dana. We sat and waited in the foyer. Aaron held my hand tightly in his. He had said very little since Martin had arrived at our home to tell us the shocking news, worrying me greatly.

'What are you thinking, Aaron? Do you know it's bad but won't say so because you don't want to upset me?' He slipped his arm around my shoulder, bringing his head closer to mine.

'I was just thinkin' that I don't believe Dana will get out of this without consequence. She's one of our best friends, an' I know this'll grieve ya deeply. I've arranged with Richard for us to pay her legal bills to take the pressure off Martin. I know better than most Richard charges like a wounded bull, the little bastard. He may be our friend, but he's a lawyer through an' through.' He smirked at me, and I smiled back knowingly.

Richard's services were very expensive; however, as far as I was concerned, you got what you paid for. If you paid peanuts, you ended up with monkeys—with the exception of Mr McPhee—who had been paid generously and still acted like a baboon.

I couldn't think straight and wasn't taking notice of anything around me. People walked past us without paying any attention—we were just faces in the crowd as they were to us. Everyone present was awaiting theirs or someone's fate, who they no doubt cared about. Dana could actually go to gaol for this, and her life would be ruined. She could get hurt in there—or worse. I couldn't imagine many of the prisoners would take kindly to an upper-class lady sharing their cell, or demanding help to dress each morning, and I tried to smother a smile. I knew this was no time for joking, and if Sister Mary Monica were here, my knuckles would be flayed until they were raw and bleeding—but only Dana could get herself in such a position. She wouldn't have cared or even thought of that small yet important piece of paper in England when she married Martin—she had put all that behind her when she started her new life here. Richard returned, appearing dejected as he took a seat next to us and opened a folder containing some papers.

'Well, it's true.' He shook his head in disbelief before meeting my gaze. 'Dana admitted to me that she knew she was still legally married to her first husband when she married Martin. She will plead guilty today and will be remanded at Geelong Gaol until she is sentenced. I will work hard to ensure she gets the absolute minimum prison time, but because she is pleading guilty, it truly is out of my hands.' Martin placed his head in his hands in despair, and Aaron squeezed his shoulder in comfort. Richard ushered us towards the courtroom door, advising us Dana's case would soon be heard.

I followed them in then sat down next to Martin, took his shaking hand in mine, and smiled at him reassuringly. Within moments, her case was called. Dana was escorted by a policeman through a door at the side of the courtroom into a secure area, then forced to stand facing the court, flanked by two prison wardens left to guard her. She looked terrible and couldn't take her eyes off Martin. Her hands were secured tightly in front of her body, the chains hanging from her wrists, an overwhelming urge to run to her and help her escape welling up inside me.

'Ease up, Abi,' he whispered. 'I can feel in your body you're wound up so tight you're about to unravel. That wouldn't be helpful for Dana, now would it? Ya need to calm yourself down an' wait to hear what the magistrate says. Richard's very good at his job, an' if anyone can help her, he can.' He kissed the top of my head and I concentrated on relaxing my body and slowing my breathing.

Richard sat at the front table and introduced himself, stating he was representing the accused, Dana Shannon. Police Magistrate T. D. S. Heron listened to the case as it was put to him, then asked Dana for her plea.

'Guilty,' she announced loudly, standing tall and proud. She looked directly at us and gave us a weak smile. As Richard had predicted, she was remanded until her sentencing date in three-weeks' time.

In the carriage on the way to drop Richard back at his office, he explained plainly what Dana had told him, holding back nothing.

'The police advised her this morning that her first husband had been seeking a divorce since she left and has been looking for her for all these years, finally tracking her down to Geelong. He sent the divorce papers to a local solicitor who, upon further investigation, found Dana had married Martin. He reported her to the police and, as you know, they arrested her this morning. In the first husband's defence, I don't think he intended for this to happen and thought it would be clean-cut once Dana signed the papers, making their marriage null and void. I will do all I can for her; however, I cannot promise that she will not serve a custodial sentence.' The carriage had stopped, and he bid us farewell and quickly returned to his office.

The three of us sat in silence on the ride home, all thinking about Dana. When we arrived, we left Harry with the horses and made our way to the front door. Aaron encouraged Martin to come inside and have something to eat, and he slowly followed us to the kitchen, appearing to be in a trance. Leo watched silently as we sat down at the kitchen table, then stopped what he was doing and quickly pranced over to us.

'How did everything go? Is she doing twenty-years hard labour for being a wanton woman and a dirty little bigamist?' Leo enquired, promptly sitting down at the table with us while Sally made the coffee and baked the scones. I rolled my eyes at him and discreetly pointed at Martin, bringing to his attention the poor man had his head in his hands and was crying once again. Leo looked at me blankly and I sighed deeply, giving up.

'No good, mate,' Aaron replied, then went on to explain the events of the morning. 'Someone needs to go an' tell Victoria.' He quickly rose to his feet just as Martin lifted his head and wiped his face.

'No, I'll go. I not only committed to Dana when I married her, I took her girls as my own daughters that day. Vicki needs to hear it from me, Aaron.' He rose unsteadily to his feet, reaching out to shake Aaron's hand before departing after thanking us for our support.

Aaron and I sat staring at each other over the warm scones and coffee, not speaking. Leo, however, couldn't help himself.

'How long do you think Dana will be locked away for, Abigail? She'll be your first real criminal friend who has done actual, real gaol time like the convicts who built this country. Don't you find that a tiny bit exciting?' he asked me gleefully, clapping his hands. I glared across at him, folding my arms against my chest as I narrowed my gaze.

'Leo, you're a fat-headed moron. Do you ever think before you speak, or does this shit just naturally come pouring out of your mouth? Here, take a handkerchief and wipe the side of your lips, because you still have brown stains there,' I spat as Aaron quickly put his arm across my chest to prevent me from getting to my feet and smacking him in the face.

'I only meant imagine the fabulous stories she will have to tell us all when she's released from a prison *with* walls. Can you imagine the type of people she will befriend? We will have convicts and tavern trollops visiting us all the time. What a delightful thought, and we'll be privy to what it's really like on the other side of those bars. I wonder if they still whip them and torture them like they did the criminals sent her after the English invasion? I can't wait until she gets out in a decade to tell us every little detail of her adventure. There may even be some same-same action, if you get my meaning?' I tried to throw myself at him in a rage; however, Aaron calmly held me where I was, rendering me useless.

'If I were you, Leo, I'd stop talkin' now. I won't be around all day to protect ya from her,' he warned as the smile disappeared from Leo's face and he immediately went quiet, noticing the look in my eyes.

'Anyway, I must get on with my day—and what a wonderful day it is. I feel all is right in the world,' he sang, rising to his feet.

'Why, you son of a... ' I started to scream, lurching forward as Aaron clamped his hand over my mouth.

'Leo, for ya own safety, walk away now,' Aaron yelled out above my angry tirade. Leo promptly turned on his heel and trotted into the kitchen, paying me no mind. Aaron waited until I had calmed down, then kissed me on the lips. 'Now, you behave. I don't want any quacks visitin' here today for either one of you.' Defeated, I nodded my assent. I sat with my head bowed, thinking about Dana. Aaron embraced me before walking out the back door to the stables, leaving me with Leo and the scones. I chose the scones—and they were far better company.

I spent the morning in the drawing room writing letters to Sister Josephine, Mr and Mrs Malcolm, and Tamara and Elizabeth. Tamara had stayed with us last week with the children, who we barely saw, and spent most of her time secretly meeting Hamish.

Hamish would see her for the time she was here, then see other women in the time she was not, and he seemed fairly happy with the arrangement. He didn't treat Tamara badly, but in public he treated her like an acquaintance, which hurt her feelings. He had tried many times to explain to her she was a married woman and needed to be discreet; however, she refused to listen. I was sick of hearing about their boring sex life, and if it had been anyone else, I would have given her some of Dana's tips.

The fact they were both my friends and were having sex upset me, and even thinking about it, let alone discussing it, left me cold. Tamara wouldn't take the many hints I'd left her and continued to talk of him incessantly every waking moment. I knew she was unaware of the other women in his life, and I kept my mouth shut, not wanting to interfere. Hamish did not appear to be any closer to settling down than he had been since we broke up, and I couldn't help but worry for him.

He would come daily to see Aaron and the twins on his way to Angus and Polly's house, and would often spend time with me, talking and drinking coffee out in the garden. He was the old Hamish again, and I enjoyed his company and treasured his friendship. He still had that golden aura radiating around him, making him look far more beautiful than what he actually was with the way he was behaving. I would always love Hamish as we were close, but I was in love with Aaron, and that's what made the difference. I felt a hand on my shoulder and jumped, almost falling from my chair.

'Sorry, Abi. I did speak, but ya were lost in thought.' Aaron gazed down at me, concern crossing his handsome face. 'How ya travellin' after this mornin'?' He sat down beside me. I remained where I was at my comfortable writing desk next to a large window, positioned there so I could be bathed in sunlight while writing my letters.

'Yes, I'm fine. It's Dana that I'm concerned about.' I swallowed hard, feeling I would burst into tears. He rose, took me by the hand, and pulled me to my feet. Then, he encircled me with his arms and kissed the top of my head.

'I was worried about ya so knocked off a bit early for lunch. I've decided to take a sickie for the rest of the day as I don't have much on. Guess who the lucky sheila is that gets to spend it with me?' he asked with enthusiasm. I couldn't help but smile at him. 'Since we have no guests stayin' with us right now, can we eat naked in bed?' I rolled my eyes at him before he hurried off to order lunch, leaving me there alone shaking my head in disbelief.

'Come on, Aaron, help me dress. The twins will be home soon.' I poked him in the ribs before trying to pry open his eyelids with my fingers. We had fallen asleep after taking a heavy lunch in our room.

'Yeah, nah,' he murmured sleepily, throwing his arm across me and pinning me to the bed. 'I wanna stay here. The twins might take the long way home—or go an' play with Willy an' Bella without askin' since they no longer need me.' I laughed and hugged his arm.

'Don't go getting all sad because they're growing up. You know they have always been independent since they were small. It doesn't mean they don't love you,' I reassured him while stroking his soft, blonde hair. He lay on his back, staring at the ceiling.

'But they called me annoyin' an' think I should be sent to Coventry,' he replied, obviously hurt. I tried not to smile.

'Aaron, get over it. They're free spirited children who want to explore, and they should be allowed to within the safety of Willow

Grove. You have to let go, my darling man.' I started to giggle before he reached out and grabbed me, pulling me close.

'It's not funny, Abigail. We need to have another nipper since the two we have are too grown up now to wanna spend time with me.'

'I haven't even thought of having more children because I'm so busy with these two, and they are still so young. Maybe we could start thinking about it, though.'

'If ya stay in bed with me, I'll give ya a surprise.' He smiled wickedly as I shook my head.

'That I doubt very much.' I pulled myself up, ready to get out of bed. He sat up, too, his hair all messy and his eyes pleading as he kissed me.

'Please, just a quarter of an hour.' He pulled me back to his chest, and I decided fifteen-minutes more wouldn't hurt anyone.

Thomas and Emmy stood in the kitchen eating strawberry cupcakes with Leo. They had a glass of milk each, which Leo insisted they drink three times a day no matter how old they were, and embraced us when we walked in.

'Daddy, can we please go for a ride before dinner? All of us together?' Emmy asked him sweetly, and he smiled down at her.

'Who wants to go? Hands up, an' majority rules,' Aaron called out cheerfully before sitting down next to them and patting the seat beside him for me to join them for a moment. Thomas and I put our hands up, as did Aaron and Emmy. 'Then it's settled. Drink ya milk an' we'll go on an adventure.'

'Can I come, too?' Leo asked as I glared across at him. I still hadn't forgotten his remarks about Dana this morning.

'No, you can't, and if you say another word about prisons, criminals, stabbings, and murders in gaol or anything more of the sort that you believe will happen to Dana, I will twist your ears off,' I warned him, then headed for the backdoor. Aaron followed, chuckling to himself while the twins ran on ahead.

'Abigail, you're frightenin' when ya get angry an' threaten people. I know he deserves it, but ya sometimes scare the shit out of me, an' I often wonder if ya really will kill him one day. Me biggest fear is you'll snap an' do him in, an' I'll be visitin' ya in gaol, ya spirited wee vixen.' He chuckled to himself as we passed through the garden, hand in hand, Leo now far behind us—although his wailing still filled my ears.

Harry saddled Rainbow and Majestic for the twins, while Aaron and I saddled Goliath and Delly.

'How are you, Harry?' I asked, holding the twins' horses by their bridles.

'I'm beaut, Mistress. I heard about your friend Dana on the grapevine an' I wanted to tell you I'm sorry for it. Did you know your great-aunt Isabelle spent time in gaol herself?' he asked with a grin. I turned my head abruptly and stared at him, unable to hide my surprise.

'Why was she in prison? You sound like you knew her intimately,' I remarked, kicking myself yet again for being so forward. He glanced across at me sadly as Aaron led Goliath out, the twins following behind leading their horses. 'I will be there in a few minutes,' I called out, and they waved to me happily as they passed by. Harry sat down while I jumped up and sat on his high workbench to listen.

'I did know her intimately, as you say. She was a very private person an' didn't talk a great deal about her past. She carried a sadness with her about it, though. I never questioned her an' only listened when she needed to unburden herself. She only ever mentioned once to me that she had spent time as a convict, but'd go no further or tell me any details. I do know she had a friend durin' this time called Abigail, who she named you for. They served their time assigned to the same master, no different from indentured servants.'

'I have found a journal written by an Abigail Sinclair, but I cannot bring myself to read it.' He nodded thoughtfully as I gazed up at the loft where the stable hands slept. I felt he knew far more than he let on, but didn't want to say anything to offend him. 'What was my aunt like?' He swallowed then wiped his mouth with the back of his hand.

'She was a mysterious woman, my Izzy, which only added to her charm. As I told you, I made her acquaintance when I was nineteen an' she was much older, but to look at her you'd never guess. She was still stunningly beautiful when I met her, with many blokes decades younger still pursuin' her.' Harry paused to blow his nose before continuing. 'I spent the last five-years of her time in Australia beside her before she left Willow Grove an' returned to England. She stayed there for just over a year, then I got word she'd passed away not long before she planned to return here. I loved your great-aunt Isabelle deeply an' never forgot her. It's why I never married, an' why I'm still reluctant to, no matter how much I adore me Jenny. Isabelle still has a big part of me heart wherever she is—that'll never change, despite her bein' gone so many years now. You favour her very much, Mistress.' His eyes shimmered with tears that he quickly brushed away, thinking I hadn't noticed.

'I'm so sorry your heart was broken,' I said sincerely, and he smiled weakly.

'Isabelle never meant to hurt me. She loved me just as much as I adored her,' he murmured, his face full of emotion. 'When she left, it was due to a family situation, an' she had every intention of returnin' to Willow Grove. She loved this place, an' it's for her memory I stayed an' attempted to carry on an' fulfil her dream for the property. I've a picture of her, which I'll show you one day. I doubt you even know what she looked like an' how much you're like her. It warms me heart that her bloodline, although not direct, has carried on with you. If you don't mind me sayin' it, you've inherited her sweet nature, as well as her beauty, an' you've got the same fire in your belly. I find talkin' about Isabelle extremely difficult, though, Mistress. I never have gotten over losin' her.'

I was stunned. This was the first time I had been given so much information from someone who knew her so intimately. Suddenly, she felt like a real person to me—a family member who had lived a life that was mysterious and intriguing. My understanding was that, although no one knew her exact age, she was well into her eighties when she passed. I had formed the opinion she must have been an extremely progressive woman to take a young lover at her advanced age. I didn't question him further, as I could see it brought up painful memories. I jumped down from the bench and, much to his surprise, embraced him. I felt he needed a friend given he had just bared his soul, being such a private person myself. He smiled at me fondly as I made my way to Delly's stall.

I wore the new riding outfit Catherine had made especially for me—a pair of tan, fitted trousers no different from what the men wore around Willow Grove, with a matching jacket in chocolate brown, cinched in at the waist with two pockets in front. The knee length riding boots that I'd had made in London and thought I would never wear were now firmly on my feet, the smell of leather all around me. Far more comfortable than wearing a dress to ride in, I had made the decision there and then when Catherine had spoken of her female relatives back in England wearing trousers when they went hunting and the world hadn't stopped.

Aaron was nowhere near as excited as I was about wearing masculine clothing, as he referred to it; however, I didn't care. I felt free and uninhibited and wouldn't go back now. Aaron strolled up behind me as I bent down in Delly's stall to pick a stone out of her hoof. I felt his hands on my backside as I let go of her fetlock and straightened up.

'I don't mind havin' a perv on ya in those trousers, but I don't want anyone else lookin' at ya in 'em. I can see the shape of ya bare arse, an' ya legs, no different than if ya were walkin' about in the nuddy. No stoppin' in the village or at the pub unless ya have a coat.' He placed his hands on my shoulders before turning me around to face him.

'Aaron, even women of nobility wear these when they go fox hunting or riding in England.' I grimaced as he stared down at me and grinned. 'This is tasteful compared to some I've seen. You will get used to them in time.' He'd made me feel self-conscious, shifting from foot to foot as I reached around and felt my backside to see if the pants were too tight. He looked me up and down, then turned me around to study my bum.

'It's the other blokes around the traps I don't want gettin' used to 'em. Just don't bend over.' He smacked me on the backside as

I pushed past him and led Delly out to where the children were waiting, already mounted on their enormous steeds and excited to get going. They looked so tiny sitting on top of them, and I still felt anxious when they rode.

I mounted ungraciously and followed behind. Aaron led the way past the house and garden and through to the back paddock, where we kicked the horses into a canter and rode toward the ocean. The children kept up with us, and at times were far ahead of me. They had a natural riding ability, just like their father, and they loved their horses and helped look after them each day. I could ride, but knew it would never come naturally to me.

At the beach, Aaron hobbled the horses, and the twins stripped off their clothes and splashed in the waves. We lay on the sand, watching them.

'Can you believe we made those two beautiful little human beings?' I remarked, kissing him on his ruddy cheek.

'I was lookin' at Emmy this mornin', an' she's a miniature you, with her long, red hair an' big, green eyes. I already know I'm gunna have a problem with the lads in the district when she's fifteen or so, just like you were when I met ya. Not that you've changed much.' I flinched slightly as he gazed across at me, the sea breeze whipping at my hair, and I thanked Bessie silently for binding it up so tight today.

'I was a child bride. Far too young when you look back. I should have been living with my family and protected from that sort of thing till I was of an appropriate age to start courting. I know you weren't much older, but you were twenty, and an adult. I will never allow my children to leave home before they turn eighteen, let alone commit to marriage and a family of their own.' He nodded thoughtfully, reaching across and touching my cheek with his large finger. 'I've said it before and I'll say it again. I'm fortunate it was you I was betrothed to, but many are not so lucky. I see so many young girls living in poverty with three or four bairns tied to their hips. Far too many are sold off to their husbands by their families, some as young as thirteen. I find it terrifying, especially when the men are so much older.' He nodded again, staring out over the ocean as the tide started to go out.

An hour passed before the children were finished playing. We hurried to their side to wrap them in a blanket before helping them dress and mount their horses. It wasn't long before we were back at the stable, the sun just starting to set in the sky when little Mary came out to collect the twins and get them ready for dinner.

Aaron and I returned to our room to wash and change before making our way to the dining room, where Leo sat with Thomas and Emmy—their faces polished clean, along with their bodies and hair from the bath little Mary had waiting for them when we arrived home. Now that the children were older, we tried to eat dinner in the dining room each evening so we could have some quiet family time without everyone around in the kitchen.

We all considered Leo to be part of the family, and he joined us regularly. He occasionally dined in the kitchen with his friends, or down at the dining hall with his mates—his secret tribe. I had become accustomed to our elaborate surroundings, and was now comfortable within its embrace. It felt like home—my home—a place where I was surrounded by my beautiful family and nurtured and protected within its walls.

I turned the page of the bedtime story I was reading to Thomas and Emmy when I felt a tear come to my eye. They were both cuddled into their father, fresh from their bath and smelling sweet—their bodies still, their mouths silent as they lay on the big, four-poster bed in the bedchamber they had chosen to share. I couldn't help but lean over and kiss them both as I saw their eyes starting to close. Once they were both snoring softly, Aaron carefully untangled himself and we tucked them in.

They had insisted on continuing to share a room, so for now we had put them in a large bedchamber off the nursery. I believed they would naturally want their own privacy as they matured. They were both doing extremely well at school and loved going there every day to be with their friends. As many of the children living at Willow Grove were born around the same time as they were, or in the years following, the school was full.

Mrs McGinty managed her students with a firm hand and an efficiency I admired. I found her stern, but fair, and had never experienced any issues with her, although other parents did. I had been called to the school numerous times to mediate between an angry parent and a just as furious headmistress—a headmistress who was stubborn and set in her ways, never backing down or giving an inch. Although the woman intimidated me a little, and she made my life particularly difficult at times, I was thrilled with the standard of education she was providing our children, which far outweighed the problems she sometimes created. My friend, Janet Russell, had reassured me she was a lovely woman underneath her hard exterior, and I trusted her judgement.

As I looked down at my sleeping babies, both growing up so fast, I thought again about Aaron's suggestion that we have another child. I was grateful for what I had been given and was uncertain if I was ready to change a thing. Aaron reached over and extinguished the kerosene lamp before leading me back to our own bedchamber, my hand tightly in his.

'I feel like we spent most of the day in here.' Seated at my dressing table, I gazed at my reflection in the gilt-edged looking glass for a moment as I ran the brush through my hair.

'We did. Our quick lunch in here turned into a never endin' feast.' I pretended to throw the brush at him as he undressed before I stood and went to his side. He stood in front of me, naked and grinning widely. 'See, ya can't keep away from me. You're mad for it, ya horny little root rat. I can't even undress without findin' ya next to me wantin' to touch me all over me special places.' His eyes twinkled as he reached out and grabbed my hands, forcing me to stroke his chest.

'Aaron, stop talking like Leo, you smug shite. All I need is for you to undo the back of my dress for me. Just because I go and stand next to you doesn't mean I'm trying to grope you or have sex with you. You have to stop saying this rubbish to anyone who'll listen, especially down at the stables. Every time I visit you there, you embarrass me with similar comments in front of everyone,' I snapped, turning my back to him.

'Well, they're all jealous 'cause ya can't keep ya hands off me an' sneak me away durin' the day to have ya way with me.'

'Stop turning it around.' I smacked him hard on the arm, his laughter filling the room. 'When I come to see you, it's because I need to speak to you about something important. You're the one who just picks me up without warning in front of everyone and takes me off to bed. Stop bragging about our sex life. You're making me feel like the blokes here know what I look like without my clothes on, and I don't appreciate it.' I turned around again, and he started to unbutton my dress—slowly and painstakingly due to his sausage-like fingers taking so long to undo each button. I waited patiently until he finished, all the while kissing the back of my neck and sending chills through me, easing my irritation only slightly. I slid out of my dress and into a negligee before getting under the covers, then cuddled into him and placed my head on his chest. 'I hope Dana is warm and safe tonight.' I had spoken aloud without realising as I thought of my poor friend, and quickly wiped away a tear that threatened to spill down my cheek. Aaron squeezed my shoulder.

'She's a strong woman an' will come through this.' A sympathetic smile spread across his face, although sadness touched his eyes. 'It may harden her, or it could break her, but I doubt it. She's been through more than most in her lifetime, an' she still keeps on fightin'. I have faith in her, as should you. Despite bein' a lady, I've every confidence she'll be able to defend an' protect herself while she's servin' her time. It wouldn't surprise me if she's runnin' the joint within a day of arrivin'. It's only three-weeks before sentencin', an' she may get off with a shorter term than expected.' I burst into tears, the emotions I had been keeping in check overwhelming me. I had tried to go about my business as if everything was normal after returning from court, but I could hold them in no longer. I sobbed, my body trembling, while Aaron stroked my back and played with my hair, holding me gently as he waited for the storm to subside. He wisely decided there was no more talking to be done, knowing mere words would not comfort me.

After minutes turned into an hour, he slowly pulled me on top of him. I lay across his solid body and absorbed his warmth as he kissed me deeply, slipping my negligee over my head. Much later as I lay in his arms, I stared out at the night sky for the longest time before drifting off to sleep—the stars glimmering like diamonds on black velvet—while dreams of a shipping company, a man named Simon, and a magpie filled my head and tormenting me well into the night.

Chapter Ten

THIS MORNING I PLANNED to visit Dana to ensure her first night in custody passed without incident, and more importantly, she was safe. I kissed Aaron goodbye before he lifted me into the carriage and waved me off, leaving me in silence, lost in my own thoughts, until I arrived at Myers Street in Geelong where the gaol stood.

Harry helped me down, my imagination running wild with terrible scenarios of what could have happened to my dear friend over the last twenty-four-hours. He smiled sympathetically before climbing back up onto his seat to await my return. I ascended the stairs, my head held high, before striding purposefully into the courthouse. I was asked at the front desk by a stern-faced officer what my business was, so I told him as concisely as possible. He glanced at me with some sympathy, but not a great deal of it, before shaking his head.

'I'm sorry, luv, but you'll have to write ya details on this form an' be approved by the Governor before we can let ya see ya friend,' he informed me politely.

I took a step back from the desk and grunted. I couldn't believe he wouldn't let me see her, especially when I knew for a fact they were holding her in the cells here. I filled out the form with a shaking hand, trying with all my strength to suppress my fury, then handed it to him, advising I would return tomorrow. He took the paper, nodded his head in dismissal, and placed it on top of a pile of other applications before attending to the person behind me. I turned on my heel and marched outside, so enraged I felt like hitting something—or someone. I burst into tears as soon as Harry shut the carriage door, sobbing the entire way to Catherine's shop. Answering the door herself, she only had to take one look at me before I collapsed into her arms and told her of Dana's terrible situation.

'There, there, Abigail. I'm sure it will be all right in the end,' she reassured me. She led me by the hand upstairs to her apartment, asking her housekeeper to bring tea and refreshments to the sitting room as we hurried past her. We made ourselves comfortable on the lounge side by side while she wiped my face with a handkerchief. 'I cannot believe Dana is behind bars.' She shook her head in disbelief and I nodded in agreement. Colin soon joined us, appearing extremely happy until she told him what had occurred. He placed his arm lovingly around her as she smiled up at him before fixing her attention back on me. 'There is something we need to tell you, and I do hope you are happy about it. I'm with child.' Tears filled her eyes as I turned and hugged her tightly, enthusiastically congratulating them both, Dana fading from my mind for a brief moment.

'What are you going to do about your family? I mean, you can't hide the bairn along with Colin in the cupboard when they come to visit,' I pointed out, my mouth twitching.

'We're taking the train to Melbourne to tell them next week, and if they don't approve, or they disown me, it's on their heads, and clearly not anything I can control.' She was full of bravado, but I knew deep down it would kill her to be estranged from her family, and although she hoped for their blessing, she did not expect it.

'How do you feel about becoming a Da, Colin?' He didn't seem concerned about facing her family, and the grin that hasn't left his face since he walked in was answer enough.

'Aye, I'm as happy as a puppy with two tails, I am, Abigail. If me darlin' Catherine is satisfied with all in her world, so am I.' I smiled while studying his bright red hair, wondering if their child would favour him over my sweet, very English blonde friend. 'I'm a qualified tailor now, as ye know, an' a professional man. Mr Montague is also a tailor, an' no different tae me. Och, except he's had decades longer tae become renowned in his field o' expertise. I've also started designin' the men's clothin' I'm producin' an' will one day be just as well known. The man's human, an' naw better or worse than me, aye Abigail?' His eyes twinkled in amusement as I smiled again. 'I'll try an' impress her kin an' prove I can support Catherine an' the bairn, but from what I know aboot 'em, it'll be as easy as spearin' an eel with a spoon. I'm tryin' tae stay focused on the most important issue here. We're havin' a wean o' our own just like ye an' Aaron, an' I still cannae believe it.'

Joy resonated from every part of him—his arm still wrapped protectively around Catherine, the mother of his unborn child. She was the happiest I had ever seen her, and I was beyond thrilled for them.

'I completely agree with you, Colin.' I smiled across at him, his eyes sparkling. 'The most important thing is you're both happy and excited about the little family you're creating all of your own. Damn anyone else who thinks otherwise. Send them all to Coventry, I say,' I bellowed loudly to no one in particular, and they threw back their heads and laughed, Catherine's melodious giggles filling my ears and easing my heart.

I reclined on my favourite chair in the sitting room, the room cosy and warm thanks to the fire burning brightly in the hearth, the day grey and cold, just like my mood. I felt melancholy and miserable beyond belief, but could do nothing to lift myself from this pit of sadness that now consumed me. I brushed away stray tears that refused to stop with the back of my hand when Hamish walked in. I sat up quickly, thinking something was wrong as he sat down opposite me and leaned forward, his elbows resting comfortably on his knees.

'Sorry, Abigail. I did naw mean tae disturb ye. Leo said ye were in here an' naw feelin' up tae visitors, but I came tae see if Aaron was around. I apologise if I upset ye.'

'No, it's fine. I'm not upset with you, just feeling down about Dana.' I sat up and explained what had happened earlier this morning.

'Aye, I know Dana despises me, but I would naw wish what she's goin' through on me worst enemy. I'm sorry fer it, Abigail, an' I'm sorry how upset ye are by it all. Yer a kind an' decent friend tae her, an' I have naw doubt will remain so, despite the fact she'll be an outcast within her own circle when she's released.' I turned my head abruptly and glared at him, his face starting to flush.

'Why should she be ostracised when she is being punished already?' I snapped, feeling extremely upset for her and offended by their ignorance. 'I'm so thankful I never became involved with these superficial, elitist, shitty, shit people of high breeding. High breeding, my big, fat, hairy arse. If you were raised right, Hamish, you would have been taught to value and treat people with compassion and empathy in all your dealings, and wouldn't partake in judging or condemning those around you for the smallest sins or transgression. I hate all that bullshit, and I thought you did, too.'

'Aye, I do, Abigail. I'm just tellin' ye what'll happen an' how she'll be treated when it's over. I'm naw sayin' 'tis right at all, so ease up.' I took several deep breaths, trying to compose myself. I knew deep down none of it was his fault, but felt so devastated by the unfairness of it all my heart physically ached.

'If you've come to see Aaron, you've just missed him. He finished lunch and went down to the stables not a quarter of an hour before you showed up.' The words had only left my lips when I burst into a flood of tears I could no longer hold back. He moved to my side and quickly took my hand in his, attempting to console me. I was immediately overwhelmed with a sensation of hot pins running up my arm and releasing warmth into every part of my body, causing me to tingle all over. An awkward silence hung over the room as he stared into my eyes, a lump in my throat I was unable to dislodge. Without warning, he pulled me in close, placing his mouth on mine before I could pull away, his tongue forcing my lips apart. I tried to push him off, despite all the old feelings I held for him rushing in and overwhelming me, but he was far too strong. For a brief moment, I kissed him back before my sensibilities returned, then violently shoved him away, raising my voice. 'Stop! Stop it now! This is not right. Not for you. Not for me. And certainly not for Aaron. He is my husband, and your best friend, and he doesn't deserve this.' My body shook as I struggled unsteadily to my feet to get away from him, my legs wobbling no different to the desserts Leo liked to make with gelatin. I felt sick to my stomach as I quickly moved to the opposite chair, trying to regain my composure but failing miserably. He glanced across at me in silence, appearing shamefaced as he averted his gaze, then stared out the window over the back garden.

'Aye, yer right. I should naw have kissed ye, an' I'm sorry fer it. I only wanted tae comfort ye by holdin' yer hand, but when I touched ye, I could naw stop meself goin' further.' I could hear the anguish in his voice and felt the pain deep within his heart, while feeling deep regret in my own. 'Are ye goin' tae tell him what passed between us?'

'I don't know. Yes. Maybe. Oh, I'm not sure. I think I'll have to, but I must take some time to think. Hamish, promise me now you will never touch me for any reason. I don't want this to ever happen again. What we just did betrayed everything I have with Aaron. Now I will have to find a way to earn back his trust before I even confess to the poor man I've played him false, and he realises what a filthy whore I am.' I sobbed softly, unable to stop the tears pouring down my face or comfort myself, while he remained where he was, his hands clenched into fists by his side.

'Again, I'm deeply sorry, Abigail. I did naw plan it, an' regret me actions more than ye'll ever know. I promise I'll naw touch ye again.' His voice low, he was visibly upset as he rose to his feet. He strode across the room and stepped out into the hallway without another word. I remained where I was, my head lowered as I continued to cry—so deeply ashamed of myself, while wondering how I would explain my actions to my beloved husband. He trusted me beyond measure, and would soon realise what a fool he truly was. His friendship with Hamish—the bond they shared close and their connection deep—would be irretrievably damaged all because of me. I needed to eat, if only to think clearly, and I struggled to my feet, any strength I had now gone. I made my way to the kitchen and silently crossed the room, lowering myself into a chair before sighing deeply. Leo hurried over and placed his hand on my shoulder.

'Hamish left in a hurry. Did you two engage in a bit of argy-bargy?' His face broke into a large grin, but I didn't smile back.

'No. I think he was just busy. He came to see Aaron, not me.' I averted my gaze, my face flushed as he gazed down at me suspiciously, but said no more. I picked up a fork and started to eat a slice of toffee tart he placed down in front of me, adding a large dollop of heavy cream. I stared out the window while the staff bustled around, lost in my own thoughts, when shouting drifted into the room from outside. The workers stopped one by one to listen, the usually noisy kitchen now silent, some straining their ears near the back door to hear what all the excitement was about. Leo rushed out the kitchen then hurried through the back door before picking up his speed and prancing down towards the stable yard. I followed behind, my heart in my throat, their voices filling my ears before they came into view at the end of the garden. I approached slowly, unable to take my eyes from an enraged Aaron, who stood nose to nose with Hamish, who appeared equally furious. I watched and listened from a distance, dreading what I was about to witness, while Leo stood within a few feet of them, unable to contain his excitement.

'Ya havin' a fuckin' lend of me, ya mug. How dare ya touch even a hair on me wife's head, let alone have a crack at her when me backs turned?' I jumped in fright as Aaron pulled back his enormous arm, then brought his fist down hard, striking Hamish in the face and knocking him backwards. He stumbled, although he remained on his feet, then stopped several feet away near the stable door, his large frame bent over, his hands on his thighs, while blood poured out of his nose and onto the gravel, a large, red stain starting to form. A number of farm workers and stable hands had stopped what they were doing to come over, seeming to enjoy the performance these former mates had decided to put on for all and sundry without shame or embarrassment.

'She was mine, an' ye stole her away. Ye cheated me,' Hamish roared before charging at him, landing a hard punch to Aaron's eye, causing the skin near the corner to split, spilling blood down his face.

'You've been waitin' in the background for years for ya chance to have a crack at Abi, an' today ya choose to take it? Or have ya had a go before this, ya cunnin' mongrel?' Aaron bellowed before running towards him, his shoulder low as he connected with his stomach, causing Hamish to grunt then double over before Aaron tackled him to the ground where they rolled around, punching each other and shouting obscenities.

Angus wasn't laughing for once, while Harry appeared shocked as they stood side by side observing their two mates beat the living daylights out of each other without warning or reason. More workers had strolled over to see what the fuss was about while behaving as if they had never witnessed an argument, although I conceded this was particularly nasty and the rarity of it was in itself intriguing. No one intervened, letting them struggle with each other in the dirt while continuing to shout and curse. Humiliation overwhelmed me as I listened to them yell private details about me for everyone to hear.

It wasn't common knowledge that Hamish and I had been courting when I arrived in Australia. Most of the workers at Willow Grove were of the belief I had only been with Aaron since the day I arrived given his betrothal to me had been common knowledge throughout the district for fifteen-years. It was no one's business other than ours, and the fact that these two idiots were revealing our private life to the world infuriated me.

'Oh, what a shemozzle. It's so exciting, I could wee my pants right here where I stand,' Leo squealed, jumping up and down beside me, while Aaron and Hamish lay on the ground still scuffling and cursing, shouting terrible threats to each other. 'I just want to scream, fight, fight, fight, and clap my hands for the winner before giving him a big, congratulatory embrace. And from what I just heard, you mad rooter, you're the one who caused this delightful dance of argy-bargy between them. It doesn't appear either is winning at this stage. It's punch for punch.' I turned and glared at him as he clapped excitedly while Aaron and Hamish continued to roll around in the dirt, their clothing soiled and torn.

'Stop saying argy-bargy, you fat-headed moron,' I snapped as he continued on, my words falling on deaf ears.

'They're just so enormous when you compare them to the mere mortals among us. I'm surprised they aren't doing more damage than they are. If that was me down there,' he remarked, pointing to them only several feet away as they struggled—behaving as if we were at the circus observing the unfortunate souls they displayed in their sideshows—before continuing with his commentary. 'All my bones would be broken by now.' He arched his eyebrow then shrieked as they grunted, roared and spat, both drenched in sweat, landing blow after blow; seemingly without much damage as he had so helpfully pointed out. 'Abigail, it's clear you are a wonderful teacher and role model. They have both committed your favourite words to memory, and you must be proud they use them with such enthusiasm and precision right at the perfect moment. Ooooh, I have never seen two men as strong, or as handsome, rolling around together on the ground. It's giving me tingles in my belly and makes me feel warm and delicious all over, like a sunrise. I'm so excited and I just can't hide it.'

'Oh, be quiet,' I snapped, glaring at him before I reached over and shoved him. He stumbled back but soon regained his balance as I bent down, glaring at the two morons rolling around at my feet. 'For Christ's own sake, fuckin' stop! As far as I'm concerned, you can stay out here and drink with the flies. Jesus, Mary, and fuckin' Joseph save me.' Leo gasped, raising his eyes to the sky and muttering a prayer on my behalf, while clasping his hands together and closing his eyes for a moment in quiet contemplation. I'd had enough of them making a spectacle of themselves—and me—yelling our private business out over the property for the entire district to hear. More farm hands had gathered around the stable-yard to watch and, more importantly, listen—I was certain, committing every word to memory to discuss with their mates down the pub at their leisure and for everyone's enjoyment but mine.

I stepped around them and hurried away, quickly bending down to pick up a silver pail full of water that had been discarded at the stable door. I marched back and without hesitation or guilt, dumped the entire contents over them. They continued to wrestle for a short time before seeing sense and rolling apart, appearing vague and confused while struggling to sit up, only then realising they were soaking wet. They sat on their backsides, their legs splayed out in front, only a few feet separating them, while slowly and silently assessing their injuries while catching their breath. They glared at each other, the awkward silence hanging heavily around us only broken by their loud panting and the occasional grunt.

'Dickheads,' I hissed before throwing the empty bucket in their direction, unfortunately missing them both by a country mile. I turned abruptly on my heel and headed towards the house, leaving them in the dirt and feeling quite satisfied in doing so. Leo followed close behind, peppering me with questions I chose not to answer. Many of our house staff walked beside us, hurrying back to work after witnessing such excitement.

'Did Hamish touch your special places? What happened, Abigail? You know I don't like secrets when these secrets are being kept secret from me.' I shrugged him off as he drew up alongside me, wishing the ground would open up and swallow me whole rather than be subject to such intense scrutiny from every man and his dog. 'What did you do? Did you grab Hamish's tallywacker? I knew you wouldn't be able to control the lust you have for him forever. It pumps through every part of you when he's near, but surely even you have some self-control. Even I would not touch anyone without consent, and here you are attacking my poor Adonis the first chance you get. Someone kissed someone, I do know that, but the who, why, when, and what of it escapes me. Tell me every detail, Abigail. Abigail?' I pushed him away violently as I stepped inside the backdoor, his shrieks piercing my ears. He was a determined little shit, though, and followed me into the kitchen. 'You have to tell me your secrets. You promised. I'll go insane and end up at Ararat before you. You must tell me!'

I ignored him and sat down at the kitchen table, trying in vain to gather my thoughts. Within moments, Aaron appeared at the door, angrier than I had ever seen him.

'I wanna see ya in the sittin' room. Now!' he roared. I cringed, but stood and silently followed him. Leo watched on sympathetically, unsurprisingly making no offer to come with me for support or protection, although I knew his ear would be on the door as soon as it closed. I followed Aaron into the room to find Hamish already seated, a cloth held to his swollen nose, now obviously broken. Their knuckles were bloodied and bruised, while they had both sustained cuts and scrapes to their arms, legs and torsos from the gravel. The physical blows they were quick to hand out, but not so willing to receive, had mostly hit their mark. Aaron didn't look much better than his sparring partner, sustaining a deep cut near one eye and long, red scratches on his neck.

I lowered myself onto a chair opposite Hamish, while Aaron sat down beside me, although he didn't touch me. The golden glow surrounding him was tinged with red, frightening me a little, as he stared across unwaveringly from his seat at Hamish, his head in his hands while avoiding Aaron's gaze.

'I warn ya now, mate. Don't piss in me pocket an' try to convince me it's rainin'. I want the dead-set truth of what passed between ya, or I'll beat the livin' shit out of ya where ya sit.' His voice low, his tone threatening, Hamish slowly raised his head and met Aaron's stare, guilt mixed with regret clear in his brown eyes.

'It's naw Abigail's fault. I offered her comfort regardin' her distress over Dana, an' I shouldn't have.' He swallowed hard before continuing, his voice barely audible. 'When she started tae weep, I reached fer her hand as a friend with naw intention o' anythin' more—of that I give ye me word, mate.' Aaron remained silent, only nodding his head slightly for him to continue. 'When I touched her, thoughts o' the times we spent together before ye came along filled me mind. 'Twas me that forced her in tae me arms, an' me that kissed her with force. I could naw help meself, an' I know there's naw excuse fer it. Abigail pushed me away, an' I came tae ye straight away with it. I'm sorry fer hurtin' ye, mate. Yer like a brother tae me, an' I dinnae want tae lose the friendship between us. I value it very much.' Aaron held his gaze, neither blinking for the longest time.

'Do ya have any plans to take another crack in the future when I'm not lookin'?'

'Naw, I give ye me word. I'll even go so far as tae promise I'll naw touch her again. Not even a bloody handshake.' Aaron remained silent and unmoving as the minutes ticked away, the clock on the mantel unusually loud. He hadn't yet spoken to me, or even acknowledged my presence as I studied him apprehensively. Finally, he leaned forward in his chair then gracefully rose to his feet.

'I'll take ya at ya word. For now. I've never known ya to lie to me yet. Come back tomorrow an' help me finish off the south paddock.' Hamish looked up at him in surprise before his expression turned to one of relief. He too rose to his feet, offering Aaron his damaged hand. Aaron leaned in to him before taking it in his own steely grip. 'But touch me wife again an' I'll do ya damage. I *will* kill ya if you're that much of a prick an' insist on a next time.' He escorted Hamish out while I sat back and waited, knowing it would soon be my turn. Shortly after, he returned and made himself comfortable opposite me. He leaned back in his chair as I squirmed under his glare, the silence almost deafening. 'He forced ya, ya said?' I could barely hear him, but nodded slightly, my body numb and my thoughts fragmented. He fixed his bright blue eyes on mine, giving nothing away. 'I only have one question for ya, Abigail. Did ya kiss him back?'

Aaron had stormed back to work, leaving me alone and crying. I had tried so hard to explain my lapse, but he wouldn't hear it and left in a rage, but not before throwing a vase against the wall, shattering it into a million pieces.

Leo had come to my side soon after witnessing him rage through the kitchen and out the back door, slamming it behind him with such great force, it now hung from the one remaining hinge. He had slipped his arm around me and remained silent as I told him everything that had passed between Hamish and I, no more than an hour before. He tried to comfort me, murmuring softly while kissing my cheek and stroking my head as I sobbed in his arms.

'Oh, don't even give it another thought.' He smiled down at me as I continued to cry, unable to stop no matter how hard I tried. 'Now who's being the big fairy? Mistress Aaron, I do believe. He needs to kick off his high heels, strip off his ball gown and harden the hell up. Be a man, as the Australians say. It was only a kiss, no different from this.' He leaned down and gently kissed me on the cheek before straightening up, leaning back against the couch, my head in his lap. 'Was there even a tongue involved? Yours or his? Oh, dear, of course there would have been. I clearly recall the horror of being forced to watch you together in steerage night after night—embarrassing for all of us still to this day. I stand by my opinion of you heteros. The way you lot flaunt your lifestyle and push your views and morals onto us normal humans, of whom,, I must remind all who will listen, suffer in silence living alongside you. This fact alone should cause you all to hang your heads in shame.' He sighed dramatically, a weak smile touching my lips. 'I don't blame you for it, Abigail, not for a minute. I truly believe you were born this way. Like you always say, you can't choose who you love.' I giggled softly before he became serious, a rare occurrence. 'Aaron will calm down, no doubt, once the dust settles. I do have to say I've never seen him so angry. I almost feared for my life as he bore down on me in the kitchen like an enormous blonde bull.' He widened his eyes, exaggerating as usual. 'The men around here can't seem to keep their hands off you, causing me to concede you do indeed have a pot of gold at the end of your lady garden.' Leo threw back his head and laughed loudly, trying without success to make me smile when all I wanted to do was crawl into a hole and stay there forever.

I met the children on their way home from school, stopping in the garden to play ball until Leo called us in for dinner. Aaron still wasn't home, so we followed Leo to the dining room and sat together down one end, the table far too large for four people. Mr Masters and the footmen served us in silence, the only sound a lonely seagull foraging in the garden bed just outside the window. Thomas and Emmy filled their plates while Leo looked on proudly, then did the same. I raised a spoonful of soup to my lips, pausing as I caught sight of the twins staring back at me, both refusing to start their dinner.

'Where's Daddy? We never eat without the old bloke,' Thomas complained, his eyes filled with concern as I tried to smile at him.

'He has some work to finish off. He'll be home soon enough, my angels.' I forced a smile, watching as they slowly picked up their cutlery and began to eat. I didn't want to alarm them, but I had not the faintest clue where he could be. Leo and I chatted with them about their day, hearing several times just how much they enjoyed school and loved their friends. No matter how hard I tried to keep my mind focused on them, my thoughts inevitably wandered off to

Aaron. He was the last person in the world I would ever hurt on purpose, the guilt I carried so heavy I wanted to burst into tears again. I knew I hadn't explained adequately that, although I loved Hamish, I was in love with him and adored only him. He was my life, along with our children, and I would never risk my marriage by betraying him. I couldn't even explain to myself why I kissed Hamish back when I didn't desire him, nor did I think of him in that way any longer.

I ate my dessert in silence as Leo entertained the twins with stories of his travels around the world, making them giggle. After dinner, I accompanied them to the nursery and prepared their baths. I always used the same products on Emmy's hair as I used on my own, giving her a head massage while Thomas relaxed in his own bath in the empty bedchamber across the hall.

'Mummy?' I brushed the softening treatment through her long, thick hair that hung around her in loose waves to her waist, before nodding slightly.

'Yes, beautiful girl?' I smiled down at her while gently washing her body with a large sea sponge I had acquired from Amelia's shop.

'I heard Christopher's dad say to Mary's dad after school today that you are the prettiest lady they have ever seen,' she announced proudly as I gently rinsed her hair with fresh water.

'Well, Emmy, that means you are the prettiest little girl, as everyone says you look exactly like me. Always remember that it is your heart and soul that are important, not your outer beauty. Treat people with kindness and compassion, remembering we all bleed the same colour. Every single person you will ever encounter deserves love and respect, with a big handful of kindness thrown in for good measure.' She giggled as I wrapped her hair in a towel, then helped her out of the bath before wrapping another large, fluffy towel around her. 'Now, I've laid out your nightgown on the bed. You dry yourself off and get into it while I go and see to your brother.' I hurried to the bedchamber next door that would eventually be used by Thomas, once they finally decided it was time to sleep apart, and entered the bathroom without knocking.

'Ma, what the bloody hell are ya doin'?' he yelled, quickly covering his private parts with a washcloth. I stood my ground in the doorway, averting my gaze to the mirror where I checked my hair then dug into my pocket and took out a jar of gloss, applying a thin coat to my lips.

'I'm sorry, my darling boy. I was only coming in to wash your hair and help you.' I smothered a smile as he raised his arm and ordered me out of the room. I stood outside with the door slightly ajar so he could hear me, although I could no longer see him. 'What's wrong with you, anyway? I bathe you every night and you've never complained once.' After some time, I heard him sit up in the bath and curse under his breath.

'I heard me mates talkin' today, an' they said we're all too old to bathe with our brothers an' sisters, an' far too mature to have any help from our oldies,' he called out, pausing for a moment. 'I was too ashamed to tell anyone ya still wash me hair for me. If I confessed ya helped me into me nightclothes, they'd take the piss outta me till me old bones rest in the soil of Willow Grove, let me give ya the drum.' I raised my hand and covered my mouth, laughter threatening to spill out of me. He was the spit of his father, becoming more like him with each passing day. 'Anyway, Ma. I told a furphy an' pretended I bathe meself. I know Bessie believes the deceitful liars livin' among us'll be struck by lightenin', but I don't believe so if ya only doin' it to protect ya pride an' reputation.' I choked on my own saliva, coughing and spluttering as he waited impatiently for me to compose myself. 'I love ya from ya head to ya feet, Mummy, but I don't want ya comin' in the washroom anymore an' invadin' me privacy. Ya have to accept I'm growin' up, an' I'll have hair on me balls soon enough. You're a mother—an' ya try so hard to be a lady—an' ladies aren't allowed to see anyone's tally whacker, includin' mine.' He went quiet for a moment, the water splashing noisily against the cast iron tub as I bent over holding my stomach, my body shaking silently. 'Well, they can look at their husband's old fella sometimes, but that's it. I was told today, if ladies see a one eyed snake belongin' to anyone else, they faint to death where they stand. Good luck explainin' that one to Mr Neilson when he comes callin'.' I erupted into loud giggles, collapsing onto the ground near the door, unable to quieten my hysterical howls. How he even knew the name of the local undertaker, I couldn't even begin to guess, nor did I want to. It took some time before he spoke again. 'I don't wanna cause ya to fall down unconscious. Ya could wack ya head an' be on ya way to meet the heavenly father before ya can count to three, or be injured an' sufferin' forever. It's sensible to stay away when ya know I'll be in the nuddy.' I inhaled deeply through my nose, willing my voice to remain even.

'I thought you liked me washing your hair.' He was silent again for the longest time.

'I do. That's the bloody problem. I don't like this growin' up thing, Mummy. Ya have to do more an' more for yourself every day, an' it's hard work I don't need at me tender age,' he complained. I abruptly clamped my hand across my mouth again so he wouldn't hear my laughter.

'All right, then. I'll bring your nightwear to you in here so you have your privacy, and so I can prove to you I'm sensible.' I got out just in time, running from the room without waiting for his response before bursting into fits of hysterical laughter on the nursery floor. Emmy heard me and came to her bedchamber door.

'What's so funny? What did Thomas do now?' She rolled her eyes, only making me laugh harder.

'You will have to ask him. I have no doubt he will be more than willing to tell you all about it.' I pulled myself together and struggled to my feet then went and placed his pyjamas on the bed before closing the door behind me. Emmy and I sat together in the nursery, our heads close as she showed me several pictures she had drawn at school, going on to hand me a short story she had written on the handmade paper produced by one of our maids. She read aloud, telling me of the adventures partaken by the bunyip she believed lived in the lake here at Willow Grove, then collapsing onto my lap in giggles when he tripped and fell into the water. Soon after, Thomas joined us, proud as a peacock he had bathed independently and would no longer have to lie to his mates—or dodge any lightning that may strike nearby.

We went to their bedchamber, and they climbed up under the covers before I slipped in between them with my book. I had introduced them to *The Secret of the Australian Desert* by Ernest Favenc, and they seemed to be thoroughly enjoying every page. I had purchased so many books written by Australian authors since I arrived in Geelong, I was filling my library and office at an alarming rate.

My children had inherited my love for the written word and, although they adored the stories their father told them in the mornings, they also loved when I would lie with them at night and read to them as they drifted off to sleep. I cuddled between them, the story coming alive as my voice rose and fell dramatically, and within half-an-hour they both snored softly beside me. I gingerly got up after kissing their cheeks and tucking the quilt around them, while finding it adorable they still slept together holding hands.

I closed their bedchamber door and walked through the nursery, tidying up as I went. Little Mary no longer slept in the children's wing. She stayed in her own room each night now that they were older and could come to my room if they needed us during the night. I went to our bedchamber to see if Aaron had returned, finding Bessie waiting for me instead.

'Mistress, what's wrong?' She hurried to my side, stopping abruptly then raising her hand to stroke my cheek.

'I don't even know where I would begin if I could speak of it.' I shook my head as she led me across the room, guiding me to the dressing table before pushing me down into the seat and undoing my hair, pin by pin. She stood behind me, staring at my reflection in the looking glass as she brushed my hair for the longest time. I told her what I could of what had passed between Hamish and I—and of Aaron's reaction.

'Oh, I always told you that splitting your heart between those two boys would end in tears. I know you consider Hamish a close friend, but it's as plain as the nose on your face he still loves you. Oh, he tries to hide it, and hide it well he does for the most part, but nought stays hidden from me. You did nothing wrong, and I have no doubt Mr Aaron will calm quickly enough. He doesn't stay angry for long, especially with you. Now, stand up and I will get you into a fresh nightgown.' I obeyed immediately, wiping my eyes with the hem of my dress before she helped me into my nightgown. I climbed up onto the bed, sighing deeply before she sat down next to me and took my hand in hers.

'Goodnight, Bessie. Thank you.'

'Thank you for what?' Confusion crossed her lovely face for a moment.

'For not judging me or being cross.' She patted my hand before kissing me goodnight—tucking me in tightly before she crossed the room and silently closed the door behind her.

Time passed. I tossed and turned, unable to sleep, my thoughts tormenting me. I was worried when he stormed out hours ago, but had become increasingly concerned with each passing minute. Aaron could be down at the pub drowning his sorrows, or he may have gone to stay with his parents to get away from me. Wherever he was, I felt sick to my stomach and lying here wondering hadn't eased my mind at all.

I struggled out of bed and quickly crossed the room, stepping inside my wardrobe as I mumbled to myself. I slipped a housedress over my nightgown, carelessly throwing my long woollen cloak over that, then made my way to the stables where I saddled Delly as quickly as I could. I mounted ungracefully before slowly guiding her down to the village, not wanting to alert anyone of the trouble between Aaron and me. She knew her way despite the darkness of the night, her footing steady and sure, delivering me to the pub safely. I tethered her to the post near the water trough and climbed the stairs, pushing open the door to the busy pub, the music filling my ears. It had become a meeting place for the single men and women in the district, and a number of marriages had occurred as a result.

I scoured the room for Aaron, but he was nowhere to be seen. He was hard to miss, standing a full head above most others. I noticed Bessie and Danny seated at a nearby table, and hurried over to them. Bessie appeared surprised, but nonetheless, greeted me warmly before offering me a seat.

'What are you doing up and out of bed? I only put you there five-minutes ago,' she remarked, narrowing her gaze at me.

'I'm looking for Aaron. Have you seen him?' I asked, starting to feel desperate.

'Aye, he was in earlier, bought a bottle o' whisky, an' rode off on Goliath. I thought he shot through for home,' Danny replied, his tone apologetic. It was at that moment I knew. I thanked him, then kissed them both before quickly hurrying out onto the street and mounting Delly, who patiently waited where I left her.

I rode across the paddocks toward the coast, tasting the salt air as we cantered through the dark. The above sky was hazy, the moon shrouded in heavy clouds, the chill in the air leaving me grateful I had remembered to don my thick cloak, the soft mink lining the hood only adding to the warmth it provided.

I arrived at the cottage, relieved to find Goliath grazing outside and smoke billowing from the chimneys. I dismounted and tethered Delly before turning on my heel and slowly making my way to the front door, my heart in my throat. I turned the handle, the door unlocked, before pushing it wide and stepping inside the cosy sitting room. I found him at our table overlooking the ocean just outside the kitchen door, half a bottle of whisky in front of him. He didn't move, although I knew he had heard me come in. I sat down next to him then reached across and picked up the bottle, raising the green vessel to my lips and taking a long swig before screwing up my face. The potent liquid burned like fire as it made its way down my throat then settled in the pit of my stomach, warming me from the inside. He didn't look surprised to see me and poured himself another drink, his eyes fixed unblinking on the dark ocean below.

'Do ya still love him, Abi?' I turned to him and placed his face between the palms of my hands, my eyes staring into his.

'No. I love you, and you alone. You are my sunshine, and I adore you. I can't change what happened, but it's a moment in time I will regret forever. I'm deeply sorry for it.' Tears streamed down my face, my head lowered in shame, guilt and regret. He raised his glass to his lips, deep in thought before taking another deep drink.

'I understand Hamish, ya know? He's loved ya for a long time an' has stopped himself crossin' the line for years, now. See, I know better than anyone what it's like, Abi—the wantin'—an' the gutwrenchin' need to be with ya. Hamish still feels it no doubt. I understand him like I said, an' can even forgive him 'cause he's like a brother to me. What's killin' me is the thought there's a chance ya still love him an' want him.' His voice broke, and he lowered his head into his hands.

'Aaron, please listen to me. I have not looked at Hamish with anything but friendship the entire time we have been married. I cannot explain what happened today, because I don't understand it myself. For a brief moment, we were back on the ship, and all those old feelings came back. I give you my word, I pulled away within a few moments when your face came to mind.' I sobbed, my head resting on my arms in front of me. 'I promise you, Aaron, it's only you I love,' I murmured through my tears. I looked up and wiped my face, glancing across to find his eyes fixed on mine.

'I love ya too, Abi, but ya bloody well shit me to tears sometimes.' He took me in his arms, kissing me thoroughly before carrying me to bed, the familiar sound of the waves crashing against the shore bringing me much needed comfort I hadn't known I was seeking.

I woke in a strange bed, my thoughts fragmented as I tried to remember where I was. I was comfortable and warm, but by myself, and I didn't recognise the room. Within moments, it all came flooding back to me. I had agreed to spend a few days with Tamara at her new property, Warwillah—an impressive red brick mansion her parents had recently purchased in her name on St Kilda Boulevard—but in all truth, I would have agreed to stay anywhere to get away from the trouble at home. I hadn't brought the children as I didn't want them to miss school, and they would have been expected to stay with Tamara's nannies most of the time, a situation they would have hated and complained about incessantly until I cut short my stay and returned home. I thought it best to leave them in the care of their father given the purpose of my stay was two-fold, and not something I wished to discuss with anyone. I had secretly resolved to pay a visit to Tatiana Starovsky—or Madame Zvezda, as she was known. A seer, or soothsayer, she had given a reading to Dana not long before Charlotte passed. I had never discussed what Dana had relayed to me weeks later, with her or another soul; however, the accuracy of her predictions had haunted me since.

I visited Dana as often as they would let me at the Geelong Gaol where she was awaiting sentencing. Relieved to find she was stoic for the most part while trying every single day to remain fierce and not lose hope, even when hope was nowhere in sight, she was coping far better than expected. She had all the support that Martin could give, along with that of Victoria and our family and friends. Aaron felt I should get away for a few days, to have a break from the stress of the responsibilities that at times lay heavy on me. He knew I would be well-treated at Tamara's due to the sheer number of staff she employed who would cater to my every need, and encouraged me to go. Tamara had been so pleased when I arrived on her doorstep, but was soon asking for word of Hamish. I didn't tell her he had kissed me last week, fearing it would upset her and preferring to keep it between Aaron, Hamish, and myself—along with, of course, the two-dozen workers who had witnessed the entire performance and hadn't stopped talking about it for days.

Hamish and Aaron had gone on as if nothing had happened, but Hamish no longer came to visit me alone during the day, which I suspected Aaron was quietly pleased about. A sharp knock sounded on my door before Tamara came skipping, a plush dressing gown draped over her dainty shoulders. She slipped it off, allowing the gown to fall to the floor before climbing up onto the other side of the bed and making herself comfortable next to me.

'I have ordered our breakfast on trays to have in here. Now, tell me more about what Hamish has been doing while I'm not there.' She threw herself back on the pillows, a silly smile on her face. I rolled my eyes then stared out of the window onto the wide road lined in elms, poplars, planes, and flowering gums. A beautiful thoroughfare into Melbourne and the Botanic Gardens, the elaborate mansions lining the boulevard housed some of the wealthiest and most powerful families in Victoria.

'I don't know, Tamara. I'm not his keeper, or his mother, and I don't keep track of him or pay attention to what he's up to,' I replied a little too sharply. She didn't notice, lost in the romance of this relationship she valued far more than its actual worth to either of them.

'I believe Hamish has fallen madly in love with me. The last time I stayed with you, he actually kissed me properly on several occasions.' Her eyes shone, while I turned over, not wanting to meet her gaze. I was uncomfortable talking about anything to do with Hamish, and politely tried to change the subject three or four times, but failed at every attempt.

Her ladies maid entered the bedchamber, another maid following behind carrying our breakfast trays. We sat up against the pillows as they silently placed them on our laps. All soon departed without uttering a word—precisely how Tamara expected her servants to behave. They would only speak when spoken to and were trained to be as unobtrusive as possible.

'Do you believe he would marry me if I wasn't already married?' she asked as I chewed my toast mindlessly.

'Probably, Tamara,' I replied before sighing deeply, deciding to concentrate on the only thing that would bring me pleasure in this room, my breakfast.

'I couldn't leave Brian, though. Hamish couldn't keep me and the children in this lifestyle, and that would never do. I do have more privacy since Papa purchased Warwillah, although I allow Brian to stay here to ensure no one suspects anything untoward. I hope Hamish will visit and stay here as my guest as I find lately I want to spend all of my time with him. When I'm away from him, all I think about is how handsome he is.' She sighed again and I turned away, sipping my cup of coffee the cook had so thoughtfully made and sent in. I had listened to her politely for long enough. If I stayed in bed any longer, I would say something I would regret.

'I think I'll go down to your library, and browse through some books, if that's all right with you, Tamara?' She rose to her feet, her food barely touched, before slipping on her dressing gown.

'Of course. You know where it is,' she called out over her shoulder before stepping out of the room. Her maid arrived soon after to help me dress and style my hair for the day. She was extremely efficient, yet didn't speak, only politely answering my attempts to converse with a word or two. I found it so very sad, but held my tongue as I gazed at the poor girl in the mirror, noting she wasn't very happy about it, either. To be surrounded by people in your own home and not know anything about them or be unable to stop for a chat or a laugh would leave me feeling so lonely and isolated. Once she had finished with me, she quickly departed.

Downstairs, I wandered through the enormous rooms until I came to what I remembered to be the library. I pushed open the door to find Brian engaged in a sexual act with the butler, oblivious to my presence. I stood stone still, unable to move my feet as my heart began to race. I slowly backed out of the room as if none of it had happened and my mind hadn't been permanently scarred forevermore. Brian turned his head just as I neared the door, his eyes widening while his face darkened to purple within seconds; however, he was clearly unable to stop or hide as the butler concentrated on his task, unaware of my presence. I stepped back and closed the door behind me to let them finish what they had begun before I so rudely intruded.

I cursed under my breath as I hurried down the empty hall. I could not understand why Brian felt the need to fornicate in front of me. Either I had very bad timing, or he engaged in the sins of the flesh a lot and was caught by other people, too. 'Lock the bloody door if you're going to be poking someone's date. That's what keys are for,' I muttered under my breath as I wandered on in search of the library, this time knocking on all the doors and waiting as long as it took to receive a response before entering.

I directed the carriage driver down Flinders Land towards Madame Zvezda's small terrace, leaving firm instructions for him to wait for me out the front. Yesterday, I had sent a message to her with one of Tamara's servants requesting a meeting, and she had agreed to see me at noon, leaving me an hour before my train departed for Geelong.

'Welcome, Mrs Cavanaugh.' Her accent was barely detectable, her face kind I noticed as she swung the door wide. She nodded politely, welcoming me into her home before silently leading me into the parlour. I was startled for a moment as I gazed around the dark room—the heavy, blood-red drapes blocking out all traces of sunlight, while enormous ivory-coloured candles burned in three corners casting a warm shadow over the room. A massive, silver samovar gleamed on a tall cabinet behind a highly polished mahogany table, and although I admired nearly everything in the cluttered room, I was uncertain how most of the items were used given I had never visited or even met a soothsayer before today.

'Thank you.' I smiled across at her as I lowered myself onto the chair at the elaborate wooden table, my back to the door. She took the chair opposite me, studying my face for the longest time while shuffling a deck of oversized cards without looking at any of them. I stared back, noting her short and stocky frame, as one might expect of a Russian peasant. Her steel-grey hair matched the colour of her eyes, unnerving me a little. The woman was undeniably compelling, yet everything about her frightened me.

'Tell me why you've come?' I shifted in my seat before inhaling deeply, taking a moment to organise my thoughts.

'Well,' I swallowed hard several times in an attempt to dislodge the lump in my throat before trying again, 'it all started when I was a wean. I started to notice a golden glow surrounding certain people, then released as I grew older that I was the only one who could see it. Over the years, I've seen other colours—grey, even black—and they have become more common since I left Scotland.

'How do you *feel* when you see such things?' I thought hard for a moment before returning her gaze.

'My emotions range from joy, to distaste, to outright fear, depending on the colour of the aura. I've also noticed my dreams often serve as signposts of things to come, both good and bad. I'm hoping you can help me understand what it all means.'

She said nothing more, lowering her head as she shuffled the cards again while murmuring a silent prayer, to whom I was uncertain, before placing them down one by one on the table in front of her, the intricate drawings and symbols unique to each card laying face up. One card in the centre of the three diagonal rows showed a figure of a skeleton dressed in black robes bearing a scythe, while the nine of swords lay across it. She glanced down and grimaced before discreetly sliding both cards back into the deck and drawing out two more. She studied the images that now lay in front of her for the longest time, causing me to jump when she finally spoke without warning.

'I can see you are pure-hearted but wilful. You are beautiful in spirit, not just in face and form. You have what we call the sight, although for some reason, you are blinded in this lifetime. It appears haphazardly, and often confuses you rather than informs, as it should. What you see is as real as this fat backside of mine I'm sitting on. I want to reinforce for your own peace of mind you have not gone mad. It's not your imagination at work, dear one. You must learn to trust your senses again, to embrace those you are drawn to, and protect yourself from those you are not—especially the dark ones. If you allow it, they can and will do you great harm.' I thought of Leroy and George Maslow, and a shudder ran down my spine. I was about to ask her about both men when she raised her finger to her lips to silence me before continuing. 'The auras you are privileged to see are the visible manifestations of each individual's soul energy. On a deeper level, all souls are part of the universal life force that connects all things. Many of those connections are a result of bonds formed during past lives we have shared—yes, we have lived before and we will again.' She lifted her gaze to mine and nodded once before raising her eyebrows at my apparent confusion. I was unsure if I believed her, but tried to open my mind and leave my Catholic upbringing behind, just as a dear friend once wisely advised me to do. 'Reincarnation is very real, Mrs Cavanaugh. If you can keep that in mind when a soul with an aura only you can see crosses your path, it will help you find understanding, along with connection to spirit, self and all beings within the universe, while providing the peace you so desperately seek in this lifetime.' Feeling disturbed by the cards she had dealt earlier, then hidden from my sight. I told her of my concerns, my stomach in knots at the thought that someone I loved may be at great risk.

'I apologise for my ignorance when it comes to matters like these,' I said, her eyes lighting up and a smile touching her lips.

'There's no need to apologise, Mrs Cavanaugh. When we don't ask, we will never know.' She smiled across at me reassuringly before settling back and closing her eyes for a moment. 'I'm uncertain what my spirit guides were trying to tell me, in all honesty. I sensed whatever it was, it did not relate to your immediate family—you, your husband, or your children, but there is a tall, dark man outside of those you hold dear influencing the direction your life will take. I cannot see much more and feel he is somehow blocking me, as silly as it sounds. The outcome seems to depend on him, yet I do not have a clue who he is, or even if he is a pure soul or a dark one we need to protect you from,' she remarked, her eyes still fixed on the cards on the table. 'There was a vaguely disturbing aspect to it appearing as it did, but there was a murkiness that prevented me from identifying any immediate danger to you or your loved ones. In saying that, be cautious, my dear. Guard yourself faithfully as you go forward in life, and please do not agree to meet with any powerful men who are strangers to you without having someone present in the room. Not for any reason, and keep your eyes open wide. Please remember that, whatever happens on this earth, transitioning to the hereafter is a natural occurrence for us all. There are several realms in the spirit world we are encouraged to go to when our time here is over, but I'll talk to you more about that when you visit me again.'

With that, she smiled, gathered her cards together, and stood to usher me out. I gratefully paid her more than the fee she had asked for and hurried back to the carriage, a number of interesting theories running through my mind before settling in to wait until I had time to explore every aspect further when time allowed, leaving me much to consider.

I woke with a start, my stomach in knots while a slight headache had settled across my forehead. It had only gone daybreak but today was Dana's sentencing, and I was far too anxious to sleep. She would appear in Geelong Court to find out if, and for how long, she was going to prison. Aaron slept soundly, his arm across my chest as I gazed across and studied his face. With his long eyelashes and beautiful features, he looked so young when he was asleep. I placed my hand gently on his cheek, trying not to wake him but needing to touch him. He slowly raised his arm, placed his hand over mine, then opened his eyes and smiled sleepily.

'G'mornin', me beautiful Abi. Are ya worried about today?

'Of course, I am. Aren't you?'

'Yeah, but what will be will be, as me Ma says. It's too early to get up, so come here,' he complained, pulling me close and holding me until I fell asleep in his arms. Hours passed before Bessie came bustling in to wake us, startling me as she busied herself around the room.

'Come on, you lazy gits. You have a big day with poor Dana, God bless her. I hope with everything in me she gets off today. I've been praying every night for her, so I hope the good Lord is listening to every word.' She lifted her face to the ceiling and raised her voice. 'Are you hearing me up there? Give me a sign or I'll be taking my business to Mother Mary herself. Women listen far better and act a great deal quicker.' I struggled to sit up, trying not to laugh aloud as Aaron stared across at her, his eyes sparkling in amusement.

'I'm sure the good Lord above is hearin' ya prayers, Bessie. If you're sayin' 'em that loud, how could He ignore ya?' Aaron called out as she disappeared into my dressing room to find me something suitable to wear in court. Aaron quickly rose and hurried to his dressing room to ready for the day. Bessie chose a navy dress for me, thinking a conservative style would reflect well on Dana, and show those in attendance the company she kept were of good morals with impeccable reputations. She hurried me into my dress then styled my hair, finishing in half the time she usually took.

Aaron and I called out our farewells before making our way downstairs. We stopped in the kitchen to see the twins before they left for school. Willy and Bella ate their breakfast alongside them every morning, the four of them rarely apart. We sat down for a few minutes to eat before leaving them with little Mary and Leo, just as Angus joined them to face his second breakfast.

Dana stood straight as an arrow, a guard on each side of her as she stood in the small box where all defendants before her awaited their fate. She looked over at me and smiled, showing me her fingers, crossed tightly for luck. I blew her a kiss, making her smile again.

The magistrate entered, and everyone stood until he sat down. Aaron sat beside me, holding my shaking hand tightly as I tried to calm myself. The judge outlined the details of her crime no different than if she had committed cold-blooded murder, infuriating me. Once he had finished taking Dana to task for her dishonesty, treating her as if she should be given the death penalty, the beady-eyed little man sat up straight with his horsehair wig slightly askew and addressed her.

'Mrs Dana Shannon, you have been charged with the crime of bigamy,' he announced without emotion. 'I have reviewed all the evidence that has been provided to me by the police and your solicitor, Mr Richard Malcolm. I have taken into consideration your sworn statement that you fled England in the dead of night in fear for your life, and that of your children. You claim to have discovered your husband in a compromising situation with another man. I recognise that you were not in a position to obtain a divorce; however, you knowingly and willingly entered into a second marriage, fully aware the first was still valid. You have openly admitted your guilt, which I must praise you for, saving a long, drawn-out trial. I hereby sentence you to six-months hard labour in His Majesty's Prison in the State of Victoria.' He banged his wooden hammer down loudly in dismissal, startling me.

I felt my stomach drop, his words sinking in as I realised my dear friend would be locked up and deprived of her liberty for half a year. Six-months seemed to fly by when you were enjoying your life, but I doubted it would go as quickly when locked in a small cell with thieves and murderers.

Dana gasped loudly, her hand clutching her throat as she lost consciousness. The guard managed to catch her before she fell to the floor, slapping her face several times until her eyes opened for a moment then closed again. She was carried from the courtroom by the two officers, dragging her away through the back door without sympathy. Martin was inconsolable, as was Victoria, who was supported by a clearly shocked Aiden. We all agreed to meet back at Willow Grove to commiserate before Aaron and I returned to our carriage. Once he had closed the door and we were finally alone, he put his arms out to me.

'Come here, *mo anamchara*. I'm sorry for it. It's longer than Richard thought she'd get, but not as long as she could've been given.'

Six-months in a tiny cell, eating awful food, and being told what to do and when to do it. It sounded worse than the orphanage, and I would think of her every day while she was serving her time and visit as often as I could. I lay back on Aaron, resting my head on his chest while he held me around the waist. There was really nothing to say. We sat side by side in silence as the horses clip-clopped their way home, a thousand thoughts I refused to think about filling my head, while my heart remained empty and hollow.

Colin and Catherine waited in their carriage in our driveway. Harry pulled the horses up behind them before opening the door and assisting me down, Aaron close behind me. They had visited her family two-weeks ago, and Colin had directly, and quite bravely in my opinion, asked Mr Montague for Catherine's hand in marriage. After several heated discussions no one else was privy to, he had reluctantly agreed. He knew well enough that, if he didn't, Catherine would go ahead anyway with or without his blessing. They were keeping the child a secret until after the wedding in four-weeks time—the grand event already being madly planned down to every last detail by Mrs Montague, much to Catherine's displeasure.

Aaron's family arrived soon after in three carriages, as did Angus and Polly, waving to us as Catherine and I stood side by side chatting quietly near the front entrance. Amelia and Tommy pulled up near the stables while Leo and Hamish strode over to the front step, greeting everyone cheerfully as they passed. As the day was warmer than expected, we decided to sit on the wide back verandah, overlooking the beautiful garden and manicured lawn. Aaron asked Mr Masters to serve the best whisky we had and to keep the supply of ale and wine flowing. Hamish carried two bottles of beer, casually strolling towards me. He stopped and offered me a bottle before making himself comfortable beside me.

'Here, I think ye need this.' I accepted gratefully, raising the bottle to my lips and taking a deep drink. We had almost returned to the comfortable friendship we once shared, and he had kept his promise to not touch me. After sitting down together a week after it happened and talking to each other from the heart—a conversation that remained private between us—we had agreed not to speak of it again. Aaron was no longer watching us like a hawk when we were together, and by the time Hamish's broken nose had healed and Aaron's split face and bruises faded, they were back to being the best of mates. Aaron had struggled seeing us together for months, even when he was present or the children were around. He hadn't taken his eyes off Hamish whenever he was near me for a moment during that time; however, now he had relaxed back into how it had been before. Hamish sat comfortably in a chair next to my sun lounge as he drank his beer thirstily while I drank mine with the same vigour.

'Six-months is a long time tae be locked up in appallin' conditions. I know she hates me, but I would naw wish it on me worst enemy,' Hamish remarked sadly, stopping Jonathon to take another beer before placing his empty bottle on the tray and thanking him again. 'Yer a good friend tae those ye love, Abigail, an' ye've been a good friend tae Dana. I've naw doubt ye'll continue tae be.' He rose to his feet, smiling down at me before striding off to find Angus.

I went over to commiserate with my sisters-in-law, Victoria, Scarlett, and Adele, who were all drinking whisky. The children had been left with their grandparents, who were all too happy to mind them all for the day and night if required. The girls were a wild bunch when together and today they were out to get drunk, using the trial as an excuse, as well as the fact that they were child-free for the night. Everyone was staying over so they could all relax and let down their hair.

Victoria, or Vicki, as her friends and family called her now, poured me a whisky and I drank it down at once. When I had met Dana's youngest daughter a decade ago, she had been a proper, well-bred young lady without a hair out of place. Since marrying a Cavanaugh, she was far more relaxed, a pattern repeated with Patrick and Luke's wives. Adele poured me another, and I drank it down just as fast.

'We hear you've been holding out on us, Abigail,' Scarlett announced, a mischievous smirk touching her lips.

'In what way, might I ask?' I was having difficulty focusing on her face and closed my eyes for a moment, already feeling tipsy.

'We heard that Hamish came into the sitting room, grabbed you in his arms, and kissed you passionately.' I reluctantly nodded as the three of them collapsed into giggles. They were all drunk, and I wasn't far behind.

'You have to admit he is a gorgeous man. All the women love him, yet he really only has eyes for one person,' Adele teased. I felt myself blush, not only from the alcohol.

'It didn't happen like that. It was just a slip, and he regrets it. I've forgiven him,' I told them firmly, changing the subject as they continued to giggle. More beer was brought over, and I went from shots of whisky to glasses of beer, and back again several times over. It numbed my pain and eased the sadness I felt at what Dana would be going through.

'Don't you think you have had enough, Abigail?' Leo sat down heavily beside me then slipped his arm around my shoulders protectively. 'You didn't touch lunch, so you're drinking on an empty stomach. You know it doesn't take much for you to get really drunk and humiliate yourself. You're funny, I will give you that, but you're embarrassing and you'll hate yourself in the morning, as will I.'

'Leo, you know I love you, and I do, but please, please, please, don't order me around. I'm not in the mood to be bossed by any man right now. Men are the reason my friend is in gaol. Without them, life would be so much simpler,' I slurred before raising my glass of whisky and lifting it to my lips. Aaron had been watching me for a while now, but didn't come over, leaving me to talk with the girls.

Everyone stayed up well into the night, talking and drinking, until they could talk and drink no more. People slowly stumbled up to the guest rooms one by one, except for Catherine, who was the only sober person there. She helped get the drunker women to bed since their husbands were well-oiled and useless. I had fallen asleep on the lounge to the sounds of my family and friends' voices and awoke to find Aaron kissing me.

'I'm not gunna even try to let ya walk.' He shook his head before bending down to pick me up in his arms, grunting to himself as he straightened up. I lay my head on his shoulder as he carried me up the stairs to our room, where he undressed me and helped me into bed then stripped off his clothes and joined me.

'I love you, Aaron. You are the only one for me,' I mumbled, feeling happy and oblivious to anything but joy.

'Shush, me darlin'. Stop talkin' an' get over here. It's me favourite thing in the world when ya drunk,' he whispered. I let him pull me up onto his muscular frame before he sat up and kissed me, his enormous arms engulfing my body. That night, I dreamed of a portrait of a woman, her face blurred, while nightmares I couldn't remember haunted me until the dawn arrived to bring comfort, if only for a time.

Chapter Eleven

WE HAD DECIDED TO go with our family and friends to our Gippsland property for two-weeks over the Christmas period to see in the new century together. I was turning twenty-five in a couple of weeks, and I couldn't believe how fast time was passing.

Thanks to my late great-aunt Isabelle, I had been left a thousand acres in an area called Rokeby in Gippsland, the pristine Tarago River running through the property. We had visited it once, many years ago when we were first married, but were unsure what to do with it at the time. Aaron had decided two-years ago to develop the land into a holiday retreat for our family to use when the children had time off from school. The money in our bank account had grown so significantly over the years, he wanted to spend some of it on something we would all enjoy, and he had spared no expense to achieve his dream.

Aaron had designed a large, two-story cottage for us, along with twenty guest cottages for our family and friends to stay in that were dotted around the property. We had not seen them finished until now, and I was thrilled at how beautiful they were. The main house was ten times the size of the cottages, but no more beautiful than each building now standing proudly on what was once empty land. Aaron had taken on the entire project from start to finish, from arranging the construction according to his specifications, down to and including selecting and purchasing all the furnishings in Melbourne.

It had cost him a small fortune to buy everything to furnish the cottages and main cottage comfortably. I was impressed by the quality he had managed to obtain, from the carved wooden furniture to the luxurious bedding. He had arranged for everything to be transported to the property, again costing an enormous amount of money. He had promised no matter how uncomfortable the cost made me feel, I would be overjoyed when it was completed—and he was right. It had turned out so beautifully I was over the moon and so very proud of him.

I stretched out on the new soft mattress while languishing under the luxurious linen and heavy quilts that lay over me, feeling my joints click. It felt strange being surrounded by new things. Despite knowing they were mine, not one thing felt as if it belonged to me yet. The main house along with the cottages were built of bluestone, reflecting the same colour as the river depending on the sky. Our house, although much larger, matched the cottages in architectural style. I adored everything about it. Although it was large in comparison to the average family home lining the streets of Melbourne and the outlying suburbs, it was a tenth of the size of our house at Willow Grove. It felt cosy and warm, and there were enough rooms to house the twins, Leo and Bessie, along with little Mary, with more to spare.

Our bedchamber was on the lower floor, with nearly all the other guest rooms upstairs. There were two main living areas and a large kitchen, with an informal dining room next to it. The main cottage overlooked a bend in the river, where it widened and slowed into a tranquil swimming hole with a sandy bottom and grassy banks.

I listened to the birds start their morning songs as I lay looking out at the idyllic view. Every single member of Aaron's family had joined us, along with Colin and Catherine and their little boy, David. Martin and Dana had agreed to come, as had Brian and Tamara. Elizabeth had only decided to join us because she couldn't bear the thought of spending Christmas without her sister. She had dragged her reluctant husband Eric along, despite his preference to stay in Melbourne with his own family. Amelia and Tommy had borrowed a carriage from us and followed behind on the long journey, while Polly and Angus, along with Richard and Jasmin had left a day earlier, wanting to spend an extra day without so many around them.

Surprisingly, Hamish and Angelique Promenade had recently begun seeing each other again—a shock to us all—and he had brought her along, much to my chagrin.

I felt a hand settle on my stomach and smiled to myself.

'Do ya think we'll have any more nippers?' Aaron murmured sleepily. I could hear the wanting in his voice as he leaned over and kissed me good morning.

'I don't know. I'm sure it will happen again eventually.' I patted his hand reassuringly. I hadn't given it much thought until now. I was more than content with my lot and was confident I would fall again at some point. I still had years of child-bearing ahead of me before I would have to worry. I pushed my pillows down and lay flat beside Aaron, placing my hand on his rugged cheek. 'Thank you for building such a beautiful place for us and our children. I want to spend as much time as we can here with our family and friends.' I leaned over and kissed him, thanking him again.

'There is nowhere else I'd rather be than here with you, *mo anamchara*. I fitted an extra lock on the door so Leo can't bother us.' I laughed aloud as he chuckled to himself before pulling me close, my body melting into his as I silently agreed with him. There was nowhere else I'd rather be either.

Later, as I lay in his arms, I heard Leo bustling around in the kitchen and smiled. He couldn't contain his excitement at the modern, spacious kitchen and appliances that had been installed. My darling friend was like a child at Christmas who couldn't wait to play with everything. No one was even awake yet, let alone ready for breakfast. The clatter of pots and pans continued to fill my ears, forcing my decision to rise from our bed to go see what he was up to. Freeing myself from Aaron's sleeping grip, I slipped out of bed and threw on my dressing gown.

Leo had coffee brewing on the stove, and I sat at the new table as he poured me a cup and added milk and sugar. The table was made from solid hardwood and, although its legs were beautifully carved, it was not ornate or gaudy. It had comfortable, matching chairs; the thick padding covered in the finest leather. It could seat twenty people; however, a larger table outside under our back verandah that overlooked the river could accommodate forty.

'How did you sleep the first night in your new bed?' He raised his eyebrows inquiringly before sliding into the chair opposite me.

'It was very comfortable, but I kept waking up, and I'm tired.' He sipped his coffee while gazing around the large room admiringly.

'I must say, it's lavish for a holiday farm, but it's so peaceful here. I enjoy watching all the children run around free, even Tamara's, who appear to have never seen or experienced the great outdoors. You have to admit her children have unfortunate personalities, along with unfortunate physical features.' He wrinkled his nose in disdain, while I tried to smother a smile and not encourage him.

He was right. Not about how they looked, but how they interacted. There was such a difference between the children being raised at Willow Grove and their Cavanaugh cousins, all free-spirited and rowdy compared to Tamara's children. Her four were reserved and quiet and didn't know how to play outdoors or with other children. They had never been exposed to these situations before. They were schooled at home by a private tutor, rarely given the opportunity to mix with other children. This appeared to only add to their isolation, leaving them withdrawn and alone except for each other and their nannies. Unlike other children, they were not allowed to get their hands dirty, let alone soil their clothes.

Brian and Tamara had brought a full complement of servants with them, including four nannies and a ladies' maid. We were asked to provide two cottages, as Tamara didn't want the children or her staff in the same room with her and Brian. I had been surprised they hadn't asked for separate cottages for themselves; however, they were keeping up appearances, even amongst our friends.

'I hope everyone settled into their cottages last night and were comfortable.' I sipped my creamy, sweet coffee as I stared out onto the wide, fast-flowing river.

'I'm sure everyone is wonderful and enjoying themselves already,' Leo reassured me, a slow grin spreading across his face. 'You worry too much. Who cares if they're comfortable or not? So long as we are, there's nothing to fret over. See, I just solved one of the problems you whine about that bothers you dreadfully. Now we've resolved that you don't have to think about it again.' I couldn't help but giggle.

Bessie and Danny soon joined us for breakfast, while Aaron arrived halfway through. I was still in my dressing gown despite everyone else gathered around me taking the time to dress for the day.

'Good morning. How is everyone on this beautiful, bright summer day?' Bessie asked cheerily, kissing Danny, who sat beside her. 'Aaron, those beds are as soft as a cloud,' she continued. 'How did you furnish all these cottages so beautifully? Most men wouldn't know where to start, and the whole thing would be a big mess and massive disaster in the end, left for a woman to fix. There would definitely be tears.'

Bessie sounded impressed, but Aaron just smiled, remaining silent on the matter.

'He had a lot of help from the shop assistants, and when they didn't know, he just chose the most expensive thing,' Leo teased, collapsing into peals of laughter. On hearing our voices, Thomas and Emmy joined us, followed by little Mary, who made their porridge.

'Good morning, Mummy and Daddy,' Emmy called out, embracing us then making herself comfortable on her father's lap. Thomas came to my side for a kiss, then went to his father and did the same.

'Daddy, can we go fishin' as soon as we finish breakfast? Uncle Hamish promised us last night, an' he said you'd come,' Thomas enquired excitedly, his shaggy, blonde hair hanging down around his shoulders just like his father's.

'Did he, now? Well, I suppose if he promised, then I'll have to come. Ya can't go breakin' promises, even when someone else made 'em for ya.' He chuckled as he reached out and ruffled Thomas' hair fondly. The twins finished their porridge and drank their milk in record time. They were already dressed in their play clothes and had done so without help from anyone, even their beloved Mary. Catherine had made Emmy some pants to make it easier for her to keep up with the boys. She loved them so much I found it hard to get her to wear dresses for school. Hamish joined us, embracing the twins before sitting down and picking up his cutlery.

'So, are ye up fer it?' Hamish asked as he shoved a forkful of buttered mushrooms into his mouth.

'Up for what, boofhead?' Aaron replied, finishing his coffee.

'Let's have a competition tae see who can catch the biggest trout.' Hamish smiled as the twins cheered.

'I'll whip ya... you know what,' Aaron replied, grinning as he gazed proudly at his offspring.

After they had departed in a flurry of excitement to gather the other children, the ladies' maids for Angelique and Tamara arrived to take each of their employers a tray in bed. I insisted they eat before leaving, ignoring their eye-rolling. They both sat at the table, one fidgeting worse than the other, as I dished their breakfast and then poured them a coffee.

'Thank you, Mistress, but if we get caught doing this by the Countesses of Collins Street, we will both be sacked on the spot,' Angelique's maid advised, her left eye twitching for a moment, unsettling me slightly.

'Don't worry about that. Neither of them can leave their cottages until you return to help them dress so they won't find out—and we won't tell,' I promised. They appeared relieved, going on to eat heartily while Leo prepared the two trays. Given the kitchen was too small for everyone to crowd into, Leo had decided he would serve banquet style on the back verandah at set times each day. It would make it easier for everyone and himself, as we wanted him to enjoy it here, too. He was almost finished preparing the food to serve breakfast outside for our guests, some only just starting to rise, while others were already sitting around outside chatting cheerfully.

Aaron had fashioned an enormous table from large slabs of wood, a number of matching benches placed around it. It seated forty people, give or take a few depending on how close they sat to one another. He had worked on it each time he'd come with Hamish to supervise the construction of the buildings and sheds. The polish had come up beautifully, and it was obvious to all it was a work of love. The table was so heavy it could never be moved from where it sat on the back verandah overlooking the river without a team of bullocks, heavy chains, and days of backbreaking labour.

Leo glanced outside at the growing number of hungry guests before heading outside to place trays filled with food on the table. Just as he set down the last dish, Aaron's parents lowered themselves into the seats next to me, while Catherine and Colin brought David to sit on my lap then seated themselves. Patrick and Scarlett, Aiden and Victoria, and Luke and Adele all arrived together with their children, quickly settling them at the table to feed them first.

'Where's Aaron, Abigail?' Patrick asked, scanning the table then out over the river. I told him about the fishing expedition, and soon after the men had devoured their food, grabbed their children, and ran off to join in without a second glance at any of us—leaving a grateful tribe of women free of their offspring and ready to enjoy the day.

Richard and Jas arrived, and within minutes Richard did the same, quickly feeding the children and rushing them along to catch up with the others.

'Abigail, it is so beautiful here hidden away among the trees. Thank you for inviting us, my dear,' Edith Cavanaugh said lovingly, stroking my hair back off my face as I ate my second breakfast. I smiled at her and squeezed her hand.

Mr Cavanaugh had recently purchased a large parcel of land, with Aaron's help, just outside of Geelong, building a processing factory for his seafood, and it was going well. He had named it Cavanaugh and Sons Seafood and business was booming. He had hired employees to run his seafood shop in town, leaving him and his sons time to invest in their new venture, which was well on its way to securing their futures.

They were no longer considered middle class—their wealth increasing tenfold over the past year—allowing Aaron's mother and my sisters-in-law to engage a small army of staff to run their sprawling homes. The Cavanaugh homes weren't mansions, but they were large and spacious with many rooms and accommodation for their staff.

Tamara's team of nannies guided her children up for breakfast, and after they had picked at their food and moved it around the plate for a while, I told them what the rest of the children were doing so they could join them. All four stared at me blankly when I tried to explain what fishing was, and I soon gave up, leaving it for the men to show them later.

Dana and Martin joined us, Dana sliding into the chair opposite me as I smiled up at her. She had served every day of her six-month gaol term, but had confided that minutes seemed like hours, hours felt like days, and the weeks passed like months, the months feeling as if they dragged on for years. It was not something she spoke of often, even to me. It had not broken her spirit, though, and she had come out stronger, with a different perspective on life. She had seen things she had never seen before and experienced the despair and terror of being incarcerated.

'It's beautiful here, Abigail. Aaron did a great job,' Dana remarked before enthusiastically dishing up not only a plate for herself but for her daughter and grandchildren, leaving Aiden to help himself. She turned to Vicki, her eyes filled with love. 'Hello, my darling daughter. Where are my grandchildren? Their food is waiting.' We explained about the early morning fishing trip. Everyone smiled at the thought of the children already having so much fun and the fact it left us girls free to gossip. Amelia and Tommy joined us, and as soon as their children had finished breakfast, Tommy rushed them away to find the others. Angus and Polly finished breakfast, too, and Angus and their children followed Tommy.

We sat at the table eyeing the few remaining leftovers that hadn't been demolished by the hungry mob. I picked up a piece of toast slathered in creamy butter and placed two slices of bacon on it before folding it in half and eating it like a sandwich.

'I can't believe we have to put up with Angelique for two whole weeks,' Polly complained loudly, appearing annoyed. 'I'd like to smack Hamish on the back of the head for going back to her. She has a dark soul, and he managed to escape fairly unscathed last time. I doubt he will be so lucky this time.' I could only nod in agreement, my mouth too full to speak.

'Polly, you can't pick your in-laws. It's just a shame you're not as lucky as us,' Scarlett teased, smiling across at me.

We relaxed down by the river on sun lounges under the trees that lined the bank. Tamara finally joined us, while Brian went to eat leftovers in the cottage and talk to Leo. She sat next to me and leaned in close, glancing around to ensure she couldn't be overheard.

'I need to talk to you. Hamish is going to leave Angelique for me. I snuck out to his cottage during the night, and although he initially didn't want to let me in, he relented like always. I stayed a while, and we did it. I think we are back together,' she whispered. I listened to her go on and on about Hamish and how much she despised Angelique, nodding while trying to concentrate on what she was saying. I wanted to be a good friend to her when it came to her affair; however, my mind kept wandering. I was worried Tamara and Angelique would come to blows over the next fortnight, thrown together with no means of escape only adding fuel to the fire considering the obvious friction between them.

While Tamara continued to talk, I heard the distant voices of my children. I couldn't see them yet, but rose to my feet and craned my neck. Soon they came around the bend and ran up the riverbank to us, so excited that we couldn't understand what they were saying. Their fathers slowly ambled up the bank to join us and showed us three buckets, all full of trout they had caught. Aaron and Hamish didn't mention their competition, so I assumed the children had caught most of them. Aaron sat down heavily behind me, slipping his arms around my waist.

'Ya should've seen 'em catch those fish. I've never seen so many delighted nippers in me life.' He gently kissed the back of my neck, sending chills through me. It was getting hot, the day set to be a stinker so all the children were ushered back inside to change into their bathers. Thomas and Emmy skipped off by themselves, hand in hand. They were eight-years old now, and felt more and more independent each day, rejecting our help more than not these days. I was proud of the fact that, despite having a wonderful childhood with all the love in the world and every material possession they could want, neither of them were spoiled like some children I'd met.

The men decided to play a round of croquet on the smooth, grassy course installed on the other side of the house while they waited for their wives to help the children change into their bathers.

'Are you going to go swimming, Aaron?' He continued to kiss the side of my neck, sending chills through me.

'Bloody oath. Are ya comin' in with me? I wanna see the swimsuit from France Catherine copied for ya,' he answered, licking my ear and making me squirm.

'Stop that! You know I hate it! If you hate the riding pants Catherine made me, then you are really going to despise the swimsuit.' I laughed aloud, quickly glancing around to ensure we were alone. He had discreetly slipped his hands under the blouse I wore, fondling my breasts while playing with my nipples as I lay back against him. We talked of my excitement that Christmas was nearly upon us when Leo caught sight of us and headed in our direction. He wore a short pair of purple pants that were so tight I could see the outline of his sausage and eggs clearly.

'Where the bloody hell did ya get them pants?' Aaron asked, his eyes wide as he slipped his hands out from the top of my blouse before tucking my top into my long skirt.

'Aren't they fabulous? Catherine made them for me just for swimming, and I have a bright pink pair, too.' He pranced around in front of us like a peacock, his bulging groin near Aaron's face. He shoved him down roughly into a seat as I began to giggle, having never seen anything like them in my life on a man or woman. I knew Catherine would give in to his demands because he would harass and constantly nag her until she did. Colin had bluntly refused to deal with him or make any of his clothes thanks to his unreasonable expectations and flamboyant taste, not to mention temper tantrums when he didn't get his way. Colin designed day suits and evening suits for gentlemen, among other things, and was extremely conservative compared to Leo.

Catherine was the opposite. She loved making clothes for him because she could use her imagination to its fullest and create what could only be referred to in polite company as distinctive outfits. Leo didn't care what people thought. He dressed in brightly coloured shirts and pants except when he went into Geelong where he would wear a plain suit.

'I saw what you were doing to her when I walked over here, you dirty little scrubbers,' Leo remarked as Aaron chuckled, but still refused to look in his direction should he be confronted by his exaggerated crotch

'What of it? It's only you who came along, an' you've felt her up a thousand times yourself, so why shouldn't I?' He took my earlobe in his mouth and sucked gently before softly biting it, sending shivers all through my body.

'Oh, stop it, you mad rooters,' Leo demanded, jumping to his feet and placing his hands on his hips. I couldn't take my eyes from the outline of his genitals, the tight shorts revealing far more than I wanted to know. 'Eyes to me. I have something important to say.' He stood over us, tapping his foot in irritation until we gave him our full attention.

'Well, get a move on,' I mumbled, his gaze narrowing before he reached over and pinched my nose. I shrieked, pushing him away before Aaron grabbed my hands to prevent me from inflicting damage on him.

'Back. To. Me! Are you listening?' he demanded to know. I nodded resentfully, knowing the sooner we cooperated and let him finish, the sooner he would leave us alone. 'You have been married so long now you should be sick of the sight of each other and barely talk, let alone touch—just like my Mumma and my Pappa. They sleep in different rooms and only say a few words to each other in passing, typical of how abnormal people behave after the first few years and the children are out of the way. You should follow in my parents footsteps as they are a perfect example of how you two should be behaving now you have your own little family. I say this with love. Stop touching each other—it's nauseating.'

'Well, so are these things ya callin' pants, an' we're all forced to look at 'em whether ya have our consent or not,' Aaron teased. I collapsed into giggles as Leo wiggled his outrageously garbed bum in my face, before repeating his performance for Aaron's benefit. He soon became bored with us and pranced off to the river for a swim, and more importantly to show anyone who would pay him a scrap of attention his new bathers.

We could hear the excited chatter of the children as they ran down to the river with their parents, all dressed in their swimwear, or bathers as the Australian referred to anything you wore into the water. Aaron's hand rested on my belly, and I relaxed back into him as

I gazed up at the red river gum sheltering us, its large branches spread wide into a glorious canopy above.

'I wouldn't believe ya carried two nippers in here if I hadn't seen it with me own eyes. Ya stomach's so flat,' he remarked, his voice low as he unconsciously caressed my belly.

'Maybe I should start wishing for more children. It seems when I really want something and focus my mind on it, it manifests and comes to be without any effort. Like conceiving the twins so soon into our marriage. It's strange looking back. I fell almost instantly, but I truly believe it was only because my desire to have children was strong at the time. But you know something, my beautiful man?' He smiled to himself before nodding, encouraging me to continue.

'I've no doubt you'll tell me.'

'I haven't given babies a second thought until recently, and maybe that's why we haven't been blessed with more. I'm now certain I want more bairns with you and am confident—don't ask me how or why—I'll be with child within the year.' He nodded, his eyes lighting up at the thought, before we turned our attention to our friends and family nearby.

The children splashed in the wide, deep river with their fathers behind them, except for Tamara's offspring—their four nannies watched on closely from the bank, all appearing ready to leap into action if required. Her children were reluctant to go in too far, their obvious hesitation I could only assume due to the other children splashing while being thrown up into the air by their uncles and fathers. It was clear to anyone who cared to look all four were averse to getting wet. Tamara had re-joined us, finding she was bored and had nothing better to do, while Angelique finally appeared, making herself comfortable next to Aaron and myself. She stared down her nose, silently judging me sprawled out on top of my husband while paying her no mind.

'Where's Hamish?' she asked sharply.

'He's swimming with the children,' Tamara interjected from a few seats away. She glared across at Angelique, who hadn't acknowledged her, and didn't seem likely to anytime soon. I was surprised she had even heard the question. Angelique rolled her eyes before waving her hand dismissively in her direction.

'Sadly, I'm not surprised. You would think he'd come to my cottage to at least say good morning, but of course he doesn't. He would prefer to be out swimming with other people's brats,' she spat. I was tempted to tell her with some delight he'd also gone fishing with those same brats earlier, but held my tongue. 'Abigail, fetch me a cold drink,' she ordered. I nodded, remaining silent as I struggled to my feet then marched down to the river, pulling out a netted bag holding bottles of beer, cider, lemonade, and fruit juice. I promptly returned and handed her a bottle of lemonade and a clean glass. She stared up, unmoving as if expecting me to pour it for her. I stood my ground, forcing her to take the bottle and empty glass, before sitting back down on Aaron's lap, his face like thunder.

I excused myself soon after, leaving Aaron to tolerate her while I went to change and swim with the children. They were so much better company than adults sometimes. I undid my top, taking it off and placing it over the back of a chair, then slipped my skirt down and stepped out of it. I went to my drawers and took out the bathers Catherine had made for me. This one was one-piece in a brilliant emerald green, the bottom coming down to my mid-thigh. The top section fitted snugly to my body and had no sleeves, only thin straps sitting over my shoulders to keep everything up and in place. The neckline was a deep V, and I adjusted the front to cover myself more. Just as I was about to put my hair up, Aaron walked in.

'Why did ya leave me with that awful bloody woman? I couldn't shoot off quick enough, ya traitor,' he complained, his eyes fixed on my bathers. 'It's a bit short, but it covers ya well enough.' He appeared confused, unable to decide whether he disapproved and would forbid me from wearing it or if he genuinely liked it. 'It's fitted a bit close to ya body, though. I thought these were meant to cover ya from ya neck to ya ankles, no different from a sugar sack, but it's nothin' like I imagined.'

'I don't know how Catherine comes up with her ideas. I only wear them.' I stared into the full length looking glass turning to and fro while studying my reflection, deciding I was respectable enough no matter what opinion Aaron formed. I was among family and friends anyway, feeling confident enough those around me wouldn't judge too harshly. I wanted to feel free in the water and not have yards and yards of heavy fabric dragging me down. Aaron pulled on his short pants, and although Catherine had made them for him, they were nothing like what Leo was swanning around in and offending every person who happened to look in his direction. Aaron strode towards me, his chest bare, then lifted me off my feet, kissing me thoroughly.

'Ya look like ya get around. I'm not sayin' ya look like the town bike or ya bang harder than a dunny door.' I abruptly turned my head to glare up at him, fury rising within me as he stumbled over his words, fear crossing his face for only a moment.

'You bloody well just did, you rude, fat headed neanderthal.' He shook his head while slowly backing away from me, his hands up in defeat.

'Stop lookin' at me with blood in ya eye. I didn't mean it the way it come out an' now ya have me fearin' for me life. I still can't make up me mind if I wanna be a party to ya goin' out there lookin' like that,' he whispered in my ear then ran his hand over my backside. I finished putting my hair up on top of my head before rising to my feet and quickly tidying the room. Once I had finished and he was ready, he took my hand and led me back outside. We found most of the women had returned to the banks of the river, leaving their children in the care of their men who were still in the water and showed no signs of getting out.

Catherine and Colin joined us, and I was relieved she was wearing a similar swimsuit in black. The other women eagerly enquired where we bought them, and when Catherine shyly revealed she had designed them, they all placed their orders with her immediately. Except for Angelique, that is. She looked me up and down disdainfully before announcing far louder than required such swimsuits were not proper for a lady to wear in public. I ignored her and followed Aaron down to the riverbank.

Patrick, Aiden, and Luke were already in the water with their children, along with Thomas and Emmy. Richard had joined us, his two children splashing around, while Tamara's children dangled their feet at the edge of the river but would not go in any further. I shrieked when Aaron picked me up, threw me over his shoulder and carried me into the water. He held me above the slowly moving current as I struggled against him, calling out for help from my children.

'Should I throw Mummy in?' he boomed above the noise as Thomas and Emmy nodded frantically.

'Yes!' they screamed, the little traitors.

Their cousins soon joined in, wanting to see the big splash I would make. They laughed and cheered as he swung me over the water three times, then cruelly let me go. My body hit the surface hard, and I felt the cold water sting for the first few seconds after being submerged. Soon, though, my body became acclimated to the temperature. It felt clean and refreshing after enduring the heat of the day. As I came up to the surface to take a breath, I found Aaron standing in front of me, the water lapping at the top of his chest while the twins hung off each arm. He threw them up in the air and into the water and, as I heard them screaming and laughing, he took me in his arms.

'I can see ya nipples through that costume when it's wet.' He pushed his broad chest into my breasts, covering me so no one else could see. I put my arms up around his neck and let my body float. 'We need to explore an' find another swimmin' hole just for us where we can swim naked an' there's no one else around to bother us, me precious Abi.' I relaxed back into the water, nodding slightly as he grinned down at me. 'I'll be jack of it all by the end of next week if I'm forced to tolerate this many drongos roamin' around freely. I need to find somewhere I can escape with ya each day to preserve me own sanity so I don't leave 'em all for dead an' shoot through by meself.'

I kissed him and promised I would make time for him later in the day, leaving him to return to the children waiting impatiently nearby. As I climbed up onto the bank, Dana marched over, her eyes wide.

'Christ on a bike, you cut a magnificent figure in that thing, whatever it is. I'm green—absolutely green,' she exclaimed, bending down to take a closer look at the hem, then the inside stitching. 'I've ordered three from Catherine and, as she already has my measurements, all I have to do is choose the colours.'

She didn't care how old she was, she would still wear the fashions of the young, impressing me no end and only increasing my admiration for her. Besides, she possessed an enviable figure herself, still appearing decades younger than she was, her body now voluptuous once more, her breasts ample and firm. As I stood on the edge of the riverbank chatting with her, I noticed Aaron staring at me—and so was Hamish. I immediately felt self-conscious and bent down to retrieve a large towel to wrap around my waist. Dana followed my gaze then turned back and noticed my flushed face. She raised her hand before gently resting her cool palm against my burning cheek.

'Ah, yes. The blaigeard's still madly in love with you, and it thrills me. It gladdens my heart that it's his burden to bear for the rest of his life. His penance is to witness your happiness in the arms of another every single day of the rest of his pathetic existence, while he ends up with the likes of a woman like Angelique. Poetic justice, I would call it, Abigail. Poetic justice.' She sighed, a weak smile touching her lip as she followed me inside so I could change.

She sat on my bed while I slipped on a fitted blouse with a slimline skirt in a lightweight cotton that had become all the fashion. Then again, so had mutton-leg sleeves. Mr Montague had predicted all those years ago when I first met Catherine that they would become the height of fashion—and they had—but I had staunchly refused to wear them to this day, no matter how much Catherine tried to convince me. I considered them ugly and cumbersome, and my opinion hasn't changed.

'I don't understand how you and Aaron have remained friends with Hamish for nearly ten-years now, and after the way he has treated so many women—not to mention the big-bottomed elephant in the room no one seems willing to acknowledge or discuss. He still wants you.' Her voice was barely a whisper as she stared out the window, her body present but her mind no longer here, while a number of emotions flitted across her face from one to another before my eyes as she allowed herself to become lost in her memories. I let my hair loose and gave it a quick brush.

'Dana, I know what you think of him and you have every right.' I straightened up and quickly pulled my hair back, securing it on the top of my head before turning to her. 'I would never try to convince you to speak to him or change your opinion. Please don't put me in that position as I would never do it to you. He is our friend, and he is not what you think; however, like I said, it's not my place to try to change your mind. I just don't want to be in the middle as I love you both dearly.'

She nodded, averting her gaze before slipping her arm through mine and leading me back outside.

'I'm sorry, Abigail. It's... ' Her voice faltered, her eyes filled with tears as she swallowed several times before continuing. 'It's just next year it will be ten-years since I lost my darling Charlotte. Do you know the pain hasn't lessened? Not one bloody bit—nor have the regrets and grief I carry over a life lost so young. Such a waste, and it served no purpose for what I can see. Not a day goes by when I don't think of her and how her life would be if she were still here with us. I like to believe she would have married and been very happy with a family of her own by now.'

I embraced her tight before she returned to Martin, while I sat down alone in my sun lounge, watching the children swim. I felt so awful for Dana, but I felt she had backed me into a corner and forced me to tell her where I stood. I looked around and noticed everyone was either swimming or had disappeared inside. Hamish saw me, bounded up onto the riverbank and, wrapping a towel around himself, strode over and sat down next to me.

'I hope ye dinnae mind that I brought Angelique here fer the holidays. I know she has strong opinions, but I'm hopin' she can keep them tae herself this time.' I turned and studied his face, searching for an ounce of sense, but finding not a drop.

'Hamish, I have to ask you as I can hold my tongue no longer. What has possessed you to reconcile with her after what has passed between you? You weren't suited then, so tell me how you're a good match now? What's changed?' He bent forward in his chair, picked up a twig, then slowly started to scratch a picture in the dirt.

'The truth is, Abigail, me parents have given me an ultimatum. I must settle down an' marry Angelique or they'll disinherit me. They feel now that I'm naw far off thirty, I must stop wastin' me time with women o' low breedin', as they say, an' get serious about startin' me own family like Angus. It's all been arranged through our parents this time.'

I could hear the strain in his voice, but didn't say more, as it was none of my business. Even though I didn't like the woman much, maybe she would be good for him. I could only hope that was the case, and he wasn't forced to endure a miserable life once they married.

Leo rang the large bell at the back door to summon us for lunch, and within ten-minutes everyone was eating, talking, and feeding their children all at once. I enjoyed the unruly noise and the raucous laughter that filled the room whenever our family and friends were around us—and I knew Aaron did, too.

Chapter Twelve

SEVERAL OF THE WOMEN, and a couple of the men, sat around the campfire, a number of animated conversations going at once. The children were off exploring with Hamish and Angus, and we hadn't seen or thought of them for hours. Aaron hurried to my side, interrupting a heated discussion between Adele and Scarlett. He carried a cane basket over his arm, and I wondered what he was up to.

'I apologise, ladies. I've come to steal me wife away for a few hours to spoil her an' make sure she knows I love her.' He smiled charmingly at them before bowing dramatically.

'Why can't your brother be more romantic like you?' Scarlett moaned, throwing a spoon at Patrick, which he dodged while chuckling loudly.

'Again, I'm sorry an' I apologise that the oldies were unable to create four perfect sons. It was a once-in-a-lifetime experience the day I was born into their arms. It's unfortunate for ya that Abigail gets the cream an' you get the milk—or possibly the way water,' he told them smugly, making me giggle as I rose to my feet and bid them farewell. They groaned as we walked away, the conversations animated between husband and wife.

'Where are we going?' There was purpose in his stride, and I struggled to keep up.

'A place out in the bush I found this mornin'. I believe it'll be perfect an' is just what we need.' He slipped his arm around my shoulders and slowed down as we stepped into a heavily wooded area on the edge of the property.

He pushed his way through the scrub with me following, and soon after we arrived at a beautiful rock face, a small waterfall splashing into the river, swirling and flowing around several large rocks that appeared to slow its momentum. Due to the thick scrub, no one would notice the oasis they lay beyond even if they walked straight past it. We sat down on a blanket that Aaron had spread out.

'What do ya think?'

'It's perfect, Aaron. Almost magical.'

'God's own country. Bloody beautiful.' He took out a bottle of Sauvignon Blanc and poured two glasses. We sat talking and making fun of Angelique while we finished the first bottle, then opened the second. I lay back, feeling warm and relaxed. Within moments he was on top of me, his lips on mine.

'I've wanted to do that since seein' ya in those wet bathers. Even me married brothers looked like they were gunna have a crack at ya for a second—an' Catherine—despite her recently joinin' the puddin' club. They'd make a blowfly sick, the filthy perverts. It took all me strength not to jump outta the water an' cover ya with a blanket.'

'Why? Are you jealous? I won't wear it again in public if you don't want me to.' I cringed inwardly, mustering everything in me to hide how hurt I felt. I considered his brothers my brothers, and our sisters-in-law my sisters, and was unable to even contemplate ever looking at them any other way no matter what they wore.

'Yeah, nah, of course not, *mo anamchara*. I'll be straight up an' down with ya, though. I've just about had a gutful of other blokes, includin' me brothers, gazin' at ya body with lust in their eyes an' thinkin' I don't notice, ignorantly believin' I'm thick as two bricks an' can't see with me own two eyes they're havin' wicked thoughts about ya—except for Brian an' Leo. Ya safe 'round them, an' I'm grateful for it.' A mischievous grin touched his lips, causing me to smile back at him. 'I heard Catherine takin' what sounded like hundreds of orders for these immoral bathing costumes today. Seems like you'll all be wearin' 'em soon enough—except for Angelique, who was as mad as a frog in a sock.' He threw back his head and howled with laughter as I tried to smother a smile. He finally composed himself, bending down to kiss me while undoing the front of my blouse and exposing my breasts. I lay back and closed my eyes, counting myself fortunate I did not have a single thought of England.

We finished off the last of our dinner—not one morsel left over from the two dozen roasted trout and boxes of vegetables cooked ten different ways. The large platters were now empty as Bessie and little Mary carried the remaining dishes to the kitchen, Danny following them in to help clean up. They had volunteered to act as Leo's assistants, finding themselves at a loose end given I really didn't need Bessie's assistance while I was here. The twins had already decided for themselves they didn't need little Mary either, other than for a few small things she liked to do for them.

We had put the children to bed straight after dinner. They were exhausted from their day, and it was nice to have some peace. I followed Aaron out to the campfire that burned warmly by the river where permanent seating, built in a large circle, had been installed. It was a lovely evening—all except for the mosquitoes—the sound of constant slapping and the occasional cursing confirming their annoying efficiency. Dana had wisely advised us to wave a white handkerchief around our face and neck, and surprisingly, it did help—but only slightly. The irritating insects didn't seem to like my blood much, but everyone around me could not stop whingeing or scratching.

'It's so enjoyable out here now that all those children have finally gone to bed. At least now we can hold a decent conversation without being interrupted,' Angelique remarked, her face relaxing into a smile for the first time today. I rolled my eyes at Aaron, a slow, sweet smile touching his mouth. Most ignored her and continued speaking between themselves—some even going so far as to turn their bodies away from her, while others stood and changed seats in an attempt to get away from her. It was blatantly obvious that I was not the only one who disliked Angelique. Hamish appeared tense, his manner abrupt while visibly squirming in his chair. I wondered what the hell could be wrong with him before raising my eyebrows inquiringly when I caught his eye. He cleared his throat several times before rising to his feet, fixing his attention on the dark, swirling river running alongside him.

'I've somethin' I'd like tae say.' A hush fell over us as Hamish cleared his throat again, his cheeks a mottled red. 'I wanted ye all tae be the first tae know. I've asked Angelique fer her hand, an' she's done me the honour o' acceptin'.'

An awkward silence hung heavy over each of us for a moment, many regarding him with sympathy before realising it was not the expected or appropriate reaction. Nearly all present jumped to their feet and burst into raucous cheers and applause, while Angelique reminded me of the cat that swallowed the canary as everyone, all except for Tamara, congratulated and wished them well.

The fire had burned down to glowing embers, the low hanging stars bright overhead taking my breath away. Aaron rose gracefully to his feet, pulling me to mine before calling out we were off to bed. After bidding everyone goodnight, we strolled hand in hand toward the main cottage.

'Strewth, poor Hamish wasn't too enthusiastic when he made the announcement. It was hard to watch.' He stopped for a moment to gaze up at the Southern Cross, the stars glinting like diamonds on black velvet above.

'Yes, and I feel just so bloody sad for him. He didn't believe in love when I first met him, and now he's completely thrown away any chance of happiness he had by marrying her. He has his own money. Why is he so scared of being disinherited?'

'It's not just about the money, Abi.' He pulled me in close and pointed up to the dark sky, naming the planets, stars and moons one by one as he went. I was unsure if he was making it up as he went along, or yanking my chain, as he often liked to say, or he was genuinely teaching me about the universe. 'It's the family name an' their reputation an' standin' in society that's important to the Makenzies. Unfortunately, Hamish has fought against 'em for a long time, an' now he's thrown his hands up in the air an' just given up. He doesn't care anymore about himself an' will do whatever shuts that old bastard up if it gives him peace. Ya don't have to be blind Freddy to see what's really goin' on. We all know when a hurricane is approachin'—an' so does he.' He closed the door to our bedchamber behind him while I stripped off my clothing then slid under the cool, crisp covers that felt wonderful against my bare skin. Aaron climbed in beside me, then leaned across to extinguish the lamp on his side table. 'It was a beaut day from start to finish. Surrounded by the nippers, you, our family, an' friends—all enjoyin' an' explorin' a new place out in the bush. It's a special privilege to be able to bring everyone together.' I kissed him deeply, and he kissed me back enthusiastically, not pulling away until much later. When I finally drifted off to sleep, a bunch of wilted roses, a broken sapphire, and a black magpie figured prominently in my dreams—yet all I could see was the darkening horizon and a storm like I'd never witnessed approaching.

Christmas morning had finally arrived to greet us and I was beyond excited. I could hear the children sneaking out to the lounge area to check if Saint Nick had visited. I laughed when I heard Emmy squeal with delight, quickly shaking Aaron awake to listen to them. Thomas sounded over excited as he examined his train set, while Emmy held her new doll in the crook of her arm as if it were made of glass. They stampeded to our room no different from a herd of baby elephants, bursting through the door and running inside our bedchamber before jumping on the bed to show us their new toys.

'There are stacks more out there, Ma, but it'd be no different than shovellin' shit uphill with a spoon if we tried to carry 'em all in to show ya. You'd make a few quid if you sold it all off,' Thomas remarked thoughtfully, while Emmy proudly showed her father her new baby doll. We hurried out of bed and followed them into the large living area, beautifully furnished with wide lounges and comfortable chairs, while low-lying tables were strategically placed in between to sit a drink or a plate of food on. We admired every present they received, then dropped to the ground to play with them, both taking it in turns to show us how their new toys worked. Shortly after, Leo came bounding down the stairs in his bright pink pyjamas.

'A Merrrrry Christ-massss tooo yoooou, a Merrrrry Christ-massss tooo yoooou, a Merrrrry Christ-massss fab-bubu-less fam-mmm-ileeeeeeeeee, a Merrrrry Christ-massss tooooooooo yooooooooooou.' He stood halfway up the staircase, his voice so loud and off key, I was forced to cover my ears. The screeching finally stopped, and he took a bow, the twins cheering loudly as we clapped before he took a final bow then joined us.

'But that's the happy birthday song, Uncle Leo. It's got nothin' to do with Christmas,' Thomas loudly pointed out.

'You can make it be whatever you want it to be, Thomas, just like everything in life. You only need to be clever like me and replace the words. Like I do to all the songs. I make up my own lyrics, which are, of course, far better than the original. I sing them to your mother; however, she runs away from me every time. Come to think of it, when I sing, no one in the kitchen seems to stay around long, either,' he remarked thoughtfully. We collapsed into giggles as Aaron thumped him on the back sympathetically before leading us back over to the lounge.

He was such a terrible singer. We couldn't get him to stop, though. The only way I personally found peace was to run—and run fast in the other direction as swiftly as possible before he physically pinned you down and forced you to listen to his terribly awful voice. It reminded me of two feral cats fighting in a burlap bag. I had never come across a worse singer in my life, and hoped not to again. A quarter of an hour passed before Leo excused himself and hurried off to prepare Christmas breakfast for one and all. Aaron stood, took me by the hand, then pulled me to my feet.

'Mummy an' Daddy are goin' back to bed to get a bit more shut eye.' They ignored him, far too engrossed in their new toys to notice their father lead me out of the room and back to our bedchamber. He closed the door behind us, but not before I heard Leo yell out a rude joke. 'The sparrow hasn't farted yet. The sun hasn't even come up, an' I haven't received me special Christmas gift. Ya know, the one ya give me every Christmas mornin'.' He smirked as we climbed back into bed.

'You mean the one you get all the time?' I laughed aloud as he pulled me in close to his naked body and I let myself melt into him, unable to imagine wanting to be anywhere else in the world.

The sound of a door opening and raucous laughter filled my ears, rousing me from a deep slumber. I was still wrapped in Aaron's arms, exactly how I had fallen asleep, while he lay beside me snoring softly. I slowly opened my eyes and gazed up to find Thomas and Emmy standing by the bed holding several boxes in their arms, both appearing quite excited.

'Wake up, Daddy. We've come to give you your present and to hear our morning story.' Emmy leaned over him, speaking directly into his ear. A slow smile spread across his face as he turned towards them, rubbing the sleep from his eyes. They kissed him good morning as I passed him his short pants, smiling to myself as he slipped them on under the covers, while I pulled on my thin summer dressing gown.

The twins climbed in between us, then excitedly handed us our gifts, their smiles wide. Thomas presented me with an exquisite gold necklace, a small diamond set into it, while Emmy gave me the matching earrings. I had taken the twins shopping for their father's present, and they had chosen well. I relaxed back as I watched him unwrap a pair of gold cufflinks with a small diamond in each, along with a solid gold watch to wear on his wrist. He grinned then spread his arms wide to embrace them, as did I, before they settled down next to us to listen to their Christmas story—a new adventure about a boy stuck on a boat on Christmas Eve left wondering if Saint Nick would find him. I lay back and listened just as intently as the twins, who lay heavy in his arms.

Aaron had already given me my Christmas present—a diamond brooch surrounded by emeralds with matching emerald earrings. I'd bought him a gentleman's carriage for when he needed to go into Geelong on business. The workmanship had impressed him beyond measure. Since our marriage, he had become a collector of carriages, and we still had every single one we had ever owned, along with great-aunt Isabelle's numerous carts and carriages I had inherited. Aaron updated them every two-years as they became bigger and more elaborate. I enjoyed travelling in my carriage, and had my favourites, too. I didn't mind at all that he spent an enormous amount of money on them as I spent a great deal of time travelling in the things and wanted to be comfortable.

'Are ya comin' out for brekkie or do ya want it brought to the bedchamber on trays?' Thomas enquired, perched up on the corner of the bed. 'Uncle Leo said ya should've been in the kitchen an hour ago, so ya missed out an' will go hungry. I told him I'd make ya up a tray with me own hands an' bring it to ya. I don't believe in starvin' people to make ya point.' I burst into hysterical laughter, while Aaron snorted in amusement before Emmy planted herself down beside me.

'Well, then, there's no point in them even getting up from their bed, is there, Thomas? Especially if Uncle Leo has made it clear he has no intention of feeding them. Come with me and I'll help you. I know how to force him to cook,' Emmy confided, taking her brother's hand before scrambling out of bed. I giggled to myself as I listened to them run from the room. Aaron leaned over and kissed the top of my head.

'I can't believe they'll be nine in a few short months. We need to have more, Abi,' he whispered, and I nodded.

'I promise you I'll make a wish at midnight on New Year's Eve to fall within the year.' I raised my hand no differently than if I were swearing an oath on the Bible in a court of law.

'I dunno if it works like that, but I trust ya. Ya seem to always get what ya want.' I felt a burning desire deep inside me to add to our family since Aaron had recently brought it up again. I lay in his arms, gently kissing his lips and exploring his mouth while we waited for our children to bring us breakfast in bed.

We exchanged presents with our friends after lunch. The children seemed to have the most fun, if we were keeping score, but the adults came in a close second. Richard sat beside me watching our offspring mess about with their new toys, often stopping to interact with each other before returning to play.

'How is everything in your world, Abigail? I worry about you sometimes. You are always looking after everyone else and putting yourself last. You have so much money you could be travelling the world, seeing places that you have only read about in books. Do you remember that you once wanted to do that?' I glanced at him affectionately then leaned across and kissed his cheek.

'That was a long time ago, Richard. Close to ten-years in fact. Fanciful dreams slip away when your happiness comes calling, and whatever that is becomes your new reality. You end up living a life far removed from the one you envisioned, but that's what life's all about. I'll travel one day, but not yet. I'm content and more than happy with how my life is now.'

'I'm pleased for you. You deserve every happiness in the world, Abigail.' He placed his large hand on mine while we reminisced about London, and the years that had passed since I was there. Aaron strolled over and made himself comfortable beside Richard.

'Ya tryin' to steal me wife or are ya both havin' a sentimental moment?' He grinned widely as Richard chuckled to himself.

'Abigail and I were talking about the dreams we all have for our lives when we're young, and how it can turn out very differently. Sometimes better than what we planned,' Richard remarked, glancing lovingly across the verandah at Jasmin and their four children.

'I always knew me life would turn out well, but I never expected it to be like this.' Aaron winked at me, taking my hand in his. He and Richard soon began talking about his law practice and our business affairs. I blocked them out as I relaxed back into my chair and dozed off. I woke with a start to find Aaron sitting next to me stroking my hair, not another person in sight.

'It's time for tea, or dinner as ya call it. I let ya sleep 'cause ya tossed an' turned like a fish outta water all night. I didn't know what was wrong with ya or if ya were crook.' He helped me to my feet, then guided me out into the hallway. 'Do ya feel better now?'

'Yes, much better than I did. Thank you for letting me sleep,' I said, and kissed him. We walked through the house then wandered outside to find them all sitting around the enormous wooden table, eating and chatting cheerfully. I could hear raised voices as we approached and sighed deeply. 'What now?' I muttered crossly as we reached the table.

'I've had just about enough of your snide comments about my wedding, Tamara. I will plan my day how I want it and not how other people want it to be,' Angelique snapped as Aaron and I sat down.

'I'm not being snide,' Tamara replied haughtily, gazing down her nose at her rival. 'I was trying to help you by making some much needed suggestions, but from what you have described of your upcoming wedding and how you envision it to be, it sounds positively awful, but I will keep my well-meaning opinions to myself.' She gave Angelique a superficial smile, then dismissed her with a wave of her hand.

'Positively awful? And which part of my day will that be?' Angelique spat, glaring furiously at Tamara. Brian and Hamish wisely kept their heads down and stayed out of it, which I thought was the intelligent thing to do.

'Where do you want me to start? The white carriage drawn by four white horses with red feathered headpieces that will transport you as if you're the Queen of England? Or the ten maids you want walking by your side down the aisle? I can't imagine you even have that many friends. You may well be forced to have your housemaids fitted for gowns so they can attend to your every whim, and why wouldn't they be there to wipe your arse on your wedding day. Why change anything?' Tamara shot back, Angelique appearing mortified. Her hands shook, her face a mottled red as Hamish tried to calm her.

'I've been tae many weddin's, an' they were all different. None were better than the others.' He gently placed his hand on her upper arm to reassure her; however, she turned and smacked his hand away, her face twisted in rage.

'Shut up, Hamish. What would you know? You're just the man who will turn up on the day, say the words you have to say, then walk me back to the carriage,' she spat, shoving him away again. I watched in fascination as the colour of Tamara's face changed several shades at once, her hateful stare fixed on Angelique, who continued to behave as if Tamara didn't exist. Hamish leaned back, withdrawing his hand from her arm, then shrugging at Aaron in confusion. Tamara sat up straight as an arrow, continuing to stare at Angelique..

'Don't you dare speak to him like that! It seems all Hamish is good for is to escort you on your wedding day and do as he's told, no different from a mongrel in the street,' Tamara hissed, picking up her wine glass and taking a slow and measured sip, not once taking her eyes from Angelique.

'What does anything between Hamish and myself have to do with you? I think you care a little too much, Tamara,' Angelique remarked condescendingly, regaining her composure. She narrowed her eyes and looked Brian up and down suspiciously before he averted his gaze, his nervousness obvious.

'I have been friends with Hamish for nearly a decade, so of course I care what happens to him and how he is treated. We all do,' she replied, her face flushed.

'Well, just so you all know, you may be Hamish's friends, but I will not tolerate anyone getting in between us, no matter who they are or what their excuse. Hamish is a grown man and he can take care of himself, so you don't need to fear that this terrible monster here is going to hurt your poor little Hamish,' she said coldly, then elegantly placed a morsel of food in her mouth. I shoved a forkful in mine, then sat back, feeling infuriated.

I abruptly pushed myself away from the table and rose to my feet, silently marching away without a glance or a word. Aaron followed me into the bedchamber, quietly shut the door, then sat down on the bed beside me.

'That was hard to watch.'

'I just don't understand how he can stay with someone so cold and devoid of feelings.'

'Look, Abi, I can't stand the woman either, an' it grieves me to watch a mate bein' treated like shit on her shoes. The poor bloke's stuck with her, though. Has he told ya the reason why? He told me in confidence, an' I can't break me word if ya don't already know.'

'Yes, he told me,' I replied flatly as Aaron put his arm around my shoulders and pulled me close.

'Ya right, *mo anamchara*. He doesn't deserve it an' what his parents are doin' to him is terrible.'

'It's no different from what was done to us, and it's worked out. I can't imagine being this happy with anyone but you,' I reminded him.

'Yeah, but we liked an' respected each other from the start, an' that grew quickly into love. He doesn't like her, an' she doesn't respect him, so how's that gunna work?' He leaned across and kissed my nose, making me smile. 'Hamish has been tryin' on an' off for years to force himself to like her, let alone love her, an' he truly believes he'll never fall in love again,' he added, shaking his head sadly. 'He thinks he just has to accept what his parents want an' make the best of it. I've talked till I'm blue in the face, but his mind is made up this time.' I nodded just as sadly. 'It's not for us to be arguin' with her no matter how rude she is, Abi. It just makes it worse for Hamish. He'll come to one of us if he needs to, so stop worryin'. She's partly right, though. He is a man, an' he can stand up for himself, an' eventually he will. Can ya see him puttin' up with this kind of behaviour after the weddin' with the violent temper the good lord gave him?'

He chuckled to himself, and I started to laugh—not because I was happy, but because he was right. Hamish was not one to take rubbish from anyone, and she would get a rude shock in the future when she did eventually experience that side of him.

'Are ya ready to go back?' he asked, a wide grin spreading across his face.

'Yes, I am now.' I sniffed loudly before he took my hand, pulled me to my feet and into his warm embrace where I wanted to stay forever.

I had left them all down by the river, most wrapped in blankets as they sat around the campfire deep in discussion. All except Tamara and Brian. I had noticed Leo's absence immediately, and soon after decided to go inside to check he was all right. Not finding him downstairs, I made my way up to his bedchamber. As was my usual fashion, I knocked once then pushed the door wide before walking straight in, a strangled scream filling the room. It took some time to realise the shrieks were my own, deafening all within a bull's roar. Summoning all my strength, I inhaled deeply in an attempt to calm myself and catch my breath, unable to take my eyes from Brian's naked body spread out on the bed. I took no notice of Leo lying beside him, or his nakedness, having been forced to gaze upon him in all his glory more times than I'd seen him fully dressed. I was unable to move, standing still as a statue in the middle of the room. I didn't know what to do or say for the third time in my life. I backed away slowly as Brian reached down and pulled a heavy quilt over them both, hiding their shame. I turned and ran out into the hallway and down the stairs to the empty living area, my heart in my throat.

I sat down heavily on an enormous couch all by myself, silently wishing someone else was in the house to talk to and try to erase the terrible image of what I had just seen from my mind. I couldn't believe it had happened again. I wondered if Brian was an exhibitionist who liked people to catch him in the act; however, I was confident after tonight I was his favourite. I started to giggle, and soon after collapsed into hysterical laughter. I howled so loudly that Leo and Brian came running downstairs, both now fully clothed. Just looking at them sent me off into peals of laughter. Tears poured down my face and my stomach muscles hurt, but I couldn't stop. Leo sat down next to me and shook me by both arms, appearing to believe what I had just witnessed had sent me well and truly mad.

'Abigail, calm yourself. You've got yourself into a state. Brian, I think you caused Abigail to go into shock. Look at what you have done to her. You should be ashamed of yourself.' Brian stared back at him blankly, setting me off once again.

I slowly walked back to the fire, still smiling to myself.

'What are you so happy about?' Aaron asked as I sat down on his lap and slipped my arms around his neck.

'I will tell you later.' I smirked wickedly, just as Dana came and sat by me.

'I'm thrilled Hamish has ended up tied to that evil, cold bitch. God has answered my prayers, ensuring he will never find peace or joy again in this lifetime. And he certainly won't love or be loved again if the angels above are smiling down on me. Even blind Bill can see there is nothing between the two of them.'

I gently placed my hand on her shoulder but didn't say anything. I wouldn't speak against Hamish no matter how she felt. I believed she was entitled to her feelings given what she had endured, but I hoped she would also respect mine.

We remained by the fire through the evening and into the wee hours, enjoying the night and the company. Everyone, for the most part, had a lovely Christmas—the last of the century and one that would live in my memory for the rest of my life.

We were returning home in a few days, but tonight we would celebrate New Year's Eve together. Tomorrow, we would enter the twentieth century, and I was excited about the changes that would bring. We had experienced a wonderful fortnight here, but it was time to disperse and have some time to ourselves. We had explored the property, finding a cave that Aaron told the children was a bushranger hideout, scaring them all away. We swam daily and walked along the riverbank together, while the children swung from ropes tied to tree limbs above the river, bravely dropping from great heights into the pristine water. We talked until there were no words left, ate great food prepared by Leo, and drank good wine.

By all accounts, everyone had an enjoyable time, apart from the tension between Tamara and Angelique, something we had all chosen to ignore. I noticed immediately that even tonight, they sat apart glaring hatefully at each other.

We gathered around the fire by the river waiting to see in the New Year. We had allowed the children to stay up late, as they were getting older now and were fairly sensible. Aaron had made sure there was plenty of grog on hand, and Leo had provided hot snacks for everyone that were passed around on platters. I was determined not to get drunk tonight, just happily merry, and refused offers of whisky, choosing to stick to beer. Elizabeth came to my side then sat down next to me.

'Abigail, I'm concerned about Tamara. I can't understand why she's defended Hamish so ferociously for the past two-weeks. I certainly understand why she would dislike his fiancé, as I think everyone here does, but we have all managed to control ourselves and be polite. I've tried to talk to her, but she only says it's not my business.' She appeared concerned, glancing across at Tamara as I patted her leg reassuringly.

'I wouldn't worry too much, Elizabeth. I think once your sister returns home she will soon be back to normal. It's difficult to spend so much time with someone you don't particularly like.' Eric strode over with a beer for each of us, then sat down, putting his arm around his wife. We chatted and drank until I was pleasantly warm, but not drunk. Gavin Cavanaugh sat with me, speaking of how pleased he was with the new factory.

'I wanted to thank you.' He embraced me for a moment, then relaxed back in his chair staring out over the river. 'I know you asked Aaron to fund our recent expansion, but of course I also know it came from you. I want you to believe me when I say this, dear Abigail. Even if you had turned up here all that time ago without a penny to your name, we still would've taken you in and loved you just the same.'

I felt tears prick my eyes. I had been a part of this family for nearly ten-years now, and I loved them as if they were connected to me by blood. His words meant more to him than he would know, and I embraced him for the longest time. He really had turned out to be the father I never had, and Aaron had given me the family I always wanted.

We sat for a time reminiscing of Hogmanays long gone that we had spent together, and how fortunate we were to see in a new century—all together, safe and truly loved. We sent the children off to bed, then Aaron took me by the hand and led me away from the group.

'I wanna dance with ya.' He smiled as he roughly pulled me into his arms. He sang a love song to me while we danced under the stars, our friends and family looking on. I heard Aaron's mother sigh, then saw her take her husband's hand in hers. Soon, they were all up dancing, whispering sweet words to each other under the romantic sky above. I could have stayed like this forever, but Aaron decided there was more beer to drink, led me back to the table, and poured another for me and himself. We sat watching the others for the longest time.

'What are ya dreams for the twentieth century?' I thought for a moment before answering.

'To be as happy as I am now. I want to watch our children grow into fine adults, then bounce our grandchildren on our knees. To have you by my side until we make old bones. To pass on a legacy to our children and their children that means something. To make a difference in this world in some positive way and leave the place better than we found it. What about you?'

I was curious about his intentions as we stepped into this new century. He was unpredictable in thought and deed sometimes, although I found his spontaneity inspiring and fun.

'Not much different to you, *mo anamchara*. I wanna see the nippers free to live as they please an' seek happiness where they find it—no matter how many we're blessed with. I wanna be as happy an' content as we are now when we are finally forced to part.' He gently stroked my hair from my face, kissing me deeply. 'Who knows what this new century will bring? Whatever happens, I'm sure it'll be excitin.'

'What's gunna be excitin'?' Angus interrupted, bringing us more beer. I decided I would drink two more glasses and then stop, not wanting to make a fool of myself on a night that would be forever etched in our memory.

I wanted to remember this night for the rest of my life. Abigail Cavanaugh—Abigail Delmont for a brief moment—an unwanted child with no surname was alive and well and standing here surrounded by love ready to see in the twentieth century. I was happy and healthy, and had everything I needed and all I could ever want. I wished my life could be frozen in time and things never changed, and I would always be this happy.

We saw in the New Year together, cheering for the future while reminiscing of the past—the festivities continuing into the wee hours. The moon was high in the sky when the celebrations started to die down and our loved ones slowly moved away from the fire one by one to find their beds for the night. Aaron took my hand, leading me up to the house and into our bedchamber. He locked the door as I slipped out of my dress and into my nightgown, joining him in bed. I cuddled into him, lay my head on his shoulder, then placed my hand over his heart.

I had remembered to make my special wish at midnight. When the clock had struck twelve, Aaron had held me in his arms and kissed me passionately under the stars, my silent prayer to expand our family sent above.

I kissed him gently on the cheek before revealing that I had caught Brian in the act for a third time, and he threw back his head and roared with laughter, his body shaking.

'I don't see the funny side to this at all, Aaron.' I screwed up my nose indignantly. 'You're not the one who has that image burned into your brain, not just once, but three times. Three different images with three different men, and none of them pleasant.' I grimaced at the memories now imprinted in my mind forever. It seemed I was making him laugh harder without meaning to. I pushed him away, turning my back to him until he had calmed.

'Happy New Year, *mo anamchara*.' He kissed my shoulder before I turned back to him. 'We haven't knocked boots since last year, so come here.' He took me in his arms and kissed me deeply. Later, as I drifted off to sleep in this new century, I dreamed of red poppies in a field, a silver spoon, and a dismal war over the ocean.

Chapter Thirteen

I WOKE TO FIND Aaron with his ear against my stomach. 'He could kick a goal for the Geelong Cats this mornin',' he announced proudly, moving up to kiss me. 'Now wait here. I've somethin' special for ya.' He jumped out of bed, quickly put more wood on the fire, then hurried out of the room.

It was June 1900, and I had fallen over Christmas when we were away with our friends and family at our Gippsland property. We had named the place Heavenly Hideaway and decided we would visit there at least once a year for a few weeks at a time given we'd all had such a wonderful time there. Our neighbour, Mr Garry Stewart, had agreed to care for our property when we weren't in residence. Aaron had insisted on paying him, which he adamantly refused, saying that was the Aussie way and the neighbourly thing to do. I was greatly impressed by his country kindness.

My pregnancy had been mostly trouble-free, but I was starting to experience pain in my back again, which was driving me mad. Other than that, I was feeling as well as I had when I carried the twins. I snuggled under the heavy covers, the only sound the crackling fire spreading warmth through the spacious bedchamber.

'I'm back,' he called out cheerfully, kicking the door closed behind him. He placed a tray holding an enormous chocolate cake down on the bed. Its ten candles burned brightly, complementing the glowing embers in the hearth. 'Happy tenth anniversary, *mo anamchara*. I love ya more now than the day we married if that's possible. Thank you for bein' you, Abi, an' for bein' the best wife an' mother a man could hope for.' He bent down and kissed me before walking over to the sideboard. He brought over a jug of hot chocolate with two cups and placed them on his bedside table, then came back to bed. 'I'll bet me left nut if ya weren't breedin', ya weddin' dress would still fit ya.'

'It wouldn't come near me now.' I laughed as I caressed my stomach. I was a little bigger this time, but not much, and I had already pulled out the dresses Catherine had made for me a decade ago when I carried the twins. I didn't care in the slightest if they were fashionable or not, when I wore them they brought back beautiful memories. We sat up in bed while Aaron cut the chocolate cake then placed a generous slice on a plate for me. 'It tastes exactly the same as the cupcakes you bring me for our monthly anniversary.' I laughed, kissing his chocolaty lips then wiping his wide mouth with my finger.

'That's 'cause it is. Leo used the same ingredients, but turned it into a big one.' He chuckled, his mouth full. 'I like the cupcakes much better 'cause I get to eat 'em while I wait. The tool wouldn't let me have even a bite outta one this mornin'. Not even a crumb. He's as tight as a fish's arsehole.'

He looked disappointed, while I smothered a smile. We drank the creamy, hot chocolate and ate half of the cake, then lay down, comfortably full.

'Are ya gunna be all right to travel an' do what ya have to do tomorrow?' His handsome brow was furrowed, concern clear in his bright blue eyes, the colour of the ocean, as he gently stroked my belly.

Over a month ago, Aiden and Victoria had accompanied us to Melbourne to spend a weekend, enjoying the hospitality of The Delmont. Aiden had gone for a walk by himself to buy Victoria a gift and found a saddled horse wandering down the road. As he didn't know Melbourne at all, he mounted the horse and rode through the streets trying to find the local police station. He wandered through the city, lost and unable to find his bearings, when two young constables saw him, recognised the reportedly stolen horse and pursued him. They soon caught up with him and violently pulled him down onto the road, where he hit his head.

He was arrested and charged with horse stealing, and his court case was being heard in Melbourne tomorrow. I had been called as a character witness. Even though Victoria and Aaron were also there that weekend, she was his wife, and he was his brother; therefore, Richard felt my account of what occurred that afternoon would hold far more weight with the jury. Richard was confident Aiden would be acquitted given he had never committed a crime before, he had no motive to steal the horse, and he was of good and decent character. We planned to catch the late train today so I could rest before court tomorrow, and also visit with William and Beatrice.

Aaron leaned over to his drawer, pulled out a wrapped box, and handed it to me. One thing I found since leaving the orphanage was that I loved getting presents. Everything I was given, no matter how small or inexpensive, I appreciated and loved. I tore the brown paper off and opened the box. I stared at the contents for a long time, unable to find the words. It was beautiful—whatever it was. Not a bracelet, yet it wasn't big enough to be a necklace, either. The fine gold chain dripped with diamonds, reminding me of the tassels that held the heavy drapes in place during the day. I stared across at my husband, still unable to speak. He noticed my puzzled expression and grinned at me, his eyes sparkling.

'I confided in Mr Dawson an' told him how much I admire ya feet an' ya ankles. He thought I was takin' the piss when I asked him to make somethin' to adorn 'em with, but soon came up with this.' He took the anklet from me and placed it around my right ankle. It fit perfectly, the glittering diamonds dangling down onto my foot. I lay back and held my leg up in the air to admire it.

'It's beautiful, Aaron. Who would have thought the day would come when you would run out of places to hang your diamonds and would have to resort to my foot? Thank you, my love.' I kissed him noisily through my laughter, then handed him the present I'd asked Mr Dawson to make for him. He opened the box, his handsome face breaking into a radiant smile.

'It's a ripper, Abi. Thank you, *mo anamchara*.' He slipped it onto his right ring finger, the thick, solid gold band holding three small diamonds in the corner representing me and the twins.

'When the bairn is born, Mr Dawson can add another diamond to it.'

'There's one more anniversary present I want.' He grabbed me by the shoulders and pulled me on top of his large frame, chuckling to himself before drawing me down to kiss him.

We sat together at the kitchen table with Thomas and Emmy when Hamish joined us.

'What do ye want done while yer away trippin' the lights fantastic in Melbourne?' He sat down in between the twins and began munching loudly on some toast.

'Just talk to Harry an' Angus when ya can catch 'em. They know what's to be done, but ya can start with the horses. Monty is due to be broken to harness 'cause he's been bought an' paid for an' they want him yesterday. I don't wanna rush him just 'cause of their impatience. They can bloody well wait till he's ready. He's goin' with three others, an' I've formed the opinion the buyer is far too wealthy for their own good, an' hasn't had to wait for a thing since the day they drew their first breath.'

Hamish nodded, finishing a large glass of orange juice before belching loudly. He was looking a lot healthier these days, and appeared far happier.

We had attended his engagement party for Angelique—a lavish affair—and tried to show our support by having them over to dinner many times. I always made certain we did everything a proper grand house should do when she was present, even though it made me uncomfortable in my own home. Angelique had remained cold and distant despite our offer of friendship and was intensely focused on herself. Hamish had lost the sparkle in his eye and the bounce in his step. He had walked around for months in a daze, his misery obvious to all, with several of the farm workers comparing him to a convict about to be led to the gallows at Melbourne Gaol.

The much anticipated event came around far too quickly, but we ensured we were there at St. Mary's Church in Geelong to witness the unhappy union. Sitting inside the beautiful bluestone church brought back lovely memories of my own wedding day. Hamish stood nervously at the altar with Angus and Aaron by his side, along with eight men I had never laid eyes on before. Even I was forced to admit the wedding was far too extravagant and was starting to look ridiculous when the ten bridesmaids came marching down the aisle then stood to the left of the altar in their oversized, cornflower blue gowns.

Colin and Harriet Makenzie were beaming as they stood looking down the aisle, waiting for the wedding they had so desperately wanted and were so willing to sacrifice their son's happiness for. Angelique slowly walked down the aisle, reminding me of an exquisite painted doll. Hamish stared blankly over her head at the back of the church, refusing to look at her even for a moment. Her father enthusiastically passed her to Hamish, who took her hand before she joined him at the altar. I could see Hamish's hands shaking, and he looked sick, sweat pouring from every part of him. Aaron noticed, too, and placed his hand on his shoulder to steady him.

The priest started the service, and when it came time for Hamish to say his vows, there was silence for what seemed like an eternity. Angelique shook his hands, trying to get a response, but he turned away and stared at the priest, then Angelique, then straight at me, shaking his head as though trying to wake from a bad dream. He turned back to Angelique, told her loudly he couldn't go through with it, then hurried down the aisle with Aaron and Angus close behind.

Furious, Angelique had screamed and cursed, then chased him down the aisle, shrieking in between her threats to make him suffer. She walloped him over the head with her bouquet several times, damning him to hell as he continued to walk away, ignoring her violent and very public outburst. I had hurried to the carriage to meet Aaron, and we had taken Hamish back to Willow Grove where he sat celebrating with Aaron well into the night before they both staggered off to find their beds.

The next day, Hamish went to face his parents, who had all his possessions packed and waiting for him, telling him bluntly he was now on his own. He returned soon after and told us of his situation, and Angus and Polly generously offered for him to move in with them, making him a permanent resident of Willow Grove from that day forward. He worked closely with Aaron from dawn till dusk, and was getting to know the running of the farm nearly as well as he did.

Hamish finished a stack of pancakes, then teasingly stole some bacon from Emmy's plate.

'Uncle Hamish, that's not fair,' she complained, her sweet little face now serious. 'You shouldn't steal 'cause it's a sin. Ask Bessie, she'll tell you true, but I'll let you have it 'cause I love you.'

Hamish smiled down at her, wrapped his arm around her tiny shoulder, then pulled her in close to his side for a cuddle, continuing to chew on her bacon. He was the happiest I had seen him in a very long time. He had spent so much time with us before he was disowned, both visiting and working with Aaron, and had settled quickly into his new life here.

Tamara, though, was a thorn in his side. She was obsessed and hounded him every time she came to stay. Long before he'd left Angelique at the altar. Although he constantly rebuffed her, she would not leave him alone. He was trying to get his life in some kind of order, and he didn't want to be sleeping with a married woman now. It was getting to the point where I would be forced to stop her visits for a while. It was becoming uncomfortable for everyone, with her turning up at the cottage at all hours, disturbing Angus, Polly, and the children.

'What are yer plans fer the day, Abigail?' Hamish asked, finishing his meal before wiping his mouth with a napkin.

'Not much. We're already packed for Melbourne, and I don't feel like walking anywhere to visit with anyone today.' I smiled weakly, reaching down to rub my aching back.

'Maybe ya should go back to bed,' Aaron suggested then winked at me. 'I'm handin' over to Hamish for the next few days. It shouldn't take too long, then I'm free to join ya.'

Bed did sound like a good idea. It was storming outside, and the wind was blowing the trees sideways from what I could see through the window. I could think of no place I would rather be than snuggled up in my bed reading a book.

'Yes, I think I will go back to bed for a while.' I covered my mouth as I yawned loudly, closing my eyes for a moment.

'Not before you eat this, fatty,' Leo teased, placing a steaming vegetable omelette down in front of me.

'But we just ate half the chocolate cake,' I protested, eyeing the delicious-looking omelette.

'Yes, and your point? When has that ever bothered you? Chocolate cake is not good for the baby. This is, so eat.' He hurried off to find my raspberry syrup, returning soon after. I ate the large omelette, so full of vegetables the egg only barely held it together. Aaron rose to his feet then bent down and kissed me goodbye, while Hamish wished me luck for tomorrow as they left through the back door.

'Now, you two need to put on your thick coats, scarves, and hats, and don't forget the gloves and the leather boots,' I called out to Thomas and Emmy, who ran to the back hallway to retrieve them. They returned wrapped in layers of clothing so thick all I could see was their little faces smiling back at me. They kissed me and Leo goodbye, met their cousins at the door, then ran to school through the wind and the rain.

Leo poured me a coffee and sat down. This was our morning time together, our ritual. We spent it mostly gossiping and laughing, but sometimes there were serious issues to discuss, or we would confide things to each other that we wouldn't tell anyone else.

'Are you sure you will be all right for tomorrow? It's just that I worry about you, Abigail,' he said sweetly, sipping his coffee.

'I'll be fine. I've had no problems at all carrying this time. There is no need to fret. It will all turn out for the best, I'm sure.' We gossiped for a time without interruption, Leo telling me since Brian had started to accompany Tamara once a month to stay with us, he was enjoying their secret bedroom romps, despite not liking the man much. I couldn't understand where his head was. Brian was the loveliest person I knew and, although a quiet man, he had an engaging personality. And I believed he deserved a medal for putting up with Tamara.

Aaron walked back into the kitchen, stopping as soon as he saw Leo and me.

'What are ya still doin' up? Talkin' about all the filthy business goin' on around here, I bet.' Leo looked up at him, a mockingly prudish expression on his handsome face.

'Why do you think that's all Abigail and I have on our minds, Aaron? Maybe you're projecting your own dirty fantasies onto us.'

'Cause that's what fills ya minds. Don't forget, I hear ya talkin' occasionally, an' it's enough to burn ya ears off. It embarrasses me to even listen, let alone talk like a bushy in public.' He laughed loudly as he poured himself a cup of coffee, then sat down. 'So, Abi, do ya still tell Leo how fantastic I am in bed, teasin' him 'cause he can never have me?' Aaron asked, a twinkle in his bright blue eyes. I rolled my eyes and made gagging sounds while Leo giggled in delight.

'No, I do not. That's all in your mind. Do you think you are the only man we talk about?' I teased, and he chuckled to himself.

'Oh, Goliath, if you only knew the filthy, disgusting things that come out of your wife's mouth.' Leo laughed again before continuing. 'Who would ever have guessed she was raised in a house of God by God's own wives? I wouldn't. It looks like religion hasn't touched her mind or that black soul of hers. She hasn't been scarred like the rest of us, who were brainwashed as children. My parents dragged me to church every Sunday, and look how I turned out.' Aaron stared across at him thoughtfully, arching an eyebrow.

'An' ya truly think Abi didn't have religion shoved down her throat a million times more than you've had to put up with? From what ya told me, ya parents are bush baptists.' Leo stared back at him blankly, his expression one of complete confusion as Aaron threw back his head and howled.

'Sunday Christians us Catholics would call it,' I interjected helpfully, smiling reassuringly at Leo as relief washed over him while Aaron composed himself.

'Kinda means that. The sayin' refers more to the souls among us with little to no spiritual conviction, or no faith at all in anythin' outside of 'emseves. Atheism is more fittin' I s'pose. I don't believe religion had anythin' to do with how ya turned out, mate. Let me try an' remember the exact words ya used.' Leo appeared curious but was clearly thrilled the attention was back on him where he firmly believed it belonged—every minute, of every hour, of every day, of every week, of every month, of every exhausting year after year after bloody year since I'd known him. Just thinking about it made me yawn and want to find my bed and nap. 'Hmm, that's right,' Aaron remarked, tapping his nostril for a moment. 'I recall that ya called 'em hypocrites who harangued an' harassed ya an' constantly gave ya the hairy eyeball. Ya also accused the people that gave ya life of possessin' black souls. Ya told me, an' anyone within a bull's roar that'd listen, ya couldn't believe the kirk they attend is still standin', confusin' ya no end as to why the roof hasn't fallen in on top of 'em before they even get the opportunity to anoint 'emselves at the door.' Aaron snorted in amusement, while Leo continued to stare back at him blankly. 'Ya clearly stated that they forced religion on ya, an' 'cause of that, ya have a morbid fear of goin' to hell, even though ya don't believe in it. See, I do listen to ya when ya spin ya yarns. You're forever accusin' me of ignorin' ya when in reality, I'm ya most loyal listener.' He took a sip of coffee before clearing his throat. 'Then there's the matter ya raised askin' why Abi isn't scarred like ya. She isn't a sheep, an' fortunately has a strong mind. I doubt anyone could force her to believe in somethin' she found inconsistent an' hypocritical. If ya actually sit down, Leo, an' listen to Abi when she speaks about it, ya would understand that she believes religion is used as a form of social control, to keep people in their place.' Aaron smiled at the vacant expression on his face.

'I believe there is something on the other side,' I added, 'but I don't know what that is yet. I hope I find out more about it before I have to go there.' I giggled as Aaron put his arm around my shoulders and kissed the top of my head.

'Oh, me, too,' Leo interjected, jumping up and down in his seat and clapping in excitement. 'I'm not stepping through those golden gates until Saint Christopher confirms in writing they have all the luxuries I enjoy and deserve, and swears a solemn oath they intend to provide them to me whenever I ring my bell to call them to attend to my simple needs.' I shook my head in disbelief.

'Saint Peter. And the gates are pearl, not gold, you fat headed moron. I don't believe for one-minute your poor parents forced religion on you. You think Arthur Conan Doyle is personal friends with Sherlock Holmes and his cast of characters?' He nodded vigorously as I shook my head again, Aaron looking on in amusement, his mouth twitching. 'My point is, you believe Sherlock and his mates commute between here and the boarding house they live in two doors down from Jesus, Mary, and Joseph, four streets away from the pearly gates. You know nothing about religion or the Christian faith. You're a hypocrite for even calling yourself Catholic.' He widened his eyes at me before pretending to yawn.

'I don't need to know anything. I make it all up as I go along, no different from the leaders who stand up the front leading their flocks to salvation. If I want to call your Saint Peter my Saint Christopher, I will.' He waved his hand in the air, demanding our attention. 'Back to me, Abigail. You've been preaching from the pulpit for far too long, so step away. Back to me I said!' I rolled my eyes but gave in and turned back to him. 'Now, where was I? Oh, yes. The peasants will clear a path for me as I approach the golden gates and check with Saint Chris they'll allow me to wear my pink pants. I will not commit to spending eternity there until they prove to me it will be fabulous.'

Aaron chuckled before rising to his feet and pulling me to mine, bidding a flustered Leo goodbye before ushering me upstairs.

'I can't think of a better way to spend our anniversary than in this cosy room with you. Have ya seen it outside? I hope the nippers got to school okay an' didn't get blown away. I wish we were still at the cottage, though.' He smiled wistfully, climbing up on the bed then settling himself next to me. He had whisked me off to the honeymoon cottage for a few days and we had only returned last night, knowing we had to be ready to leave for Melbourne. 'Turn over an' I'll get the knots out.' I moved closer and made myself comfortable. He pushed firmly on the areas he knew pained me, instant relief washing over me and almost sending me to sleep. He stopped suddenly, placing his hands on my cheeks and kissing me gently on the lips. 'Come an' sit on me. I just wanna look at ya belly.' He pulled me close, then wrapped both hands around my stomach. 'Ya look even more beautiful when you're carrying me child.' He stared in wonderment as my belly moved in his hands to the kicks of the baby. I leaned down and kissed him for the longest time until he no longer noticed my stomach.

Thomas and Emmy stood on the front steps with Leo, Hamish, Bessie, and little Mary waving us off. I hated leaving the twins behind.

'Do you think we should have taken them with us?' I asked Aaron as I waved goodbye through the open window before the carriage abruptly pulled away.

'Do ya need spectacles? Did they look like they'd notice our absence, let alone fret for us? They couldn't give a fat rat's arse whether we're there or not.' He chuckled to himself, shifting in his seat and trying to get comfortable in our new carriage. 'Nah, Abi. This sorry business is not for the nippers to witness, an' we'd only have 'em locked up in the hotel with little Mary. It's best they stay home, an' it gives us a couple of days together without work an' constant interruptions.'

We arrived soon after at the station in Geelong. We bid Harry farewell then made our way onto the platform, stepping up into the first-class carriage before finding our compartment. Aaron sat in his usual place next to the window, while I took the seat next to him, leaning in close as he slipped his arm around my shoulders. As the train started to pull away, I wondered as I so often did when we travelled to Melbourne if Aaron had booked the entire compartment. Not once in all these years had we ever had to share a compartment, and I had my suspicions.

'I'm confident they'll drop the bullshit charges once ya give ya evidence. It's been a circus from the start,' Aaron growled, his jaw set. 'The coppers wouldn't listen to anyone, not even the witnesses who came forward to say they saw the beast wanderin' alone for hours before poor Aiden mounted him. They were set on chargin' him from the start. They're corrupt bastards, bashin' his head into the ground, then claiming he fell. There were a hundred witnesses to it, but they're too intimidated by the Victorian police to come forward an' tell the truth. 'Twas only the luck of the Irish that saved him from bein' killed that day.'

I nodded, shifting again in my seat to get comfortable, my head on his shoulder, then closed my eyes. I was nervous about tomorrow. I had never given evidence in a court of law before. It wasn't the legal terms they used. I'd read a number of law books and understood their implications. It unsettled me when anyone, stranger or neighbour, focused on me. I hated to be the centre of attention, and they would be listening to every word I said. I feared I might say the wrong thing by mistake and ruin everything. I would never forgive myself if I caused Aiden to lose the case.

'What do ya wanna do for tea, *mo anamchara*? Go out or stay in?' Aaron asked, stroking my head.

'I'm happy to see what's new on The Delmont menu once we arrive,' I murmured, feeling ravenous all of a sudden.

The moon was high in the sky when we stepped into reception and were shown to our usual suite on the top floor at the front of the building, looking down over Swanston and Flinders streets and the Yarra River. The bright city lights twinkled beneath us as we stood watching the people and carriages down below still filling the streets.

'Did ya wanna see Dana an' Vicki tonight? We could meet 'em in the restaurant here if you're up to it?' Aaron asked as he stood behind me, his hands placed firmly on my rounded belly.

'Yes, I would love to. I am really worried about Victoria and the children with Aiden being locked up for all this time.' I placed my hands over his and sighed deeply.

'I'll go ask 'em now to meet for dinner in an hour.' He prepared to leave, his hands dropping to his side. I turned and kissed him before making my way over to the bed.

'Thanks, my love. You are a wonderful husband, and I love you.' I lowered myself onto the bed and stretched my back.

Dana, Victoria, and the children had been staying at The Delmont since Aiden's arrest, visiting him daily. He was being held in the cells at Pentridge prison in Coburg, just on the outskirts of Melbourne. I was looking forward to seeing them and finding out how they were holding up. I put my feet up on a pillow, admiring my ankle bracelet, the light glinting off it, while I waited for Aaron.

'It's arranged. Are ya feet sore, Abi?' He closed the door then silently crossed the room to my side, his brow creased in concern.

'Just a bit. They are a little swollen.'

'Here, let me take a squiz.' He sat down heavily on the end of the bed and took my feet in his enormous hands. He gently massaged them, providing instant relief. I lay back down in bliss as he rubbed his fingers over them hard then tried to massage the fluid from my ankles. 'Does that feel better, *mo anamchara*?' He continued to hold my feet in his large hands, his eyes sparkling as he stared across at me.

'Yes, much better,' I struggled to sit up, but somehow managed to climb up on his lap and wrap my legs around him before placing my lips on his.

'Ahh, it's like that, is it?' I ignored him and continued kissing him till he kissed me back.

We met Dana and Victoria, who were enjoying a small pre-dinner drink in the bar, then joined them at a table for four. Aaron ordered a twenty-five-year-old scotch for himself and a lemonade for me, into which I discreetly poured some raspberry syrup, then drank thirstily. Aaron then ordered me a jug of lemonade, knowing how much raspberry syrup I was going through lately. I finished the jug before dinner arrived and he ordered another.

'Thank you so much for coming and speaking for Aiden tomorrow, Abigail,' Victoria said, holding my hand. I squeezed hers and smiled.

'Please don't think anything of it, Vicki. We are family, and of course I would come and try to help in any way I can,' I replied, to which she smiled half-heartedly.

'You're looking tired, Abigail. Are you getting enough rest?' Dana asked, her brows furrowed as she examined my face closely.

'I'm older than I was with the twins, and I tire far easier. I shouldn't complain, though. Compared to others, my pregnancy is wonderful.'

'Well, you certainly look amazing. You have the same curved stomach you had with the twins. It's so sweet and lovely,' Dana remarked, placing her hand on my belly and waiting for the baby to kick. Other guests watched us intently, some whispering behind their hands. I was obviously with child and not confined, or restrained, at home. We ignored their judgement glances and snide remarks and chatted cheerfully throughout our meal. 'Well, you go and get your rest for tomorrow, sweetie. We don't have to be there until ten o'clock in the morning. Aaron, you make sure she sleeps as long as possible,' Dana ordered, and he smiled down at her.

'Anythin' ya say, Mother,' he teased, his eyes twinkling.

'And you'd be a fool to forget it,' Dana called over her shoulder before disappearing into the elevator, always wanting to have the last word.

I woke to find Aaron lying on his side, not taking his eyes from my face, even when I stared back at him and arched my brow inquiringly.

'What?' I asked sleepily.

'You'd better go back to sleep. It's too early. Dana will strike me down dead, an' the last thing I need is her breathin' down me neck about ya. I thought me life would be easy since ya didn't have parents, leavin' me without a mother-in-law to contend with. I have to admit, I was grateful for it, too. I've heard far too many stories about the interferin' an' general nuisances they make of 'emselves. Little did I know I'd end up with two of 'em, each as fierce an' unreasonable as the other.'

'Bessie and Dana?' I giggled to myself, and he nodded, pretending to grimace in pain as I smacked him on the arm.

It was just getting light outside, the day overcast and grey. I had hours before I was required to get up and prepare myself.

'All ya have to do today is tell the truth,' he reassured me, gently stroking my face with his finger.

'Thanks, Aaron. I wasn't even thinking about court until you brought it up, and now I feel all nervous again.' I playfully smacked him on the arm a second time. He pulled me up onto him, turning me to face him. He stared at me intently, then placed his hands on my stomach.

'You do look tired, *mo anamchara*,' he observed, caressing my belly as he lay back down to look at me. This pregnancy must have been taking more out of me than I realised.

'Honestly, I feel fine,' I assured him.

It probably was time for me to start slowing down a little. I rose early every day, and once I had seen the twins off to school, I would oversee the running of the main house, then visit the village to check on the welfare of the residents. Some just enjoyed sitting and having a chat, while others would come to me with problems and complaints, expecting me to resolve them within the hour.

It took a lot of my energy to remain calm and not lose my head due to the frustrations the petty squabbles and gossip caused me. I found some of the women the most difficult to deal with, especially when it involved an argument with another of the village wives. I had my favourites, like Jenny, Margaret, and Maisie, along with Patty, and Amelia, who I now considered close friends and confidants. For some reason, despite all my efforts, the other wives weren't as friendly towards me.

Margaret had explained to me during one of our wine-drinking visits that some of the wives were intimidated by or jealous of me, going on to assure me I wasn't to concern myself with any of it as my real friends knew my heart. These women supported me unconditionally when it came to my involvement in village life and being appointed, albeit against my will, as the unofficial caretaker of all our workers and their families.

Aaron now had his hands behind me, massaging my lower back. It was such a relief. The doctor had already said I was carrying the same way as the twins, confirming in my own mind I had a few more months left to suffer. I knew that it got worse before it got better. As I sat on top of him, I sighed deeply as my body relaxed under his touch. Soon after, I had fallen back into a fitful sleep, dreams of sugarcane, ships and chains filling my head.

I gazed into the oval mirror as I sat at the dressing table while the hotel ladies' maid silently attended to my hair. I had put on the dress Catherine had made me especially for court. It was conservative, but I felt comfortable and wanted to make a good impression on the jury. The maid wound my curls up and bound them at the nape of my neck, which I liked very much. I now planned to show Bessie how to recreate the style once we returned home and this sorry business was behind us. I thanked her and rose to my feet, turning to find Aaron at the door, shifting from foot to foot impatiently.

'We'd best be off, then.' He took my hand and kissed me firmly on the lips, smearing the gloss the maid had applied. 'Ya look like a very wealthy, respectable lady.' I looked down and studied my dress then turned back to him.

'Don't I look like this at other times?' He raised his eyebrows, his wide mouth twitching.

'Yeah, nah. When ya go ‘round in bare feet with ya hair down, ya look like a free-spirited gypsy. Don't ever change, me girl.' He smiled and kissed off the rest of my gloss.

The carriage stopped outside the Melbourne Supreme Court, the street bustling with people, while up ahead there seemed to have been an incident, bringing the carts, trams and carriages to a standstill. Aaron helped Victoria and Dana out of the carriage, then lifted me down onto the street. We found the courtroom where Aiden's case was to be heard and sat down on the seats provided just outside to wait. A well dressed clerk stepped out into the wide hall, announcing the court was now in session. I remained where I was while everyone around me shuffled into the room. There were several others called to bear witness, who were also not allowed in until called to give evidence. Aaron decided to wait with me, reluctant to leave me alone in my condition. He held my hand firmly in his while I rested my head on his shoulder.

'Vicki's wound up tighter than a ball of string,' he remarked, leaning back in his seat to observe the odd person hurrying past us.

'The poor darling. If I were in her position, I would be far worse.' I swallowed several times in an attempt to remove the lump in my throat, anxiety settling in the pit of my stomach and refusing to leave.

'Ya know, Leo tried to convince me to bring him to the trial. He reckons he can win the case for Aiden by givin' evidence.' I turned and gazed up at him, unable to hide my confusion.

'But he wasn't there. As usual, the fat headed moron makes no sense.'

'He seems to think you'll ruin the case by openin' ya fat mouth, but he also believes if he got into the witness box an' told all present what a lovely boy Aiden is, he'd get off. Even blind Freddy would take anythin' he says with a grain of salt.' He chuckled quietly, while I shook my head and rolled my eyes but said nothing.

We sat together in the now empty room talking quietly until we noticed Dana and Victoria hurrying towards us, both appearing strained.

'Richard wants to meet for lunch,' Dana advised before sitting down beside me, taking my hand in hers.

Richard joined us shortly afterwards and led us out and down the busy road to a coffee palace a few streets away from the courthouse. We placed our orders while Richard poured sweet water from a blue bottle for everyone as we sat around the large, round table.

'I know it appears it hasn't gone well due to this morning's events, but once we have Abigail testify, I am positive we will win.' Richard leaned back in his chair and sighed, his shoulders visibly relaxing. I drank my water, enjoying every refreshing sip. We chatted animatedly through lunch about everything except Aiden's case, before Richard stood to go and pay the bill.

'Thanks for lunch, Victoria,' I called out as I took Aaron's hand in mine then started to walk back towards the courthouse, chatting with Dana while Vicki hurried to catch up with us.

'What do you mean? I didn't pay,' she asked as she fell into step with us, staring across at me, her big, blue eyes wide.

'Oh, but you did. Richard paid, and don't think he won't charge you like a wounded bull when it comes time to pay him for his services. He may be our friend and we love him, but at the end of the day, he is still a lawyer.'

Chapter Fourteen

I WAS THE LAST to be called in to testify. I felt my stomach drop at the thought of being alone in front of so many people and having to speak. Aaron squeezed my hand and kissed me good luck, then I followed the court officer inside. Aaron wasn't far behind and took a seat beside his family, many who had arrived this morning for the trial. They all appeared calm, and seemed so confident Aiden's name would be cleared, it eased my nerves a little.

I made my way to the witness box, my head down and my eyes fixed on the polished floor. I couldn't look at anyone, although I could feel all eyes were on me. I stepped up inside the little box, held my right hand on the Bible, and gave an oath to the court officer that I would only tell the truth, or my soul would be immediately sent to Hell. Well, that was how he made me feel, glaring at me suspiciously before whisking the Bible away and returning to his seat at the side of the courtroom.

I turned to look up at the judge sitting only a few yards when I began to shake uncontrollably, my heart in my throat. I held onto the side of the witness box to support myself, my vision starting to blur.

'Excuse me, Mrs Cavanaugh. You have gone pale. Please be seated in the chair provided for you. I can see we have brought you out of your confinement,' the judge remarked plainly. I sat down heavily on the chair that had just been placed behind me, feeling more and more panicked as I tried to catch my breath. My heart raced and my hands trembled, my eyes going wide as I tried to clear my vision and slow my breathing. Within a few moments, I had managed to regain some control. Aaron, along with every single soul present, stared silently at me across the large room with great concern but were unable to help even if they wanted to intervene.

I felt a wave of fear crash over me as I slowly raised my head to look at the judge, the swirling black aura around him the colour of ebony, affecting me so deeply and without warning I felt I would vomit on the floor in front of him. The judge sitting before me—a man we had crossed paths with at Tamara's engagement party more than a decade ago—now identified as the Honourable Judge George Maslow.

His dark eyes were fixed on me, but I couldn't focus or even look in his direction. All I could see was that black aura, giving me knots in the pit of my stomach, a feeling of dread running so deep I felt it touch every part of my being. I forced myself to turn my head away and look towards my family and friends, locking eyes with Aaron immediately. I was uncertain if he remembered this man or not, but he had certainly noticed my reaction once I recognised him.

The prosecution stood and questioned me first, asking me personal questions about Aiden. He tried to insinuate my brother-in-law lived a secret life none of us knew anything about. I strongly denied this, and told them everything I knew about Aiden—what a hard worker he was, and that he was a good and decent husband and father. After he sat down, it was Richard's turn, who smiled reassuringly as he approached. I had managed to calm myself a little, focusing my attention on anything but the Judge.

'We have heard you say here today, Mrs Cavanaugh, a number of positive things regarding your brother-in-law, Mr Aiden Cavanaugh.' I nodded before Richard turned back to the court as he stood in front of me, then towards the jury..

'Yes, because it's true.' I too looked across at the jury made up entirely of men.

'You appear to be a woman of means, Mrs Cavanaugh. My understanding is that you are one of the wealthiest women in the state of Victoria, and most likely Australia.' I flinched then felt my face start to flush, not wanting to answer. I couldn't understand why Richard was bringing up my own personal business when it had nothing to do with Aiden's case.

'I'm not sure about that.'

'I can stand here, your honour, and stake my life on the fact this is true.' Richard strode theatrically up and down in front of the jury, raising his arm as he spoke to emphasise his point.

'Where are these questions leading, counsellor? I'm finding them quite irrelevant?' Judge Maslow snapped, and I felt myself silently agreeing with him even though the man terrified me.

'I am about to tell you, your honour. Mrs Cavanaugh, if Aiden needed any money—or a horse—would you help him?' I saw a twinkle in his eye and smiled back weakly.

'Certainly. We own a stud of rare breed horses. We would help in any way we could if that ever happened, and would provide him with one of our own horses at no cost.' I glanced back across at the jury, most with kindly faces.

After I had answered a few more questions, Richard returned to the table where he sat next to the police prosecutor, he advised he had nothing further to add. I sighed in relief, my head lowered and my eyes fixed on the floor. The judge loudly announced I was dismissed, but motioned for me to stay where I was.

'We will adjourn until tomorrow morning at ten o'clock. I would like to see Mrs Cavanaugh in my chambers immediately. The court is dismissed.' He slammed down the wooden gavel then left through a back door in all his glory, his robe swishing behind him and his horsehair wig slightly askew. I stared across at Aaron, who shrugged his shoulders, his expression just as puzzled as my own.

I was led by a court officer through a door, down a hallway, and into a wood-panelled office with shelves lining every wall, filled to the brim with leather-bound books, and an expensive leather lounge behind me. The large, carved desk made of solid wood, a high-backed leather chair behind it, took up half of the room. I noticed there was nothing out of place on the desk as I sat down on a smaller leather chair, waiting to see why Judge Maslow had summoned me. The entire room was meticulous in every way, from the furnishings to how spotlessly clean it was kept.

The door opened and George Maslow entered, the wig gone and his dark hair now combed neatly, a warm smile on his lips; although he still wore his robe. I attempted to smile back while I waited for him to sit at his desk. As he closed the door behind him, I saw him turn the key in the lock then place it in his pocket. My stomach dropped, and I could feel fear rising in me. He removed his robe then sat down behind his desk, leaned back, and stared at me in silence for the longest time. He was a handsome man, although his brown, almost black eyes were cold and devoid of emotion.

'Do you remember me?' His voice was low and charming, taking me aback for a moment. I swallowed hard, attempting to control the fear rising up in me by breathing deep and slow. And I held onto the fact he had not acted in any way to justify the irrational terror I felt when in his presence.

'I believe we have met, but that was a long time ago.' My voice faltered, my hands folded in my lap so he couldn't see that they were shaking.

'Not from then, from before that?' A strange look settled on his face as a chill ran through me. I hadn't a clue what he was referring to, and the confusion showed clearly on mine.

'To my knowledge, we were not acquainted before the night of Tamara and Brian's engagement party.' I stared up at the books behind him, unable to look directly at him. His great height, dark hair, and confident manner stood out, leaving me convinced I would remember him no matter what the circumstance.

'It's true then. You came back without your memory. Why would you choose to do that?' He shook his head in disbelief and let out a long, slow whistle. I had no idea what the hell he was talking about, and the more he spoke, the more confused I became. 'Damn it, Abigail,' he snarled, and I jumped, startled at his manner. 'I have every memory we ever shared stored in my mind for eternity. Because of your unbelievably foolish decision to wipe your memory in this life, I am unable to tell you anything of what we shared, or when this lifetime even occurred. Whether it was five-hundred-years ago or fifty, I'm unable to speak of it. Damn you to Grimsell, Abigail. I have spent a long time waiting for this moment. You are the reason I came back to complete another life cycle. Have you no memory whatsoever of Hiriarni or any of your past lives here on this planet?'

My mouth dropped open in disbelief and I felt all the blood drain from my face. I was convinced this man who sat so calmly before me was a lunatic, and I was seriously frightened. I considered for a moment if a black aura signified some sort of mental deficit, while noting everything about him appeared normal—although he clearly believed everything he was saying.

'I'm sorry. You may have mistaken me for someone else,' was all I could think to say. He stared at my face, then my breasts, causing the hair on my neck to stand up. I felt as if he was undressing me with his eyes, and I shifted in my seat, squirming under his stare.

'Oh, my dear, simple, servant wife, I remember *you*. Right from the minute I saw you again at Tamara's engagement I wanted to fuck you like you've never been fucked in this lifetime, but you always had that rather large husband of yours around. What? You're shocked? Surely you've had many men approach you over the years. I know for a fact you have, but you wouldn't remember that now.' His eyes bored into me, appearing as if in a trace, while my fear continued to rise. I doubted very much I would be believed if I relayed this conversation to anyone, even my closest friends. He appeared quite normal to those around him, and obviously had the skills to hide the fact he was a raving lunatic underneath the cloak of respectability he shrouded himself in.

'Yes, I am shocked, and highly offended. I have never had anyone be so blunt with me. But I can assure you that you will not get to fuck me, as you so crudely put it. I'm married and I love my husband. I don't know who you believe me to be, but you're wrong.' My voice shook with anger and fear. He abruptly rose to his feet and walked around the desk, then sat back on it in front of me.

'I can assure you I will. We can do this the easy way or the hard way. I didn't want to come back here, and only did so because you drew me back, you wicked bitch. You bewitched me, triggering an obsession I can't control. You thought you could get away from me, but I followed you back after escaping from where my soul was being held in Grimsell. It's not a place you have ever been, and I wouldn't wish it on anyone. It's almost impossible to escape from, and it took me a very long time to achieve; however, as you know, I am a very determined man. I refuse to return there after this lifetime or the next.' His dark eyes glinted dangerously, and I shivered, averting my gaze. Leaning forward, he slowly ran his finger along my jawline, sending cold chills through me.

'I will not let an evil bastard like you touch me, even with someone else's syphilis-infected prick,' I spat, attempting to stand. He swung his arm back and struck me in the face, my eye stinging. I felt warm blood trickling down my cheek, my body frozen with fear on the chair.

'Does that change your mind?' he enquired, brazenly running his finger down my collar bone.

'No. Fuck off, you filthy cocksucker,' I screamed and tried to stand up again. He shoved me back down hard, then struck me again with his fist, splitting my lip. I could taste blood and one of my teeth felt loose. I burst into tears as he remained where he was staring down coldly from where he sat on the desk.

'I detest women with foul mouths. You will stop it now or I will seriously harm you, do you understand? If you had kept your memory like the smart woman I thought you were, we wouldn't be having any of these problems. You knew me well, Abigail, and were acutely aware to not ever go against or vex me. Do not try it now. Do you understand?' His voice was eerily calm, a similar tone to how I remembered Leroy speaking to Polly in the tavern cellar. I nodded silently, mustering all my strength to hide the terror I felt. He handed me a handkerchief to wipe the blood from my face. 'You are still the most beautiful woman I have ever seen, but with a vocabulary no different than if you were raised in the slums. You have always had a big mouth and are far too free with your opinion.' He grinned down at me while I sobbed, then reached out and grabbed me hard by both arms, violently yanked me to my feet. 'Those eyes, those eyes, they are bewitching. You love to cast your spell over men then betray them, don't you, you little bitch?' His face had turned from red to a deep mottled purple as he spat on me, gripping my upper arms so tightly I could hardly feel my hands. He kissed me forcefully, shoving his tongue into my mouth as far as he could while squeezing my arms even tighter, making me cry out in pain. When he let me go, I stepped back and slapped his face as hard as I could, then turned and ran to the door, my screams filling the room as I fumbled with the door knob. He remained where he was, appearing unperturbed. 'No one will hear you, Abigail. There is no way out unless I allow you to leave. Settle yourself down now and let's get this over with. I don't want that husband of yours coming here, I've always detested him. It makes no difference how many lives he leads, he is still a smug bastard. I hate him for what he did to me, and will find a way to ensure he suffers now in this life. He has not evolved spiritually like he could have because of what he did. You, on the other hand, my dear, are a highly evolved soul—only you can't remember. What a waste. You will do as I say calmly and without complaint, and maybe it will jog your memory.' He watched from a distance, appearing amused as I continued to shake the handle of the solid wooden door, but it wouldn't budge. I turned my head and glared at him hatefully.

'I will not do anything calmly with you,' I spat, then screamed and thumped as hard as I could on the door, trying to make someone, anyone, hear me.

He got up, casually strode over to my side then hit me with such brute force in the stomach, I doubled over, unable to breathe. He took me by the arms, dragging me back to the desk while muttering under his breath. He raised his arm and punched me hard in the face again as, clawing and kicking, I struggled against him. He forcefully turned me around and brutally threw me face-down on the desk, holding my wrists behind me as I screamed in terror. He held me down, placed all his weight on me, squashing my unborn child, then grabbed a fistful of my hair and shook me violently in an attempt to stop me fighting him.

'Stop the hysterics, Abigail, or you know what I will do to you.' He lifted his hand and pointed to the centre of my forehead, and I flinched in fear. 'Deep in there somewhere you must have memories of me. For your own sake, I hope you remember what happens if you cross me. There was many a time I was forced to teach you a lesson with my fists due to how outspoken you are. Stop making me hit you. You always did this. Pushing me to the edge until I would explode and hurt you. Why are you doing the same thing again if you don't remember? I had hoped that part of you would have changed, that you would have learnt your lesson in your previous life after what happened and the consequences you suffered, not bring it with you to the next. You, of all souls, know that better than anyone.' I lay still on the desk, sobbing uncontrollably.

He lifted up my skirts while continuing to hold my arms behind my back in his vice-like grip. I screamed again, my voice hoarse. I struggled against him as he grabbed my breast hard and twisted it, causing pain to shoot through me. He placed one hand firmly around my mouth and pinched my nostrils, trying to stop me breathing. Within moments, I felt lightheaded and dizzy, my vision turning to grey. He let go of my mouth just as I was about to sink into unconsciousness, leaving me gasping, trying to take in as much air as I could all at once. He dropped my wrists then placed his hands around my throat, shaking me violently and cutting off my oxygen again.

I continued to resist him with every bit of strength I had in me, but he was far too strong and more than double my size. He hit me hard in the side of the face again as I lay on the desk, then shoved his hand between my legs. I went rigid as he jammed his fingers inside me, roughly and callously, causing me to scream again in pain. Within moments he had dropped his pants and forced himself inside me, thrusting so deep and hard the pain was unbearable. I let my mind float away to a place where everything was warm and happy, and no one could hurt me, as he did disgusting things to my body.

When he was finished, he let me go, throwing me to the floor. He buttoned the front of his trousers and returned to the chair behind his desk, opening a large folder. I sobbed uncontrollably, too weak to get up. I couldn't think straight, but knew I had to get out of that room.

I struggled unsteadily to my feet, feeling pain in far too many places to count, standing silently and unmoving as I watched him write in a leather-bound book, almost as though he had forgotten I was there. I was too distraught to speak, supporting myself on the back of the chair, while I waited to see what he would do next. He pulled the key from his pocket and placed it on the desk, not bothering to look up at me—my whimpering the only sound in the eerily quiet room.

'There you are, Mrs Cavanaugh. I look forward to seeing you in court tomorrow. Good day.' I silently took the key with a trembling hand and hurried to the door, trying desperately to stop my hand shaking long enough to put the key in the lock, but my first attempts were unsuccessful. 'Oh, by the way, Abigail. I really enjoyed our little reunion. That was all I needed from you. For now. I would say pass on my regards to your husband; however, Aaron and I have known each other for a long time now, and I doubt he would want to hear a false greeting from me. I know for certain he doesn't have his memory. He was never and will never be evolved as you and I,' he murmured, a smug look on his face.

He appeared satisfied as I stared back at him before turning the key again. This time I heard a loud click. I flung the door open wide and ran down the darkened corridor, sobbing in relief I was still alive. I had never come face to face with a raving lunatic before, and I found it the most terrifying experience of my life. The things he had been talking about hadn't made sense to me at all. And nothing Madame Zvezda had said sounded remotely like this.

I opened the courtroom door and rushed out into the foyer. My body trembled, and I felt cold. There were several people still in the foyer who looked at me in horror when they saw the blood and bruising to my face. I stumbled along, pain in my stomach intensifying, and knew I had to find Aaron as quickly as possible. He wasn't anywhere to be found inside, so I continued on, staggering out onto the street where I found him standing next to our carriage. He took one look at me, dropped the newspaper he was reading and ran up the steps, fear in his eyes.

'Christ, Abi, what's happened? I've been lookin' everywhere for ya. No one would tell me where ya went.' He took me in his arms just as I started to lose consciousness, quickly picking me up and carrying me towards the carriage. I shook my head in an attempt to clear my mind and speak, my voice barely above a whisper.

'Aaron, I can't tell you anything right now, but I need you to get me to the closest hospital immediately. I think I'm going to birth this child here in the street. It's too early. We need the doctors to try to stop whatever is happening. Please concentrate on that first and I will tell you what happened as soon as I can.' I closed my eyes again, pushing everything that had just been done to me to the back of my mind. I had more important things to think about now. He quickly placed me in the carriage and ordered the driver to take us to the hospital as fast as possible.

Aaron carried me through the front doors of The Alfred Hospital on Commercial Road, and I was immediately placed on a trolley bed in a large room. The nurse put a screen by the bed for privacy, but hurried away when I asked to see my husband. They wouldn't let Aaron in, and I could hear him arguing with the medical staff while I was being examined by a doctor. He spent the longest time taking notes, before advising me he would be writing a report. For whom, I was uncertain, nor did I ask or care. I told him what George Maslow had done to me, and of the pain I was experiencing. The nurse felt around my stomach, appearing concerned.

'I have given you something in an attempt to halt the contractions,' the doctor said, gently patting my arm before he excused himself to go and speak with Aaron. I lay unmoving, the pain easing as I listened to them outside my door. 'I'm Doctor Brown. I have examined your wife and spoken to her at length. I'm sorry to have to tell you this, Mr Cavanaugh, but your wife has been brutally attacked... physically and, ah... sexually. I have found cuts and bruising to her face and an injury to her stomach. Her body is covered in bruises and she has been manually choked to the point of passing out. She has been violently raped and the blow to her stomach has caused her labour to start.' He paused, allowing Aaron a moment to absorb the unimaginable before continuing. 'Your wife has injuries to her genital area as a result of this attack. She has been struck in the face and body many times, causing significant damage that will take weeks to heal. I apologise again for being so blunt. I think it's best you not discuss the attack with your wife at this present time. It will only cause her further distress.' Aaron stomped into the room and over to my side, his face like thunder.

'I know the bastard who did this, but I need to make sure. Tell me his name so I can go an' cut his throat,' Aaron whispered, his eyes glinting dangerously.

'Please, please, please, Aaron. Do not speak like that. I need you here beside me, not in a gaol cell, imprisoned for murder. Or worse. Without you, the children and I would be hopelessly lost. You must promise to stay with me no matter what happens,' I begged, clinging to his hand as tears poured down my face. He stared at me for the longest time.

'All right,' he said slowly and with great reluctance. 'I'll stay me hand for now, but only 'cause it's you who asked it of me. An' 'cause I know ya need me here beside ya.'

I was experiencing contractions every five-minutes or so. They were not as intense as I remembered the first time. I muttered a prayer to Sister's God, asking him to protect our unborn child and stop the labour, hoping against hope he would hear me.

A great deal of time had passed before Dr. Brown came back in with a copy of his report. I took it before Aaron could read it, putting it away in my purse—surprisingly still in my possession.

Two police constables entered the room soon after and took my statement, although I was forced to pause each time the pain came. They provided me with a copy, listing Judge George Maslow as the perpetrator of the violent attack, and advised me he would be taken in for questioning.

My contractions were getting stronger and closer together, and my concern increased with each passing moment. Aaron could see the fear in my eyes as he sat by my side, holding my hand in his until Dr. Brown returned to examine me again.

'I need to conduct an examination, Mrs Cavanaugh. It may be slightly uncomfortable, but for only a moment. I apologise in advance,' he said kindly before he slipped a gloved finger inside me—and it *was* bloody uncomfortable. Dr. Brown appeared worried as he straightened up and covered me with the sheet. 'We must move your wife into a private room right away.' Two young nurses came to my side and prepared to move me. They pushed my bed out of the room and rolled me down the hall, Aaron walking along beside me, his face as white as a ghost. Once settled in a private room, Dr Brown hurried in, shaking his head apologetically. 'I'm sorry, but I cannot stop the contractions. You are going to have this child, and soon. There is nothing we can do to prevent it, unfortunately. The infant most likely be born dead, or die soon after. Its lungs are too underdeveloped to breathe on its own. I need you to be prepared for what is to come.' His manner was gentle, and very, very kind, but even that did not soften the blow.

I turned my head to face the white wall and started to sob. Aaron bent down and placed his forehead on mine, holding me close as our tears mingled together, both silently hoping despite what the doctor said, everything would be all right and somehow our child would survive. I knew miracles did happen, especially when you wished for them hard enough. Another contraction began, and I pulled away from him, groaning loudly.

'Now, Mrs Cavanaugh, I need you to push. You know how to do this,' the doctor called out from the end of the bed.

'I don't want to push,' I wailed, crying out in distress. 'I want our child to remain safe inside me.' I sobbed like I had never sobbed before, my heart broken, Aaron discreetly wiping a tear from his cheek as he watched on helplessly. Despite refusing to cooperate, my body was making its own decisions—pushing by itself and without my consent, while brutally trying to expel the child from me.

'Nearly there. One more push, Mrs Cavanaugh,' I heard from somewhere in the room, my face covered in sweat, my vision blurred.

'No,' I screamed as our child was born into the world. Aaron watched closely, his eyes red, his hand trembling. The doctor sighed deeply as he gazed down at the little boy, then slowly and silently shook his head. Aaron's eyes filled with tears once again, while Dr. Brown handed him to a nurse and asked her to wrap our son in a towel. He turned back to me, then bent down to push on my stomach, quickly conducting another examination.

'Mrs Cavanaugh, you have another coming. I need you to push again.' His eyes filled with sadness, pity clear on his face, while he gently patted my hand as I burst into loud sobs. A second set of twins. How wonderful that would have been. My heart, soul and body were completely shattered, and I feared at that moment I would never recover. My body pushed the second boy out without my consent, who also did not cry. Aaron returned to my side and sat with me, appearing broken-hearted. Kissing my forehead as we both cried, we were unable to comfort ourselves let alone each other.

'Please clean and wrap our boys in blankets and hand them to us,' Aaron requested as politely as he could, holding my trembling body while trying to quieten my sobs. The nurse turned to Aaron, advising it was not their usual practice, that they believed it best that grieving parents did not view their stillborn child. She then explained that the hospital disposed of any foetuses, immediately angering Aaron.

'Are you lot the full quid? These boys are our sons, and we love 'em livin' or dead. They're not somethin' to be disposed of like scaffy. Mind me now so we've no problems between us in the future. They'll be collected from here by an undertaker in the mornin' to be taken home for burial.' Aaron's voice was low but calm, his eyes glinting dangerously. The nurse turned to the doctor for support, while keeping a wary eye on Aaron, who did not take his eyes from either.

'If that's what they want, and they have the funds to carry it out, then I see no harm in it, nurse.' Dr. Brown nodded compassionately, patting my arm in comfort. The nurse brought the two tiny boys, each wrapped in a blanket, and handed them to us. I moved over to make room for Aaron to sit down on the bed beside me.

'What'll we name 'em?' Tears spilled down his ruddy cheeks as he held his tiny son to his chest. The wean looked as if he were sleeping, and I wished again he was.

'I want to name this little man Harrison,' I replied, kissing his perfect little lips, tears pouring down my face unnoticed.

'Well, then, this little bloke has to be Jack.' Aaron stared down at him, unwrapping the blanket then gently running his hand along his tiny arms and legs before stroking his chest. He climbed in bed with me and we cuddled our children together, telling them how much we loved them and how wonderful their lives would have been had they not been forced to join the angels. A nurse hurried in, quickly apologising for the intrusion.

'There are two policemen here to see you.' She had barely uttered the last word before they unceremoniously pushed past her and stood at the end of my bed. They appeared senior in rank, unlike the constables who had taken my statement earlier.

'Good evening. I am Inspector Peter Caville and this is Inspector Ralph Walker. We understand that you made a statement earlier to police reporting that you were assaulted. We have a signed report here from a Dr. Brown that states quite clearly you were attacked on the street and your memory is impaired due a head injury you have sustained. He advised us that the perpetrator is unknown at this time. Do you believe that to be true, Mrs Cavanaugh?' He looked down his long straight nose at me, his voice dripping with menace.

I felt sick. I didn't want him to know I had a copy of the first report as evidence of my complaint. By the look of him, he was likely to take them from me by force. Aaron remained silent, his jaw clenched while the colour had started to rise in his face. I gave him a look that only married couples understood, and he nodded slightly, attempting to hide his rage.

'What would happen if I said that was not the case?' I asked ingenuously, looking not at them but down at my tiny son, dead in my arms.

'Then we would have to consider your mental stability. We would have you hospitalised to be examined and treated.' The other officer with him had not said a word since arriving and appeared increasingly uncomfortable the longer they stayed. I knew exactly what this Inspector Caville was threatening me with. I had heard it a thousand times before when Leo threatened me with the same thing, often offering to drive me to the Ararat Asylum himself. If I didn't go along with this arrogant, and obviously corrupt policeman, he planned to have me committed to an asylum far closer, where I would be kept at their mercy indefinitely. I smiled weakly at the inspector and spoke up as best I could.

'It was all a misunderstanding. I was in a great deal of pain at the time. Judge Maslow was the last person I remember seeing today because I was in his court before I was attacked. This bump on my head has really confused me,' I rasped, my throat sore. Aaron gritted his teeth, his hands curled into fists by his side, but he remained silent much to my relief.

'Are you prepared to sign a sworn statement to that effect?' he asked, his face relaxing into a warm smile.

'Yes, I am,' I replied without emotion, cradling wee Jack in my arms as my tears continued to fall. Inspector Caville left the room to prepare the statement I had just made and returned shortly after. I signed it and he gave me a copy, which I left on the bed.

'You don't happen to have a copy of the first report so we can file it away, do you?' He studied me suspiciously, his offsider preparing to leave.

'I'm sorry. In all the muddle of giving birth while making a statement, I forgot to get one.' I widened my eyes innocently as I stared up at him, wishing I could hurry him along. I knew my body and mind had gone into shock, but somehow I was still functioning. I wanted them gone so I could be with my boys, who hadn't had a chance to draw breath. 'Does it matter that I don't have a copy of the first statement, Inspector?'

'No, it doesn't matter at all.' He smiled, patting my hand before they turned to leave.

'They cover their arses, don't they?' Aaron whispered bitterly the moment they stepped out into the hallway, lowering his head to kiss Harrison on his tiny face. We spent the next hour with our beautiful, lifeless babies before handing them over to the nurse. 'I'd like to see Dr. Brown now, thank you,' Aaron told her quietly.

'I will see if he is available.' She gently carried our babies out of the room. Aaron put his head on my stomach and sobbed while I ran my fingers through his hair, talking softly to him. I felt in some way this was my fault and blamed myself, although I couldn't come up with an exact reason why I was culpable.

'Are ya all right after givin' birth?' He raised his head for a moment and gazed up at me, his eyes red and swollen.

'Yes, I am. I'm sore all over from where he beat me, though, but nothing seems broken.'

'I hope ya face looks worse than it feels, Abi, 'cause from where I'm sittin, it looks painful,' he whispered, caressing my cheek gently with his thumb.

'It will heal. Aaron, look at me. All this will heal, and we still have each other. I don't want you doing anything stupid. Like I said, I need you, and Thomas and Emmy need you. I will be all right if you promise me that you won't do anything to seek revenge,' I begged him again, holding both of his hands in mine. He remained silent for the longest time before nodding his head slightly.

'I'm not gunna lie to ya, Abi. I can't give ya a false promise that if I see him in the street, I won't harm him.'

I sighed deeply but nodded my head and tried to smile. As long as he stayed with me and had time to calm down, all would be well. He would promise me eventually, so I let the subject drop. Dr. Brown paused at the door, avoiding our gaze before hesitantly stepping inside.

'How could ya, doc? Lie like that?' Aaron demanded to know. Dr. Brown stared down at the floor, appearing nervous, his face flushed.

'I'm sorry, but you must try to understand. You don't know the kind of pressure these men placed on me. They made threats against my family. I had no choice but to do as they asked, and for that, I deeply apologise.' I believed his sincerity was the only thing that stopped Aaron from beating him to death with his fists.

'I'm takin' me wife back to The Delmont to care for her, so I want ya to examine her again an' give her a large injection of that morphine ya hand out so freely. Ya can provide me with a bottle to give her until she's recovered. I'll not leave her in a hospital where the doctors lie an' cheat 'cause they don't uphold the Hippocratic Oath. Do as I say, Dr Brown, an' you'll have no more trouble from me,' Aaron growled, his eyes glinting dangerously. Dr. Brown appeared nervous but made the wise decision to comply with Aaron's demands and released me immediately.

Aaron carried me from the carriage into the hotel. Not a soul was about except the night clerk, who greeted us politely while trying not to stare. I felt like I was flying and couldn't feel any pain after the injection I had been given. I relaxed into him and cuddled into his chest until we arrived in our suite. He gently placed me on the bed and kissed me lightly on my broken lips. He carefully removed my dress and undergarments, placing them outside in the hallway to be burnt in the morning. He bathed me and washed my wounds, then dried me with a warm towel and slipped a nightgown over my head.

He helped me into bed and I slipped under the covers, placing my hands on my flat stomach. My poor babies—gone, just like that. This time last night they were happily kicking away in my belly with a future and infinite possibilities, and tonight they had passed into the beyond without even a brief moment shared with us.

I knew deep in my soul there would be consequences in the future, and I would do everything in my power to ensure that Aaron didn't seek revenge. The problem was, I knew the man as well as I knew myself—he wasn't one to let things go without having the final say, whatever that might be. We had already lost so much. I couldn't face losing anymore. It was something I couldn't think about now. I was exhausted and could no longer think straight, so I pushed it all to the back of my mind to consider once I was strong enough.

Soon after, Aaron carefully climbed into bed, gathered me in his arms, and we cried together over all that had happened and all we had lost. As I drifted into a fitful sleep, I dreamed of two cherubs flying above fluffy white clouds, a rope, and a big-bladed knife suddenly descending into my heart.

A Word from the Author

THANK YOU FOR TAKING the time to read my series 'Samsara-The First Season'.' It's been nearly a decade since I wrote the first sentence of Abigail's story, and it is a privilege to share it with you.

If you have a few moments, I would be deeply grateful if you left a review on your chosen platform or website. It will help other readers find books that they may never have discovered otherwise. Your feedback means the world to authors and we cannot thank you enough for your support! Thank you for investing your valuable time and money in this story and I hope you enjoyed reading it.

If this series was not for you, that's perfectly okay. We all have different tastes as readers and we can't please everyone all the time. Thank you again for your support and I wish you well in finding novels that bring you joy. Much love to all xx

To find out more,

go to www.jlmartinauthor.com

Samsara

The First Season

Unconditional Love
Volume One Book Five

What if you could remember a past life?
Or worse, what if you couldn't?

Abigail and Aaron grieve for their stillborn twins, and the aftermath of the brutal attack on her leads to further trauma that will have life-changing consequences. Hamish remains a steadfast friend to both Abigail and Aaron, moving to Willow Grove permanently to help run the property, while Abigail tries to keep life as normal as possible for those around her, particularly the twins, under impossible circumstances. Faced with the very real chance she could forever lose someone she loves, she goes to extremes to keep them by her side, prepared to lose everything she owns to save those close to her.

Continue the journey alongside Abigail and the cast of characters she calls friends through the first season of 'Samsara' and find out what thousands of readers are talking about.

Want to stay up to date and be the first to hear about Samsara? Go to jlmartinauthor.com to sign up for her newsletter and receive alerts and updates, along with bonus content. Links to social media and bookstores available here too.

jlmartinauthor.com

www.ingramcontent.com/pod-product-compliance
Lightning Source LLC
Chambersburg PA
CBHW030802200726
48285CB00014B/461
* 9 7 8 1 9 2 5 8 5 2 2 8 8 *